The Holiday Cottage

Also by Sarah Morgan

The Summer Swap
The Book Club Hotel
The Island Villa
Snowed In for Christmas
Beach House Summer
The Christmas Escape
The Summer Seekers
One More for Christmas
Family for Beginners
A Wedding in December
One Summer in Paris
The Christmas Sisters
How to Keep a Secret

For additional books by Sarah Morgan,
visit her website, sarahmorgan.com.

SARAH MORGAN

The Holiday Cottage

CANARY STREET PRESS

CANARY
STREET
PRESS™

Recycling programs
for this product may
not exist in your area.

ISBN-13: 978-1-335-49909-7

The Holiday Cottage

Canary Street Press
22 Adelaide St. West, 41st Floor
Toronto, Ontario M5H 4E3, Canada
CanaryStPress.com

Printed in U.S.A.

To Flo, Ali and Dora, with much love xx

1

Imogen

It began as a casual conversation and Imogen wasn't quite sure at what point things had started to go so wrong. It wasn't her fault. At least, not *all* her fault. She'd wanted to be friendly, that was all. To form a bond with her colleagues. That wasn't a crime, was it? It was almost a requirement of open-plan offices. They created an atmosphere of familiarity. Sitting side by side and across from the people you worked with encouraged confidences and chat, and allowed for the gradual absorption of tiny granules of information that you didn't even realize you'd overheard. It was intimacy by osmosis.

"Hey, Imogen." Anya glanced at her across the desk. She was a makeup addict and spent at least half an hour of every day extolling the virtues of her latest find. Today her eyelids glittered like an ornament on a Christmas tree. "Did you see the email from the boss? She's planning a 'bring your dog to work day' the week before Christmas."

"I saw the email." Her day had gone downhill from there.

Bonding with her colleagues was important, but she liked to keep her work life and her homelife separate. "Did you get the costings for those venues, Anya? I have to send that proposal to Rosalind to check before it goes to the client at lunchtime."

Pets, clothes, makeup, diets, travel, food, movies, books, bad dates and irritating clients. That covered the bulk of the conversation that bounced around the office.

"Just waiting on the last two. Isn't it a brilliant idea? Every dog wears a festive outfit and Rosalind picks the winner. All for charity. It will be so much fun. I'm wondering whether I can persuade my little Cocoa to wear antlers. Generally, he hates having his head touched, so maybe not. But we get to dress up too. I bought a new sparkly highlighter on Saturday. Perfect for Christmas. There was a discount if you bought two, so I got one for you too." She passed it across the desk to Imogen.

"That's for me?" She took it, surprised and touched. "Why?"

"Just because." Anya shrugged and grinned. "Call it a thank-you for helping me out of that sticky client situation last week. Also, you have great cheekbones and it will look good on you."

Imogen felt an unexpected sting in her throat. She remembered her first day at the company when Anya had presented her with a frosted cupcake and a pen that glowed in the dark. *You're going to be working late so you'll need this.*

It was hard to believe she'd been here for almost a year. She'd started her new job a few days before Christmas and had barely got started before the office had closed for the festive break.

"I love it, thank you." She checked the time and felt a flash of panic. She didn't miss deadlines. Not ever. And this one was too close for comfort. She wanted to call and get the costings herself, but she was Anya's manager and was supposed to be helping her develop, so she needed to stop doing things herself. The restraint almost killed her. It was so much easier and safer to do it herself. At least then she could be confident it would be done on time, with no mistakes. "Will you chase those venues urgently? Those are the last numbers I need to finish this."

"Sure, I'll do it now. I saw a lipstick that would look great on you, Imogen. Maybe we could go shopping together one lunchtime. And if you're looking for doggy outfits, I saw a cute red Santa coat on the internet that would look great on a golden retriever. Or do you already have something in mind?" Anya was more interested in the idea of everyone bringing their dogs to work than she was in doing actual work. "You will be bringing Midas, won't you?"

Realizing there was no chance of getting those costings until she finished the dog conversation, Imogen glanced at the photograph on her desk.

Huge brown eyes gazed back at her and she felt a sudden pang.

Bring your dog to work day.

She touched the photo with the tips of her fingers. "I'm not sure if I'll be able to bring him." She definitely wouldn't be bringing him, but she still had to work out how best to present that fact to her colleagues without alienating them. And then she had a brain wave. "He's not been well. The vet has kept him for a few nights."

"What? No! Midas is ill? And you didn't tell us?" Anya put her pen down and looked at Janie. "Janie, did you know Midas was ill?"

Janie glanced at them, her ponytail swinging across her back. She was a fitness fanatic and used the gym for an hour every morning when everyone else was still asleep. Occasionally, she paced up and down the office just to get her step count up.

"Midas is ill?" Janie rejected a client phone call and focused on Imogen. "That's awful. What happened? Was it the dog walker's fault? Did she let him eat something he shouldn't have eaten?"

"No, nothing like that." Maybe illness hadn't been the best

way to go. She should have played along and then found a reason for Midas to be absent on the day. *He stepped on something and he has to rest his paw.* "It's not important. Look, if you could get the last of those costings that would be great, because I need to finish this document and the deadline is—"

"Of course it's important! This is your dog we're talking about. What is more important than that? The client can wait."

"The client can't wait," Imogen said. "We're in a competitive business. There are new events companies springing up every day. It's important that we exceed expectations."

"We will. We'll do a great job on the event itself. We always do, particularly with you in charge. But this is just a proposal. No one is going to die if it's a few hours late. You can pause for two minutes, Imogen," Anya said. "You worked over the weekend supervising those events, and you didn't take a day off on Monday. You work too hard."

Too hard? There was no such thing as *too hard.*

She loved her job. Her job was *everything.* She was a natural multitasker and handled twice as many accounts as everyone else. She did whatever it took to win business and keep the client, and she did that through experience, attention to detail, creativity and sheer hard work. She was good at what she did. And that wasn't only her opinion. In her previous company she'd moved up to the lofty heights of management so quickly a jealous colleague had left an oxygen mask on her desk.

But now she had a team of six to manage, and occasionally she wished she could just do all the work herself rather than delegate. Anya, in particular, seemed to feel no particular sense of urgency about anything. She was generous and kind, but maddeningly slow to complete tasks. She told everyone that work-life balance was essential to her, but Imogen rarely saw her focus on the work side of that equation.

It was like trying to run a race with six weights attached to her waist.

She was going to have to speak to Anya. There was no avoiding it. She needed to have a "conversation" about commitment and goals. Managing Anya would take her away from doing actual client work, which meant she'd be working longer hours.

Work-life balance? There was no balance for Imogen, but she didn't mind. This was her choice.

"The deadline is lunchtime, Anya. We can do this!"

"Relax, Imogen. You're going to get white hair and wrinkles before your time. You have so much energy you make me want to lie down. It will get done. It always does." Anya dismissed the deadline, and Imogen felt her stress levels ratchet up another notch.

It did get done, but only because she invariably ended up doing it herself. She really liked Anya, which made it even harder. "Anya—"

"I know. You're stressed. And I understand why."

"You do?" Hearing that came as a relief. Maybe Anya was more aware of work pressures than she'd thought.

"Of course. How can you be calm when your lovely Midas is ill? I can't believe you've been keeping this to yourself. I'd be totally freaking out."

Midas?

"I—"

"What does the vet say? When will they let him out? You must be worried sick. It's okay to be honest. We're a team. We're here to support each other. You're allowed to be human, Imogen. We can cover for you if needed. We can do your work."

Imogen blinked. Anya didn't seem able to do her own work, let alone anyone else's, but this probably wasn't the time to point that out.

"Well, I—"

"Anya's right," Janie said. "You don't have to hold it in. I mean, this is Midas. He's your baby." She reached across the desk and picked up the photo Imogen kept on her desk. "Look at that face. Poor boy. I'm sure Rosalind would give you time off if you explained. She was amazing when Buster had that lump on his leg. I suppose because she's a dog lover herself. She gets it."

"That's why I love this place," Anya said. "Everyone is so human. The last place I worked no one talked about anything personal. It was like working with a bunch of robots. Nightmare."

A place where no one talked about anything personal? Imogen was starting to wonder if that might be preferable. She loved her colleagues, but she would have loved them even more if they shared her work ethic.

But there was no denying that her colleagues were good people, even if most of the time they seemed to fit work around their personal life.

Janie looked close to tears as she held the photo of Midas, and Imogen reached across and gently removed it from her fingers.

"I'd rather not talk about it." She placed the photograph back on her desk, next to the one of her family. In her last job they'd had a hot desk system, and no one had been allowed to display a single personal item. RPQ Events was a very different place.

There were plants and a fish tank, and people were encouraged to personalize their workstations. Anya's computer was framed by fairy lights, and no one seemed to mind.

Glancing around her on her first day, Imogen had seen everything from fluffy mascots to family photos. She'd stared at her stark, empty desk and decided she needed to do something about it.

Come on, Imogen, show us your family, Janie had said cheerfully, and Anya had nodded agreement. *Do you have any pets? We're all animal lovers here. Even Danny. He'll tell you he bought the rabbits for his daughters, but don't believe him for a second.*

She'd never had a personal photo on her desk before, but here the absence of it drew attention so she'd done the same. She'd appreciated how welcoming they were and wanted to be part of the team, so she'd carefully selected one photo of Midas and one family photo taken at Christmas. Everyone was huddled together, laughing for the camera as they struggled not to lose their footing in the snow. Imogen loved that photo. Everyone looked so *happy*.

"We're here for you, Imogen." Janie reached across and rubbed Imogen's shoulder in a show of solidarity. "You're so brave and strong. It must be awful not having your furry friend there to greet you when you get home. I'm sure you miss him horribly. We had no idea you were going through this. You seem so *normal*. Honestly, you're amazing, although I'm sure it helps having such a close family."

Imogen started to panic. She found personal conversations like this really unsettling. Any moment now they'd be suggesting grief counseling. She needed to shut this down before it went any further.

"I do miss him, but he's in good hands and I'm sure he'll soon be home. If you could get those costs, I'd be able to send this through to the client by lunchtime."

"Working on it now. What's wrong with him?"

"What's wrong with who?"

"Midas." Anya's eyes were wide with sympathy. "Nothing serious, I hope. I don't know how you can concentrate on work when he's ill."

"They're not sure what's wrong," Imogen said. "They're running tests."

This was the problem with working in an open-plan office. People wanted details.

Much of her time was spent out and about with clients at their offices, visiting venues or supervising events, but eventually she had to return to her desk, and that meant being cocooned with her colleagues. And it wasn't that she didn't like them, because she did. She liked them a great deal, but there was a fine line between fitting in and being welded together. If someone wanted to talk, then she was always willing to listen, but sometimes the level of information became *too much* (close physical proximity didn't seem to be the moderating influence it should have been).

Take Janie for example. Because Janie never bothered to leave her desk when taking a personal call, Imogen knew that Janie lived with her mother, had one sister who was married and that she was currently dating two different men so that she had backup in the event that one of them ghosted her (Janie's father had walked out when she was ten, leaving her with a perpetual mistrust of the opposite sex).

Then there was Peter. Peter was head of tech, and he sat to her left. He'd been with the company for six months, yet despite this relatively short acquaintance she knew he had an appointment with his doctor on Friday to talk about a part of his body Imogen tried never to picture in a colleague. She knew his girlfriend wanted them to move in together, and she knew Pete had no intention of doing that because she'd heard him on the phone to his landlord renewing his rental for another year.

And there was Danny, another account manager, who spent a large part of the day arranging gym sessions and after-work drinks so that he could arrive home after his wife had put their four-year-old twins to bed. Yes, he had rabbits, but judging from the conversation, he'd never contributed to their care. That was his wife's responsibility (and his wife seemed to have a great number of responsibilities).

Imogen filed all the things she heard into a compartment in her brain labeled *things I wish I didn't know* and tried to forget about them. The thing she found less easy to handle was the fact that they wanted to know about her too.

She was a private person and, given the choice, she would have revealed nothing about her personal life, but she wanted to fit in. She wanted people to like her. So she did what everyone else did and put photos on her desk. She chatted. And the chat requirement was about to escalate because they were heading into the worst month of the year for team bonding activities.

December.

Imogen knew that the "bring your dog to work day" would just be the start of many Christmas celebrations. There would be the office Christmas lunch, the Secret Santa, the charity quiz night (*which one of the following is not one of Santa's reindeer?*). The list was endless and, although her colleagues knew a few things about her, the one thing they didn't know was that she dreaded Christmas. Last year had been easy because she'd only joined a few days before, but this year promised to be more of a trial.

"At least you'll have time off with him over Christmas." Janie flashed her a smile. "Only thirty-six sleeps to go. We're spending Christmas with my sister this year. I can't wait. She has a bigger house and a bigger TV. How about you, Imogen? Please tell me you *are* taking time off. The office closed for a week last year, but still you sent emails on Christmas Day. I mean, who does that?"

"I'd just joined the company. I was keen." That wasn't really the reason, but it worked well enough as an excuse. "I didn't expect you to look at them. But with the office closed and clients enjoying the holidays, it seemed like the perfect time to catch up. I wanted to be able to hit the ground running in January."

"But it was your holiday too. Why weren't you just hanging out with your family?"

"I was." Imogen moved the photo of Midas next to the family photo. "But there were a few hours in the day when everyone was either watching a movie, or sleeping off too much food, so I opened my laptop." And she didn't want to think about it. She really didn't.

"You're obsessed," Anya said. "Don't take your laptop this year, then you won't be tempted. It was a bit startling to turn on my computer on January 2 and find fifty-six emails from you waiting in my inbox."

"I like to end the year with everything tidy," Imogen said. "I still spent plenty of time with family, don't worry."

Janie sat back and shook her head. "I don't know how you do it all. You hardly ever come out with us after work because you're either babysitting your niece and nephew or you're visiting your grandmother. You have a dog. You do everything for everyone, and still handle an inhuman workload. And you never take time off. How many holiday days are you carrying forward into next year?"

"Er—I don't know. Most of them I think."

"Exactly! Would you slow down? You make the rest of us feel inadequate."

"You're all great," Imogen said. "We're a brilliant team."

"We are, but if you're not careful you're going to burn out. You've been working every weekend, so you deserve a good break. Your family home looks like a dreamy place to spend Christmas. That gorgeous big house. All that countryside. Midas must love it. Are you excited?"

Christmas, Christmas, Christmas.

As far as her colleagues were concerned, it was never too soon to talk about Christmas. It made her want to scream.

This year the conversation had started in July (July! What was wrong with people?) when Anya had indulged in a Christmas movie marathon over the weekend and proceeded to talk about it for several weeks after.

In October, Janie had returned from a trip to the supermarket to buy a salad and pointed out that the shelves were already lined with Christmas decorations and Christmas chocolate. She'd placed her plastic-looking salad on her desk, along with a garishly wrapped chocolate Santa.

"I normally avoid chocolate, but Christmas is the exception," she'd told them happily as she'd stripped the Santa of its red foil and bitten off the head. "How about you, Imogen?"

Imogen had focused on her computer screen and hoped they'd lose interest.

"I refuse to think about Christmas in October. It's too soon." It was okay to say that, wasn't it? Plenty of people refused to think about Christmas in October.

A month later, when someone had asked her about plans for the office Christmas party, she'd said the same thing.

"I refuse to talk about Christmas in November. It's too soon."

But next week it would be December and Imogen would have run out of viable excuses. Decorations glittered in shop windows. Christmas music boomed relentless cheer over loudspeakers.

She could no longer avoid the topic.

She'd have this one conversation and hopefully that would be it for a while.

"I'll be going home, yes. It will be chaos as usual. You know how it is. Big noisy family gathering. Tree too big for the room. Log fire. Uncle George singing out of tune. I'll be spending most of my time trying to stop the nieces and nephews squeezing the presents and making sure my mother isn't burning the turkey." That was enough information to keep them happy, surely? "We really need that costing, Anya."

"I'm on it. Oh, and I forgot to tell you that Dorothy Rutherford called for you earlier. You were on the phone to that tech guy from the lighting company."

Imogen felt her breathing quicken. "You forgot? Dorothy Rutherford is an important client, Anya. When she calls, I stop what I'm doing and take her call. If I'm on with another client, then I call her right back when I'm done."

"She was fine about it. She loves you. We all know you're the reason she gave us the business. She wanted to carry on working with you when you left your last place. You can do no wrong. Also, you're the only one of us who genuinely loves her alcohol-free wine."

"I don't mind it," Janie protested. "It's a refreshing drink. But it's not—you know—alcohol. It doesn't give me the buzz I need on a Friday night. I know those bubbles aren't going to give me the headache I need the morning after."

"Just Friday?" Anya grinned. "What about the other nights of the week?"

"Those too. It's the first thing I do when I get home. My mum and I open a bottle and share it. That's why I go to the gym every morning. I'd have more willpower if I lived on my own. You're so lucky to be able to afford your own place, Imogen."

Imogen waited for a break in the conversation. "What did Dorothy want?"

"She wanted to talk to you about the proposal you sent. Sounds as if she wants to go ahead with everything you suggested. She was impressed. She asked for a bespoke and original concept and you gave her one. The outdoor festival, complete with a stage and tents and the works. Like a rock concert. She thinks it's a perfect way to showcase their products to customers and have a party for locals at the same time. And she loved the idea of fireworks and the drone display. This will be a huge piece of business, Imogen. Congratulations. You turned a virtually impossible brief into reality. We should celebrate—" She grinned at Janie. "Fancy a glass of nonalcoholic wine?"

"No thanks. I'd rather have a double espresso. I'll say this though, I love their packaging. Those bottles are classy. They *look* like champagne."

"And their sales are rocketing, so someone is loving it."

Anya rested her chin on her palm. "I wonder if it's because the marketing is so clever. She has tapped into the whole healthy living trend. Pictures of her estate in the Cotswolds with its vineyard, lots of cool people toasting each other with glasses of Spearcante. I look at the ads and I want to be there, even if there is no alcohol on offer. I wonder how she came up with that name?"

"I think spearca is from an Old English word meaning spark," Imogen said and they both stared at her.

"How do you know these things?"

"Dorothy is my client. It's my job to know as much about her as possible. She hasn't always been in business. Originally, she read English Literature at Oxford. And then she did Medieval studies, which included Old English and Old Norse. I think she also studied Anglo Saxon prose and poetry. I guess etymology was part of that."

Anya frowned. "Isn't that insects?"

Janie grinned. "That's entomology. Etymology is the origin of words, and I'd rather talk about that than insects, thank you very much."

Right now, Imogen didn't care about the origins of the name. The only thing Imogen cared about was that Dorothy had been kept waiting. Dorothy wasn't only an important client, but she was Imogen's favorite client. She was smart, interesting and surprisingly easy to work with. She embraced Imogen's ideas and rarely reined her in. Dorothy had been running the family vineyard in the Cotswolds for many years, producing award-winning wines, before deciding to experiment with extracting the alcohol from the wine. She'd been producing no-alcohol wine long before it had become something of a cultural movement, but lately the business had taken off.

Imogen had worked with her for several years and found her enthusiastic, encouraging and supportive. She never whined and complained, which was more than could be said for most of their clients.

"I'll call her now."

"No point. She said she'd be tied up for the next couple of hours, but she'd call you from the car on her way home."

Imogen managed to hide her frustration. If Dorothy was in a meeting, then it would have to be later and she would have to try not to stress about it.

And in the meantime...

"Anya, if you could get those costings now it would mean I could finish this document..." She had a sudden brainwave. "And then I'll be able to make the call about Midas."

"Of course! Anything for Midas."

"Great. Thanks." As she'd hoped, the mention of Midas galvanized her colleague into action, and ten minutes later Imogen had all the costings incorporated into the document.

Relieved, she sent it through to Rosalind for final approval and sat back in her chair.

Done. Finally. Maybe she should try using Midas as a motivator more often.

She felt uncomfortable talking about him at work, but she badly wanted to fit in, and if that required a little personal sacrifice on her part, then fine. She'd do whatever it took, even pretend to be enthusiastic about Christmas.

Her colleagues would never know the truth.

Soon a giant tree would arrive in the foyer and she'd admire it along with everyone else. Mistletoe would be hung in strategic places, even though office romance was banned (and, as Janie had once pointed out after several glasses of wine that most definitely had retained all its alcohol content, the number of kissable people in their office was depressingly limited).

And there would be the "bring your dog to work day."

Midas.

She sighed and glanced at the photo on her desk. The photographer had captured the exact moment his tail had been suspended in mid wag.

He really was a gorgeous dog.

It was just a pity he wasn't hers.

Also a pity that her Christmas wasn't going to be a big, noisy family affair.

She loved the family photo she'd placed on her desk, but they weren't her family. She had no idea who they were (although they looked like lovely people).

She'd described someone else's Christmas, not hers.

There was no big house in the country. There would be no oversize tree or a log fire. Uncle George wouldn't be singing out of tune because she didn't have an uncle called George, or any other uncle. She wasn't going to have to stop her nieces and nephews squeezing the presents, because she didn't have nieces or nephews. There would be no games of charades, and no burnt turkey because her mother had never cooked a turkey in her life.

But right now that wasn't her biggest problem. Her biggest problem was "bring your dog to work day."

Everyone was expecting to meet Midas, but there was no Midas.

Imogen didn't have a dog. Imogen didn't have a loving family.

Imogen had no one.

The personal life she'd created for herself was entirely fake.

2

Dorothy

Dorothy eased into the line of traffic and was heading out of London when Imogen returned her call.

"I'm sorry I missed your call, Dorothy. You know how much I enjoy talking to you." Imogen sounded breathless and apologetic, and Dorothy smiled. It would have been hard not to admire and respect someone who was as relentlessly upbeat and positive as Imogen. Her energy transmitted itself to the people around her. Added to that, she always had a smile on her face and was ferociously committed to her job.

"It's not a problem. I only rang to tell you in person that I loved your proposal, so consider this a green light. We can talk details in due course." She glanced briefly at her daughter, who was seated in the passenger seat next to her, hands clasped in her lap.

Sara gave her a look.

Dorothy ignored it. This was her decision. She could do as

she pleased. And it pleased her to give the business to Imogen. No one deserved it more.

"Brilliant! That's the best news. I'm excited." Imogen's enthusiasm filled the car. "I'll start working up some of the detail over the weekend and let you have that on Monday."

"There's no hurry. Take the weekend off, Imogen. You've been working too hard." Dorothy checked her mirror and pulled into the outside lane. "I was thinking that maybe we should have lunch next time I'm in London. We can toast our excellent partnership and also Christmas."

"That would be great. Just name the day and time, and I'll make the arrangements. I'm already looking forward to it."

"I'm in the Cotswolds for the next week, but I'll be back in London the week after that. Does that work for you?"

They firmed up plans, Dorothy wished Imogen a pleasant weekend and then ended the call.

Silence echoed around the car.

Dorothy waited. She didn't have the energy for the conversation she knew was coming. Not tonight.

Finally, Sara spoke. "Mum—"

"I don't want to hear it, Sara."

"But—"

"Imogen is doing a great job. She is smart, hardworking and creative. There is no one I would rather be working with. You heard her just now—her enthusiasm is infectious."

Sara took a breath. "She is good. I'm not arguing that point, but—"

"Do you know that our suppliers and customers still talk about the event she ran for us last year? Even the ones who didn't come talk about it, because they regret not having made the effort. It's a shame you missed it."

Sara turned her head away and stared out of the window. "Ava was sick."

"Yes." Dorothy opened her mouth and closed it again. *Let it go, Dorothy.*

"I know you want to give the business to Imogen," Sara said, "but don't you think we should at least ask a few other companies to pitch?"

"No." Dorothy kept an eye on the car ahead that was weaving in and out of traffic. "Imogen is excellent at what she does, the costings are in line with our budget and I'm confident the project will run perfectly if she is in control. Why put it out to pitch? We're a small family business and I don't have time for all that. What *is* that guy doing? Does he really think he's going to squeeze through that gap? Friday afternoon does strange things to people." She wanted this conversation to end, but it seemed she didn't get that lucky.

Sara tapped her fingers on the file in front of her. "All I'm saying is that—"

"I know what you're saying, and I'm grateful for your opinion, Sara, always. But this decision is mine, and I've made it." She said it as if it had been easy, but it hadn't. She wondered if Sara knew that she questioned herself every moment of the day. Big decisions, important decisions, should be clear, but this one was murky and opaque. "Those concepts are perfect. The drone display is inspired. We're holding it on our own land, which will keep the costs down. And I love the fact that we'll be able to invite our neighbors and everyone in the village. It will be quite a party."

"It is clever, I admit it. This isn't about Imogen's work, you know that." Sara sighed. "I'm worried about you, that's all."

"You don't need to worry about me. I know what I'm doing." If only that were true. She had no idea what she was doing. She was winging it. Doing her best. Making her best guess and hoping that instinct served her better than it had in the past. Mistakes should make you wiser, surely, but in her case they'd just made her wary.

"Mum—"

"More importantly, give me the latest sales figures and then we can switch off and get ourselves into weekend in the country mode." The traffic finally eased and she headed out of London, leaving the city behind her.

She could feel Sara's gaze on her, but finally her daughter turned her attention to her phone.

"Patrick sent the numbers through an hour ago. Sales are up 40 percent on this time last year. Orders are going through the roof, but that's Christmas of course. I spoke to the agency— the new ad, *Christmas without the headache*, seems to have resonated with the forty- to fifty-year-old age group, which is good because we were aiming to increase sales among that group."

Dorothy smiled. "All those parents cooking the Christmas dinner. And your new social media campaign?"

"It has been a hit with influencers. We've had some dreamy lifestyle photography, the new bottle and label looks great in photos. There was a brilliant one taken on a Christmas tree farm. I'll send it to you. The half size gift bottle with the Christmas label has almost sold out. We have more on order—" Sara talked for the next hour, and by the time she'd finished updating Dorothy, they'd left the motorway and were weaving their way along country roads toward the Cotswolds.

Dorothy felt the stress of the city leave her and a new stress form behind her ribs.

It wasn't the place, it was the time of year.

"It's cold today," she said briskly. "I can't believe it's December next week. It will soon be Christmas." The moment she said the words she felt Sara's hand on her leg, comforting.

Any tension that the earlier conversation might have caused fell away.

"I know." Sara gave her leg a squeeze. "But it's going to be fine. We're going to have a good time, you wait."

"We are. We always do." What would she do without her

daughter? Dorothy sat up a little straighter and focused on the road. Sara was better than she was at compartmentalizing. She'd managed to lock the past away. Dorothy wished she was able to do the same. "Are the girls excited?"

"*Excited* doesn't cover it. They've made a chart so that they can count the sleeps until Santa comes. They've made more Christmas cards than we have people in our lives. I have no idea what we're going to do with them all."

"Get the girls to send them to the animals. The alpacas would love to have a Christmas card, I'm sure."

"That's a great idea, although you'll have to make sure they don't eat it." Sara laughed. "And talking of alpacas, Mrs. Nolan wants to know if they can borrow Benson for the play at school. As you'll be in the audience, you can supervise him."

"Goodness. They have a role for an alpaca? What exactly is this play?"

"The kids have written the story," Sara said. "All living things welcome. They created a part especially for Benson because the children love him, and no matter how much they fuss over him, he never bites them."

"Of course he wouldn't bite them. And yes, they can borrow Benson."

"Do you think he'd tolerate wearing a pair of antlers?"

"There's only one way to find out." Dorothy smiled at the thought. "Anything else? The Herdwick sheep are friendly. You could borrow a couple."

"I did wonder about taking Romeo and Juliet."

Dorothy winced and shook her head. "Not unless you want the play to turn into a pantomime. You know what goats are like."

"They're adorable."

"They eat everything in sight, Sara."

"That's true. I suppose you're right. Fine. Just Benson then. And maybe a sheep. I'll ask."

"I could invite Miles to join us," Dorothy said. "It would be useful to have a vet there."

Sara laughed. "There is no way Miles would say yes, not after that incident a few years ago when Bryony Wilson had a glass of wine in the interval and cornered him in the corridor."

"You're probably right. I'll be the alpaca wrangler then."

"Great. Thanks, Mum. Now that the renovations are finished on Holly Cottage, are you going to give it back to the letting agency?"

"No. I'm going to deal with it in January."

Holly Cottage had once been the gatehouse for the estate, and Dorothy had been offering it as a holiday let for the past ten years. Over the summer she'd employed a local builder to update it. The work had taken much longer than anticipated thanks to the unpredictability of old cottages, but she was thrilled with the result. They'd kept all the character and charm, but updated everything from the heating system to the plumbing.

"It's looking great," Sara said. "While we're on the subject of Christmas, we haven't firmed up details for this year. The girls are hoping we could all stay with you at the house if that works."

Dorothy felt a lump form in her throat. "You don't have to do that, Sara. I'll be perfectly fine. You were with Patrick's family last year. You should have Christmas in your own home for once. I'll come for the day."

"I spend plenty of time in my own home," Sara said. "We'd much rather come to you. If you can bear to have us, of course. That way I can have a blissful Christmas lying around on the sofa doing nothing, while you run around the kitchen and entertain your hyperactive grandchildren. Who'd say no to that?" Her phone pinged and she checked her message, while Dorothy wondered how it was that Sara always managed to make her smile and feel positive about Christmas.

It was a miracle really because part of her was dreading Christmas, the way she always dreaded Christmas. It didn't matter how many years passed, it was still painful. And Sara knew that of course. In many ways it was as difficult for Sara as it was for her. They'd lived through those days together. She sometimes wondered if she would have survived if it hadn't been for her daughter.

She felt a rush of love, and also pride.

What a star Sara was, and never more so than at Christmas. She'd made a conscious decision that they were going to turn Christmas into something wonderful, and instead of keeping it low-key she always insisted that they celebrate in a big way.

She glanced briefly at her daughter. Sara was replying to the message on her phone. Her head was down and her hair had slid forward, a curtain of pale gold, leaving Dorothy with a glimpse of just her long eyelashes and the curve of her cheek. For a moment Dorothy saw her as a young girl, not as a married woman with two children of her own.

Sara. Always so responsible. So caring. Some children were nothing but a worry. Sara had never been one of those.

"Patrick says it's pizza night." Sara sent the message. "You're invited. He and the girls have already made the dough and the tomato sauce. Which basically means I'm going to have to redecorate the kitchen when I get home. Do you see now why I'm desperate to come to you for Christmas?"

Dorothy laughed and for a moment she was tempted by the invitation to join them for pizza. An evening with her grandchildren was guaranteed to distract her and lift her somber mood, but she was ready to spend some time at home.

"Not tonight, but I appreciate the invitation."

"Are you sure?" There was concern in Sara's voice. "Are you going to sit and feel sad?"

"No. I've been in London all week. Far too long. I'm going

to spend the evening checking on the animals and finding out what has been happening in my absence."

"If you change your mind, come on over. You know Patrick always overcaters."

"I know. Thank you."

"And will you let us come to you for Christmas? Is it too much of an invasion? Be honest. I promise I won't really lounge on the sofa. We'll all help, including the girls, although their kind of help often ends up doubling the workload."

Dorothy smiled. "You know I'd love to have you." The idea of it lifted her mood. She'd make a big fuss, as Sara always did. She'd choose a huge tree. The girls would love that. "It will be fun. The girls can help me decorate the house over the next few weeks."

There was an ache behind her ribs. She was lucky to have them. Her wonderful daughter and son-in-law, her two adorable grandchildren. The Estate, the business, her beautiful home in the country. The animals. She smiled. The animals were the reason she never felt lonely. She really was fortunate in many ways, and she knew it. But still—

It was possible to be fortunate and grateful but also feel an ache of regret for the past. And at this time of year that ache became more acute.

She dropped Sara at her house in the village, stopped long enough to hug her grandchildren and then headed back to the car to drive the few miles home to the Winterbury Estate.

Her parents had bought the house and grounds in a tumble-down state and had gradually restored it. It had been her father who had planted the vines. He'd returned from a holiday in France, inspired by what he'd seen. He'd been convinced that the sheltered aspect of the estate and the soil quality would produce an excellent wine, and time had proved him right.

Dorothy drove down the narrow country lanes, her headlamps picking out dry stone walls and thatched cottages as she headed into the small Cotswold village of Winterbury. She felt an immediate sense of serenity and calm. Despite all the advances of the modern world, it sometimes felt as if time had stood still in this quaint little corner of England.

A river bubbled through the middle of the village, flanked by houses of honey-colored stone. There was a village green, a pub that drew people from miles around, an excellent bakery and various independent stores that stocked local produce, including wines from the Winterbury Estate. In the summer months the streets were swollen with tourists keen to absorb the atmosphere, but in winter the place mostly returned to the home of her childhood.

They were forecasting a cold snap, but it had been a good year for the vines. In fact, Patrick, who was her winemaker as well as her son-in-law, had told her last month that it had been their best year ever, with their highest yields to date. June had been dry and warm, allowing for flowering, and then they'd had heavy storms but by then the vines were flourishing. They'd had a bumper harvest.

A mile beyond the village she turned off the main road, drove through the gates of the Winterbury Estate, past Holly Cottage and along the tree-lined avenue that led to the house.

The prospect of a weekend alone didn't worry her. She'd lived alone since Phillip had died and she was used to it.

Sara was worried she was lonely, but Dorothy never felt lonely here. Partly because there were usually people around— the small staff who helped her around the estate, and Jenny, her housekeeper who lived in the village—but mostly because this was her home.

She pulled up in front of the house. The front door opened, and a welcoming glow of light spilled down the steps. A spaniel sped across to her, tail wagging furiously.

"Bailey." She bent to make a fuss of him. "I missed you."

She reached for her luggage. She made a point of traveling light and only had a single small suitcase.

"He always behaves as if you've been away for a year, not a couple of nights. Good trip?" Jenny stood on the steps waiting for her, her coat already buttoned.

"Very good. Thank you for keeping an eye on everything, Jenny." She hugged the other woman warmly. They'd known each other for decades, and their friendship had sustained them through tough times. "Everything okay here?"

"Yes. I checked the alpacas earlier. Everything seemed fine. I gave them extra hay."

"Thanks, Jenny. Drive carefully. I'll see you on Monday." Dorothy watched as Jenny drove away and then headed to the house with Bailey at her heels.

It felt good to be home.

She walked through to the kitchen and was wrapped in a welcoming warmth.

Jenny had left a stack of mail for her on the table, but she decided to tackle it later and instead made herself a mug of creamy hot chocolate, which she took to the library. This was the room where she felt closest to Phillip, and she still did feel his presence here even though it had been so many years since he died. She'd been a widow for more than twenty years and she still missed him every day, even though she'd made a good life for herself.

She sat in the nook that overlooked the gardens and the paddock. In summer she could watch her small herd of alpacas from this spot, but tonight they'd taken refuge from the cold in the small barn that she'd had built for them when they first arrived.

To the right of the paddock was the vegetable garden, and behind that the orchard and then the vineyards.

Bailey joined her in the library and settled at her feet.

"We ought to have an early night." She reached out and stroked his head. "Busy day tomorrow."

Every day was busy, and with Christmas approaching it

would get busier, although nothing like harvest, of course, which always involved brutal hours and little time off. She left the logistics of running the business to her small team of staff, of which Patrick was a key member, but she still kept an eye on everything and occasionally she helped prune the vines. It took her back to those exhausting but happy days when she and Phillip had done so much of the work together.

It was time she started to give proper thought to Christmas. If her grandchildren were coming, then she needed the house to be extra festive.

It was time to start baking and freezing food so it would be less frenetic while they were staying.

No doubt it would mean working from dawn to dusk, but that didn't worry her. She needed it.

And even though she knew Sara had been teasing her with her jokes about lounging on the sofa, she badly wanted her daughter to be able to relax and enjoy Christmas. She wanted her to be able to spend time with the girls and Patrick. Focus on her children and not spend her time welded to the stove. Family time was so important, and those early years passed so quickly.

She picked up her empty mug and walked back to the kitchen.

She reached for her laptop bag and pulled out the proposal that Imogen had sent through. The concept and details were inspired, but no less than she'd come to expect from Imogen. She was an impressive young woman and she deserved the volume of business, and the trust, that Dorothy gave her.

She knew Sara was worried that she'd allowed herself to get so close to Imogen.

It was the one thing, the only thing, on which they disagreed.

Dorothy understood Sara's concern, but that didn't alter her resolve.

She was doing what she needed to do.

3

Sara

"So how was the big bad city?" Patrick grabbed her and kissed her as she walked through the door.

"Big and bad." She abandoned her suitcase and kissed him back. "I think it might have corrupted me."

"Yeah?" He lifted his mouth from hers and smiled. "That's the best news I've had in a while. Care to elaborate? Or better still, give me a physical demonstration?"

"Maybe I will."

"Mummy!" There were shrieks and then both girls came thundering out of the kitchen.

"Or maybe not," she murmured, smiling at him before she turned to hug the girls.

First was Ava, six years old and the more boisterous of the two sisters.

"We're making pizza!"

"You are? Then I can't wait to join you." She kissed Ava and held out her arm to Iris. At nine, Iris was quieter than her sister. The girls smelled of shampoo, sugar and innocence.

She held them close. Only one thing truly mattered to Sara, and that was family. There wasn't a day when she didn't feel grateful for it. They were her whole world. She'd never let anything come between her, Patrick and her girls.

"We've started making yours," Iris said. "We thought you might be too tired to make it yourself. We hoped Granny might come."

Iris. Always kind. Always thinking of others.

Sara kissed the top of her head and stood up. "Granny was a bit tired and she was keen to get back to her animals."

"Come *on*," Ava said to her sister. She grabbed Iris by the hand and dragged her back to the kitchen.

Ava. Always restless. Always moving on to the next thing.

Sara felt a pang as she watched them, hand in hand. She wanted her girls to always be as close as they were now. To always be a support to each other. *Sisters.*

Wishing she could freeze time, she walked with Patrick to the kitchen. "Have they been good?"

"Pretty good. You know how it is. They're excited to see you. I don't know how we're ever going to get them to bed on time."

"One late night won't hurt." Sara slid off her shoes and grabbed an apron. It felt so good to be home. Worry about her mother still nagged at her, but here among her family she was able to push it to the back of her mind. "I don't want tomato sauce on my best silk shirt."

"You could always take it off." Patrick gave her a look and she gave him her own look back.

Maybe they should have booked a babysitter for the evening and gone out.

"I took mine off. I dropped tomato on it." Ava scattered cheese over her pizza. "I was sad, because it's my best one."

"It will wash." Iris moved the pizza base closer to her sister so that less food fell on the table. "I put it to soak in the bathroom. She was crying, but I told her you'd get it clean again. You always manage to get things clean."

Sara smiled at her. She was pleased she hadn't booked a babysitter. Tonight was family time, and later—later, when the girls were in bed, she'd have time alone with Patrick. "You are so kind to your sister."

"Here's your pizza." Patrick put it in front of her and she blinked. "Wow. That is a lot of olives."

"Is it too many?" Iris looked at her anxiously. "We know you love olives so I gave you my share. But maybe it's too many."

"It's the perfect amount. And that's so generous of you." Sara duly admired the pizza. "I don't know how you got it so exactly right."

Iris flushed with pride and returned happily to her own pizza.

The pizzas said everything about the personalities of her girls, Sara thought.

Iris's pizza was neat and symmetrical, divided into quarters with strips of ham, each quarter decorated with the same precision.

"Your pizza is a work of art," she said as she admired it and Ava pushed hers forward.

"How about mine? Is mine a work of art?"

"Modern art," Patrick said, winking at Sara.

Ava's pizza looked as if all the ingredients had been dropped from a helicopter.

"It looks delicious." Sara slid the pizzas into the oven and sat down at the table.

"Long week? Have a glass of our best Winterbury White." He put the tall long-stemmed glass in front of her and Sara studied it.

"It's a good color."

"The taste is better." He sat down next to her and gave her hand a squeeze. "This has been our best year at the vineyard. Incredible. For once, the weather was our friend. Thanks for your update email, by the way. Sounds as if your meeting with the buyer went well."

"Really well. He's knowledgeable about the low- and no-alcohol sector. Sees it as a massive growth area for them." Sara picked up her glass. "I'm hopeful."

Ava covered her ears. "Stop talking about work. Work is boring."

Sara put her glass down. "You're right. No more work."

"And the weather can't be your friend, Daddy, that's silly." Ava picked up her crayons. "You can't do a sleepover with the weather."

"You might if you were camping," Iris said. "Remember that storm the night we camped out in the vineyard? We were almost blown away. Daddy had to come and rescue us."

"I don't remember." Ava covered the paper with green crayon. "I'm drawing a Christmas tree."

Iris glanced across. "That's pretty. You need to give it some decorations."

"When can we have our real tree?" Ava added random pink splodges to the tree.

"Not yet," Iris said. "Or the needles fall off. But soon."

"I love having a tree," Ava said. "I wish we could have a Christmas tree all year."

"Me too." Iris leaned across and mopped up a splash of paint that had landed on the table. "Do you want to share my room on Christmas Eve?"

"At Nanna's house?" Ava's face lit up. "Yes!" She glanced at Sara. "Can I? Please?"

"Of course you can, if it's all right with Iris."

"It will be fun."

Their enthusiasm was infectious, and Sara felt a glow of warmth and anticipation. She knew her mother found this time of year hard, and part of her did too, but she'd learned to block it out and not give it a moment of her attention. The faint shadow of sadness was easily forgotten when she was with the girls. Their excitement seeped into her, blasting out the wisps of darkness.

"We'll get the tree soon. We'll choose the biggest one in the forest."

Ava clapped her hands, knocked over her drink in the process, and Iris went running for a cloth to mop up the mess.

Patrick helped her. "You were the one who said you wanted a little sister."

Iris dropped the cloth into the pools of juice. "I didn't realize a little sister would be so messy."

They ate their pizza together, and by the time the girls were settled and in bed, Sara was almost ready to collapse into bed herself.

She loaded the plates into the dishwasher, cleared the kitchen and made coffee.

"Tell me that's decaf," Patrick said, "although nothing is likely to keep me awake tonight."

"Have they been waking you up?"

"Ava had a couple of bad dreams. You know how she is. Active imagination. I probably did too much with them. Wound them up playing. That's the downside of working too hard— when I'm with them I overcompensate." He reached for the cups and she poured the coffee.

"How could we produce two children who are so different?"

"I don't know, but I happen to think they make a perfect pair. You don't have to be the same to be good together. Think of fish and chips. Scones and cream."

They carried their drinks into the living room and Sara collapsed onto the sofa. "I worry about them. Iris is so sensitive, and Ava is capable of getting herself into so much trouble and she's only six. What's it going to be like when she's sixteen?"

Patrick stroked her leg. "They're going to be fine."

"You don't know that. No one ever knows what is round the corner."

"Whoa—" he shifted position so that he could look at her "—what's brought this on?"

"Nothing. It's just that sometimes I worry that—"

"I know what you worry about, but you don't need to. That isn't going to happen. Is this because you were trapped in the car with your mother for hours? Did she put those thoughts in your head?"

"No." She was quick to defend her. "Obviously she worries—"

"And she infected you with that same worry. So now I'm going to tell you not to worry. The girls are fine. They dote on each other." He put his cup down and pulled her into his arms. "How is your mother?"

"Oh, you know—the usual." She snuggled against his shoulder. "Putting on a brave face. She's busy, so that's good."

"Did you persuade her to let us spend Christmas Day with her?"

"Yes, I think so." She glanced up at him? "You're sure that's okay with you?"

"Of course. The girls will love it."

"How about you?" She reached for her coffee. "You work with my mother. Are you sure you want to spend Christmas with her too?"

"Yes. She's good company. And she is great to work with. Not that I see that much of her. Talking of work, that proposal that the events company put together for our summer party next year looks great."

"You read it? Between the vineyard and the girls, I didn't think you'd have time."

"You were away. My nights were long and empty. I missed you. And I was interested." He paused. "It's amazing how fast we're expanding. If that guy you had your meeting with puts in an order—"

"I know! Our little Cotswold winery hitting the big time." She grinned. "Merry Christmas."

"And did your mother meet up with Imogen?"

"No, not this time, although they are going to arrange something before Christmas." She felt a flicker of unease. "They're getting pretty close."

"And that bothers you?"

"I don't know." She paused. "Yes, it bothers me."

"Imogen is good at her job."

"I know. She is good. That's not what worries me." Sara's head started to throb. "You know what my mother is like. Waifs, strays, anyone in need, anyone vulnerable—human or animal—and my mother is there."

"Which category does Imogen fit into?"

"I'm not sure. But when Imogen moved companies, my mother didn't hesitate to move our business with her."

"Because she's competent and enthusiastic. Not exactly a waif or a stray, Sara. It was a sound business decision."

She welcomed the reassurance and the logic, but still, anxiety gnawed at her insides. "You're right, but we both know her reasons for using them are more complicated than that."

He was silent for a moment. "In the end, this is your mother's decision. She's doing what she needs to do. What she feels is right."

But what she was doing could have difficult consequences.

"I want to protect her." And herself. She wanted to protect herself. Was that selfish?

No, it was survival.

"I know you do. But your mother is as stubborn and determined as you are, and she isn't going to change her mind. All you can do is go along with it."

"You're right. There's no point in worrying." She snuggled closer. "The time of year doesn't help."

"I know." His arms tightened. "But it's going to be fine. We're going to have a great Christmas."

There was no reason why that shouldn't be the case. So why was she feeling so uneasy?

4

Imogen

Imogen switched off her computer and yawned. It had been a long day, and she still had to put together some ideas for a client's centenary celebration the following summer, but she didn't want to stay any later because the walk from the station to her home became steadily less safe as the evening progressed.

"Imogen?" Rosalind called to her from her office. "Can you come in for a moment?"

They were the only two people left on the floor. Desks were deserted, and beyond the windows the city stretched, tall buildings glittering against the night sky.

Far beneath them the River Thames snaked its way past Tower Bridge and down toward Greenwich. It was a stunning view of London, showcasing all the best parts, and sometimes Imogen wondered if anyone would notice if she tucked a sleeping bag under her desk and lived here. It would be so much better than her current accommodation, which was an example of London at its least appealing.

Imogen paused in the doorway of Rosalind's office. She felt the usual flash of envy. Rosalind was the only person who had her own protected space. She had a door (an actual door!), although to be fair she rarely closed it.

Imogen sometimes imagined how much more work she could get done if she had her own office. No more chitchat. No more having to be creative about her life. No more trying to fit in. What would that be like?

She'd hate it.

She was lonely at home; she didn't need to be cut off and lonely at work too.

"Is everything all right, Rosalind?"

"Couldn't be better. I have good news, and as you are a large part of the reason for the good news, I thought I'd share it with you first." Rosalind sat back in her chair and slid on the glasses that gave her the look of a serious academic. "We won the Noop account."

Imogen felt a surge of triumph. "We did?" This was why she worked all those hours. Nothing beat that adrenaline rush that came with winning a big piece of business.

"We did. And it was a six-way pitch, so even more impressive. They loved you. Congratulations, Imogen."

"It was a team effort."

"But you headed up that team." Rosalind beckoned her into the office. "Come and sit down for a moment. I want to talk to you."

Imogen walked into the room and sat down opposite Rosalind.

Yes, she was going to be very late, but it was almost worth being mugged on the way home to savor this moment of achievement.

"That is great news. When did you hear?"

"Just now. The CEO called. There's just one condition. They want you to handle the account personally."

"No problem." Imogen didn't hesitate and Rosalind leaned forward, studying her closely.

"Are you sure? I must admit I'm concerned. You already have almost twice the number of accounts as Danny, and he told me this week he is too stretched to take on anything else."

"Danny has two kids and a busy homelife." Imogen didn't mention the gym or the after-work drinks. "He has a lot on."

"Danny also has a wife who does most of it," Rosalind said dryly, "but we'll ignore that. I'm not one of those bosses who thinks that employees should have no homelife, although I suspect Danny's contribution in that department is minimal. But it does make me wonder how you manage to handle so much."

"I'm single. It helps. Also, I love my work. I enjoy every moment. I suppose I'm a bit of a workaholic." With no homelife, work was her priority, not least because she had no choice but to be financially independent.

Rosalind narrowed her eyes. "I thought you had a boyfriend. Jack, wasn't it?"

Damn. She'd forgotten about Jack, which would have been a red flag had the relationship been real, but like most things in Imogen's personal life, Jack wasn't real. Having listened to all the ups and downs of Janie's love life, Imogen was almost relieved he wasn't real.

"We're casual. He works for one of the big management consultancy firms. You know how it is. The main job requirement is that you have no life outside work."

"Even so, you're already over capacity," Rosalind said. "Don't think I haven't noticed. It's a heavy workload for anyone, even someone with your talent and work ethic. I don't want you to burn out."

"I don't know what that is, Rosalind, but I can assure you I'm nowhere near burning anything." She perched on the edge of her chair and tried to project an aura of high energy.

"You're sure you're handling everything?" Rosalind persisted. "You'd tell me if you were struggling?"

"I would." *She definitely wouldn't.* If she found herself struggling with workload she'd go to bed later to give herself more time to get things done. "I'm not sure why you're asking. Is there something I haven't done? Something I haven't delivered?"

"No. You deliver every time." Rosalind looked at her steadily. "In fact, you usually overdeliver."

"Good. I'm a fast worker, you know that. And if I need to work a few extra hours to get things done, then I'll do that."

Why was Rosalind asking all these questions? Imogen resisted the temptation to check her reflection in the mirror. Did she look tired? What was going on? Maybe she needed to wear more makeup. She'd talk to Anya about blusher.

"You're already working more than a few extra hours." Rosalind tapped her keyboard with her finger to wake up her computer. She checked the screen. "I couldn't help noticing that you sent me an email at three in the morning last week. And another the following night at four. As a matter of interest, when do you sleep?"

"I'm one of those lucky people who don't need much sleep," Imogen assured her. "And if something comes to me in the night, then I'd rather just deal with it right there and then."

"Mmm." Rosalind looked at her over the top of her glasses. "Do you have a time when you switch off?"

"Of course." *Never.* "I do yoga, meditate, walk the dog…"

"Ah yes, Midas." Rosalind removed her glasses. "Janie mentioned that he's sick. Have you had news from the vet?"

A fictitious boyfriend was manageable. Boyfriends were notoriously unreliable so there were no end of options for getting rid of them quickly without raising eyebrows, but the dog had been a mistake. She could see that now. She should have picked a less complicated pet like a rabbit or a hamster. Maybe even a stick insect, although it was hard to be appropriately gooey about a stick insect and having that particular photo on her desk would not have endeared her to Janie.

Basically, she should have picked any pet that would have allowed her to bond with the staff, without creating all this complexity.

"The vet says Midas is going to be fine."

"Right. So when are you picking him up?"

"Picking him up?" As the web of lies tightened around her she felt a flicker of panic.

"I assume the vet isn't going to deliver him to you personally?"

"Oh—no, of course not. I'll be going there myself. Although now you mention it, it would be great if they could deliver. Like pizza." *Stop talking, Imogen.* "I'm going tomorrow. They want to keep him for one more night. To be sure."

"To be sure of what? What was wrong with him?"

"They still don't know exactly. They said they'd give me a full report when I'm there in person." She made a mental note to research a few doggy illnesses sufficiently serious to require observation, but not life-threatening.

"If you need to work from home on Monday so that you can look after him, that's fine."

Work from home? If a fictitious dog was this demanding, it was a good thing she didn't have a real one.

"I don't need to work from home, Rosalind. I have a brilliant dog sitter and she is always happy to help me out with situations like this. I have three events on Monday, so I'll be zipping around London trying to be in three places at once. You know how it is." Actually, Rosalind probably didn't know how it was, because Rosalind never attended events in person anymore. She'd set up her own company and proceeded to recruit good people who did the bulk of the client-facing work.

"Your dog sitter sounds like a treasure. You must give me her details," Rosalind said. "It's a constant struggle to find anyone reliable. The last dog walker I used was a disaster."

Imogen made a sympathetic sound, as if this was a topic she understood. *Ask an open question*, she thought. That way she wasn't the one doing the talking. "What happened?"

"She walked so many she lost track. And sometimes she lost the actual dogs. Fortunately, they're all tagged. But I'm on my fifth this year."

"Your fifth?" Imogen was about to say that was a lot of dogs to get through, when she realized Rosalind was talking about dog walkers. "Right. Well, yes, it's always hard finding good people."

"Do you think yours might be able to fit my Daisy in? She's good with other dogs. Usually. Bites very rarely."

"I think the person I use is full at the moment," Imogen said quickly, "but if she gets a space, I'll let you know."

"Yes, do that." Rosalind smiled at her. "Well, if you're sure about the account."

"I'm sure." Imogen saw the time and realized how late it was. She was approaching the time when mugging might become murder. She stood up. "Thanks, Rosalind. I'll see you on Monday."

"Yes. And I hope Midas is okay and your vet bill not too scary!"

At least fictitious dogs were cheap. That was one thing. Complicated, but cheap.

Imogen left the office feeling buoyant. They'd won another account!

She smiled as she took the stairs down to the ground floor (Janie's obsession with her step count had rubbed off on her). Her footsteps echoed in the stairwell as she headed down to street level, thinking about the conversation with Rosalind.

For a moment there she'd been afraid that Rosalind wasn't going to give her the account, which was ridiculous because she was *fine*. And she definitely wasn't burned-out, or even on the edge of burning out.

She had no idea what had stimulated that conversation, but she needed to be more careful.

She'd stop sending emails in the middle of the night. It drew attention that she didn't want or need. Same with sending emails on Christmas Day. It seemed that normal people didn't do that. At least, not people with the type of life she pretended to be living. If she was really who she pretended to be, she'd be walking Midas in the crisp cold winter air and returning to the big house in the country to gather round the kitchen table with her loved ones. It was family season and she wouldn't even think about work because she'd be so caught up in the festivities.

That was a slip on her part, but she wasn't going to slip again.

This year she'd write all the emails she needed to write and save them in drafts. Then she'd send them on January 2. Anya would still return to the same number of emails, but it would raise fewer eyebrows.

She walked across the foyer, said good-night to the staff at the desk and did the dance of death with the revolving glass door that threatened to end people's careers and lives on a daily basis.

The cold punched her, and she buttoned her coat and wrapped her scarf around her neck.

They were forecasting an exceptionally hard winter. The bookies had stopped taking bets on the chances of a white Christmas in London, even though such a thing was a rarity.

Maybe she should get a real dog to keep her warm. But given that she didn't have a family who would step in and help when she needed them, that wasn't an option. She kept her life as simple as possible.

The train was crowded and she stood squashed between commuters, avoiding eye contact. She was wedged between the metal pole and a man in a suit, and it occurred to her that this was the closest she'd been to a man physically in a long time. Maybe she should try dating again, although last time that hadn't worked out so well. It seemed easier not to.

The train rattled its way through dark tunnels under the city, spewing out passengers at different destinations. As they drew farther away from the glamour and wealth of the city of London with its glass offices and sense of purpose, the crowd thinned a little and Imogen was finally able to sit down.

She stared straight ahead, careful not to look at anyone. Careful not to attract attention.

Finally, the train reached her stop and she was one of only a couple of people left on the train.

She left the station and buttoned her coat over the bag she wore across her body. She'd been mugged two months before and had her bag stolen, so now she stayed alert for the five-minute walk between the station and her home. The contrast between the glitzy glass building where she worked and the area where she lived couldn't have been more marked. Even the overoptimistic letting agent had choked on the words "up and coming" as he'd shown her around. It said a lot that the apartment had even been available for her to look around. The rental market in London was so hot that the moment something became available, desperate people offered up overinflated deposits in order to secure it, often without even viewing. No one had viewed Imogen's place. Apparently, even desperate people had limits.

She picked her way along the street, past the rubbish that hadn't been collected, past the two houses that were boarded up and the shopping trolley that someone had abandoned. A streetlight flickered, throwing dark shadows across her path. The temperature had plummeted during the day, and it promised to hit freezing overnight.

Heading down the steps that led to her tiny studio flat in the basement, she wondered what her colleagues would say if they knew the truth about her life.

She didn't live in a pretty garden flat with room for Midas to run around. No self-respecting dog would have set a paw inside her cramped living accommodation.

But that was all fine because she'd chosen to live here for a very good reason. Financial security. She could have afforded somewhere closer to the center of London, but that would have taken a large bite out of her salary. This place enabled her to save a good amount each month and, in her opinion, it was worth the sacrifice. She already had almost enough for a deposit on a modest place, but she was more ambitious than that. She wanted to fall in love with somewhere. She wanted a *home*. Somewhere that was all hers. Whenever she had doubts about her accommodation, she checked her savings account and felt a surge of pride and satisfaction.

She bolted the doors and took off her coat.

Living here wasn't so bad. It was a step up on most of the places she'd lived as a child, and she was used to surrounding herself with things that made her feel soothed and safe. She'd painted the walls green and bought two large plants so she could pretend she was in the countryside and not living alongside an abandoned parking lot and a railway line. The plants were fake, like most other things in her life, although in this case they'd been chosen not to deceive but because there was too little light in her flat for a real plant to survive. One entire wall was taken up by her bookcase, stuffed with books she'd bought at markets and charity shops. Knowing that someone had owned the books before her gave her a sense of connection. Someone else had turned those pages. Someone else had lost themselves in the same worlds she escaped to when she was alone.

The kitchen was tucked into one corner and she'd placed a small round bistro table by the only window. That was where she ate her meals. It was a lonely setup, but it worked for her.

She put her laptop on the table, made herself a slice of toast and sat down to check on the proposal they'd put together for the new client.

It was going to be a lot of work to implement the ideas they'd outlined, but she'd handle it.

Her phone pinged and she saw a message from Anya.

How is Midas?

She groaned and ignored it. Hopefully, Anya would assume she was busy.

How had she ever got herself into this situation? This couldn't carry on. A conversation was harmless enough, but things were getting complicated.

She needed to get rid of Midas, but how did you get rid of a fictitious dog? Maybe he could die of his fictitious illness. She felt guilty that she was thinking of killing an animal and had to remind herself that this wasn't a real animal.

No, she couldn't do that. If she went into work and told people he'd died, they'd be smothering her with sympathy and offering her time off, and time off was the last thing she wanted.

She took a bite of toast and gazed at the wall. Maybe she could give Midas to her "family" in the country. But that just made the whole lie even more complicated.

And then she had a flash of inspiration. She'd say he'd run away. Yes, that was good. That would work. It was clean, neat and no one would be hurt. She could blame the dog walker (she felt bad about that too and had to remind herself that her dog walker was as fictitious as her dog).

She'd be sad for a while to have lost her best friend, but also stoic. It was just one of those things. *Don't give me sympathy or I'll cry.* And no, she wouldn't be getting another pet. It was just too heartbreaking. Problem solved.

It would be a relief to get rid of at least one of the lies.

Maybe it was time for Jack to break up with her. No, that

wouldn't be good. Losing your dog and your boyfriend in such a short space of time either made you look sad or incompetent. She should be the one to break up with him.

Either way, it was time to simplify her life. She'd keep the family and the family home in the country, because they were useful conversation points at Christmas and other holidays and no one was ever going to find out the truth. But the rest of it was going to go.

Satisfied with her plan, she picked up her toast.

She'd taken another bite when her phone rang. The caller display said "Tina" and her mood plummeted.

Why now? Why today?

She stared at her phone, her stomach tense until it stopped ringing. Despite the freezing temperatures she was drenched in sweat.

It rang again, and she curled her fingers into her palms to stop herself from picking it up.

She didn't have to answer. There was no obligation. She'd answer it when it suited her to answer it. When she was ready. And right now she wasn't ready.

The ringing stopped, but then her phone alerted her to a voicemail.

Tempted to delete it without listening, she paused for a moment and then played the message, hating that part of herself that made it impossible for her to step back from it.

"Hi, Imogen, it's Tina. I need you to call me back as soon as you get this. It's urgent."

Imogen played the recording a second time, and then a third, although why she had no idea. It wasn't as if the words would change.

Hi, Imogen, how are you?

Hi, Imogen, just wanted you to know I've been thinking of you.

Hi, Imogen, I know I should have said this before now but I'm sorry about everything.

But of course the message hadn't said any of those things. She'd known it wouldn't, but still she felt disappointment every single time. Even though she knew better, she couldn't totally extinguish the glimmer of hope inside her. And maybe that was a good thing. You had to believe things could improve. You had to hold on to that hope. Otherwise, what was the point? Without hope, you lived your life in the dark, and she wasn't prepared to do that.

She reached out and deleted the message so that she wouldn't be tempted to replay it and sink lower than she was already.

This was why she'd invented a fictitious life, because her real life was something it was better to hide. To her colleagues she was Imogen with the dog, and a big loving family who had a swoon-worthy home in the country. It sounded so great that she was starting to feel envious of herself.

Still, she couldn't think about that now.

Her phone rang again and this time she answered it, as she always did eventually.

"Imogen?" The voice was raspy and hoarse. "Is that you?"

Imogen closed her eyes. She wouldn't call her Tina. She just wouldn't. Not on a day when almost everything in her life felt fake.

"Yes, it's me. Hi, Mum."

5

Dorothy

Dorothy pulled on her ancient down jacket and a scarf and headed outside with Bailey by her side. The dawn sky was milky white and the ground and the trees were covered in a silvery frost. She loved the hushed stillness of these early winter mornings, the sense that the world around was snuggling down. The trees around had shed their leaves, as if tired of carrying them all year.

"It's a cold one today." She talked to Bailey the way she talked to all her animals. As if they were family. Which to Dorothy, they were.

Every animal she cared for had a story, usually a tragic one. They'd come to her because no other help had been available to them. She'd given them a home and a second chance.

Dorothy believed in second chances.

These animals needed her, and she needed them every bit as much. Every animal she rescued gave her a small degree of exoneration for her failures. She didn't need a psychologist to analyze what she was doing. Even now, twenty years later, she was trying to make amends. Saving as many as she could to make up for the one she hadn't been able to save. And it didn't make up for it, of course. Not really. It didn't compensate. But it helped. The animals benefited, and they kept her busy. And Dorothy needed to be busy. Busy was her therapy. Busy had saved her.

In those early days when her mind and her thoughts had tortured her, when her heart had broken, and then broken again, there had been days when she'd thought she wouldn't survive it all. When she hadn't wanted to survive it. But she'd always found a reason to carry on.

First it was Sara. Then Sara's children—her grandchildren. The vineyard. The animals. They were her life now, and despite everything that had gone before, it was a good life. She was content. Yes, she thought about that time. She thought about it more often than she would have admitted to Sara, but the pain had settled into a dull ache that on some days she barely noticed.

But at this time of year, she noticed.

Christmas. The moment the berries on the holly bush turned red, she started to feel it. Her solution was to make sure she was even busier than usual. She spent more time in London. She involved herself more in the business. She filled every hour of her day and a fair few of her nights.

It was hard, but ultimately she knew she'd be fine. She'd done this before, so many times. If you survived something once, you could survive it again. And again. She couldn't block it out in the way that Sara did, but she'd learned that the way to make it through the season was to focus on what she had, and not what she'd lost. Gratitude, not bitterness.

She crossed the yard cautiously because it was icy underfoot. As she approached the paddock, the alpacas came to greet her and her mood lifted.

It was impossible to feel low when you were in the company of such beautiful, gentle creatures.

It hadn't started with alpacas. It had started with a donkey, and a call from the local animal shelter. Then it was a litter of kittens someone had tried to drown. She'd had sheep, an old police horse who needed a quiet life in the country, a donkey, chickens and a couple of rabbits.

Never an alpaca.

As was so often the case with all her animals, it was Miles McEwan, her vet, who had called her. He'd visited a smallholding where a couple keeping alpacas had lost interest because of the work involved. The alpacas were in a bad state. They needed to rehome them. Could Dorothy help?

She'd heard the anger in his voice, which was unusual because Miles was always calm and levelheaded, particularly in a crisis. But something about the plight of these animals had touched him, and it had touched her, too, as he'd known it would.

He'd known she wouldn't say no. Dorothy could never have said no to anything that was lost and needed her, and these alpacas seemed to need her. Miles had waited for her to agree before breaking the news that there were four of them.

Dorothy had known nothing about alpacas, so she'd quickly taken herself on a course, visited an alpaca breeder locally for advice and prepared the paddock closest to the house.

The alpacas had arrived on a bright, sunny spring day, and Miles and Dorothy had transferred them to their new home. They'd been in poor condition then, and Miles had visited regularly for those first weeks and months. Together they'd done what needed to be done, and before long the alpacas were thriving. A year later she'd taken in Benson, so now she had five of them.

Looking at them now, so healthy and alert, she found it hard to remember those early days.

She fed them, checked their hay, cleared the barn area where they sheltered overnight and gave them fresh water. While she was doing that she talked to them, checked their coats and general health. Miles visited frequently when he was passing on his way to visit farms, and anytime she was worried all she had to do was call.

But she didn't call him often. She'd learned all she could about them. Studied what they needed. Spent time with them.

She was closing the gate to the field when she saw Miles's car approaching down the drive.

It had been a few weeks since she'd seen him and she brightened at the prospect of his company. She felt more than a little maternal toward him, which was ridiculous really because he certainly wasn't a man who needed mothering. But he was the son of her oldest friend and she'd always looked out for him. She felt a pang as she thought about Sybil. It had been five years since her friend had died, but she still missed her every day. Seeing Miles somehow kept a small piece of her in Dorothy's life.

She smiled and waved as he parked and strode across to her, crossing the icy yard in long confident strides, not picking his way as she had done.

"Morning, Dorothy." He was wearing a thick sweater and heavy boots, and there were mud splashes on his trousers.

"Good morning, Miles. It's good to see you. Have you been up all night?"

"Most of it."

She couldn't resist teasing him. "Hot date?"

"She was a stunner. Legs like a racehorse." He grinned and leaned on the gate. "Which could have been because she was, in fact, a racehorse. I've been at the Morton Stud. Horse with colic."

"Oh dear. Is she going to be okay?"

"I think so, although I wasn't so sure of that at 2:00 a.m. Long night."

And now she could see how tired he was. His jaw was dark with stubble and his eyes were shadowed.

"You're not part of the equine team anymore. Why you?"

"I used to be, as you know, and we had a busy night so I stepped in. I'll be calling in the favor at some point."

But she knew that wasn't why he'd done it. He had a generous nature. He'd always been the same.

She put her hand on his arm. "You must be exhausted. And hungry, I'm sure. I was just about to put the kettle on and make some breakfast. Would you join me?"

"Why do you think I'm here? I was about to go home and put my own kettle on, but then I remembered that my cupboards are bare and so is the fridge, so I thought I'd drive here and look pathetic in the hope that you might take pity on me."

"Why are your cupboards bare?" Maybe he did need mothering. "Aren't you looking after yourself?"

"Barely." He gave her a sad look. "It's possible that I'm slowly starving. Look at me. Emaciated."

She looked and saw long legs, broad shoulders and strength honed by a life spent outdoors doing hard physical work. She thought about the incident in the summer, when he'd been called to help rescue a cow from the river. He'd waded waist deep into the river, sedated the cow just enough to stop her from trying to kill him and herself, and then hauled her to safety with the help of the farmer. The story had been all round the village before the evening, and Miles hadn't had to buy himself a drink in the pub since.

Sybil would be proud, she thought.

"You're positively puny," she said briskly. "It's a wonder you have the strength to lift your own mug of tea."

"I struggle. Cake might help."

"Cake?" She tutted her disapproval. "For breakfast?"

He shrugged. "I've been up all night so technically this could be dinner. I suppose I could force down a large bowl of porridge too if that would make you feel better. That special version you make with cinnamon and maple syrup. And maybe a bacon sandwich."

Now she was frowning. "Do you seriously have no food at home?"

"Of course I have food at home, but my food never tastes as good as yours." He leaned on the gate and studied the alpacas who had emerged from their shed to investigate the noise. "They're looking good, Dorothy. You're a wizard."

"Teamwork." She patted him on the shoulder. "Benson is going to have a starring role in the school play at Christmas. I don't suppose I can tempt you to join me for animal duties."

As Sara had predicted, he shuddered. "No thanks. Not after last time. I'm sure you'll be fine, Dorothy. You don't need me."

"I'm sure you're right." She smiled. "Come on. If you eat a decent breakfast, I'll give you chocolate cake to take home."

They headed to the house, and he took his boots off by the door before following her through to the kitchen.

The table was covered in branches of holly and mistletoe that she'd cut the day before and she pushed it to one side, making room for him.

"Ignore my Christmas preparations. Sit down."

"Now I'm feeling guilty for taking your time." He washed his hands and then rescued some holly that had fallen onto the floor. "You're busy."

"Nothing that can't wait. And it's always good to see you."

Not just because he was a connection to the past, but because she genuinely enjoyed his company.

She busied herself in the kitchen while he sprawled in a chair at her kitchen table, telling her about his week.

Soon the room was filled with the smell of fresh coffee and the sounds of bacon sizzling.

She enjoyed having someone to feed and spoil and watched with satisfaction and amusement as he devoured everything she put in front of him. He'd been the same as a boy.

"You're not at all hungry, then?" It delighted her that he considered her home and company a respite.

"No." He cleared the porridge bowl and reached for the bacon roll she'd placed in front of him. "I'm only eating this to be polite."

"Tell me honestly—are you cooking properly for yourself?"

"Honestly? Not much. Too tired." He finished the bacon roll and closed his eyes. "When I get home from my calls I collapse on the sofa. And this is supposed to be a quiet time of year. That was delicious, Dorothy. Marry me."

"You're thirty-two," she said dryly, and he opened his eyes.

"So? I'm an old thirty-two. And given the number of nights I work, I've crammed an extra life into the years I've lived, so if you do the calculation based on waking hours and life experience, I'm probably closer to fifty." He smiled at her and she thought to herself, not for the first time, that the woman who eventually persuaded Miles to leave behind his bachelor ways would be a lucky person.

"When did you last go on a date? A proper date."

"What's that?"

"Dinner? Movie?" She made him a fresh cup of coffee. "Remember that?"

"Not really. When am I going to fit that in?"

"You make the time." She put the cake on the table and cut him a thick slice. "Where are you spending Christmas?"

"I'm on call, so probably in a stable, pretending I'm a wise man." He suppressed a yawn. "Animals don't stop being sick just because it's Christmas. You are an incredible cook. Have I told you that?"

"Flattery like that will get you an invitation for Christmas lunch. Spend the day with us, Miles. Sara, Patrick and the girls will be here." She was about to wrap up the cake for him to take home, but he put it on his plate and started to eat it. She hid the smile and cut another generous slice for him to take with him. "We'd love you to join us."

"Do not invite me for lunch. You know what will happen.

You'll put the most delicious meal I've ever seen in front of me and then my phone will ring and I will have to leave to tend to a cow or some other four-legged beast who doesn't know it's Christmas. And you won't speak to me again." He licked chocolate from his fingers. "Trust me when I tell you that I have offended more people than I've charmed in my life. If you need proof, I can give you the number of the last woman who made the mistake of trying to live with me. I believe she has only recently stopped therapy."

She wasn't fooled by his flippant tone. She knew the end of that particular relationship had hurt him and made him wary. It had ended almost three years ago, and to the best of her knowledge he hadn't dated anyone seriously since, which was surprising because she knew for a fact that he was the object of fantasy for all the single women for miles around, and a good proportion of the married ones. Plenty of people would be more than willing to tolerate his occasionally antisocial work hours in return for being able to spend time with Miles McEwan.

"If you're called out, then I'll keep your meal warm until you're back to eat it. And I won't need therapy. I don't stress about small, unimportant things." She sat down opposite him, nursing the cup of coffee she'd poured herself. "I mean it. Please join us. In fact, I insist."

He sighed. "Dorothy—"

"Turkey, stuffing—"

"I don't—"

"Maple roasted parsnips—"

"Damn you, woman. Fine, I'll be there." He stood up and loaded his bowl and plate into the dishwasher. "Will you be inviting any other waifs and strays? Just checking this isn't a setup."

"I thought I might invite Erin."

He paused, eyes narrowed. "Erin from the bakery? Erin who is in her late sixties?"

"Is there another Erin?"

The sudden streak of color on his cheekbones told her that there was, or had been at one time, another Erin. Maybe his love life was more active than she'd thought.

"Erin from the bakery is a warm and wonderful woman," he said. "I look forward to the pleasure of her company. Particularly if she brings one of her sourdough loaves. And maybe a cinnamon twist." He closed the dishwasher and bent to make a fuss of Bailey. "Do you know how lucky you are living here? Having food put in your bowl every day?" Bailey's frantically wagging tail suggested he did indeed know.

Miles straightened. "I should go."

"Hold it right there. I want to hear about the other Erin."

He grabbed his coat from the back of the chair and gave her a wicked smile. "You definitely do not."

"I'm a lonely old woman who deserves some excitement in her life."

"My love life wouldn't excite anyone, as you well know. And if you're lonely I could bring you another animal. Paula Lightfoot's cat had a litter of kittens this week. She can't cope with them all."

Dorothy felt a pang but ignored it. "Sara would kill me if I took in another animal. She keeps telling me I must learn to say no. Also we both know that if Paula can't find homes for them, she will simply keep them."

"That's true." He walked across the kitchen, but then paused in the doorway and turned to look at her. "Are you really feeling lonely?" The sudden concern in his eyes made her all the more determined to find him someone deserving. He was a good man, and good men were not to be wasted.

"No. I don't have time to be lonely."

"But this isn't your favorite time of year."

She shrugged. "In the past, no, but Sara and family are coming to me at Christmas, and the girls are so excited it's hard not to get caught up in that. Better to focus on what you have than what you've lost, I always think. They'll be here soon. We're going to start decorating the house for Christmas. They come every Saturday."

"I know." He smiled. "How is the riding going? Is that pony behaving itself?"

"Thelma is a gem. Iris is doing well. She's a natural. She reminds me so much of Sara at the same age. I can't thank you enough for finding the perfect pony."

"She needed a good home and you gave her that. It's an arrangement that works for everyone." He suppressed another yawn and she gave him a little push.

"You're asleep on your feet. Go to bed."

"Good idea." He headed to the front door. "Thanks, Dorothy. That was delicious. You should open a café."

"If all my customers ate as much as you, I'd be out of business within a week." She waved him toward his car. "Drive carefully." She couldn't help saying it and he leaned in to give her a hug.

"I always do. You take care of yourself."

She watched him go and thought about Sybil. She missed their chats over a glass of wine. Missed sharing books and recipes and going for country walks together.

She was about to distract herself by taking a bale of hay to the field for Thelma, when she heard Sara's car.

Moments later she heard the children calling her.

"Nanna!"

"I'm here. I was about to feed Thelma."

"I'll do it." Iris took the animal duties seriously, paying attention and giving Dorothy a full report on how each animal was. "Can I ride her later?"

"I was hoping you'd want to. The exercise will do her good."

It was a routine that at weekends her grandchildren came over to help. They didn't mind getting muddy or cold. They just loved being near the animals. Dorothy enjoyed seeing them absorbed by outdoor, wholesome endeavors. She hoped that never changed.

Most of all, she liked seeing the way they were together.

"I want to ride Thelma too!" Ava danced across the yard, oblivious to patches of ice and mud. "But first I want to feed Benson."

"We'll feed Benson together. And it's not your turn to ride today, it's mine." Iris took her sister's hand and they walked together to the alpacas. She helped her sister climb onto the gate. "Hold on tight. Don't fall."

"She's always helping her," Dorothy said to her daughter. "Always looking out for her."

"I know. Iris is very protective. Oh, and while we're on the subject, you only need to make up one room for them at Christmas because they want to share." Sara watched the girls and so did Dorothy.

It warmed her to see the two sisters as close as they were.

They were so innocent, their lives simple and uncomplicated. It was about playing, school, ponies, friends. Home was their safe place, their parents a loving barrier between them and the harsh realities of life. It was impossible, looking at them, to think that things could ever go wrong. But she knew that they could. And they did.

"How is Iris doing at school? Does she have a nice group of friends?"

Sara looked at her. "Mum—"

"I'm sorry. Ignore me." She cursed herself for allowing her anxieties to spill out and infect the happy atmosphere.

"Her friends are lovely," Sara said gently. "Stop worrying."

"I'm not worrying."

"I know you are, but it's fine. I understand." Sara paused for a moment, watching Iris take her sister's hand and hold it flat so that Benson could eat the carrot she was holding. "Iris is sensible. She's not afraid to stand up for herself when the need arises. She will say no if she doesn't want to do what they are doing. I've heard her. She isn't easily led."

"That takes real strength." Dorothy felt emotion threaten to choke her. "You're a good mother, Sara."

"You were a good mother too. You still are." Sara gave her arm a squeeze. "Enough of this. We have alpacas to feed and ponies to ride."

"You're right, we do."

"I passed Miles on my way here. Is one of the animals sick?"

"No. He just came to check everything was okay because he happened to be passing."

Sara laughed. "You mean he was hungry, and he knows you always bake a cake for the weekend."

"That too. But I don't mind. I love seeing him—you know that. I worry about him. He's working too hard."

"He's a brilliant vet."

"Yes, but that doesn't mean he shouldn't have a social life."

Sara looked at her, amused. "I think Miles is big enough to take care of himself."

"Maybe." But sometimes when you'd been hurt, you needed a nudge. She knew that. It was simpler and safer to protect yourself than take a risk again, and she had a feeling that was what Miles was doing.

Benson, having dutifully eaten all the food offered to him and gifted the girls with his best soppy look, wandered back to the rest of the herd, and Iris and Ava headed to the next paddock.

"I don't see why I can't ride too." Ava was saying as they walked toward Thelma.

"I told you. Today is my turn."

Ava thought about that. "I could just have a quick turn."

Iris sighed. "Why does she never listen to no, Mummy? She argues all the time."

"She's persistent, that's for sure." Sara scooped up Ava. "No means no. Not maybe. And while Iris is riding, I need you to look after Bailey."

"I want to watch Iris." Ava wriggled and twisted, but Sara held her firmly.

"We will watch together."

Dorothy slipped a head-collar over Thelma's head and led her to the stable block. Mostly it was used for storage, but two of the stalls were kept for horses. One for Thelma, and one in case she had a call from Miles or one of the animal charities asking for her help.

Iris picked up the brush and started brushing the mud from Thelma's coat with a practiced movement.

"You're so muddy. What have you been doing?" She giggled as Thelma turned her head and gave her a gentle nudge with her nose.

Sara stepped closer so that Ava could stroke the pony. "Gently. And not near her eyes because she doesn't like that."

Ava stroked Thelma's neck. "She's soft."

"It's her winter coat. It helps to keep her warm." Dorothy tacked up the horse, led her into the yard and helped Iris mount. "Hitch your leg forward while I tighten the girth."

She made sure the saddle was secure and then walked with them to the small indoor school.

Ava was talking nonstop and Sara listened attentively, occasionally responding, asking Ava's opinion and listening to the answer.

Dorothy felt a rush of love and pride. Sara was always engaged with the girls, and careful to be evenhanded with her attention. She treated them as individuals, but made sure they knew they were both equally important. And she never seemed daunted by the responsibilities of parenthood. She was kind, practical and remarkably relaxed.

Dorothy admired her. It wasn't easy, she knew that. You did what you thought was right, but then when things went wrong you wondered what you could have done differently. How much of it was your fault. Nature versus nurture. She'd read so much about it in her search for answers. What could she have done differently? To what degree was she responsible for everything that had happened?

There were words she wished she'd never said. Wished she could unsay.

"Nanna?" Ava wriggled out of Sara's arms and ran to Dorothy. "You look sad."

She pulled herself together. "I'm not sad at all. Just a little cold. I'm thinking maybe hot chocolate would be a good idea." She was grateful to have her grandchildren to bring her back to the present. "We'll just wait for Iris to finish riding."

"I'll stay with her," Sara said. "We'll join you when we're done." She glanced at her daughter who was trotting round the school, a look of determination on her face. "Hands down, Iris! Shorten your reins. That's good."

"She's a natural. Just as you were."

"I loved it. The animals. The outdoors." Sara paused. "It was a great childhood. The best. And you and Dad were wonderful parents. I know how much you miss him. I miss him too. Which is crazy, given how long it has been. Or maybe not so crazy."

The memory of it made her eyes sting. Phillip taking Sara swimming in the sea for the first time. Dressing like Santa while he'd stuffed stockings just in case she'd peeped out of her bedroom and saw him. Teaching Sara to read. "He was proud of you, Sara."

"I wish he could have met the girls. Ava is so like him."

"She is. She has his exuberance and zest for life. Your father never used to take no for an answer. No matter what the objection, he'd find a way to talk someone round."

Sara nodded. "I don't know if that's good or bad—certainly tiring for the person on the other end."

They exchanged a look and Dorothy smiled.

"My fingers and toes are freezing. Time for that hot chocolate, I think. Ava and I will go ahead and start making Christmas decorations."

"Beware glue and glitter," Sara warned and then stopped as Dorothy's phone rang.

Dorothy checked the number. "It's Imogen—I should take this. I promise to be quick."

Sara's expression changed from warm and happy to wary. "Mum—"

"It's fine, Sara. Hello, Imogen? Is everything all right?" She listened as Imogen spoke and then nodded. "That sounds perfect. I'll see you then. I'm looking forward to it." She ended the call, aware that Sara was still watching her. "She was just confirming our lunch next week, that's all."

"I can't believe you're going back to London just for that. It's Christmas. The streets are packed. Why don't you stay here and push your lunch with Imogen into the new year?"

"Because I made a commitment and I always honor my commitments. And I like London at this time of year. I enjoy the buzz and the atmosphere, and I enjoy Imogen's company. She has been working hard for us."

Sara sighed. "We both know that's not why—"

"Can we have hot chocolate now, Nanna?" Ava, bored with horses and her sister, reached for Dorothy's hand. "I'm cold."

"I'm cold too." Dorothy took her hand. "We'll see you indoors, Sara. Don't stay out too long."

She knew there was more Sara wanted to say. She knew Sara didn't want her to go back to London again, but that wasn't going to stop her going. She would do what she needed to do.

You couldn't undo the past, but you could do your very best with the future.

6

Imogen

It promised to be the busiest day of the year so far. Imogen had three events taking place at different times, in different parts of London. Not ideal, but it sometimes happened that way. Clients didn't always have flexibility with their dates, and she was the one who had to make it all work.

Her schedule had required intricate planning to ensure she could spend some time at each event and even when she wasn't physically present, she intended to be fully available to the client if needed. Experience had taught her she probably would be needed. That was life. And it was her job to smooth out any wrinkles.

Imogen wasn't worried. She was prepared for every eventuality, and there were few emergencies she hadn't encountered at some point in her career. Most memorable was the keynote speaker at a pharmaceutical conference who had suffered a heart attack on stage. Imogen had located the defibrillator, ripped open his designer shirt and delivered 200 joules, which had brought him back to life. It had been a shock to both of them (also to the audience, and the applause had raised the roof), because that happened far less frequently than TV medical dramas led you to believe. Imogen had then escorted him to the ambulance, while simultaneously locating a substitute keynote speaker. Despite the drama, the event had been declared a success. The company had been clients of hers ever since, and the CEO sent her an extravagant gift every Christmas.

Then there had been the event where the hotel had suffered a kitchen fire an hour before a celebratory lunch for the board of a leading investment bank. Imogen had tapped her many contacts, pulled in favors and produced a four-course lunch worthy of the royal family.

She'd held an event at a zoo (client's request) where one of the delegates had drunk too much and tried to climb into the enclosure with the penguins.

And then there was the minor stuff. She'd dealt with broken heels (she'd had a pair of shoes couriered from a store in Knightsbridge), sore throats (lozenges), lost notes (she insisted clients gave her backups of all presentations), apocalyptic weather (moved the event from outdoor to indoor with two hours' notice). The list was endless. But Imogen was confident she could deal with anything that was thrown at her (or blown at her in the case of the weather). She enjoyed the challenge. She liked proving to herself, and others, that she could handle anything. *Bring it on.*

This was her job, and she was good at it. Not just good. *The best.*

Clients assumed their events would run smoothly and usually they did, but when things went wrong it was Imogen's job to fix it, preferably without the client being aware.

She worked on the principle that there was always a solution to every problem, and usually more than one. It was simply a matter of picking the best.

And even when she wasn't physically present at an event, she was always available for advice and troubleshooting. She carried two phones, just in case one of them was lost, stolen, or she needed to field two calls at once (it happened).

Each event was allocated its own team from RPQ and they were present the whole time. Imogen's job was just to show her face, take a few photos of the event, troubleshoot anything the account manager couldn't handle and generally give the client confidence that everything was in hand.

Her first event today was an all-day sales conference in a smart hotel just outside London. The company was celebrating their best year ever, and her brief had been to design an event that was both a company celebration and a Christmas celebration.

It was one of their most ambitious projects of recent months, not least because of the time pressures.

The theme of the event was Winter Wonderland, and the hotel and the gardens had been decked out like Lapland. There had been no ceiling to the budget, and Imogen had arranged for snowmaking machines to transform the grounds into a snowy paradise. There were sleigh rides and reindeer and stands offering everything from mulled wine to creamy hot chocolate. Inside, the ballroom, which only two days before had hosted a gala dinner for five hundred, was now Santa's workshop, complete with areas where the delegates could make their own toys.

Mindful of the pressures at this time of year, Imogen had arranged for a major toy store to run a stand so that people could do some Christmas shopping, and next to it a giant Santa sack so that they could donate an extra toy to a local children's charity.

The middle of the ballroom had been turned into a skating rink, and in the far corner of the room was a grotto, where elves were serving champagne and nonalcoholic cocktails to people queuing to see "Santa." Each staff member visited Santa to get their bonus for the year. Imogen had wondered if that was a little creepy, but the CEO, Angus Fitzgerald, had refused to let go of that idea, mostly because it was his idea.

"Imogen!" Angus Fitzgerald made his way across to her, looking totally out of place in a formal suit. "This is fantastic! You're a superstar."

She shook his hand, accepted his praise with a warm smile and glanced around her. "Everyone seems to be having fun, Mr. Fitzgerald."

"How many times do I have to tell you to call me Angus? They're having the best time. You've created a perfect fantasy Christmas. How do you do that?"

A perfect fantasy Christmas.

"It's my job, Angus." It helped that she was intimately acquainted with fantasy Christmases. They were the only ones she'd ever experienced. A real family Christmas had only ever happened in her imagination. She felt a tug of emotion, a sense of loss, and killed it dead. Everyone knew that Christmas was usually a time of pressure and stress. The snow-dusted beaming family type of Christmas that played a starring role in movies was fictitious. She believed that. She had to believe that, or she might start feeling sad about what she was missing.

Angus was still gazing around him. "Genius idea to have the toy store here. My wife is always complaining that she has to do all the Christmas shopping, so I bought a stuffed lion for my granddaughter. That's my contribution." He saw her looking at him and narrowed his eyes. "You have that look on your face."

"I have a look?"

"Yes, it's the look you always get when you're about to suggest something and you're not sure how I'll react."

Imogen pushed aside the image of Angus presenting his little granddaughter with a stuffed lion on Christmas Day. "You know me so well."

"Go on. Whatever is in that head of yours, say it."

She paused. "That's a smart suit, Angus."

He fiddled with the knot of his tie. "But?"

"This is a relaxed event. It's corporate, but not corporate."

"Meaning?"

"I'm wondering if you might connect with the staff more easily if you were dressed a little less formally. It might make you seem more approachable."

At that moment the VP of sales skated past them in a red sweater emblazoned in a giant snowman.

Angus watched him. "He's in sales. It's his job to connect with the sales force."

"You're the boss. This is a reward for a brilliant year. You need to connect too. This is about them."

"I'm not arguing with that," he said, "but not even for you am I wearing a snowman sweater. I need to be able to have difficult conversations. Sometimes I have to fire people. That's harder to do when they've seen you wearing a snowman sweater."

"I agree there is a line between connecting and losing respect. We're not going to cross that line. The snowman is definitely too much. But still—" She tapped her finger to her mouth, thinking, then pulled out her phone and called one of her junior team members. "Nick? Can you bring me one of the spare navy sweaters. Yes, the cashmere one. Thanks."

"You have spare sweaters?"

"Always. Things happen. Red wine on white shirts. Lost buttons. Torn sleeves. The possibilities are endless. Ah, Nick, thanks—" She took the sweater from her colleague and held it out to Angus. "Try this."

He took it from her and studied it. "The logo is a Christmas tree."

"Small, barely perceptible, but just enough that it counts as a Christmas sweater. It says, 'I'm approachable, but I'm still the boss.'"

He laughed. "I never thought clothing could say so much."

"You'd be surprised. Nonverbal communication can be as powerful as the words that leave your mouth." She took his jacket from him and held it as he pulled on the sweater. "That looks good on you."

"It's more comfortable than the shirt and tie, that's for sure. That's Christmas Day sorted too then." He beamed at her. "Can I keep this?"

As if the guy wasn't worth a gazillion. As if he couldn't have bought several tons of cashmere sweaters with the change in his wallet. What he was short on was time, and her efficiency bought people time.

"Of course." She handed the jacket to Nick and made a mental note to add the sweater to the final invoice. "Nick will hang your jacket somewhere and you can collect it later. Or we can have it delivered back to your office. Whichever works for you. In the meantime, everything looks in order here. We've checked the sound system, and everything is looking good for your speech at twelve."

"You won't be here for that?"

"Sadly, no. I have to be in Knightsbridge for eleven forty-five, but I'll be in contact with my team the whole time if you need me. But you won't, because everything is going to run perfectly."

"Because of you. You're one of a kind." He shook her hand again. "Do you ever rest, Imogen?" His voice was caring, but she assumed it was a trick question.

If she said yes, then he'd wonder if she wasn't giving her all to his account. If she said no, he'd start worrying that she might suffer burnout and his account would suffer.

"I rest when I need to, and when the time is right."

He laughed. "And that's a diplomatic answer if ever I heard one. Anytime you want to leave all this behind and come and work for me, give me a call. You must be looking forward to taking a well-earned break at Christmas."

"That's still several weeks away." She tried not to think about it, because she wasn't looking forward to it. And she didn't plan to take a break. Christmas was bad enough without having time off to sit around and think about how bad it was.

"Where do you spend Christmas, Imogen?"

It was the question she hated most, but she had her answer prepared.

"With my family in the country." She'd said the words so often, she almost believed them. And the lie was better than the truth. The truth made people feel awkward, and she didn't want people to feel awkward. Nor did she want people feeling sorry for her.

"So you'll be getting out of the city. That's good. We've worked together all these years. You know everything about me, and yet I feel as if I know so little about you. What do you do to relax, Imogen?"

"Lots of things. Jujitsu. I'm a black belt." It was the truth. The one honest thing she revealed about herself among a bushel of lies. It was her only hobby. The only thing she made time for other than work.

"Jujitsu?" His eyebrows rose. "What made you choose that?"

A need to feel more in control and able to handle herself.

"It's a great way of keeping fit." She tried to think of more hobbies. She needed to look more rounded. What did Janie do? "I do yoga several times a week. I read. I walk my dog. Pretty normal things."

"You have a dog?" Angus looked interested. "Breed?"

Oh good grief. "Golden retriever." She shouldn't have mentioned the dog. Those life details were for colleagues, not clients. She gestured to a couple of his executive team who were hovering. "I've taken enough of your time, Angus."

"I enjoy talking to you, but you're right—I should mingle. Thank you again, Imogen." He glanced around him, taking in the winter theme park she'd created. "This is the perfect ending to a perfect year."

Imogen decided it was time to extract herself before he started crying. "Enjoy yourself, Angus. This isn't just for your staff. It's for you too. You've had your best year ever. You've earned the right to enjoy this. Go and treat yourself to a sleigh ride." She gave his arm an encouraging squeeze and left him to mingle with his staff while she checked the rest of the event.

She was genuinely fond of Angus, and there was a certain thrill that came from seeing all the plans come to life so successfully.

She checked in with the account manager in charge of the event, assured herself that all was well, and then jumped on the train back into the city.

Her next event was an awards lunch held at a five-star hotel overlooking Hyde Park and she arrived in plenty of time. So far so good.

She was halfway up the steps to the entrance when she had a call from the account manager in charge of her evening event. This particular client was difficult, so she was planning to be there for the whole thing to smooth over whatever wrinkles occurred.

"Imogen?" The voice was urgent and high-pitched. "Crisis!"

Imogen paused on the steps. "Breathe, Sophie. Stay calm. Remember, we talked about this. Calm. If there's a problem, then we look for solutions. We solve it a piece at a time."

"What do you mean 'if'? There's a *huge* problem."

"Everything is going to be fine."

"It's not fine. It's unbelievable. Of all the—"

"Facts, Sophie. Give me the problem in five words or less."

"My keynote speaker for tonight is stuck in Edinburgh. There has been an incident at the airport. All flights canceled until further notice. She's panicking, the client is panicking and I'm panicking. I mean, the whole thing revolves around this woman. We've been planning this event for so long! We booked her eighteen months ago. It's not like anyone else can give her speech." Sophie's voice wobbled. "Alan Marsh is going bananas and blaming me, although why it's my fault I have no idea because I don't control the airports. But he doesn't care about that. He told me I'm useless and that he's going to fire us unless you get here in the next ten minutes."

Imogen felt a ripple of annoyance. Exacting clients she could cope with, but she had a visceral loathing of bullies. "He had no right to say that. You're very good at your job, Sophie."

"No, I'm not. He's right. I get a problem like this and I just panic. I'm not like you. We're going to lose the client and I'm going to be fired and—"

"Stop!" Imogen cut her off in mid flow. "I need you to listen to me, Sophie."

There was a sniff. "I'm listening."

"Alan Marsh can be a difficult client, but try and look at it as a learning experience. Stay calm and handle him."

"Handle him how? Can I just tell him you're coming? That will calm him down."

"No, because if you do that you're basically telling him that you don't have the confidence to do the job."

"I don't have the confidence to do the job."

Imogen's heart softened. "Yes, you do. He's just shredded it, that's all. But we're going to put it back together."

"We are?"

"Yes. And you're going to start by stating the problem as briefly as possible."

"I thought I already did."

"No, you are so flustered by the fact the client shouted at you and distracted by imagined consequences that you're not focusing on the actual problem. Your mind is all over the place and your panic explosion is stopping you focusing on what needs to be fixed. Tell me the problem. The thing that started all this."

"I don't have a speaker!"

"You do have a speaker."

"Not in the right place!"

"Right. Your speaker is in the wrong place. *That's* the problem that needs solving. So what you have here is a transport issue."

"Sure, but I don't see how—"

"So instead of worrying about losing clients and losing jobs, you need to think about how to solve this transport issue."

"I don't see what else I can do. I've already called the airport, but no one can tell me anything."

"The problem that needs fixing is not the airline's schedule, it's the fact that your client is in the wrong place. Forget the airline. Figure out how to get your speaker from A to B in the time frame available. Find a solution to that, and everything will be sorted." It was how she handled her life. Outline the options. Pick one. "Possible modes of transport—plane, train, car. Car would take too long, so that leaves planes and trains."

"But the airport has delayed all flights from Edinburgh—"

"So now the problem is that there are no flights from the airport. One solution is to consider another airport." Imogen checked the time and did some calculations. "Have you checked flights from Glasgow?"

"Glasgow?"

"Yes. Check availability. If it's an option, then arrange for a car to pick her up and take her there." She gave Sophie the name of an executive car company she'd used before and knew to be reliable. "What are you going to do when she lands?"

"I'm—er—I'm going to arrange for a car to pick her up from Heathrow. And I'm going to have one of the team meet her at Arrivals so she can relax and focus on her keynote and not logistics. That way she won't be standing at that podium flustered and stressed."

"Brilliant. You've got it." Imogen showered her with praise, trying to build up the confidence that client had shattered.

"But it won't be enough. The speaker is stressed too. In fact, she's so irritated she is threatening to give up and go home."

"Of course she is. Business travel is always stressful if you have to be somewhere by a certain time and everything is delayed. She probably feels embarrassed, even though none of it is her fault. So our problem here is to make her feel special and valued. Any suggestions?" She stepped to one side to allow a small group of guests to pass and pulled her coat around her. It was too cold to be standing outside.

"Um. She's staying here at the hotel tonight. The room is nice, but it's nothing special. The client wouldn't give us the budget." Sophie paused. "I suppose I could talk to the hotel and see if I can get her room upgraded. We do use them a lot for events."

"We do," Imogen said. "And that is excellent thinking."

"Maybe they have a suite."

"Worth checking."

"And we could offer her a complimentary spa treatment."

"That's a genius idea. Brilliant." Imogen saw one of the team gesturing to her from the doorway. "I need to go. I've just arrived at the graphic design awards. I'll be here for the next couple of hours."

"But will you be contactable?" The panic was back in Sophie's voice.

"At all times. But you won't need me, because you've got this. And if the client is rude, just listen, keep calm and assure him that you're doing everything you can to deliver the very best outcome. You're doing well, Sophie."

"It doesn't feel that way. I wish I was as calm as you. You will be here, won't you?"

"I have never missed an event, Sophie." She wasn't sure if that meant she had a sad life, or that she was efficient.

She was going with efficient.

"I know. I'm sorry. It's just that the client keeps asking for you, like the rest of us don't know what we're doing and that the whole airline debacle wouldn't have happened if you'd been there because you're like some sort of wizard problem solver—" Sophie cleared her throat. "I need to calm down. Problem, solution, problem, solution."

"That's right, and you're doing a great job." Imogen raised a finger to indicate to her hovering colleague that she'd be done in one minute. "I'll see you soon."

"Right. Because you'll be here. Of course you will. I'm going to make all those arrangements and I'll see you in a few hours."

"Keep me updated." Imogen slid her phone back into her bag, sprinted up the steps and into the hotel. She felt a wave of dizziness and realized she hadn't eaten anything since the night before. She'd grab a snack before heading to the big evening event. She wasn't surprised Sophie was finding the client difficult. Alan Marsh was difficult. One of those annoying people whose glass was always half-empty even when you'd filled it to overflowing. He found fault with every small thing and seemed to be looking for an excuse to fire them. Imogen had been careful never to give him that excuse. And she wasn't going to start today.

"Hi, Arthur." She waved a hand to the man behind the concierge desk and he waved back.

"Good to see you, Imogen."

They used this venue so frequently that she knew the staff well.

She headed straight to the ballroom where the event was taking place, spoke to the tech point person and the account manager and slid into the back of the room for five minutes. The atmosphere was buzzing.

"The tables look great." The centerpiece of each table was a hologram of a snowflake.

Christmas was already dominating her life and there were still weeks to go until the day itself.

She stayed long enough to speak to the client, check everything was exceeding expectations, and then she headed upstairs to the room they were using as their HQ for the duration of the day.

As she'd hoped, the place was empty because the rest of the team were now at the event.

Imogen took off her shoes, poured herself a large glass of water, ate a banana and a chocolate bar and then sprawled on the sofa.

She was exhausted. Her mind was racing, her heart was racing, and she still had to find time to check through the plans for her events the next day. This close to Christmas the events they ran were almost always back-to-back.

She thought about Rosalind. *Are you sure you haven't taken on too much, Imogen?*

She could not afford a single misstep. Although she'd reassured Sophie, she felt uneasy about the event tonight. The client was tricky. She needed to bring her best self.

She closed her eyes.

Five minutes, and then she'd head over and give Sophie some support.

She must have fallen asleep because she was woken by the sound of the door opening.

By the time the person entered the room, Imogen had her shoes back on and was poring over her emails. Her head was muzzy and she could feel the beginnings of a headache. She was beginning to wish she'd eaten something other than chocolate.

"Hi, Imogen. I didn't know you were still here. I love your suit. That shade of green looks good on you. You look like a very sexy elf." It was Janie, looking professional in a tailored black dress, her hair twisted into a knot on the back of her head. "I just came up to grab my stain remover. Client dropped raspberry juice on his shirt. Next time I'm suggesting a cheese plate for dessert." She rummaged in one of the bags. "Agh, where is it? I know I had one."

Imogen reached into the oversize bag she carried everywhere and handed her a stain remover. "Raspberry isn't easy to shift. You might be better off providing him with a fresh shirt."

"That's my backup. Problem—solution, right? Thanks, Imogen." Janie pocketed the stain remover. "I'm all over the place because Mum just rang, and guess what? She's getting married again."

Imogen wasn't sure how to react. Was that good or bad? "Wow. And how do you feel about that?"

"Excited! I like Ray, and she's been on her own since Dad died. All I want is for her to be happy. Sometimes I think we're more like best friends than mother-daughter, you know?"

No, she didn't know. She had no experience of that sort of relationship.

On a good day her relationship with her mother was distant and chilly. On a bad day—she didn't know how to describe it.

"I'm pleased for you."

"I'm going to be bridesmaid. We're picking out dresses next week. I love a good mother-and-daughter shopping trip, don't you?"

"Doesn't everyone? I'm holding you up," Imogen said, "I know you need to get back to the client so you can sort out that shirt."

"Yes, you're right. I should." Janie patted the stain remover in her pocket. "I'll see you back in the office tomorrow. Let's grab lunch together if there's time. Are you all ready for Friday?"

Friday? What was happening on Friday? "I—"

"You haven't really forgotten?" Janie laughed. "'Bring your dog to work day.' The day we get to meet Midas. We're all more excited than you are!"

Midas.

Enough. She had to put an end to this, she really did. "I can't do that, Janie."

"Why not?" Janie's expression shifted from anticipation to alarm. "Midas isn't ill again?"

"No, not ill." She floundered. One small lie led to another and then another. She wished she'd never started it, but she had, and now she didn't know how to end it. "I didn't really want to talk about it. It's too awful."

"What?" Alarmed, Janie sat down next to her. "You're scaring me. Of course you don't have to talk about it if you don't want to, but you know you can, don't you? You can tell me anything. We're friends."

Imogen felt her throat thicken. "Are we?"

"What's that supposed to mean? Of *course* we are." Janie took Imogen's hand, and Imogen was suddenly choked by the gesture of friendship.

She had a sudden urge to tell her everything. Would that be so bad? Janie was a kind person. She'd understand.

She tried to figure out where to start, but Janie was still speaking.

"I knew from the moment you put that photo of Midas on your desk that we'd be good friends. We're both dog people for a start!"

She wasn't a dog person. At least, not a real dog person. She was a fake dog person. She was a fake generally. An imposter. A real dog would have sniffed her out in a moment.

"And we're similar in other ways too." Janie was in full flow. "We're both home-loving people. I'm not saying I don't enjoy a good night out as much as the next girl, but I also love an evening in snuggled on the sofa watching a movie with my family. I know you're the same."

She wasn't the same, although she would have liked to be. When Imogen watched a movie on the sofa she was always alone.

She pulled her hand away from Janie's. "You're a wonderful person, Janie. I'm lucky to work with you."

"Right. So now tell me what's happened with Midas."

If she told Janie the truth, then that would be their friendship over. Janie would discover she wasn't a dog person. She'd be hurt that Imogen had lied. She'd never trust her again. The atmosphere in the office would change.

Imogen couldn't bear that. For now she needed to keep up the charade.

"He's gone. Midas has gone."

"Gone where?"

"He ran away."

"Ran away?" Janie looked at her in horror. "I thought you said your little garden was secure?"

"It is." Maybe the running away excuse hadn't been such a great idea. It made her look careless. And blaming the dog walker wasn't a good idea because Janie would want to know which dog walker so that they could all leave bad reviews. But she just needed Midas out of her life and she couldn't bring herself to kill him. "Honestly? I think maybe someone might have climbed over the fence and taken him, but I don't have security cameras or anything so I don't suppose I'll ever really know. But he's gone."

There. It was done. Goodbye, Midas.

It was almost a relief. No more lying about the dog.

And no, she wouldn't be getting another one.

She hoped that was the end of it, but one glance at Janie's face told her that was wishful thinking.

"Gone?" Janie's face turned puce with outrage. "You think someone stole him? I've read about a few cases lately. So shocking. These people who think they can take something that doesn't belong to them! And it's not like they're taking a piece of garden furniture or a TV. I mean, pets are family. They're taking a family member. It's kidnapping. Oh, Imogen—" she flung her arms around Imogen "—I can't imagine what you're going through. What did the police say?"

"The police?"

"You have reported it to the police?" Janie let go of Imogen, her mind in overdrive. "Do you have one of those pet tracking tags? Can you track him on your phone?"

Imogen stared at her. Track your dog? That was a thing? "Er, no. I never saw the need. He always stayed so close to me when we were out. He never ran away."

"So you can't track him. Oh, poor you. And poor Midas. If he wouldn't naturally run away someone *must* have taken him. What must he be going through?" Janie was silent for a moment. "There must be something we can do."

"There's nothing," Imogen said. "I just have to learn to live with it. I only told you because I won't be bringing him to Rosalind's 'bring your dog to work day.'"

"Of course you won't." Janie squeezed her hand. "We should tell Rosalind and she'll cancel it. It would be too upsetting for you to be there and see everyone else's dogs."

"No, really, I don't want it canceled. I need to get on with life."

"You're so brave. In your position I'd be a sobbing mess."

"I'm trying not to be. I'm keeping busy. That's the best way. I don't want time to think." That part at least was true. Her phone buzzed and she reached for it gratefully. "Sorry, Janie, I need to take this. Poor Sophie is having a bit of a nightmare with the event this evening. Keynote speaker is AWOL and client is difficult. I need to head over there."

"Is this The Work Nook? They're horrible. My friend used to do their PR. And I know you want to support Sophie, but I don't know how you can think about work at a time like this."

"Work takes my mind off things. Life sends you challenges, doesn't it? All we can do is weather them."

And stop making up pets and family members. That was

another thing she could do. It turned out that unpicking lies was a lot more complicated than telling them in the first place.

It was relief that Midas was gone now. That part of her fictitious life was behind her. She felt lighter for it, although weirdly sad that she'd lost her dog.

She stood up and swayed slightly.

"Are you sure you're okay?" Janie was on her feet in a moment. "Because you don't look okay. You look white. And exhausted. It must be the shock. Sit down. I'm going to make you a drink."

"I'm fine, honestly. I really need to get going."

But she did feel a bit strange. The back of her throat hurt, but she assumed that was too much talking.

With a final nod to Janie, she grabbed her coat and headed back down to the lobby. She popped her head into the back of the room where the lunchtime event was already underway, satisfied herself everything was fine and then left the hotel.

She'd support Sophie and deal with the horrible client, and then she'd go home and collapse for a few hours. Fortunately tomorrow was clear. No events. She just had to survive a few more hours and then she could use her office day to recover.

She stood on the street for a moment, debating whether to use the train or taxi. In the end, she went with a taxi. She didn't feel well enough to cope with the Christmas crush on the train.

In the taxi, she relaxed back against the seat and checked her emails.

She'd had ninety-six in the short time it had taken her to get from the hotel to here, almost all of them marked urgent. She scanned them all, selected the ones that related to the events she had today and answered them swiftly. She was in the middle of composing a reassuring response to a panicked email from a client about a budget change when a call came in.

Tina.

She rejected the call. The only time her mother called her

was when she wanted something, and there was no way she was taking a call from her in the middle of her working day. It would unsettle her too much and she needed to concentrate.

She went back to her emails, but she felt on edge and she hated the fact that a call from her mother could still have this effect on her. It wasn't just an emotional reaction, it was a physical one. Her heart was banging against her ribs, pounding out an alert. *Disaster incoming.* Her palms were sweaty (*drop what you're doing and run*), and her breathing felt as it did when she ran up the stairs too quickly.

She took several slow breaths, and then the call came again, and again she rejected it.

To begin with it had felt weird and unnatural to be rejecting a call from her mother, but that had been before she'd been forced to acknowledge that everything about her mother was weird and unnatural, most of all their relationship.

Call me Tina, was one of the earliest things Imogen could remember her mother saying to her. *I don't want people knowing you're my daughter.*

It had been confusing when she was six and hadn't become any less confusing at sixteen. But she'd weathered it. It wasn't as if she'd been given a choice. No one had said, hey, which one would you prefer? This warm loving mother who will hug you and read to you and show interest in everything you do, or this young angry individual who blames you for coming along uninvited and ruining the best years of her life?

Her phone buzzed again and this time it was Sophie.

ETA? Client asking for you.

The event wasn't for another five hours, but if the client needed her to hold his hand she'd hold his hand.

She was about to type her reply when her phone rang again. This time it was from an unidentified number.

Concerned that it might be a client, she answered it. "Hello?"

"Is that Imogen Thorne?"

"Yes. Who is this?"

"I'm a doctor and I work in the emergency department." He named the hospital. "Are you Tina Thorne's sister?"

Sister? She leaned her head against the seat and closed her eyes briefly. Her mother had been at it again.

"I'm her daughter." In her time she'd played the part of sister, best friend and a distant cousin from Scotland, but those days were gone. She was done with all that. "What happened?"

"She has had an accident. When she was brought in, she mentioned a sister. We found your number in her purse. We tried calling you from her phone, but you didn't answer."

That had been the hospital? She felt a flush of guilt. She'd assumed it was her mother asking for money. "I was in a meeting. And she doesn't have a sister."

"You're sure? Because she mentioned it specifically. She was adamant."

Pretend you're my sister.

"She doesn't have a sister. You mentioned an accident. What kind of accident?"

"If you come to the hospital, we can discuss this face-to-face. She does have a head injury, and the fact that she thinks you're her sister might indicate an element of confusion."

Delusion, more like, not confusion.

What did it say about her that she immediately suspected a trap? Was this guy really a doctor or was this one of her mother's elaborate manipulations?

"When?"

"Right away."

"Right away? You mean *now*? That's out of the question. I'm at work, and I won't finish before midnight and—"

"Miss Thorne—" his tone was scalpel sharp "—your mother has incurred some injuries. We're running tests and depending on what those tests show she'll need suturing and she will have to have someone with her when she goes home."

"You're sure she asked for me? She doesn't normally want—" She stopped. What was she going to say? *She doesn't normally want me around.* It was too embarrassing to admit that to this man, and she could already feel his judgment pulsing down the phone. He probably had loving parents, a couple of doting grandparents and maybe a wife and kids of his own. People like that didn't understand that not everyone was so fortunate. That some families were made in hell, not Hollywood. That not every problem could be fixed, nor every sin forgiven. "She may not want me."

"In my opinion, you should be here."

He didn't have a clue. He didn't know how many times this had happened to her before. He had no idea how many taxis she'd taken across the city in the middle of the night to get to whichever hospital her mother had been taken to. And each time her mother would swear it would never happen again. Occasionally, she meant it and the phone would go quiet for a few months. But then the call would come. Sometimes from a neighbor, sometimes from the police, sometimes from a strange man her mother had picked up in the bar where she worked. The end result was always the same.

Imogen took her home, did her best to tidy up the place, filled the fridge with food (she'd learned the hard way that giving cash wasn't a good idea) and then waited for her mother to sober up and tell her to get out of her life. Which she did. Until next time. And there was always a next time because no matter how hard she tried, Imogen couldn't bring herself to cut those ties completely.

She believed in family, even though hers fell short of her ideals. She tried to behave the way she felt a family member should—by offering loving support, no matter how hard that sometimes was.

She was her mother's only relative. All they had was each other. That might not mean much to her mother, but it meant a great deal to Imogen. She wouldn't give her mother financial support because that always led to bad things, but nor would she cut her mother out of her life completely. That wasn't what family did. Family should stick together through thick and thin. She believed that, even if her mother didn't. And she wanted her actions to reflect her beliefs, which was why she still had contact with her mother even though most of the time it would have been more comfortable to lie on a bed of rocks. It wasn't easy and she wasn't blind to reality.

"Was she drunk?"

There was a pause. "If you come in, we can update you properly."

Which probably meant she had been drunk. That wasn't a surprise.

But this doctor was asking her to come in. He was impartial, and he believed she should be there. What tests were they running exactly? Doctors weren't allowed to lie, were they? Hippocratic oath and all that.

She checked the time. The hospital was virtually on the way to her next event. She could take a minor detour, drop in for half an hour, talk to the doctor and then wait for her mother to tell her to get out of her life. That normally took a matter of minutes.

"I'll be with you in twenty minutes."

She ended the call, then messaged Sophie.

"Keep client calm. I'll be with you in an hour."

She'd deal with her mother and still arrive at her event in good time. No problem.

7

Sara

"We should get the Christmas tree next weekend." Sara spread butter onto toast and deftly cut it into the shape of a house. She was not going to worry about her mother driving up to London. It was ridiculous. What exactly did she think was going to happen?

"Is that mine?" Patrick sounded amused. "Nice house."

Sara stared at the toast in disbelief as she realized what she'd done. "Sorry. I was operating on automatic."

"I know. You obviously have a lot on your mind." He looked at her thoughtfully. "Do you want to offload some of that anxiety that is making your forehead crease?"

"No, but thanks."

"Fine. But at least drink your coffee. You know you're not human until you've had your first cup of the day." He put a cup down next to her. "Drink. It might help."

She felt his hand on her back, the gentle rub of his fingers against her spine.

Comfort.

She could never hide any of her moods from him. Happy, sad, worried, thoughtful—he recognized them all. And she was grateful for that. She'd known him since she was four years old and they still had the same circle of friends they'd had back then. Lissa, Shona, Paul and Rick. They'd met in kindergarten and moved through school together as a tight-knit group until university had finally forced them to take separate paths. Paul and Rick had got together almost immediately and now ran the bookshop in the village. Sara and Patrick had lived together and then married a few years later. Lissa now had her own interior design business and was based in London, but she'd renovated a cottage in the village and came down once a month for "respite" as she called it, and also to see friends and her younger brother Miles, the vet. Lissa threw stylish dinner parties, with elegant food and extravagant flower displays courtesy of Shona, who was a florist. Shona mostly handled weddings and large events and traveled a great deal, but every three months the six of them got together no matter what and caught up on life. Lissa provided the food and the elegance, Shona the flowers, Sara and Patrick the wine, and Paul and Rick were the entertainment. They kept everyone supplied with their favorite books, and Sara knew for a fact that the closest Shona got to "Christmas shopping" was sending a list of people, ages and interests through to Paul and Rick. They chose an appropriate book, gift wrapped it and delivered the whole box back to Shona to mail. Since she was on that list, Sara had started dropping hints to Paul about the book she'd like from Shona. Which reminded her, she still needed to do that.

"Have you given Paul your book hint this year?"

"No. But I saw a book on volcanoes reviewed last week. Thought it looked interesting." He scooped up his plate and studied the toast. "This is an architectural masterpiece. I want to eat the door, but if I eat the door how are we going to get into the house?"

Ava gave a gurgle of laughter. "It's just toast, silly."

Patrick studied it and shook his head. "It's a house. It has windows, chimney, doors."

"You have to eat the whole thing."

"I do? Well, if you insist." He bit into the house and Sara rolled her eyes.

"Send me the link for that book and I'll send it to Paul. I've fixed a date for our next get-together, by the way."

"Good."

"I still can't believe I cut your toast up."

"No worries. Ava was given a toast house, so I deserve one too. It's called equality." He leaned across and kissed her. "It's great, although next time could I have a castle with battlements? Or maybe a toast yacht?"

"Go and sit down." She gave him a gentle push. "You're lucky I made your toast."

"I know. But I made you strong coffee, so that makes you lucky too." He carried his plate to the table and sat with the girls. "You were saying something about Christmas trees."

"We should get one at the weekend. Make a trip of it, like we usually do. Forest. Hot chocolate." She sipped her coffee, inhaling the smell. "What do you think?"

"Why would you want a tree? You don't like Christmas." He winked at her as Ava gasped.

"Mummy loves Christmas."

"Does she?" Patrick bit into a toast window. "I didn't know that."

"You do know that." Ava frowned at him. "She decorates everywhere, and she makes a big cake and she cuts all that green stuff from the garden and wraps it around the stairs. And she puts lights everywhere. We make Christmas cards, we do paintings and make decorations and we count how many sleeps there are. She reads us Christmas books and we have twinkly lights at bath time."

"That sounds like altogether too much fun," Patrick said. "But if we're going to Nanna's for Christmas, perhaps we don't need our own tree this year."

Sara shook her head, smiling. "Patrick—"

"We're not having a tree?" Ava's lip wobbled and Iris put her toast down and patted her hand.

"We are having a tree," she said. "Daddy is just joking."

"I don't get it. Why is that funny?"

"He's teasing us."

"Nine going on ninety," Patrick murmured and finished his toast. "Iris is right. I'm joking. We're going to get the biggest tree in the forest. So big that we're going to need a ladder to put Iris's fairy on top. And I know Mummy loves Christmas. It's one of the reasons I married her."

Ava sprang up and hugged him and Iris smiled quietly.

Sara felt a glow of contentment. She did love Christmas. For a good few years that hadn't been the case. After her father's stroke and the dark days that followed, the emphasis on family had been bittersweet. But so many years had passed and she'd taught herself to compartmentalize. She ignored the bad memories and focused on the happy ones. And she had many happy ones.

Patrick had proposed to her at Christmas. She'd discovered she was pregnant with Iris at Christmas. And children had given her the excuse she'd needed to indulge her own love of the festive season. The truth was she wanted to enjoy Christmas. She made an active choice to enjoy it and ignored any feelings that threatened to dampen that enjoyment.

Patrick checked the time and stood up. "Time to move or we'll be late. Ava? Teeth."

She bared them at him and growled like a tiger.

"Great. Now go and clean them."

Ava ran off and Iris picked up the breakfast plates and carefully loaded them into the dishwasher.

"Thank you." Sara gave her a hug. "Don't forget to take your project in today."

"It's already in my bag." Iris followed her sister out of the room and Patrick raised his eyebrows.

"The arctic project is finished?"

"It's done."

"No more drawing polar bears?"

"You have drawn your last polar bear. The next time you see those bears will be at parents' evening in a week. They are having an exhibition of all the projects."

"Hers is the best."

She tilted her head. "You don't think you're biased?"

"No. Did you see how hard she worked on it? She gives everything her all."

"I know."

He put his plate on top of the dishwasher, caught her eye and loaded it inside instead. "So now tell me what's wrong. Is this still about your mother?"

"She still punishes herself, and I hate it. Even after all these years, she still thinks it was all her fault."

"Maybe that's part of being a parent. I suppose it's natural to ask yourself what you could have done differently."

"Maybe, but I also think there's a point where you have to accept that your children are individuals. You can raise them with all the right values, but you're not responsible for their choices." She stopped herself. "Let's not talk about it. You know I hate talking about it. I've learned to lock it in a box that I never open. I wish my mother could do the same."

"It's the time of year, you know that. She always finds this time of year difficult." Patrick's phone rang, but he ignored it and tugged Sara into his arms.

"You should answer that."

"It can wait."

She leaned her head against his shoulder. "I hate the fact that she feels guilty. It actually makes me angry that she blames herself."

"I know. You feel helpless and you want to fix it, but you can't, honey." He rested his chin on top of her head. "Remember that there are plenty of good things in her life. For a start she has you. And you're pretty great."

"Pretty great?" She lifted her head to look at him. "I'm more than pretty great."

"You are. You're certainly great at making toast houses." He trailed his fingers over her cheek. "Is there something more? Tell me."

She sighed and rested her hand on his chest. Part of her didn't want to bother him with her anxieties, but another part of her needed his reassurance.

"She makes me worry about the girls. She's always asking how they're doing, if they're getting on well, if they have good friends. And I know why, of course, but it makes me jumpy. I find myself analyzing everything they do and say." She felt a rush of frustration. "It makes me wonder if I need to visit all their friends' houses spontaneously just to check things out. It makes me wonder if I'm doing enough as a mother."

"We do visit all their friends' houses." As always, Patrick was calm and logical. "This is a village. We know almost everyone."

"I know. But still—"

"Just because something bad happens once, doesn't mean it's going to happen again."

"I know that too. I didn't say any of this was rational. But it's how she has made me feel."

"I know." He stroked a strand of hair away from her face. "We're going to do what we've always done. We're going to be the best parents we can be to the girls. We're going to pay attention and make sure they know they can talk to us about anything. We're going to keep talking to each other. Keep checking in. We're going to encourage them to look out for each other. And it's going to be fine. Everything is going to be okay."

She knew he believed that, and she loved that about him. He looked for the good. Expected the best. And she was grateful for it. She needed that.

Patrick didn't do what she did and wait with her breath held for life to crumble in her hands. He didn't touch wood or wear a lucky snowflake charm or look desperately for a second magpie when just one was perched outside the window.

He pulled her closer. "I do know that. I mean, look at us. And look how great our friends are. There aren't many people who have known their friends since before they could tie their own shoelaces."

"I know. And I want the girls to have that. I want them to have what we had. Good people in their lives who know them well and love them."

"They have that. The girls have great friends. They're lucky."

It was true, for the moment at least. But luck, as she knew, could change. And sometimes there was nothing you could do about that.

8

Imogen

Imogen paced the corridors of the hospital. She'd spent far too much of her life in places like this, waiting for news on her mother. She'd eyed enviously the anxious relatives who formed small groups, supporting each other through their own crises. Imogen had stood by herself, handling it alone.

In the beginning it had been fine, mostly because of Terry, the man her mother had married when Imogen was seven. Imogen had liked Terry. He'd read to her, helped her with homework and took her to the park, although for some reason she hadn't understood, his attentions seemed to annoy her mother.

Leave the kid alone. She's fine.

Her mother had been relatively stable during those years and Imogen's homelife fairly normal, if lean on affection and warmth. Occasionally, her mother would drink and she and Terry would have a huge fight about it, but they always seemed to make up.

And then when Imogen was eleven, two things happened.

Her mother lost her job, and Terry decided he'd had enough of Tina and walked out.

Imogen had been bereft. It had felt like losing a father.

Things had gone downhill from there. For the next few months her mother was drunk more than she was sober. On one occasion, Imogen had taken her mother to hospital to be stitched up after a fall and someone had called social services. A woman had arrived and had asked awkward, probing questions about Imogen's home life and Imogen had smiled and made up a story that seemed to satisfy her. *This has never happened before. Yes, things are fine at home. My aunt comes to look after me when necessary, and I can always stay with my grandmother.*

That was when she'd learned that sometimes presenting a fictitious life was better than revealing the truth. She'd read enough to be fairly sure that if they knew the truth about her homelife they wouldn't be happy. Her mother, while far from the figure she read about in storybooks, was her only family. And even though her mother would never admit it, Imogen knew she was needed. It was the two of them against the world.

Gradually, her mother had got herself back on her feet. She'd found another job. Stopped drinking. It was a nonstop struggle, but she'd gone a whole year before lapsing again.

And that was how it continued.

Whenever things were bad, Imogen had reminded herself that this was not all her mother's fault. She'd been abandoned by her own family at a vulnerable age, and that was inexcusable in Imogen's opinion. No wonder her mother knew so little about stability. She didn't know how to mother because she hadn't really been mothered herself. She didn't know how to give unconditional love because she hadn't received it from her own family. Her own mother had thrown her out of the house when she'd become pregnant.

Imogen had constantly reminded herself of that. Her mother had no faith in family. It was up to Imogen to fix that and heal her. It was up to Imogen to prove that some family could be relied on to step up and be there.

It had sounded straightforward, and it had been anything but.

When she was twelve, social services had done a spontaneous home visit, possibly triggered by another trip to the hospital with her mother, but by then Imogen was keeping house. Their small apartment was clean and tidy. Her schoolbooks were stacked on the small kitchen table, and a pot of homemade soup was bubbling on the stove. Fortunately, it had been one of her mother's good days. Her hair and her clothes were clean, and she'd returned to her job in the local pub (Imogen had tried to persuade her to take a job in a bookstore, or a coffee shop—anywhere that didn't have temptation under her nose—but her mother loved the pub). Often she'd come home with someone she'd met there and Imogen would lock herself in her room and try not to listen.

Social services had apparently been satisfied with what they'd seen because they never came round again, and for much of the time Imogen's homelife had been uneventful, if lonely. Despite her best efforts, her relationship with her mother was never more than transactional.

And it was still that way.

Imogen sighed. This whole scenario was wearyingly familiar.

Her mother. In hospital.

The staff kept asking her to take a seat, but sitting just made her agitated. She'd thought this would be quick. She'd thought she'd be able to see her mother and leave, but it hadn't worked that way. They'd asked her to wait. And wait a little longer. Things were taking time. Her mother wasn't back from having her scan. Her mother needed a blood test.

To make matters worse, her phone was exploding with messages from Sophie, each more urgent than the last. She'd switched it to vibrate, but then it kept buzzing against her thigh like an angry wasp.

Imogen, how long until you get here?

Imogen, can you call me—it's pretty urgent.

Imogen, where are you?

Imogen, call me VERY URGENT

IMOGEN HAVE YOU DIED?

A fierce-looking nurse approached. "You can't use your phone in here, it interferes with hospital equipment."

"I thought that was a myth." Imogen had worked for a pharmaceutical client and had watched entire box sets of hospital dramas. She knew how things worked.

"You can't use your phone. It disturbs the patients."

"I need to be somewhere urgently. I'm in the middle of work." She gave a pleading smile, hoping to appeal to the nurse's good nature. "Do you have any more information on how long it will be?"

"Since you asked me three minutes ago?" The nurse didn't return the smile. "No. You're not a special case, you know. Maybe you haven't noticed, but we have a department full of people waiting to be treated. I'm going to have to ask you to sit down. When I have information, you'll be the first to know."

Imogen watched her go and wondered what it was about hospitals that made her feel so helpless.

That was pretty easy to answer. Some of her worst moments had happened in hospitals, and her mother had played a starring role in all those moments.

But honestly it could have been worse. Her mother had never been violent. She'd always had enough to eat. And there had been plenty of fairly long spells where her mother was fine.

Not warm or affectionate or even particularly engaged, but at least things had been relatively calm.

Her phone vibrated again and she checked that the nurse wasn't watching her and sneaked a look.

She was going to have to reply before Sophie had a meltdown.

She turned her back on the nurse and typed quickly.

Sorry. Dealing with minor crisis. Will be there soon.

Hopefully Sophie would assume it was a work crisis.

She still had more than three hours until the event started. That was plenty of time. She could do this.

How badly injured was her mother? What was taking so long?

Apparently, she'd fallen onto a train track. Fortunately, there had been no train in sight, and by the time the 12:46 had hurtled toward the station her mother had been rescued from her drunken mishap and transferred to an ambulance.

Imogen had been given no more information than that. Other than the fact she'd asked for her sister. She didn't know if her mother had lost her balance, or if she'd thrown herself onto the track. Emotion knotted itself in her stomach. Had her mother done it on purpose?

It was that thought that kept her here. Her chest ached and she felt torn between wanting to be there for her mother and needing to protect herself. And she did need to protect herself, because if there was one lesson she'd learned in childhood it was that no one else was going to do it. There was no one supporting her. No one standing by her side. Still, on the positive side she'd learned self-reliance and she considered that nothing but a good thing. She didn't have to learn how to look after herself. She'd been doing it since she was twelve years old.

It was one of the reasons she worked so hard. She had no backup.

She checked the time again.

Maybe she should leave. But if the doctor was right then her mother had been asking for her, even though she was still maintaining that ridiculous charade that Imogen was her sister. It was a change to be asked for something other than money.

Maybe this latest incident had shaken her mother and reminded her that she had a daughter. Maybe her mother was trying to reach out.

Another hour passed, by which time Imogen's stress levels were soaring. How much longer? She couldn't miss tonight's event, she just couldn't. The best plan would be to leave and come back later.

Decision made, she went and found the nurse.

"I need to leave for work, but I'll have my phone with me at all times and I will be back later to—"

"Your mother is back from her scan. You'll be able to see her in ten minutes. We'll be keeping her overnight."

Ten minutes. Imogen did some calculations. Ten minutes of waiting, twenty minutes of conversation, twenty minutes in a cab to the venue—she could still make it in time. She could still do this, and no one would be any the wiser.

She messaged Sophie.

I'll be there within the hour.

Sophie immediately called her.

Deciding that she couldn't put this call off any longer, Imogen lifted the phone to her ear and then caught the nurse's eye.

"Sorry." She rejected the call. "I'll go outside and take it there."

"You can see your mother now. But don't upset her."

Don't upset her? That was rich. Imogen wondered what the nurse would say if she was aware of the reality of her relationship with her mother. It was far likely to be the other way round.

A few minutes, she promised herself. That was all this was going to take, and then she'd go back to work and hope no one would ask her too many questions about the missing hours in her day.

She followed the nurse down the corridor and up a flight of stairs. Her knees were shaking and her brain was telling her to run fast in the opposite direction. But this was her mother and what sort of a person would she be if she didn't respond to a call from a hospital? This was a genuine medical situation.

And yes, she could have refused to come, but what if her mother had died? Would she have been able to live with that decision? All they had in the world was each other.

Her mother was lying in a bed, surrounded by machines that beeped and flashed. Her eyes were closed, as if she was determined not to look her predicament in the face. She was wearing a printed shirt that was badly creased and there were stains that probably preceded her recent misadventures. Stains that suggested the shirt had been worn long after the time it should have been consigned to the laundry pile. Her appearance told Imogen everything she needed to know about her mother's current state.

"Mrs. Thorne?" The nurse adjusted the flow of her drip. "We have your daughter here to see you. Just a short visit as you were asking for her. You need to rest."

"My daughter? I didn't ask for my daughter." Tina Thorne opened her eyes and slowly turned her head, and Imogen was eleven years old again.

I'm in the school play, Tina. Will you come and watch me?
Why would I want to do that?

Terry would have been there, but Terry was gone.

She'd told her school friends that her mother had a big job and couldn't make it, and she'd pretended that she didn't care that she was the only person in the cast who didn't have someone who loved them watching from the audience.

Imogen had done it alone, the way she did everything alone.

She taught herself to cook because her mother couldn't be bothered. She did the laundry and the shopping. As soon as she could, she'd got herself a Saturday job and she'd started saving. She loved working and getting paid for it and she'd loved school. She'd been saved by school, or more specifically by Miss Winston, her English teacher. Miss Winston had seen something in her that no one else had. Deprived of any positive reinforcement at home, Imogen had discovered that school was different. The harder she worked, the more she achieved, the more she was praised. She aced every exam she took. She was easily the best student in the school, and the better she did, the more delighted and proud they were. Imogen was never happier than when she was at school. Working hard didn't worry her. Working hard brought rewards. Validation. There was a point to it. A purpose. And she didn't care that she had to work so hard at home that keeping up with schoolwork ate into her sleep time. She was just relieved to have something that was hers. Something she could control.

It was the staff at her school who had encouraged her to apply to university and helped her navigate the system. She'd had offers from all the colleges she applied to, but she'd picked one far from home. And she'd built a life and grabbed every opportunity that came her way. Her years at school had taught her how different her homelife was from most people's, and she'd learned to hide that fact. She learned how to blend, and how to fit in by studying people and copying them. The way they dressed. The way they talked. The things they talked about. She became someone people might want to spend time with and developed a small friendship group of similarly studious people. She participated fully in most aspects of student life, although when other students experimented with drink and drugs, Imogen walked away. That was a path she was never going to tread. She'd seen where it could lead. She was looking at it now.

She pressed her fingers into her palms and forced herself to stand her ground. She was an adult now with her own job and her own home. She didn't need to feel afraid.

Her mother's stare was blank. "What are you doing here?"

"The hospital called me when you were brought in."

"Why?"

"Because you had my number in your purse. I'm your next of kin." And for a moment she wished that wasn't the case. As a child she'd sometimes wished her mother would disappear overnight and be replaced by a different version. A better version. And then she'd feel guilty for thinking that and modify her wish to having a sibling. It would have been easier if she'd had someone to share it with. *Our mother is in hospital again.*

"I'll leave you two alone for a moment." The nurse checked the monitors one more time and glanced at Imogen. "Don't tire her out."

The nurse was probably wondering why she didn't give her mother a hug, but Imogen knew a hug would be as welcome as a mosquito bite.

She waited for the nurse to leave. "They told me you fell on the train line."

"I don't remember. And I still don't know why you're here."

Imogen took a breath. She was not going to let her mother upset her. "I'm here because they called me. You were asking for your sister. I explained you didn't have a sister." When her mother didn't answer, she sighed. "Had you been drinking?"

Tina's eyes narrowed. "Don't you stand there judging me. You have no idea what my life is like. Did you bring the money I asked you for?"

Her heart was thudding. "No. I told you when you called last time, I won't give you money. I'll buy you food, I'll pay your rent or your bills, but I won't give you money to spend on drink."

"How I spend my money is my business."

"When it's your money that's true, but not when it's *my* money." She shook as she said the words. It had taken her years to learn to say no to her mother, and even though she did it, it never felt easy. It left her insides feeling twisted and tense. "My money is definitely my business."

"You patronizing little—"

"Mum! There are other people in this ward, trying to rest." She'd discovered early in life that it wasn't possible to die of embarrassment, but that didn't mean she didn't occasionally wish it to happen.

"Stop calling me Mum! You don't get it, do you?" Her mother was pale and hollow eyed. Blood had dried on her hair and the strands clumped together, matted and tangled.

It would have been unsettling and scary, except Imogen had seen her mother in a similar state before.

"I d-do get it. You're feeling really bad and you're taking it out on me." She tried to sound firm and in control, but all the confidence, all the joy, everything she'd ever made of herself and achieved was sucked from her in her mother's presence. She was a little girl again, feeling completely alone. "And I understand that you don't want people knowing you're old enough to have a daughter my age, but—"

"That's not it. For a supposedly smart girl, you're very stupid. The reason I don't want you calling me Mum is because I don't want to be your mum."

Imogen flinched. "I—"

"I *never* wanted to be your mum, and now that you're an adult I don't have to pretend anymore, so go and live out your happy family fantasy somewhere else. *Do you hear me?*"

"I h-hear you." Everyone was hearing her. Her mother had finally made a public announcement that she didn't want Imogen. That she'd never wanted Imogen. She'd said it before, but never in public and never when she was sober.

Imogen stood there feeling vulnerable and exposed, the

last of her protection ripped to shreds like wrapping paper on Christmas morning. She tried to summon up some of the strength and determination that had kept her going through tough times, but there was nothing there.

And now her mother was glaring at her, as if she was expecting Imogen to do something, or say something.

"Mum— Tina—"

"Just go. I don't even know why you're here. You're like a barnacle! I can't get rid of you."

Imogen tried to formulate a reply, but she couldn't. Why *was* she here? There had been many times over the years when she'd asked herself that question and today was another one.

They'd had bad exchanges before, plenty of them, but never quite like this. Never as brutal, and never in public.

And there was no point in pointing out her mother's inconsistencies. No point in reminding her that she regularly called Imogen when she wanted something or was feeling vulnerable. That she might not want Imogen, but she definitely seemed to want what Imogen could provide.

She was shaking and her chest felt tight. She was conscious of the three other people in the ward who were probably listening to every word. She might as well have painted a sign on herself. Unlovable. She tried hard to detach from the emotion, but it was too big. It filled every corner of her.

And then something, the part of her that was an adult, not a frightened child, flickered to life.

"I'm here because they called me. Because I'm your only family." And that should mean something, shouldn't it? However messy, however tangled and imperfect, it should mean something. She'd always hoped that eventually her mother would realize that not everyone walked away. That Imogen really *was* family and that she wasn't ever going to walk away.

"Family? No. What you are," her mother said slowly, "is the worst thing that ever happened to me. If I could change one thing in my life, it wouldn't be meeting Terry, or the drink or any of that. It would be you. Because it all started with you. You ruined everything. I lost my own family because of you. Because of you, they wanted nothing to do with me. They kicked me out. And every time I see you, I think of how my life might have looked if you hadn't been in it. I think of the life I might have had, and how much better it would have been. I could have gone to college. Got a good job. But instead I had you. Why do you think I didn't have any more kids? Because when you make the biggest mistake of your life, you don't do the same thing again."

Imogen couldn't catch her breath. There was no oxygen in the air; either that or her lungs had forgotten how to work. Her head spun and her vision was blurry. Dizziness? Tears? She had no idea.

Intellectually, she knew that what her mother was saying was ridiculous. Of course it wasn't her fault. Plenty of people had babies and still went to college. Or made the most of other options. Night school. Online courses. There were so many opportunities. The world was full of them. You just had to grab them and go for it, and that was something her mother had never done. For Tina it was easier to blame Imogen than face the fact that she lacked the motivation. And whatever her family had done, however they had failed her, her mother could have chosen to do it differently. She could have chosen to be all the family she and Imogen would ever need. The situation could have brought them closer. They could have been a tight, unshakable unit. Instead, Tina had done exactly the same to Imogen as her parents had done to her. She'd rejected her daughter.

"You don't mean it." Imogen hated the fact that her voice wasn't steady. "It's the drink talking."

"I do mean it." Her mother's expression was blank, and she looked at Imogen as if she was a stranger. "You ruined my life."

That simply stated fact hurt more deeply than anything that

had come before. It didn't matter that it was unjust. It didn't matter that Imogen could hardly be held responsible for her own appearance in the world.

"Do you know what, Mum?" The words burst from her, "You could have ruined *my* life, too, but I wasn't going to let that happen. I *chose* not to let that happen. Because there is such a thing as individual responsibility. There are many things in this world we can't control, but you can still make choices. But you choose to blame me for everything instead of taking responsibility for your own bad decisions."

Her mother stared at her for a moment and then turned her head away.

Imogen stood there, frozen. She couldn't believe she'd said those words. She shouldn't have exploded like that. Already she felt terrible about it, but she felt even more terrible about the words her mother had said to her.

I don't want to be your mum.

You ruined my life.

She badly wanted not to care. If she was as indifferent to the whole concept of family as her mother seemed to be, none of this would have mattered. But Imogen longed for family. She ached to have people around her who were connected to her life, part of her history. She wanted to be part of something bigger than herself. She wanted to buy Christmas gifts for a whole bunch of people, she wanted conversations that started *do you remember when...*

And she knew that even "normal" families had their stresses and problems, but she would have gladly embraced those problems if it meant having people around her who had her back.

But she had no one, and she was so tired.

Tired of doing everything by herself. Of carrying every worry herself, of crying every tear by herself. What did she want for Christmas? Someone to lean on. Someone who wasn't going to walk away when things got tough. Someone who wasn't going to tell her she was the worst thing that had ever happened to them.

What was she doing here?

Her mother didn't want her loyalty. Her mother thought she was a barnacle, not a support, so now was probably a good time to do something about that.

She had to leave. She had to get out of here, but she couldn't quite bring herself to make that final move.

She heard the beep of machines and focused on the white walls and white coats of the doctors who bustled in and out. The atmosphere was sterile and cold, exactly like her relationship with her mother.

A woman who had been hovering in the doorway, presumably visiting a relative, approached and put her hand on Imogen's arm. "Are you all right, love?" There was warmth and concern in her tone and she shot a look of disapproval toward Imogen's mother, but Tina either didn't notice or didn't care.

Imogen felt her face burn. If there was one thing worse than being unwanted it was people knowing she was unwanted. She wanted to defend herself. She wanted to shout out that she hadn't ruined her mother's life on purpose, that she was an okay person and the worst thing she'd ever done was invent a dog. But she didn't, because what was the point? "I'm totally fine."

And she should be. She should not be feeling this shocked and vulnerable. Even though her mother had never spelled it out quite so clearly, she'd always known. There had been no point in her childhood, not a single day, when Imogen had thought that maybe Tina was pleased to be her mother.

With a last look at her mother, she stumbled back along the corridor. She knocked into a visitor, and then into a nurse carrying a bunch of files.

"Sorry," Imogen mumbled, "so sorry." She was walking blind, everything blurry, her whole world fuzzy and unfocused.

Somehow she made it through the waiting area and out

into the busy street. The cold air whipped under her coat and chilled her, but she didn't care. She walked until she reached the park that was adjacent to the hospital and then she sat down on a bench.

People scurried past her, wrapped up against the bitter winter wind.

Occasionally, people glanced at her, but that wasn't surprising. Only someone with a death wish would sit outdoors on a park bench on a day like this.

Eventually, someone sat down next to her and she felt a hand on her arm.

It was the woman who had been on her mother's ward. She'd followed Imogen outside. "I'm sure she didn't mean it, love. People say things when they're unwell and hurt."

That was true, but Imogen knew her mother had meant every word.

Imogen said nothing. She just wanted to be left alone, but the woman didn't seem inclined to leave.

"Is there someone I can call for you? A family member? A friend?"

A family member. *If only.* Unfortunately, her only family was lying upstairs in that stark hospital room wishing Imogen had never existed. That was it. There was no one she could call. No one who knew the truth about her life. No one who knew who Imogen really was, or where she'd come from.

She really was alone. There was something touching, but also bleak and depressing, about the fact that the only person who had shown her any care and attention was a stranger.

"I'll be fine," she said. "But thank you for your kindness."

After a moment's hesitation the woman left, and Imogen sat alone on the bench shivering. No one else stopped and she was grateful for that. She didn't want to engage with strangers. Or anyone.

Bad things happened in life, she knew that. Accidents, illness, bad choices, bad luck. It was all part of being human. But when your own mother thought you were the worst thing that had ever happened? When you were the bad thing that life had delivered?

That was a tough one to deal with. That was hard. Mothers were supposed to love their babies unconditionally. Whether they were small, bald, ugly, loud—whatever—the one thing that was supposed to be guaranteed in life was a mother's love. That was the basic requirement for a parent, wasn't it? The whole job description. Forget reading together, or playing in the park, or eating vegetables—those were all nice to have, but not essential. But love? That was essential.

And when you'd never had that, when your mother had come without that guarantee, you never really trusted anything again, because if she couldn't love you what possible chance was there of anyone else loving you?

In that moment, Imogen wished she did have a dog. Not fictitious Midas, but a real dog who would wag his tail and be pleased to see her no matter what.

The irony was that the life she'd invented for her colleagues had made her yearn for family even more than usual. Every time she described a family gathering, or a family member, she found herself wishing it was real.

She'd woken the other morning convinced that Midas was in the room, and she'd opened her eyes expecting to see those big brown eyes and wagging tail, but of course the room was empty, and the only noise came from the train, which ran so close to her apartment that the whole building shuddered every few minutes.

Snow dampened her hair and trickled down her neck.

She should move, she thought dully as she felt her fingers slowly start to freeze. She couldn't feel her toes at all because her boots were built for fashion, not cold weather. She'd dressed to look smart and professional, not so that she could withstand arctic winds and barely above freezing temperatures.

Professional.

There was somewhere she was supposed to be. Where? She'd forgotten. Her mind was still in the room with her mother. No, not her mother. Tina. If she was the worst thing that had ever happened to Tina, then the best thing she could do was remove herself from her life permanently. She needed to stop pretending that they were a family.

She had no family. She had no one.

It was Christmas, and she'd never felt more alone.

In her pocket her phone buzzed, but she couldn't summon the energy to answer it. The encounter with her mother had burned through the person she'd created, and all that was left was reality. She'd lost her energy and her confidence. She'd lost her drive and her belief in herself. There was nothing left except the stories she told herself. And they were as fake as the rest of her.

9

Dorothy

At the same time that Imogen was shivering alone on a bench, Dorothy was loading her overnight bag into her car.

She took a last look at the house, illuminated and glowing in the winter darkness thanks to Patrick, who had strung Christmas lights around the door and the eaves. It had never looked prettier, with its roof white from the light dusting of snow they'd had during the day and the trees gleaming white.

"Do you have to go tonight?" Sara huddled inside her coat. She'd been fretting for the past hour as they'd checked on all the animals. "I know it's only six o'clock, but it's already dark, the temperature is dropping and you have a couple of hours of driving ahead. Why not wait until morning and go in daylight?"

"Because then I'll have to contend with traffic. This is the best time to drive into London. By the time I reach the outskirts all the commuter traffic will have died down. And I enjoy the journey. I'm listening to an excellent audiobook." She checked that she had her phone and her laptop. "I do feel a little guilty leaving you to keep an eye on the animals while I'm gone. It's a lot to ask."

"It's not a lot to ask. We're family. I couldn't even begin to list all the things you do for us. Don't worry about a thing. We'll be fine, won't we, Ava?" Sara turned to smile at her youngest daughter only to find she'd disappeared. "Ava? *Ava!* Oh, where has she gone now? I need eyes in the back of my head and the sides. She was here a moment ago. Did you see her?"

"I was too busy loading the car. She can't be far." Dorothy felt a flash of disquiet and calmed it. Overreacting wasn't going to help. "Bailey has gone too, so I assume they're together."

"Ava!" Sara yelled her daughter's name and then gasped as a snowball hit her squarely in her chest.

Ava appeared from behind a bush, grinning, Bailey by her side. "Surprise!"

"Mmm." Sara brushed snow from her coat. "You shouldn't wander off, Ava. Not when it's dark."

"Bailey and I went to say good-night to Benson, and to tell him I'll be looking after him for the next few days. I thought he should know."

"I'm sure he was reassured to hear it."

"It's a very responsible task, Ava." Dorothy bent and brushed snow from Ava's hair. "I'm relying on you."

"Don't worry." Ava patted her arm. "Everything will be fine."

Dorothy straightened and looked at her daughter. "You're sure you can manage?"

"Of course we can manage. It's just a couple of nights. Stop worrying." Sara grabbed Ava's hand to stop her disappearing again. She'd pulled her wool hat down over her ears and the strands of hair that had escaped flicked and curled around her face like wisps of gold. "Everything is going to be fine."

"Be careful with the bolt on Thelma's stable. You know she has learned to let herself out."

"I know."

"And if you have any worries at all about the animals, call Miles."

"I will." Sara shivered as thick flakes of snow started to fall. "Mum, it's icy and the forecast is terrible. Why don't you call Imogen and postpone?"

"Because I don't want to postpone. This is an enormous project. I want to stay on top of it, and anyway I'm looking forward to seeing Imogen. It will be the last time I see her before Christmas. It's not just work, it's also pleasure. This is my opportunity to thank her for all her hard work. I'll take my time driving, and the roads will be clear once I'm away from the country lanes." She didn't tell Sara that she had already called Imogen to confirm because of the weather, but hadn't had a reply. It was unusual, because Imogen always answered Dorothy's call immediately, and on the odd occasion when she hadn't she'd called right back. But not this time. Dorothy had left three messages, and Imogen still hadn't returned her call. She'd almost contacted Rosalind to check everything was all right, but she didn't want to risk getting Imogen into trouble by revealing that her calls hadn't been returned. She was probably in the middle of supervising an event. She'd mentioned that she had a busy December.

Dorothy intended to drive to London, spend the night in the little apartment she'd bought many years before and then tomorrow she'd head to the restaurant as agreed. Imogen would be there, she was sure.

She knew so little about Imogen's life outside work, but she did know that she was reliable.

"Message me when you arrive," Sara said. "That's if you're not stuck in traffic until Christmas Eve. Everything is crazy at this time of year."

"I enjoy my trip to London at Christmas. Stop worrying. And anyway, this isn't just about meeting Imogen. I need to do some Christmas shopping. A certain toy shop is calling me." She winked at her granddaughter, who grinned back.

Dorothy cleared the snow from her car.

"Have you called to confirm?" Sara looked troubled. "You should call and confirm."

"The table is booked. Imogen has never in her life not done something she said she was going to do. She is the most reliable person I have ever worked with." She bent down and kissed Ava. "Remember. You're in charge."

"Got it." Ava saluted. "I'm the boss."

"You are the boss." Dorothy hugged her, and then her daughter. "I'll be back before you notice I'm gone. And I'll be bearing gifts."

"Go, Nanna," Ava urged. "Go now!"

"Ava, that is not polite." Sara spoke firmly although the effect was slightly lessened by the fact she was trying not to laugh.

"Nanna said it, not me. I didn't ask."

Dorothy smiled and gave them a wave as she drove off. She knew Sara worried, but that was because they were so close. After Phillip had died, it had been just the two of them. She worried about Sara just as much.

Once she reached the main roads, her drive was easier than Sara had predicted and she reached London in good time.

She parked in the underground garage and headed up to the top floor.

She'd bought the apartment the year after Phillip died. It had been a sound financial investment, which also gave her a London base. She'd never been a lover of impersonal hotels.

The apartment wasn't large—just one bedroom—but it had a glorious roof terrace with expansive views toward the River Thames. And she didn't need anything large. This place suited her purpose perfectly, and when Sara stayed too she slept on the sofa.

Dorothy unpacked the homemade soup she'd brought with

her and heated it on the stove in the kitchen while she checked her phone. Imogen hadn't returned her call and she turned the stove off and called again, promising herself this would be the last time.

Imogen's voice sang cheerfully out of the phone.

You've reached Imogen. Please leave a message and I'll get right back to you.

Dorothy didn't leave another message. Instead, she ended the call and poured the soup into a bowl. She wasn't the sort of person who expected the people she worked with to be available 100 percent of the time. She knew Imogen was in demand and busy, but still this was unusual.

She told herself that if something was wrong, Imogen would have found the time to call.

And anyway, even if Imogen had rung her to cancel, she still would have come to London.

She planned to do some Christmas shopping and enjoy the lights and festive displays in London.

Everything was going to be fine.

10

Imogen

Imogen braced herself and pushed through the revolving glass door that led into the foyer of the office building where she worked. Her head throbbed after a night without sleep and she felt nauseous as she contemplated what lay ahead. She half expected to be apprehended by security, or to discover that her pass had stopped working, but she made it through the barriers without incident. No one gave her a second glance as she headed to the elevator. To an outsider it probably looked like a normal day.

It wasn't a normal day for Imogen. It was going to be her last day.

Today was the day she was going to be fired. And there was no one to blame but herself. She'd dropped the ball. Let everyone down. She'd loved this job more than anything and she'd blown it. The one good thing in her life, and she'd destroyed it.

If she'd been the one sitting in Rosalind's chair, she would have fired herself, which was why her letter of resignation was typed and ready in her bag. She was here not to try and persuade them to change their minds, but because she always owned her mistakes. She didn't make excuses. When she was in the wrong, she said so. She was honest about that, even though she hadn't been exactly honest about anything else in her life. But what was she going to say? *I wanted to fit in. I wanted to seem normal so that you'd all like me, so I made up a few things about my life and then it got complicated.*

Complicated was an understatement.

Maybe leaving would be a good thing. The way she felt right now she didn't have the energy for work. The fire and enthusiasm that had driven her this far had gone. She felt exposed and vulnerable. Too much like her real self, and nothing like the persona she'd invented. She wasn't Imogen the events management genius. She was Imogen the unloved. Imogen the fake.

She wanted to crawl under her bed and stay there until she could work out what to do next. She didn't want to be here.

Coming into the office was the toughest thing she'd ever had to do.

The elevator doors opened and she stepped onto the floor that was taken up by RPQ.

A few people gave her a sympathetic glance, but most just kept their heads down, studiously avoiding eye contact, which told her everything she needed to know.

There was no sign of Sophie, and she felt a pang of guilt and concern as she looked at the empty desk. The knowledge that she'd let down a colleague hurt more than anything. Sophie was probably off sick. And then a worse thought flashed into her head. What if they'd fired Sophie?

"Imogen?" Rosalind's voice came from her office. "I'm taking a call from Evelyn Barker and then I want to see you."

Of course she did.

Rosalind wanted an explanation and Imogen didn't have one.

But in the meantime she might as well clear her desk. Once

her conversation with Rosalind was done, she'd want to be out of here as fast as possible. She was going to have to find another job. But who would employ her? Rosalind would give her a terrible reference.

Angus Fitzgerald had virtually offered her a job so she could potentially contact him, but he probably wouldn't want her either once he found out the reason she was job hunting.

She reached her desk and saw a large box of chocolates with a note attached.

She picked up the note.

We're here for you, Imogen. Anya and Janie. xx

The tears she'd been holding back threatened to spill over. Oh God, they were such great people and she'd been telling them nothing but lies. They deserved better.

Anya was on the phone, but she gave Imogen a smile and a thumbs-up as Imogen sat down.

That was when she noticed the stack of leaflets on her desk.

Each bore a large photo of Midas copied from the one on her desk, and above it in bold lettering STOLEN—HAVE YOU SEEN THIS DOG?

What the—?

Confused, she turned to look at Janie. "What is this?"

"We're going to find him for you, Imogen. Whatever it takes." Janie's eyes glistened with tears of sympathy. "We've put them everywhere. All over social media. Stuck them on lampposts, handed them in at office buildings and hotels. The whole team helped."

Wait. What?

"The whole team has been out looking for my dog?"

"Yes."

All over social media?

Could this get any worse?

"Janie—"

"Don't say a thing. I know you'd do the same for one of us. We're a team, aren't we? And this has basically gone viral since we posted it, so I'm confident someone is going to recognize Midas and call me. I put my number on the flyer so that you're not upset by time wasters. I'll let you know if someone genuine calls. Now, just get your head down and clear your emails or whatever. We are totally on your side, Imogen. You were going through hell yesterday. How you could focus on work when your dog was missing, I have no idea. You were looking awful when I saw you. I should have done something then. I blame myself."

"Janie—"

"I told Rosalind this morning that Midas had been stolen. She didn't know. She was sympathetic. She even shared it on her own social media. If we can get enough people to share Midas's picture, no one can sell your baby on it."

This was a nightmare. She'd thought her life couldn't get worse, but this was worse. And it was all her fault. She was choked that her colleagues had done this for her. That they cared this much. And she felt such a fraud, because the person they thought she was didn't exist. She wasn't Imogen dog girl. She was Imogen the fraud. Imogen the big fat liar.

The only consolation was that no one was likely to call about Midas because he wasn't real. You couldn't find a dog that didn't exist.

Maybe it was a good thing she was about to be fired because there was no way she was going to be able to talk her way out of this.

"Imogen!" Rosalind bellowed her name across the office, and Imogen slowly rose to her feet, ready to tell more lies. At this point she was struggling to separate the lies from the truth.

"Tell her the truth about Midas," Janie hissed. "Your dog was missing. Anyone would have screwed up in those circumstances."

Imogen didn't even have the energy to respond. She couldn't stop thinking about poor Sophie.

She walked into Rosalind's office and Rosalind gestured to her to close the door.

Rosalind never closed the door. And she never closed the blinds on her glass-fronted office, but today the blinds were closed. No doubt so that there were no witnesses to the verbal mauling Imogen was about to receive.

Imogen dutifully closed the door. "Before you say anything, could you tell me where Sophie is? Is she okay? I've been worrying about her."

Rosalind looked up from the stack of paperwork on her desk. "Sit down, Imogen."

"But Sophie—"

"She's fine. She has a migraine, which after yesterday is hardly surprising. We agreed that she'd have a day in bed, and I'm expecting her back at her desk tomorrow, raring to go."

Sophie hadn't been fired. Imogen was flooded with relief.

But having reassured herself about that, there was no more avoiding the moment.

Deciding that she might as well get it over with, Imogen reached into her bag and put the letter on Rosalind's desk. Hopefully that would speed up the inevitable.

Her boss frowned at it. "What's this?"

"My resignation. And please don't blame Sophie for anything that happened yesterday, because she wasn't responsible. In fact, she was brilliant. It was all my fault. All of it."

Rosalind didn't open the letter. "Sit down, Imogen."

So this wasn't going to be speedy then.

Imogen perched on the edge of the seat, her back straight. "I'm sorry for everything, Rosalind."

"I'm the one doing the talking."

"Yes, Rosalind."

She'd learned early on that if Rosalind talked, you listened. No one messed with the boss, not even the clients.

Rosalind sat back. "I had a call from The Work Nook this morning. Alan Marsh himself, which wasn't the best start to my day. They're not at all happy that you didn't show up last night. They are no longer a client of ours."

It was what she'd expected, but that didn't stop her from feeling mortified and sick. She did some mental calculations and felt even sicker because she knew what the loss would do to the bottom line. The Work Nook wasn't their biggest client, but still their contribution was substantial. Word would get around. RPQ's reputation would be damaged and so would Imogen's. She'd be lucky to ever get another job in event management.

But that was her future, and her immediate problem was the present.

"I apologize."

"You already did that. What I haven't heard yet is an explanation for the fact that you suddenly disappeared and were uncontactable in the middle of a working day."

"There are no excuses."

"I wasn't asking for excuses. I was asking for an explanation. I assume there has to be one, because people like you don't just suddenly decide to stop doing your job for no reason." Rosalind paused. "I understand that Midas is missing—"

"That's not the reason."

"Then what is?" Rosalind removed her glasses and rubbed her fingers across the bridge of her nose. "I can't force you to give me that reason of course, but I believe I deserve to hear it."

Imogen stared at her miserably. She did deserve to hear it.

She'd worked hard to keep strict divisions between her work and homelife, but now they'd been well and truly breached. And she was out of a job anyway, so there was no longer any reason not to tell Rosalind the truth except that it revealed her for the total fraud she was.

But she still couldn't do it. She just couldn't.

She thought of her colleagues, out there now doing everything they could to find her dog. Her fake dog. Having her back when she made a mistake. Leaving chocolates on her desk. Her eyes filled. She couldn't bear to see their faces when they found out that everything she'd told them about her homelife was a lie. Their support comforted her, even though it was based on a lie.

She blinked hard. She wasn't going to cry. No way.

"Imogen?"

Imogen flinched. Rosalind was waiting for an explanation.

And she needed to give her something so that this could all be over. She'd tell a part truth, and maybe Rosalind wouldn't ask too many questions.

"I was on my way to the Work Nook event when I had a call from the emergency department at the hospital."

Rosalind frowned. "The hospital? Someone had an accident?"

She licked her lips. "My mother."

"I thought your mother lived in Dorset."

"She was in London." Imogen improvised, although this time she did it with caution because her overenthusiastic spontaneity with Midas hadn't worked out so well. "Christmas shopping. She fell."

Rosalind stared at her for a moment. "I'm sorry to hear that. No wonder you were concerned. I know what a close family you are. So why didn't you just call and explain you needed time off?"

"Because I didn't think I needed time off. I'd had several conversations with Sophie, and I'd promised to go across early to try and calm the client down. I was in the cab when I got the call from the hospital and I thought I could see my mother and still make it to the event on time."

"But that didn't happen. Clearly, you were delayed. What I don't understand is why you didn't call someone and let them know that you had a family emergency. We would have covered for you. Was no one else in your family able to help?"

Imogen fixed her gaze on the photographs on Rosalind's desk. It was of Rosalind and her two daughters when they were young. Rosalind had parents, siblings, a whole network of people connected to her. She had a stack of Christmas cards on her desk ready to send. A list of gifts to buy.

Imogen didn't send Christmas cards. She didn't have any gifts to buy apart from the single Secret Santa for work.

Rosalind wouldn't be able to begin to understand Imogen's life.

"It turned out to be—more complicated than I was anticipating. I was upset."

Rosalind's expression softened. "Having a relative in hospital is always upsetting, naturally."

Not "naturally." Nothing about her relationship with her mother was natural.

"If you were upset," Rosalind said, "then that was all the more reason why you should have phoned for support. We are a team, Imogen. We support one another."

"I wasn't myself. I wasn't thinking."

Rosalind paused. "Your mother is lucky to have such a loving and caring daughter."

Yes, she was. It was just a shame she didn't appreciate it.

I don't want to be your mum.

You ruined my life.

Her mother's words had hammered down the defenses she'd built over the years, and now, on top of the emotional hurt, she was going to lose her job. So her reward for family loyalty was to be punished. She shouldn't have gone to the hospital. When the doctor had asked her to come, she should have refused.

Imogen felt a rush of frustration and outrage at how unfair this all was and then felt angry with herself. She knew life was unfair. She'd known that for a long time. Bad things happened to good people, and people didn't get what they deserved. She couldn't do anything about that, but she could choose not to let her mother continue to do this to her. What had her mother said? *Go and live out your happy family fantasy somewhere else.*

Well, no more fantasy. From now on she was facing reality, no matter how ugly it looked.

Rosalind sat back in her chair. "How is your mother now?"

Imogen chose her words carefully. "She's more herself."

Which basically meant she was as frustrating and imperfect as ever.

Rosalind nodded. "Good. You're probably looking forward to Christmas so that you can spend proper time together."

After last night, Imogen doubted she'd ever be seeing her mother again. And that was fine. The only thing worse than spending Christmas all alone, would be spending it with her mother.

But that wasn't the response Rosalind was expecting, so Imogen managed a smile.

"Yes," she said. "I'm looking forward to Christmas."

Rosalind was watching her closely. "I can understand that concern for your mother drove all other thoughts from your head, but we both know there's more going on here."

Imogen stiffened. She couldn't possibly know, could she?

"There's nothing more, Rosalind."

"There is. And if you won't admit it, then I'm going to spell it out." Rosalind leaned forward. "You are close to burnout, Imogen."

"Excuse me? I am— What?"

"Burnout. I'm concerned you're on the edge of it, and my job is to catch you before you topple over the edge. It's been worrying me for a while. You're a phenomenal worker with huge talent, but everyone has their limits and these last few weeks you've gone way past yours. The hours you're putting in, and the workload you're handling, is inhuman. And of course I'm responsible for that workload—" a flicker of a smile touched Rosalind's mouth "—but so are you. It's important to know your limits."

Burnout.

Imogen stared at her. She was most definitely not on the edge of burnout. Not with work, anyway. Her mother, yes. When it came to her mother she was so burned-out she was charred to a cinder.

She opened her mouth to deny it and then realized that if Rosalind thought she had burnout, then she would stop looking for other reasons for Imogen's massive screwup. She could use this, and it wasn't as if she wasn't stressed out of her mind. It wasn't a lie exactly.

"That might be true." She said it with reluctance. "I have taken on a lot lately. Maybe too much."

Rosalind gave a nod of agreement. "You give everything to your work, and these extra challenges in your personal life have been the final straw."

Well, *that* was true. "You're right, they have."

"Everyone has tough moments in their lives, Imogen, and what you should have done was reach out and share that with me so that we could find a solution together, but I realize that concern for your mother drove all that from your head and on top of worrying about Midas it was all too much. Which presumably is why you dropped the ball."

Imogen wasn't sure what she was supposed to say to that, so she simply nodded.

Rosalind studied her, always a slightly unsettling experience. "How long have you worked here, Imogen?"

"Almost exactly a year." If only all questions were that easy to answer.

Rosalind's mouth twitched. "And in that year, how many times would you say that you've dropped the ball?"

Imogen stared at her. Was that a trick question? "I—I think this is the first time, Rosalind."

"It *is* the first time." Rosalind sat forward. "So why aren't you fighting to save your job? Instead of marching in here reminding me what an asset you are, you come in clutching your resignation. Why?"

"I assumed you were going to fire me."

"Why would you assume that?"

Because her mother had stripped away her self-esteem.

When Imogen didn't answer, Rosalind frowned.

"I don't get it, Imogen. I don't understand what's happening here. I've seen you fight for your clients. I've seen you handle obstacles and objections that would floor most people. You are a champion problem solver. Why aren't you fighting for yourself?"

Imogen swallowed. "I lost a client."

"Even if that were the case, why aren't you sitting there telling me how many clients you've won for us this year alone? Why aren't you slapping numbers on my desk and forcing me to acknowledge that you've won far more than you've just lost? Because that's what you should be doing. And normally that's what you *would* be doing."

Imogen stared at her. That would have been a good tactic if she'd thought of it. And maybe she would have thought of it if her recent encounter with her mother hadn't left her feeling so worthless. She hadn't gone about this the right way at all. She hadn't tried to save herself because she hadn't felt she was worth saving. But Rosalind seemed to be doing it for her. Rosalind was giving her the tools she should have reached for herself.

Her mouth felt dry. "I won four major accounts in the first half of this year."

"You did, indeed." Rosalind's expression relaxed slightly. "And all those accounts are showing excellent growth."

"I won another two in September."

"Yes. You're an asset, Imogen. Which is why you won't be losing your job, and why—" Rosalind reached for the envelope Imogen had placed on her desk and tore it in two "—I won't be accepting this."

Imogen felt dizzy with relief. She wasn't losing her job. She felt a rush of emotion and had to stop from flinging herself across the desk to hug Rosalind.

"But what about The Work Nook? They fired us."

"They didn't fire us."

"You said we no longer have the account."

"We don't. But that's not because they fired us," Rosalind said. "I was given a detailed account of what happened by Sophie, including the degree to which they were hounding her all of yesterday, which in turn led her to hound you. And your advice, even from a distance, was excellent by the way. The speaker arrived on time and the event went off without a hitch. Sophie stepped up."

Imogen felt relief flood through her. At least no one could say the event had been a failure.

"So why have we lost the account?"

"Because I told them we could no longer work together." Rosalind's tone was clipped. "No matter what the stress, I won't have any member of my team spoken to the way they spoke to Sophie. There is no excuse for it, and that's what I told Alan Marsh when he rang to complain. We're an extension of the client's team, not a punching bag. I expect civility and respect. If they can't behave professionally, then we won't deal with them."

Imogen felt her jaw drop. Rosalind had resigned the account? That was either brave or stupid. Brave, she decided, remembering Sophie's voice as she'd told Imogen what the client had been saying to her. But most bosses would have swallowed the insults for the sake of the business.

Not Rosalind.

Imogen's respect for her boss grew still further. "That's—surprising."

"If you think that, then you don't know me as well as you should. I don't tolerate abusive relationships in my private life or my business life. What sort of a team would we be if we didn't defend and take care of one another? Our business works because of excellent teamwork. My job is to nurture that. And anyway, his team need so much hand-holding it's hardly a cost-effective account for us. I'm sure you'll come up with some ideas for how we might plug the gap left by their departure."

Imogen's head was reeling. "I will. I definitely will. I'll get onto that right away, Rosalind."

"No, you won't."

"I won't?"

"No, because you won't be working for the next month. At all. On anything. You won't be looking at emails and you won't be taking calls."

Her sense of relief evaporated. "But—I thought I wasn't fired."

Rosalind sighed. "You're not fired. But although we agree that you're an asset, there is still the problem that you are overloaded, and I'm not convinced that you're actually capable of slowing down the way things are at the moment. If we carry on like this, something is going to give, and I don't want that to be you. So I'm going to do you a favor, although I'll probably curse myself for it. You're taking a month off."

"A month?" She must have misheard that, surely. Rosalind couldn't possibly have meant a month.

"Yes. You've accrued holiday. I'm insisting that you take it."

"But we're not allowed to take more than two weeks in one go." She knew for a fact that Rosalind had refused to give Janie a month off to go to New Zealand in the summer. No one ever took more than two weeks at a time. "Those are the rules."

Rosalind tapped her pen on the desk. "I make the rules, Imogen. It's one of the advantages of being the boss. And I'm giving you special permission to take all the leave owing to you."

"Oh, but it's fine, Rosalind, and I don't want—"

"A month, Imogen. I checked with HR. You have taken two days so far this year. It's not healthy. You'll take the rest of the holiday now. It will give you time to focus on yourself and family, have a good rest and return refreshed in the new year. Have a wonderful Christmas with that family of yours. Breathe fresh air, go for long walks, bake cookies, do whatever it is you like to do to relax—" she waved a hand vaguely, clearly unsure as to what people did do to relax "—and return to work refreshed. We'll see you back here in the second week of January and at that point we will sit down and work out how to make your workload more manageable."

Imogen was appalled. "The second week of January?"

"Yes, and I don't want to see a single email from you in my inbox before that date."

This was a nightmare. Christmas was always a difficult time of year for her, and she normally only had to survive a few days. But a month? A whole month of watching other people getting excited, decorating their houses, Christmas shopping, getting ready for the big day. A whole month to sit alone in her tiny apartment, staring at the same walls she stared at all year, dwelling on what had happened with her mother.

"It's kind of you to offer, but I'd rather work, Rosalind."

"This is not a negotiation. It's an order and it's not open for discussion." Rosalind stood up, indicating that the meeting was over. "I believe you have lunch with Dorothy today. You'll keep that meeting as the two of you have such a good relationship, and then you'll go home afterward. Explain to Dorothy that you are taking leave that is owed to you. If any work issues arise, she can contact me."

She didn't want leave. She didn't want to focus on herself, and she definitely didn't want to focus on the family she didn't have. It was going to kill her. This was almost worse than being fired. At least if she'd been fired, she could have filled the time looking for another job. Kept busy. Had a purpose.

The small child in her wanted to blame her mother, but the adult knew that would achieve nothing. Rosalind clearly wasn't going to budge, so all she could do now was accept it and find a way to fill the next month.

Could life get any worse?

There was a tap on the door, and Imogen glanced up as the door opened and Janie tentatively poked her head round.

Something about her expression made Imogen think that her life was about to get worse.

"Sorry to interrupt, but I have some sort of good news about Midas. As you know, we've all been working to track him down."

Imogen relaxed slightly. She wasn't worried. You couldn't track down a dog that didn't exist.

"And we've found him."

Rosalind raised her eyebrows. "You've found Midas? Janie, that's wonderful news."

Imogen froze. It wasn't wonderful news. In fact, it wasn't possible. She had no idea what was coming next, but it couldn't be good.

"Yes." Janie gave a helpless shrug. "But it's all a bit weird and awkward. A woman phoned. She lives somewhere in Suffolk. How Midas got himself all the way out there I have no idea, although you did always say he was an intelligent dog, Imogen, so maybe he snuck onto a train or something—anyway, this woman says she has Midas."

"Good work, Janie," Rosalind said, "although I don't see why that's weird or awkward."

Janie sneaked a look at Imogen. "It's awkward because she's claiming that Midas is hers, except that his name isn't Midas. She calls him Hunter. She recognized the photo we posted and said we stole it from her Facebook page. Which is obviously total nonsense. I told her, it's the photo Imogen has on her desk, but she insists that Midas-Hunter is her dog. It's disgusting the lengths some people will go to. Anyway, I took her number and said Imogen would call her back. I'm sure it's all a misunderstanding. Or maybe you should call the police and let them handle it."

Imogen couldn't formulate a response. She'd taken the photo from social media, not thinking for a moment that the decision would come back to bite her. What were the chances? She shouldn't have told people he'd escaped. She should have just had him put down. *But then she would have been a dog murderer.*

Rosalind spoke first. "I'm sure there is a simple explanation."

There was a simple explanation. She was a fake. Her entire life had been cracked wide-open and eviscerated. Her lies exposed. The irony was that she'd only told the lies in the first place so that she'd be accepted by her colleagues. And now those same lies were going to ensure they never accepted her again.

But that was a problem for the future. Right now she had to figure out how to handle this latest crisis.

"If you give me the number, I'll call her. Thanks, Janie." She took the piece of paper Janie proffered. The number swam in front of her eyes. What was she going to say to the woman?

"Take the meeting with Dorothy and then make the call about Midas. And after that take the month off," Rosalind said gently. "You need it."

They thought she was losing it, and maybe she was.

This time Imogen didn't bother arguing with her boss.

She was going to need a month off to figure out how to unravel the mess she'd made.

11

Dorothy

Dorothy arrived in the restaurant early and settled herself at the table by the window that Imogen had reserved. She'd had an excellent morning and managed to finish her Christmas shopping. She'd bought far more for the girls than she should have done, but she hadn't been able to help herself. She intended them to have the best Christmas ever, and the thought of creating that for them raised her own spirits.

This weekend she intended to make a start on decorating the house. She'd already raided the garden for greenery, but she needed to dig out the boxes of decorations from the attic.

She checked the time. Imogen still hadn't called, but she had no reason to think she wouldn't be here. And after a hectic morning it was nice to sit for a moment and absorb her surroundings.

Every corner of the restaurant sparkled and all around her people were enjoying themselves. The place echoed with conversation and laughter. There was a small group enjoying an early Christmas office celebration, and a couple facing each other with bags of Christmas shopping stacked at their feet. They'd refused to leave their parcels at the desk and Dorothy wondered what could be in them that was so precious.

Christmas was supposed to be a time of giving, but for her Christmas was the time when everything had been taken away.

She took a breath and drank some of the water the waitress had poured on her arrival.

She wasn't going to think about that now. She was going to do what Sara did and block that time of her life out and focus on the present. This Christmas was going to be wonderful, and in the meantime she was looking forward to a celebratory lunch with Imogen.

She studied the menu briefly, and when she glanced up again Imogen was standing in the doorway.

She was wearing a scarlet coat and she handed it to the girl at the desk, revealing long black boots and a well-cut wool dress that skimmed her figure and ended midthigh. She looked smart and businesslike and then she turned and Dorothy felt a flicker of concern because she could see even from this distance that Imogen was stressed. *Upset?*

She watched as Imogen smoothed her dress, pulled herself together and then spotted Dorothy. She crossed the restaurant in quick strides, a bright smile on her face.

"Am I late?"

"No, I was early."

Goodness, the girl looked exhausted. As if she hadn't slept at all. As if her world had somehow fallen apart since Dorothy had last seen her.

What could have happened?

Concerned, Dorothy stood and gave Imogen a hug even though she knew it would probably be considered unprofessional. She could almost feel Sara frowning. She expected Imogen to pull away, but instead she stayed there, hugging Dorothy as if she was the last human on earth.

Dorothy felt a lump form in her throat and she rubbed Imogen's back.

"It's good to see you. Is everything all right?"

"Oh. Yes, it's fine. Sorry. Christmas hug." Imogen cleared her throat and pulled away suddenly as if she'd just realized what she was doing. She sat down, her cheeks flushed. "It's been a bit of a week, that's all. You know how it is at this time of year. Chaos. I've been looking forward to this. Looking forward to seeing you." She blinked several times and studied the menu hard.

She was so obviously struggling with her emotions that Dorothy felt an ache in her chest.

"Is it work that has been busy? Or all the Christmas preparations?"

"Mostly work, although some of that is linked to Christmas, of course. I had events back-to-back yesterday—" Imogen's voice was overly bright "—but it was fine."

Something in her tone told Dorothy that it hadn't been fine at all, but she knew Imogen wouldn't tell her the truth. She was the consummate professional. She didn't confide or gossip, which was appropriate of course because Dorothy was a client. Still, she sometimes wished she could break down that barrier between them. There were so many things she'd like to know. So many questions she would like to ask.

Imogen put the menu down. "Have you chosen, Dorothy?"

"I think I'll have the soup and the duck. You?"

"The same."

They ordered their food and a burst of raucous laughter from a table close to theirs drew Imogen's attention.

A party of ten were wearing silly hats and exchanging gifts. Imogen stared at them for a moment, then looked away and focused on Dorothy. "How has your trip been so far, Dorothy? Successful?"

"Very. I did some Christmas shopping this morning, for my granddaughters. It was unbelievably crowded, but I did manage to get the last few things I needed. Next year I might bring them on a trip to see the Christmas lights. I think they'd enjoy it."

It was small talk, but she sensed Imogen needed it.

"How are Ava and Iris?" Imogen remembered every detail of every conversation. It was one of her many strengths.

"They are excited about Christmas. They're still at that age where the anticipation of Christmas is as exciting as Christmas itself."

They paused as their starter arrived.

Imogen stared at her soup, as if she was trying to remember why she'd ordered it. Then she picked up her spoon. "Will you be spending Christmas with them?"

"They're all coming to me, which will be chaotic no doubt, but also fun. Last year they spent Christmas with Patrick's family—Patrick is my son-in-law, as you know—and to be honest, because I was on my own I didn't bother too much. I had a tree, because I thought it would be nice when the children visited, but I didn't do much more than that in the way of decorations. But as they're all staying and we're having a family Christmas, I'll make more of an effort. I love to cook so there will be plenty of food involved."

Imogen put her spoon down without touching her soup. "That sounds nice. It's a wonderful time of year." Her tone was warm and her words perfectly appropriate, but there was something in her eyes—something lost and sad—that made Dorothy put her spoon down too.

She'd never seen anyone trying so hard to be strong when she was clearly at the breaking point.

She felt the same emotion she felt when Miles called to tell

her he had an animal who was unloved and needed a home.
Which was ridiculous, because Imogen was an independent
and successful woman.

Still...

"Are you sure everything is all right, Imogen?"

"Absolutely. Tell me more about your grandchildren."

Dorothy paused and then picked up her spoon again. If that
was what Imogen wanted, then she'd play along. "They love
making homemade decorations and cards. My daughter, Sara, is
drowning under paper chains and snowmen cards. How about
you?" She asked the question casually. "What are your plans
for Christmas? I assume you won't be working?"

"The office closes for the week between Christmas and New
Year."

Their starter was removed, Imogen's mostly untouched.

Dorothy decided not to comment. "You're ready for the
break, I'm sure."

"Actually, I'm very lucky," Imogen said in an unnaturally
high voice. "Rosalind has given me a whole month off. An
extended break. I've accrued some holiday and she wants me
to take it before next year. But of course you have my mobile
number so if anything at all comes up, or you're concerned
about anything, all you have to do is give me a call. Or call
Rosalind, obviously."

"A month? What a treat." Dorothy could see from Imogen's
expression that she considered it to be anything but a treat.
"Where will you go? Will you be spending it with family?"
The moment she said it she wanted to snatch the words back.
She shouldn't have asked that question. It was too personal.

"No. Not this year. It will be just me."

Just me.

Those two little words were loaded with emotion, and Dorothy had an overwhelming urge to invite Imogen to spend

Christmas with them, but she managed to stop herself. That would not be appropriate.

She wanted to ask why Imogen wouldn't be spending it with family, but she knew that question would also be inappropriate.

The main course was placed in front of them—glazed duck with fondant potatoes.

"What will you do?"

"I haven't finalized my plans." Imogen's head was tilted down, her focus on her plate. "I'll probably just stay at home," she said. "Lie in. Read some books. Catch up on sleep and TV. All the things I don't normally have time for. It will be fantastic. The great thing about spending Christmas on your own is that you can be entirely selfish. You can watch whichever TV program you like with no disagreements over the remote control, you can cook or not cook. Only yourself to think about. If I can't be bothered I can just make a grilled cheese sandwich and no one will care. Brilliant."

A grilled cheese sandwich. *No one will care.*

Dorothy cared. And she sensed Imogen cared too.

The ache in her chest intensified and she put down her knife and fork.

She couldn't stand this.

"Imogen—"

Imogen put her knife and fork down too and looked up. "I'm really sorry, Dorothy, but I'm not feeling well. Headache. I didn't sleep well last night. I should have canceled, but—"

"I'm glad you didn't cancel, because I really wanted to see you." Dorothy paused, unsure how best to handle this. "We've known each other for a while now, Imogen. I know that technically I'm a client, but I hope I'm also a friend. You can trust me."

"Oh, I do. You're always so kind." Imogen picked up her glass and took a sip of water. "You're my favorite client, but don't tell anyone that obviously. Sorry. This is so unprofessional."

"Not at all." Dorothy ignored the people around her. "Why didn't you sleep well? Is something wrong?"

"No. Well, maybe a few things, but nothing important. A few personal issues." She hesitated and then put her glass down and gave Dorothy a tired smile. "Honestly? I don't want a month off. I'd rather work. I like to stay busy, you know? Things feel easier when I'm busy."

Dorothy did know. "When life is hard, it sometimes helps to have no time to think about it. I understand that. What I don't understand is why are you taking a month off if you don't want it? I'm surprised Rosalind would allow it."

"It was her suggestion." Imogen scrunched her napkin into a ball, her knuckles white. "Actually, not a suggestion. She thinks I need it. I don't think she's right. I mean, Rosalind is *great*," she said hastily. "Really brilliant. Best boss ever. And it's true that I have been busy. We won a few new clients, and maybe I've taken on a bit too much, but I love it so it didn't seem like a problem to me."

But it had clearly seemed like a problem to Rosalind. Dorothy had the utmost respect for Rosalind. If she was concerned, then there must be a good reason.

"What do you do in your free time, Imogen?"

"Free time?" Imogen had a glazed look on her face as if she was trying to remember what that was. "I do loads of things. I have a black belt in jujitsu—the Japanese variety, not the Brazilian. I started in my last year of school, and I've done it ever since. I train with a club here in London and usually I go a couple of times a week, although when I started working for Rosalind it became more like once a week. Less than that sometimes." She paused, thinking. "In fact, I haven't been since April because I've been super busy. But I keep meaning to go. It's a great way to keep fit, as well as being useful for self-defense. I prefer it to the gym."

But she hadn't been since April. And it was now December.

"It sounds like a fun thing to do. And being based here in London you have so many options for entertainment. Do you like theater?"

"*Love* it. The last thing I saw was that controversial staging of *Hamlet*." The napkin was now so twisted that Dorothy doubted that even a steam iron would restore it to its previous state of pristine smoothness.

"The one last year?"

"No, it was this year." Imogen frowned. "Or maybe it was last year. Time flies."

By the time they'd finished their duck, Dorothy had ascertained that not only had Imogen all but given up martial arts and hadn't been to the theater for over a year, she'd also not been to the cinema and had only read one book since the summer.

She was starting to understand why Rosalind had insisted Imogen take a month off.

"So what will you do with your time? A month off is a real chance to recover. Will you stay at home?"

Imogen seemed to pull herself together. "I haven't decided. This only happened this morning, so I haven't had a chance to get my head around it. I'll probably stay in London. Maybe I'll finally manage to see a play or go to jujitsu." She put her knife and fork down. "The duck was completely delicious."

She'd eaten about two mouthfuls, but Dorothy didn't comment on that.

She couldn't bear to think of Imogen on her own in London eating a grilled cheese sandwich on Christmas Day.

"Have you considered a break in the country? I have a holiday cottage on my estate." The words were out before she could stop herself. "You could use it."

"Use it?"

"Stay in it. Holly Cottage. It's pretty. Cotswold stone. Open fire. Thatched roof." Her mind drifted back to the few months when she'd lived there herself. After Sara had left for college and she'd been on her own, the place had been a comfort. It might be just what Imogen needed. "It's idyllic, really. Popular with honeymooners, and the social media generation who love to take selfies because the place is so welcoming and cozy. It's normally booked solid all year, but I had to have some work done in it so I stopped taking bookings in the summer. If you fancied getting out of London, then you'd be most welcome to use it. I wouldn't charge you."

Imogen stared at her. "You're offering me your cottage?"

"Why not? It's empty. And if you're looking for fresh air and relaxation it fits the brief. And the village is only a ten-minute walk away across the fields. We're in the country, but the village has everything you could possibly need. In the summer it's ridiculously crowded, with tourists trying to photograph it from every angle, but at this time of year it's at its most charming. It has an excellent farm shop, a few gift shops, a vintage clothing store, a wool shop—do you knit?"

"I— No, I don't knit."

"There's a library, an independent bookshop and a café that sells the best gingerbread you've ever tasted. They switched on the Christmas lights last week and the village looks so pretty. And if you don't feel like leaving the cottage it's the perfect place to curl up and read, or catch up on TV."

Imogen took a sip of water. "And you'd let me stay there?"

"I'd love you to stay there. You'd be doing me a favor to be honest, because it isn't good for the cottage to be empty in this cold weather."

Imogen put her glass down. "How long were you thinking?"

"Stay the whole month if you like. You don't have to decide now. See how you feel."

Imogen took a breath. "When would you want me to come?"

"Whenever you like. The cottage has everything you need so all you have to pack is warm clothing."

"I could come on Friday?"

"Perfect."

"Friday it is," Imogen said. "If you're sure. Thank you. It will be great to get away from London." She smiled at Dorothy. A real smile this time, not the forced overcheerful version she'd produced at the beginning of their lunch.

"I can meet you at the train station."

"There's no need, but thank you. I'll rent a car," Imogen said. "It will be useful to have one while I'm there, and I don't want to make extra work for you."

"It's no work at all. It will be a treat to have you in the cottage."

And only in that moment, when it was all agreed, did she realize that Sara was going to kill her.

She felt a flicker of trepidation and also guilt. She should have thought about that, and normally she would have done, but she'd been so stressed at the thought of Imogen sitting alone with a grilled cheese sandwich on Christmas Day that she hadn't been able to help herself.

But what was Dorothy supposed to do? She could not enjoy Christmas knowing that Imogen was all alone in London. And it wasn't as if she'd invited Imogen for Christmas or anything. She was simply lending her the cottage. It was no different to renting it out to a stranger.

What could possibly go wrong?

12

Imogen

Imogen drove carefully down the icy lanes toward Winterbury. She'd left early and the drive from London had been easy, but as she drew closer to the address Dorothy had given her, the impact of the overnight snowfall was visible everywhere.

The roads were glassy in the pale winter sunlight, the hedges and fields white with snow. She drove through picturesque villages with rows of pretty cottages and shops with windows illuminated and decorated for Christmas. She passed an ancient church, its roof coated with snow, and crossed a bridge over a stream that was frozen.

She'd thought that by leaving London she'd be avoiding Christmas, but it seemed as if this place had been designed for the season, and as if that wasn't enough, nature had added the final sparkly flourish to the landscape. And with that pale winter beauty came the cold.

Fortunately years of saving on heating bills meant she'd amassed a wardrobe of warm clothing.

Her suitcase was full of wool sweaters and outdoor gear. She'd also packed sturdy boots because she liked the idea of walking to the village Dorothy had described.

Fresh air, country walks, maybe a few hours with a book in the village café—it all sounded perfect. Not completely perfect, of course. Completely perfect would have been spending time with family, but for someone spending Christmas alone, this was good. Better than being alone in London.

Alone.

The word seemed to settle on her like one of the snowflakes drifting in front of the car.

Perhaps because of that encounter with her mother, she was more aware of it than usual. Everywhere she looked, people seemed to be in groups. There was a woman with two excited children trying to feed ducks that stood bemused on the frozen surface of a pond. A family laughing together as they dragged an oversize Christmas tree along a snow-covered path and a couple walking hand in hand looking like something from an ad for vitamins (or maybe winter coats).

Imogen watched as the woman laughed up at the man, and he lowered his head to kiss her slowly.

"Ugh," she muttered. "Get a room." And they probably had a room, most likely in a five-star hotel where they'd order room service and sip champagne and talk about how much they loved everything about Christmas. Perhaps he was going to propose and they'd remember this particular Christmas forever.

Everyone seemed content.

Everyone had someone.

Imogen felt a pang of envy and forced herself to focus on the road. She knew that wasn't true, but right at that moment it *felt* true. Part of her hoped to pass a couple in midfight, or a child having a tantrum. Anything that might remind her that she wasn't the only one living a less than perfect life. She knew

Christmas was a difficult time for many people, but there was something about snow and sparkle that made her forget that.

As she left the village, the roads worsened. She gripped the wheel, hoping she didn't slide the rental car into a ditch. Trees bordered each side of the narrow road, their snow-covered branches creating a frozen archway. It was pretty, but also deadly, and she slowed as snow fluttered down, reducing her visibility. Maybe driving hadn't been such a great idea. She was used to living in the city, where snow swiftly melted and rarely interfered with daily life.

"You have arrived at your destination," said her phone and Imogen breathed a sigh of relief.

"Thank you."

She shook her head. And now she was talking to her phone as if it were a person. She was losing it.

She took the turn indicated, past a stylish sign saying Winterbury Estate and Vineyard and then stopped. A pair of large wrought-iron gates had been left open and she could see the driveway winding ahead through an avenue of snow-laden trees.

Dorothy lived here?

It was a good thing she was on her own in the car because she was pretty sure her jaw dropped. She'd seen pictures, of course, when Dorothy had explained that she wanted to hold the summer event on her land, but pictures didn't capture the magical setting or the sheer scale of the place.

She drove through the gates and there to the right, sheltered from the road by a dry stone wall and mature trees, was Holly Cottage. The name had no doubt been inspired by the large holly bush that dominated the front garden. It was crowded with scarlet berries, although with weather this cold she had no doubt the birds would soon strip it bare.

She pulled into the parking space and gazed at the place that would be her home for the next few weeks.

The cottage was chocolate-box perfect, brimming with

Cotswold charm. Snow clung to the roof and dusted the rose that climbed its way up the pale stone walls, and she could see in a single glance that everything Dorothy had said about it was correct.

It was the perfect Christmas cottage. The ideal romantic bolt-hole. The dream honeymoon destination. A paradise for the selfie obsessed. But Imogen didn't fit into any of those categories, and there was something about the idyllic cottage that intensified the ache of loneliness inside her.

Maybe this hadn't been such a great idea.

By coming here all she'd really done was change her surroundings. Everything else had come with her. All her feelings about this time of year, her guilt at having deceived her colleagues, the hurt caused by her mother. The whole mess that was her life. Had she really thought that "getting away from it all" would actually mean getting away from it all?

She sat for a moment, feeling sorry for herself, and then remembered that feeling sorry for herself achieved nothing.

She turned off the engine and took a deep breath. She'd made it through Christmases that were worse than this one. So her mother didn't love her. That wasn't exactly a shock, was it? Deep down she'd always known that. There was no reason why hearing it spelled out so brutally and publicly should have this effect on her. What did it matter if a bunch of strangers knew her sad tale? Hopefully, it would make them appreciate their own families, and in a way her mother had done her a favor because now she was going to stop deluding herself that this little "family" of hers existed. It existed only in her head, a figment of her imagination, conjured by yearning and hope. Her mother was so damaged by her own family's rejection that she was incapable of trusting anyone with her love.

She was on her own in the world, and the sooner she accepted the reality of that, the sooner she'd stop feeling so bruised.

And she had much to be grateful for. She still had a job she loved (she wasn't going to think about how she was going to unravel the lies she'd told her colleagues, at least not now). She had somewhere to live, and she could afford to feed herself.

And for the next few weeks she was going to be staying here, in this wonderful place.

Yes, she would still be alone, but it would be better than London. The wintry isolation was glorious, and so much better than streets crowded with stressed-out Christmas shoppers. And it was all hers.

Having given herself a sharp talking-to, she stepped out of the car and stepped onto a soft blanket of fresh snow studded with pine cones from the surrounding trees.

All she saw for miles around were snowy trees and fields. It was blissfully peaceful, the air cold but crisp and clean.

Her spirits lifted and with a surge of new determination, she dragged her case to the cottage. Dorothy had left it unlocked and she opened the door, tugged off her snowy boots and stepped onto the stone floor. Warmth seeped through her socks and she stood for a moment, savoring the welcome heat. At least she wasn't going to be cold.

She abandoned her suitcase and explored the cottage. The place was flooded with natural light, something that was lacking in her home in London.

There was a stylish living room with oak beams and windows that overlooked a walled garden, now covered in snow. Deep, comfortable sofas faced each other across a low coffee table stacked with books, but the focus of the room was an inglenook fireplace that was home to a wood burning stove. She imagined curling up in the evening in front of that fire, snuggled under one of the warm throws with a book. Leading off from the living room was a pretty kitchen. The cabinets were painted a soft creamy shade, there was a small kitchen island and everywhere she looked there were stylish hints of country living. In a corner nook by a window there was a dining table that overlooked the fields beyond.

There was a door on the far side of the kitchen and she opened it, expecting a storage cupboard.

"Oh—" She stared and then smiled, because the door led to a cozy den with a large flat-screen TV and an enormous modular sofa that encouraged the occupants to sprawl. Two of the walls were exposed stone, and the third was covered in well-stocked bookshelves.

She could happily have spent the entire holiday in this room alone, but she still had the upstairs to explore, so she headed back through the kitchen and up the stairs, feeling considerably more cheerful.

How lucky was she that Dorothy had offered this to her? How completely perfect.

She opened the door to the master bedroom. It had a vaulted ceiling and views across the countryside. Across snowy fields she could see a church spire. Presumably that was the village Dorothy had mentioned.

The bed was large and draped in pale shades of duck-egg blue. She was so tired after a run of sleepless nights that she had to stop herself from sliding between those sheets and closing her eyes. There was a bathroom tucked into the eaves and a small second bedroom, which had a desk facing across the garden.

The place was small, but luxurious and infinitely welcoming. She could see why it was popular with the influencer generation.

"Imogen?"

Dorothy's voice carried upstairs, and Imogen took a last wistful look at the bed and headed back down the stairs to the front door.

Dorothy was standing in the doorway, wrapped up in a thick coat and a warm scarf. She was clutching a cake tin and by her side was a spaniel, who bounded across to Imogen, tail wagging.

Delighted, she stooped to pet him, comforted by his enthusiasm and the warmth of his greeting. "Aren't you gorgeous?"

Dorothy looked interested. "This is Bailey. You like dogs? Do you have one of your own?"

Imogen straightened. "I do like dogs, and no, I don't have one." She wasn't going there again. From now on it was the truth all the way.

She'd called the woman from Facebook and explained that it was all a big mix-up. Fortunately, the woman hadn't questioned her too closely on how her dog had featured in the "missing dog" post. Janie had been messaging her, and Imogen had told her that it was all a misunderstanding and that she'd explain when she saw them next.

Exactly what explanation she was going to give was something she had yet to figure out.

She felt Bailey nudge her leg with his nose, and for a moment she wished he was hers.

Dorothy tugged off her boots and left them on the doorstep. "How was your journey? The roads are pretty icy around here. They clear the main roads first when there is a snowfall, and we're often last."

"It was fine, thank you. I only arrived about ten minutes ago."

"And you've looked around? Is everything all right for you?"

"It's gorgeous, Dorothy. I can't believe you're letting me stay here." It was something she'd wondered about frequently over the past few days. She and Dorothy had always got on well, but still—lending her a cottage?

Why?

Dorothy was obviously more generous than even Imogen had thought, although she did intend to pay her, obviously.

"It's my pleasure, Imogen. I brought you a cake I baked earlier." She held out the tin. "Shall we have a cup of tea and I can tell you a little about the place? There's a local map in the file in the living room, but it's almost easier if I point out of the window."

Imogen made tea, finding her way around the kitchen under Dorothy's direction, and then they sat at the table together.

"The village is worth a visit." Dorothy stirred sugar into her tea. "It dates back to Roman times and it's pretty, with some interesting shops. It's an easy walk from here. Even with snow on the ground the footpath should be easy to find. It leads straight across the fields. You'll see the church spire in the distance. It's visible from everywhere. Use that as a landmark to guide you."

"It's so cozy and comfortable here I might not step out of the front door for my entire stay." Imogen leaned down to stroke Bailey.

"I should have said that if there is someone you want to invite—" Dorothy picked up her mug "—a friend—someone special—please go ahead. Treat the place as your own."

Who would she invite?

She spent most of her life at work, and the people she was closest to were her work colleagues. She was fond of them, but she couldn't imagine inviting Anya or Janie to stay here with her. For a start, they didn't really know anything about her. And anyway, they both had family and plans for Christmas.

"There isn't anyone. But I'll be fine."

Dorothy cradled her mug. "I don't like to think of you all on your own."

All on your own. Why did people say that? Why not just *on your own?* Did the sentence really need the extra emphasis?

"There's no need to worry about me. I like my own company. It will be good to just relax."

Dorothy put her mug down. "Come for lunch tomorrow," she said quickly, "up at the house."

"Lunch?"

"Yes. I insist. It will be wonderful."

Imogen had the sense it was a totally impulsive invitation, driven by the fact she'd said she would be alone. What Dorothy didn't realize was that she was almost always alone. She was used to it. And she liked being alone most of the time. It was only at Christmas that she found it difficult.

"Honestly, I'll be—"

"It will be fun. I can introduce you to the animals. Have you ever met an alpaca?"

"You have an alpaca?"

"Five of them. Also two goats, a couple of sheep and a Shetland pony much beloved by my granddaughters. Sara says that soon I'll be able to open a petting zoo."

Imogen was intrigued. "It will be good to finally meet Sara. I've heard so much about her. It's a shame she couldn't make the event last year."

"Mmm. She had…complications."

"That's right. I remember you telling me." Still, it seemed odd that she'd never met Sara. But it was a small family business, so maybe not. She knew Dorothy didn't believe in wasting people's time unnecessarily. "So you care for all the animals yourself?"

"Mostly. I occasionally enlist the help of family, and my vet, Miles, is very good. Do you like animals?"

"I don't really have any experience with them." Apart from fake ones, and presumably that didn't count. "I'm a city girl."

"Why don't you come a bit early tomorrow and I can show you around before lunch? It's easy to find. Carry on up the driveway and the house is directly in front of you. It will take you about ten minutes to walk, or you could drive it if you prefer." Dorothy finished her tea. "I think you'll love the alpacas. Everyone does. They are such characters, particularly Benson."

"You name them?"

"Technically, my granddaughters named them, but yes, they all have names."

Lunch at Dorothy's and a meet with a herd of cute alpacas. It was too tempting to refuse.

"I'll be there."

13

Dorothy

"Imogen is joining us for lunch?" Sara dumped the bags on the kitchen table and sent her mother a look of despair. Snow clung to her coat and her hair and a large overnight bag bulged on her shoulder. "No! Why? What were you thinking?"

"I wasn't really thinking. It was all very spontaneous." And now Dorothy felt terribly guilty. "When I visited yesterday, she looked so alone. I asked her if there was someone she'd like to invite to join her in the cottage, but she said there was no one. No one! Can you imagine having no one to invite? I couldn't leave her like that, Sara. I couldn't do it. If you'd seen her, you would have invited her to lunch too."

"I would not." Exasperated, Sara dropped the overnight bag in the corner of the kitchen. "Maybe it makes me a terrible person, but I would have had no problem *not* issuing an invitation for lunch. You've already been more than generous offering her the cottage."

And Dorothy knew Sara was upset about that too. "I couldn't

bear to think of her spending a month alone in London," she said unhappily. "If you'd seen her—"

"I would have suggested that four weeks is a great opportunity for long-haul travel. The Caribbean is great at this time of year."

"Maybe I should have said that, but there was something about her. She seemed—" Dorothy rubbed her fingers across her forehead. "Why isn't she spending Christmas with family, Sara?"

Their eyes met and held.

Then Sara looked away, as if she couldn't bear the question in Dorothy's eyes. "I don't know. And that is not our business. She's a stranger. A stranger." She enunciated the word carefully. "She's not your responsibility, Mum."

"I know that. But—"

"Mum!"

"I'm sorry." Dorothy had a knot of anxiety in her stomach. "Having her in the cottage shouldn't interfere with you at all, but I shouldn't have issued the invitation for lunch. I see that now. I didn't think it through. I didn't mean to upset you."

Sara's expression softened. "I know that." She crossed the room and hugged her mother and Dorothy hugged her back.

"Forgive me."

"Forgive you for being kind and generous?" Sara eased away. "It's who you are, and that is never going to change. But I must admit sometimes I wish you weren't quite so generous."

"I'm going to change. I am going to learn to say no. And I think I'm getting better at it. I did say no to Miles the other day when he tried to tempt me with a kitten."

Sara shook her head, but this time there was laughter in her eyes. "That's the best you can do? You are a lost cause."

"Maybe." Dorothy glanced at the corner of the room. "What's in the bag you brought?"

"The girls' clothes for their party later. Ava can't stay clean for five minutes so if she wore her dress now she'd look like a wreck by the time we get there. She can change before we leave."

The village Christmas party. She'd forgotten, probably because all the room in her head had been taken up by Imogen. "What fun for them. I roasted a chicken for lunch." Dorothy opened the oven to check on the chicken. "Doesn't it smell delicious? Organic, from the farm. It was a gift from Valerie for the casseroles I made her. And I've made an apple pie."

"It does smell good. I brought extra carrots and parsnips, as requested." Sara opened the bag on the table and then stopped. "What are we going to talk about? This is awkward. I actually feel nervous."

"She's very easy to get along with. It will be good for you to have an opportunity to get to know her properly."

"I don't want to get to know her properly." There was a note of panic in Sara's voice. "What am I supposed to do? What am I supposed to say?"

"Just be your usual kind, welcoming self and leave the rest to me." But she could see now that this did have the potential to be awkward.

Sara sat down at the kitchen table, her shoulders slumped. "What time is she arriving?"

"Any moment." Wishing the whole thing was over, Dorothy sprinkled a few extra sprigs of fresh thyme onto the chicken and carefully returned it to the oven. "What time do you have to take the girls to the party in the village?"

"Four o'clock." Sara looked at her. "I can't do this."

Dorothy closed the oven door and straightened. "You don't have to do anything. Just enjoy lunch."

"But that's the point. I can't enjoy it. I'm so tense and stressed I feel as if I might explode." Sara's voice wobbled. "I think I'll go home, Mum. Tell her I didn't feel well. Tell her one of the girls was sick. Tell her anything you like, but I'm not staying.

I'm sorry, but I can't do this." She stood up just as Ava skipped into the room with Bailey at her heels.

"What can't you do, Mummy?" Ava did a twirl and almost fell over the dog. "You can do anything if you try. That's what you always say to me. I'm practising my ballet, Nanna. Watch me."

"I'm watching, sweetie. Move away from Bailey or you're going to pirouette right into him." Dorothy was also watching her daughter. She saw Sara pull herself together. Swiftly the emotion was masked with a smile, albeit a strained one.

"We're not staying for lunch, Ava. I have a headache." Sara looked so pale and tired it wasn't a claim anyone was likely to argue with. "Where's Iris?"

Ava stopped twirling and frowned. "But Nanna made chicken with my favorite potatoes. And you said I have to eat a proper lunch or all the sugar at the party will make me sick."

"I'll make you something at home. Iris!"

"But I want chicken."

Iris appeared in the doorway. "What's the matter?"

"Mummy has a headache and now we can't eat the chicken." Ava looked desolate and Dorothy felt terrible that she'd caused so much friction. She and Sara were close. She should have given more consideration to the fact that she might find this difficult.

"Oh, Mummy." Iris was by Sara's side in an instant, her arms around her. "Can I get you tablets or a glass of water?"

Dorothy saw Sara's eyes mist.

"No, honey. I'll be fine. But I'd just like to go home if you don't mind."

"Of course we don't mind." Iris stroked Sara's hair. "We'll go right now. Do you want me to call Daddy?"

"No, I'll be fine. But thank you for asking."

"I mind," Ava howled. "I mind a lot. I want to stay here with Nanna and Bailey and eat chicken."

"That's bad manners, Ava. We're a family," Iris said firmly, "which means we always stick together and support each other. If Mummy needs to go home, then we go home."

Dorothy met Sara's gaze. *We're a family, which means we always stick together.*

Ava looked chastened. "Are we still going to the party later?"

Iris shushed her. "Don't worry about the party."

"But—"

Sara gave a wan smile. "I'll be fine to take you to that, I'm sure."

Dorothy was about to try one more time to persuade her to stay when the doorbell rang.

"I'll go." Ava sprinted out of the room before anyone could stop her, and she reappeared moments later with a nervous Imogen.

"Hi. I hope I'm not early?" Imogen was clutching a box of chocolates. Like Sara, her hair and coat were dusted with snow. "I thought it would take me longer to walk here." Under the warm coat, she was wearing a cream cable-knit sweater with black jeans and fur-lined boots. The cold had given her cheeks a pink tinge.

Ava took the chocolates. "Thank you. How do you know my Nanna?"

"Imogen and I work together, and she will be staying in Holly Cottage for a few weeks." Dorothy pulled herself together. "Thank you for the chocolates. That's kind of you, Imogen. You've already met Ava. This is my daughter, Sara, and my other granddaughter, Iris."

"Pleased to meet you." Iris shook Imogen's hand carefully while casting anxious looks toward her mother.

Sara was gazing at Imogen and there was something in her eyes that made Dorothy's heart break.

She never should have done this. Sara was right. But it couldn't be undone now. All they could do was get through it.

"I've heard a lot about you." Friendly, Imogen extended her hand to Sara who somehow roused herself enough to shake it.

"I hope you're settling in to Holly Cottage."

"It's a beautiful place."

"Do you have a tree yet?" Ava was oblivious to any tension in the room.

"A tree?"

"A Christmas tree."

"Oh—no." Imogen looked uncomfortable. "I don't usually bother."

"You never have a tree? Why not?" Ava's appalled expression would have made Dorothy laugh in different circumstances, but she'd never felt less like laughing.

She was conscious of Sara hovering, white and tense, of Iris worrying about her mother, and Imogen awkward and unsure.

"I live alone. Just me." She gave Ava an apologetic look. "It never seems worth it."

Ava frowned. "But if you live alone you can do exactly what you want to do and not think about anyone else—" she gave her sister a look "—so I'd have ten trees and no one would be able to stop me."

"Ten?" Imogen laughed. "You don't think that's too many?"

"No." Ava looked suddenly excited. "We can choose you a tree when we get ours. We're going tomorrow, aren't we, Mummy? You could come too."

Sara's expression would have been comical if it hadn't been so heartbreaking. "Let's see how we all feel in the morning."

Ava looked puzzled. "But—"

"Enough." Iris hugged her. "Mummy has a headache. You need to stop talking for five minutes." She gave Imogen an apologetic look. "She's excited because it's our Christmas party this afternoon."

"A party? That does sound fun." Imogen smiled and glanced at Dorothy. "It's kind of you to invite me to your family lunch. I hope I'm not intruding?"

"We're delighted to have you. But Sara was just—"

"Going to peel the carrots." Sara pulled herself together and reached for the bag she'd bought with her. "Anything else you'd like me to do, Mum?"

Dorothy felt a rush of gratitude and admiration. Sara was going to stick with it.

The sense of relief was enormous.

"No. Everything else is in hand." Maybe this wouldn't be awkward after all. A simple lunch. They'd make Imogen welcome and that would be it.

Iris looked at Sara, puzzled. "But you have a headache."

"It's a little better, thank you." Sara kissed Iris on top of her head. "We'll stay for a while."

"You should drink a large glass of water. I'll fetch you one." Iris fetched her mother a glass of water and watched her drink it.

"I want to see Benson," Ava said. "I drew him a picture. And I want to tell him about the party later. Santa might be there, but he might not be the real Santa because he's busy. I'm going to wear my new dress, but I'm not wearing it now in case I make it dirty."

"We can't see Benson. I have to help Nanna with lunch." Having dutifully drunk the water, Sara was rapidly peeling and chopping carrots.

"I could take her," Iris said. "She can show Benson her ballet."

Ava beamed at Imogen. "You could come too. You'll like Benson. He's friendly."

"I'm looking forward to seeing him," Imogen said.

"We can go right now!" Ava's eyes were round. "Can we go, Nanna, *please*?" She grabbed some of the chopped carrots and pushed them into her pocket. "He loves carrots, but they have to be chopped small or he chokes. You can have some too. Then he'll like you right away." She grabbed a few more carrots and thrust them at Imogen.

Imogen looked startled, but then took the carrots with a smile. "Thank you. And for the useful information."

"Benson will be eating more carrots than we are," Sara said mildly, but she chopped an extra one and pushed the pieces across to her daughter. The rest she transferred into the oven tray with the parsnips Dorothy had already prepared.

"Why don't we all go for a quick walk before lunch? The food will be fine for a short time." Dorothy decided that a distraction would be good for all of them. "Has it stopped snowing?"

Iris looked out of the window. "It's not snowing, but it looks cold. Will that make your headache worse, Mummy?"

"It will be fine, I'm sure." Sara wiped her hands. "I think it's a good idea."

"We'll all wrap up," Dorothy said briskly. "It will be good to show Imogen around a little. I can point out that path across the fields to the village so that you know where you're going when you explore."

And maybe visiting the animals might be good for Imogen. Dorothy always found them to be an excellent cure for a low mood. And even if Imogen didn't feel the same way, it would make conversation easier for Sara.

And there was Ava, of course. It was hard for anyone to be reserved or awkward around Ava.

She checked that everything was in order with the lunch, and then they pulled on coats and boots and ventured outside.

Snow blanketed the fields and clung to trees and hedges. Soon the ground would be stamped with footprints, but for now it glittered, pristine and untouched.

After the fresh fall of snow the air was cold and crisp. It made eyes water and cheeks turn pink, but Ava didn't care as she skipped happily toward the field where the alpacas lived, tugging Imogen by the hand as if she'd known her for her whole life and not just five minutes.

"They have a shed to live in for when it's really cold, but they like being outdoors too, and they have fur so it's like wearing a coat the whole time." Ava clambered onto the first bar of the gate and called across the field. "Benson!" Her high-pitched voice carried through the air and all the alpacas immediately headed for the gate.

"The big brown one is Benson. Isn't he lovely?" Ava poked her little arm through the bars of the gate, and Iris approached.

"Be gentle, Ava."

"I'm gentle. He's very friendly," Ava told Imogen, "and in the summer we take him for walks. When I grow up I'm going to have a hundred alpacas."

"A hundred alpacas and ten Christmas trees." After the initial shock of having carrots thrust at her, Imogen seemed smitten with the little girl. "You're going to need a big garden for that."

"I'm going to live in the country like Nanna." She climbed a few more bars of the gate and reached out to Benson, who nudged her with his nose.

"He obviously likes you a lot." Imogen placed a steadying hand on Ava's back as she wobbled on the gate.

The protective gesture brought a lump to Dorothy's throat. She felt a rush of emotion and she caught Sara's eye.

She didn't know what her daughter was thinking, but she had a good idea.

Ava was holding Imogen's hand and Dorothy felt a warm glow as she listened to Imogen engaging her in conversation.

"Do you have a favorite alpaca?"

Ava shook her head hard. "I love them all the same. If I had a favorite, that might make the others sad."

"Are they related to each other?"

"Basil and Sage are brothers. That's Basil." Ava pointed to the cream alpaca at the back of the herd. "The other brown one is Sage, then there's Dill and Pepper. Pepper is short for Peppermint. They're all named after herbs except for Benson."

Imogen studied the alpacas. "Can they jump out?"

Dorothy joined them. "They've never tried. Miles, our vet, tells me they're rather reluctant jumpers. Either way, I've never seen them bother the fence at all."

"What about foxes?"

"Oh, they see off foxes." Dorothy rubbed Benson's neck gently. "They work as a team. They make quite a din. But we try and keep away animals that could spread bovine tuberculosis, like badgers."

Imogen gave Benson a tentative stroke. "They have such thick coats."

"Yes. And that can conceal problems, so we watch out for that. They were in a terrible state when they arrived with me, although not Benson. He was well cared for."

"What happened with Benson?"

"He was one of three, but the other two sadly died. Alpacas don't like to be alone. They're herd animals," Dorothy told her. "Miles tells me they should never be kept in herds of less than three, which is why he asked if I'd take him."

"I'm a herd animal," Ava said. "I have a sister. We're fine being a two. We don't need to be three. Do you have a sister, Imogen?"

"No. It's just me," Imogen said. "I'm an only child."

"What's an only child?"

"It means my mother only had one child and no more. I don't have brothers or sisters."

Ava wrinkled her nose. "I suppose you have to find yourself a herd, like the alpacas." She fed Benson a carrot. "My mummy had a sister, but she went away, so she's an only child too now."

"Ava!" Sara's face was as pale as her surroundings. "That's enough."

"I was just saying—"

"Ava, stop," Iris said quickly, "you know Mummy doesn't like to talk about that."

"I know. Because it makes her sad. But she has us, and Daddy, so she's not sad now. We're her herd." Ava jumped off the gate and tugged at Imogen. "Come and see our pony, Thelma." Oblivious to the tense atmosphere, she skipped through the snow toward the stables.

Dorothy put her hand on Sara's arm, but her daughter shook her off and walked quickly after Ava.

Dorothy watched in despair. Ava was too young to know what to say and what to keep back. This wasn't Ava's fault, it was hers. Sara was right. She never should have invited Imogen. She'd stirred up a hornet's nest and that was not a good thing.

Iris, sensitive to everyone's moods, looked unhappy. "Shall we have lunch, Nanna?"

"Lunch?" Dorothy dragged her gaze from Sara's stiff shoulders to her granddaughter's worried eyes. "Good idea. Let's do that."

Iris followed her mother and sister, picking her way carefully so that she didn't slip.

Ava was stroking Thelma, having seemingly forgotten the conversation about siblings.

"It's time for lunch," Dorothy said. "You need to come in and wash your hands, Ava."

"Iris needs to wash hers too." Ava gave Thelma a final pat and they all headed back to the house.

"I had no idea you had so many animals," Imogen said. She looked flushed and happy as she glanced back at the pony. "This is a beautiful place."

"I'll show you around the vineyard at some point," Dorothy said. She'd be able to make that a purely professional trip. "It would be interesting for you, particularly as you've been working on our products for so long."

"I'd like that."

Back in the kitchen they savored the warmth and the delicious smells of cooking.

The girls washed their hands, supervised by a subdued Sara, while Dorothy busied herself putting the finishing touches to the lunch.

"Five-minute warning. Wash your hands, girls. Imogen, there's a cloakroom right across the hallway if you need it. The towel is clean."

Imogen vanished and Dorothy put the chicken in the center of the table, followed by dishes of roasted vegetables and potatoes.

Sara looked exhausted, and Dorothy felt guilty because she knew she was the cause of it.

Once lunch was over, she'd take Imogen back to Holly Cottage and that would be it. She'd give her a phone number in case of emergencies. Other than that, she'd be leaving Imogen alone.

"That looks yummy." Ava knelt on her chair, and Sara gestured to her to sit properly.

Dorothy pulled the warm plates out of the oven, while Iris and Sara finished laying the table.

There was no sign of Imogen.

Dorothy glanced toward the door, hoping she was all right.

She was about to carve when the cloakroom door finally opened and Imogen appeared.

She looked ashen.

Concerned, Dorothy immediately put the knife down. "Whatever is the matter, dear? Are you feeling unwell?"

"The pictures on the wall of the cloakroom—"

Pictures? "You mean the family photos?"

"Did you see the one of me with Benson?" Ava plopped a roast potato onto her plate. "I like that one, and the one of Bailey in the snow. He looks so funny covered in white. Like a snow monster."

And suddenly Dorothy knew. She knew why Imogen was looking so shocked.

Her stomach lurched.

"Imogen—"

"I can see that they're family photos," Imogen said, "but what I don't understand is why there is a photo of my mother on the wall?"

Dorothy felt her heart skip, and for a moment she thought it might stop altogether.

Why hadn't she thought of that? Photos. They were everywhere, and such an important part of her life that she never questioned their presence.

Sara stood up quickly, and for a moment Dorothy thought she was going to walk out and leave Dorothy to deal with this crisis. And she wouldn't have blamed her if she did. Sara had warned her. Sara had thought it was a bad idea right from the start. And she was right.

But Sara didn't leave. Instead, she beckoned to the children. "Girls, I'd like you to go and watch TV for a few minutes."

Ava held tightly to her plate. "But we're having chicken."

"Lunch will be a little bit later."

"But—"

"Iris, could you take your sister for me, please?"

Iris looked confused, but nodded and took Ava's hand. "Come on. We'll watch cartoons."

"I'm hungry. And we're not allowed to watch cartoons in the middle of the day."

"Today we are. Special treat. And we'll eat in a minute." Iris coaxed her sister out of the room and once the door closed behind them, Dorothy pulled out a chair.

"Come and sit down, Imogen."

"I'm fine right here." Imogen stood without moving. "There were four people in that photo. My mother, a younger girl and an older couple, a woman and a man. You're the woman."

Dorothy wished she could rewind the clock and do things differently. Unfortunately, it wasn't the first time in her life that she'd felt that way. "Yes, I am. And this is my fault. I should have said something before now, but it's complicated."

"You're the younger girl." Imogen turned to look at Sara.

"Yes." Sara held her gaze without flinching. "Tina was my older sister."

"Sister." Imogen rubbed her fingers across her forehead. Her hand was shaking. "She asked for her sister. I told everyone she didn't have a sister." She seemed almost to be talking to herself.

Dorothy forced herself to speak. "Tina is my daughter. My eldest daughter."

Imogen was breathing rapidly. "So that makes you my grandmother."

Had there ever been a more awkward moment?

"Yes." Dorothy felt pressure in her chest. Terror, anticipation, but also relief because the moment that had been hovering in her future was finally here. "I'm your grandmother. I hadn't intended for you to find out this way, obviously, but—well, maybe it's a good thing. There was no easy way. And now it's out in the open I really hope we can get to know each other." The words felt so inadequate and far too small for the hugeness of the moment.

"My grandmother." Imogen's tone was flat. "We've worked together for almost two years. We've sat in meetings together, run an event, had lunch—and you never once said anything? Why? You obviously knew who I was the whole time."

"Not immediately, but it didn't take long for me to figure it out." And she had so many regrets. The whole situation was such a mess she couldn't see how they were ever going to unravel it, but if there was to be any chance of a future relationship it had to be based on a foundation of truth.

"That's why you gave us the business."

"No." It hadn't occurred to her that Imogen might think that. "I gave you the business because you are the best at what you do. When you moved to RPQ, I wanted us to continue working together. I'm proud of you, Imogen."

Confusion and pain flickered across Imogen's face. "Proud? Why would you be proud? I'm nothing to do with you. You didn't want me in your life. Anything I am, *anything I've done or achieved*, is despite you, not because of you." Her eyes shone with hurt, but there was also determination there, and Dorothy saw that whatever vulnerability she had, she also had a core of steel. If she hadn't been so worried, she might have been impressed and a little in awe.

"You're upset, and I can understand that—"

"Upset? Yes, I'm upset, but mostly I'm angry. You lied to me."

"I didn't exactly lie, but it's true there are many things I haven't told you and there are reasons for that. Good reasons." Dorothy felt sick and shaky. She pulled out a chair and sank onto it for support, ignoring Sara's quick look of concern. "It's complicated, Imogen. If you sit down, I'll tell you everything and I will answer any questions you have."

"What questions would I have? I already know everything I need to know. You abandoned my mother." Imogen's voice broke. "You were her family, her only family, and you threw her out when she needed you most. Families are supposed to stick together no matter how hard it gets, but you left us to struggle. And I'm sure it wasn't an easy situation, but even if you didn't like what she was doing you should still have loved her and made it clear that you loved her. She had *no one*. We had no one. You're the reason she is the way she is! You're the reason she has always been incapable of forming a proper relationship with anyone, including me."

Dorothy felt as if she'd been punched. The shock of it made it hard to breathe. Whatever reaction she'd expected, it wasn't this. Or maybe she'd been ridiculously hopeful. Naive. "Imogen, sweetheart—"

"I'm not your sweetheart. You made up your mind about that a long time ago." She turned to Sara. "And I always thought it was a little odd that we'd never met, but now I understand. You were purposely avoiding me. You didn't want anything to do with me, did you?"

Sara was white. "Imogen—"

"I have no idea what's going on. I have no idea why I'm here now, what exactly has changed, but I'm not interested in being part of your bizarre social experiment. It's too late. You weren't there when my mother needed you, when *I* needed you, and I certainly don't need you now. I'll pack my things and leave, and you can call Rosalind to discuss any business issues, if you're even interested in that side of things." Imogen snatched up her coat and ran to the front door, narrowly avoiding Bailey, who was on the hunt for food.

Dorothy opened her mouth to say something that might stop her leaving, but all that emerged was a feeble croak.

Silenced by all the terrible accusations that Imogen had thrown at her, she couldn't find any words.

Where should she start? What could she say or do to make this better?

By the time she was finally able to make her voice carry sufficiently to be heard, it was too late.

The front door slammed, the sound echoing through the house.

Imogen had gone.

14

Sara

This couldn't be happening. Not now, after all these years. She'd kept the trauma firmly in the past. She'd spent decades learning to block it out. She'd built friendships, and a family. She'd built a life.

If thoughts about that time ever entered her head, she ruthlessly ignored them. She didn't talk about it. She was proud of the way she'd locked it all in a box and refused to give it even a morsel of her attention. It was a form of self-protection, and it had mostly worked. On the rare occasions her mother tried to talk about it, her response was visceral and physical. She was right back there, living that awful moment, feeling control slip away from her. She started to shake. Her heart pounded. Her palms became sweaty. She felt a tightening in her breath and a desire to run to a safe place and hide until the memories were back in the box. It was a scary experience and one she tried hard to avoid. She was sympathetic with her mother, but firm. She gave her the same message. *You were not to blame.* But then she moved her on. Not dwelling on it had been an important element in her ability to function normally.

She'd been doing well, but then her mother had struck up a relationship with Imogen.

This was the outcome she'd been afraid of for so long. From that first day when her mother had come home from a meeting with the conference company they were using and told her that Imogen was handling the account, she'd had a sense of impending doom. She'd known, deep down, that it was just a matter of time before the whole thing exploded.

And now it had.

She didn't want to think about it. She didn't *want* to remember.

Her mother's actions had flipped open the lid of that box, and now the past was spilling back into her life. Wounds that she'd thought were healed opened up again, and she realized she hadn't healed at all, she'd just bandaged it well and continued to function.

Panic closed over her, threatening to drown her. She wanted to call Patrick. She wanted to feel him wrap his arms tightly around her and promise to keep everything bad away. And she knew he'd come in an instant if she called.

She reached for her phone, but then she saw her mother sink onto the nearest chair and all thoughts of calling Patrick vanished from her mind.

However bad she was feeling, it was clear from her mother's face that she was feeling worse.

She put her phone down.

She needed to hold it together for her mother's sake if not her own. She would *not* fall apart. She would not let Tina do this to her, or her mother, again.

When her mother had told her she'd offered Imogen the cottage, she'd been horrified and more than a little angry, but even in her most pessimistic moments she wouldn't have predicted an outcome quite as brutal as the one she'd just witnessed.

Sara took a slow deep breath, and then another. To calm herself, she thought about Patrick and the girls. She thought about Christmas and how much fun they were going to have.

"Mum—"

"Are you angry with me? You must be so angry with me."

"Of course not." Her anger evaporated in a moment. How could she be angry with her mother for being warm and generous? For always wanting to reach out and help anyone in trouble? It was one of the many things she loved about her, and the fact that this time it had backfired so badly wasn't her fault. "You were trying to help. It's not your fault. Just as it wasn't your fault last time."

"It was. Some of it was. I said terrible things on that dreadful day."

All justified in Sara's opinion, but she knew better than to say that.

"We all have moments when we say things we regret. That's part of being human. It's impossible to go through life always saying the right thing. It doesn't change the fact that people make their own choices, and Tina made hers. To think that your actions could have influenced those choices is fanciful. You can't control everything, Mum. People aren't puppets. You need to forgive yourself and move on. Instead of blaming yourself, you should try acceptance. It happened. It was messy. But in the end Tina made her own choices."

"Yes. You're right. But those choices have impacted on poor Imogen. Right now she is our priority. I have to go after her." Her mother stumbled to her feet, the suddenness of the movement knocking the chair over.

Sara shot out her hand and caught it before it could hit the floor. "Mum, just take a moment. Let's talk about this. Think about the best approach."

The sight of her mother's face scared her. She was taken back to that awful night. The memory of it all blurred together. Tina shouting. Little Imogen screaming her lungs out and clutching her stuffed bunny, her father collapsing. The shriek of an ambulance siren, the flash of blue lights and then bleak hospital corridors and her mother's white face as she tried to hold all of it together.

Seeing her mother so upset scared her. It couldn't happen again. She wasn't going to let it happen again.

"Breathe, Mum. Please stay calm. It's going to be okay." She was saying that for her own benefit as much as her mother's. "We're going to fix this."

"How? Those things she said—" Her mother clutched her arm. "I'm going to find her and explain. She doesn't understand any of it. I need to make her understand."

Sara didn't voice her own fears—that Imogen would never understand because the only family member she could remember having in her life was Tina. Unlike her mother, Sara harbored no illusions about her sister.

But she knew better than to raise that now.

"We will talk to her, but for now you need to calm down if you possibly can." It wasn't going to be easy to talk to Imogen, because she'd walked right out of the door without giving them a chance to explain.

But that was shock, Sara reminded herself. They were all in shock.

There were things she needed to process herself, but right now her priority was her mother.

"I can't calm down until I've seen her. Spoken to her. She left her coat. We need to take her coat or she'll freeze. And she left her bag, with her phone." Her mother looked around her, panicked and distracted. "Where did I put my car keys?"

Sara's heart sank because she knew she was the one who

was going to have to do this, even though all she wanted to do was hide.

"You're not driving anywhere."

"I have to. I have to go after her."

"I'll go." She had to force the words out. The last thing she wanted to do was have another encounter with Imogen that involved raking up the past. She didn't even want to think about Tina, let alone talk about her, but if the alternative was letting her mother do it, then she was just going to have to face her fears.

Her mother didn't argue. "Yes. You'll be faster than me. Go after her, Sara. Tell her how worried we are about her. Apologize from me. And I should be apologizing to you, too. You said this was a mistake and you were right. I should never have offered her the cottage. But when she said she wouldn't be spending it with family—" Her mother's hands were shaking, and she was breathing much too rapidly for Sara's peace of mind.

"It was a difficult situation. And I know you still feel a sense of responsibility."

"I do, particularly as she seems so alone. Why isn't she spending Christmas with family? Where is Tina? Are they not close?"

"I don't know, Mum. I don't have any answers." And she didn't really want answers. She didn't want to think about it at all, but she had no choice now.

"I assumed she was doing fine. That she'd built a life." Tears fell, and her mother pressed her hand to her mouth, trying to stop the sobs.

"Oh, Mum, please—" Sara put her arms around her mother, offering what support she could. "Please don't cry. I can't bear it. This is not your fault."

"Oh, it is." Dorothy sniffed and rummaged for a tissue. "We both know it's my fault. Even the way Tina left was my fault. The things I said—"

"You told the truth, that's all. And she needed to hear it."

She really didn't want to talk about this. She didn't want to *think* about it.

"And telling it did no good at all. If I could change one thing about that time it would be the words I said to her that night."

Sara felt her mother cling on to her, and she tightened her hold, not knowing what to do or say. She felt helpless and more like a child than a grown woman with a family of her own.

She worked hard at never thinking of her sister, but when she did it was almost always with anger for the destruction she'd wrought within their family.

After a moment, Dorothy took a deep breath and pulled away. "I'm sorry. This isn't about me. It's about poor Imogen. Go after her, Sara. Please. Right now."

"In a minute. I'm not leaving you like this, Mum." She didn't voice her worries that her mother might collapse, just as her father had. "I can't believe she spoke to you like that." She was a little shocked by it.

"We mustn't blame her. It's not her fault, poor thing. She was hurt. Shocked. And there was some truth in what she said."

"There was no truth in it." Sara chose her words carefully. "You didn't abandon Tina. The idea of it is ridiculous." She tried hard to control her own emotions on the subject. She could vent at Patrick later. Poor Patrick.

"But Imogen felt it so strongly." Her mother dug her hand into her pocket and found a tissue. "You saw her. She was furious with us."

"I think we should leave her to calm down a little, get used to the idea, and then we should all sit down and have a conversation."

"We can't do that." Dorothy blew her nose. "You heard what she said. She's leaving. She is probably packing as we speak. You have to stop her."

There was a noise from the doorway, and Dorothy quickly turned her back and tried to pull herself together.

"Mummy, when are we going to eat? Ava is really hungry." Iris stood there, Ava by her side.

For a moment Sara was thrown.

She'd forgotten about her children. When in her life had she ever forgotten about her children?

She swiftly pulled herself together. "Nanna is going to serve lunch, while I just pop down to Holly Cottage for a minute."

Iris was looking horrified. "Is Nanna crying? What's the matter?"

"She's probably hungry," Ava said helpfully. "I feel like crying too. Chicken would help."

"Oh, you poor things. Come and sit down and eat some lunch." All bright smiles and willpower, Dorothy carved chicken onto plates and added vegetables.

Sara quickly reheated gravy and poured it into a jug. "Help yourselves. I'll be back in a moment."

"Where are you going?" Iris poured gravy on Ava's chicken and then on her own. "Aren't you having lunch too?"

"I'll join you in a minute. There's something I need to do."

"Where's Imogen? She's probably hungry too." Ava stabbed a piece of chicken. "I like Imogen. And Benson liked her. She's very pretty. She has golden hair like yours, Mummy."

Iris caught the look on her mother's face and pushed the plate closer to her sister. "Eat your lunch. You've been complaining about being starving for the past hour, so eat."

Sara took advantage of the moment and left the room. She grabbed her car keys. Holly Cottage was only a five-minute walk down the drive, but she'd be there in less than a minute if she drove. For her mother's sake, she didn't want Imogen to leave before she'd had a chance to talk to her.

What exactly was she going to say?

Sara closed her eyes for a moment, dreading the forthcoming encounter. Imogen was her niece. Her sister's child. She still remembered every detail of the night Imogen was born. She remembered holding her in the hospital. Remembered the precise moment the midwife had carefully given her Imogen to hold.

She'd been swaddled in blankets, a tiny innocent little bundle oblivious to all the complexities that her arrival had created.

And then she'd opened her eyes, and nothing had prepared Sara for the rush of feeling that had engulfed her.

Sara had gazed into Imogen's blue eyes and realized that love at first sight really could happen. It was a thing. Right there in that moment she'd given her whole heart to her sister's child.

And four years later her heart had been broken.

And it was probably about to be broken again, because whenever Tina was involved, that was what happened.

Bracing herself for what came next, she stepped outside and shivered. While they'd been inside, the temperature had dropped and it had started snowing again. She was glad now that she'd decided to drive and not walk.

But Imogen had been walking, and she'd left her coat in the kitchen.

Sara felt a flicker of concern as she turned the car and headed back down the drive to Holly Cottage. It wouldn't have taken Imogen long to walk home, but it would have been long enough for her to get cold. If she was sensible, she'd take a hot shower before packing up the car, which at least gave Sara a little more time.

If necessary, she'd beg her to have at least one calm conversation with her mother. She'd explain that Imogen had some of the facts wrong (some! Ha. All of them, more likely) and that it was important that she listen to Dorothy.

But what if she refused to listen?

The trees that lined the side of the drive were coated with fresh snow, and normally Sara would have taken a moment to admire it. Snow had a certain magical quality, and it made her happy. Or, to be more precise, it made her girls happy, and anything that made her children happy made Sara happy. But today she wasn't thinking about snowmen, or snow angels or snowballs. She wasn't thinking about Christmas.

She was thinking about her mother. About how white she'd looked. How stressed.

And she was thinking about Imogen, and the shock of that interaction they'd just had. She'd done everything she could to avoid meeting Imogen face-to-face because she just found it all too difficult. At the event last year she'd made the excuse that Ava was ill because she hadn't trusted herself to come face-to-face with Imogen and not react. And her mother had known it was an excuse.

She felt an ache deep in her chest.

Part of her wanted to pull over and have a good cry as her mother had, but she couldn't do that. She didn't have time to waste. She needed to talk to Imogen.

Sara gripped the wheel more firmly and told herself that this was not the same situation they'd faced with her father. Her mother didn't have high blood pressure or any of the other medical issues that had affected her father.

Her mother was going to be fine. But the sooner they could have a conversation with Imogen and set her straight on a few things, the better Sara would feel.

You were her family, her only family, and you threw her out when she needed you most.

She didn't have to ask herself why Imogen would have believed all those awful things. She already knew.

She clenched her jaw. It had been decades since she'd seen Tina, but she was not going to think about her sister now or she'd be the one with blood pressure problems. She needed to focus on Imogen. Imogen was an innocent victim of very unfortunate circumstances. She deserved to hear the truth. Whether she chose to believe it or not was outside Sara's control.

She approached Holly Cottage and felt a rush of relief as she saw Imogen's car parked outside the cottage.

At least she hadn't left. That was good.

She parked, picked her way along the snowy path and pushed open the door of the cottage. "Imogen?"

There was no reply, and Sara tugged off her shoes and stepped into the hallway and then into the kitchen. It was empty, and there was no sign that anyone had been here in the past few hours.

Maybe she was upstairs using the bathroom.

Sara walked to the bottom of the stairs. "Imogen?"

She went from room to room, which didn't take long because the cottage was small.

A quick glance told her that Imogen's suitcase was still in the bedroom, her clothes neatly folded into the drawers.

Sara walked back downstairs, confused.

Imogen's belongings were still here, but there was no sign of Imogen herself. So where had she gone?

15

Imogen

Imogen stumbled through the snow. Her eyes stung, and she wasn't sure if it was the cold or tears. She was going with the cold. She *never cried*. Even when her mother had publicly announced that Imogen was the worst thing that had happened to her, Imogen hadn't cried. But surely crying right now would be understandable.

Dorothy was her grandmother. Dorothy!

It didn't make sense. None of it made sense.

Dorothy, whom she'd worked with for almost two years and trusted, had lied to her. Not for one minute had Imogen suspected she was hiding such a big secret.

But why would she have suspected?

Who would ever think that a person would be hiding something like that?

It felt worse because she didn't usually allow herself to get close to anyone. She was cautious. She kept her real self hidden behind the persona she'd created. She considered herself pretty much invulnerable. She wrapped and padded her feelings and then encased them in solid steel so that no one could get to them. She didn't give people the ability to hurt her, but Dorothy had hurt her.

She'd trusted Dorothy, and it turned out that all this time she'd been keeping a huge secret.

Lying. Was it lying? Maybe not exactly, but it amounted to the same thing.

All those meetings they'd had together, all the laughter they'd shared, and it turned out that all along this woman who Imogen had liked and admired more than anyone she knew, wasn't who she seemed.

She'd sneaked her way into Imogen's affections by not being honest about who she was. She'd obviously known that if she told the truth, Imogen would want nothing to do with her. What other possible explanation was there?

She'd thought Dorothy respected her work, but maybe it wasn't that. Would she have moved her business to RPQ if it hadn't been for their relationship?

She felt betrayed and shaken. What was real? What was true?

Was Dorothy in contact with Tina?

The ground gave way beneath her, literally this time, and she yelped with shock as she slithered down a short bank and into a ditch. Her feet broke though the thin layer of snow and ice and she lost her balance and sat down hard in the freezing water of the stream she hadn't even known was there.

Shocked, she didn't move, but then she felt icy water seeping through her boots and her clothes.

Great. Just great.

She scrambled to her feet and squelched her way up the bank to the other side. She'd been so upset and deep in her own thoughts she hadn't noticed that she'd gradually veered toward the edge of the field.

And now she was soaked as well as miserable, which just proved that life had a grim sense of humor.

Shivering, she looked around her and tried to work out where she was, but it was snowing hard now and there were no landmarks visible, just trees, fields and snow. She'd walked *much* farther than she'd thought, and there was no sign of the cottage.

Follow the church spire, Dorothy had said, but where was the church spire?

You can see it from everywhere.

Not when it was snowing, apparently.

She didn't even have her phone because she'd fled the house without remembering to grab her coat and bag.

For a brief moment, anxiety swamped misery. She was freezing cold and she had no idea where she was. Storming off across the fields had been another of her less than brilliant ideas, not quite as bad as Midas the fake dog, but pretty close.

She hadn't been thinking of anything except the fact that Dorothy was her grandmother, and that she'd hidden that fact.

There was so much she needed to digest. Rosalind had let her keep her job, but there was no way Imogen was going to be able to work with Dorothy now. What would happen?

It was too much. Too *big.*

Shivering, her survival instincts kicked in and she forced herself to concentrate on the moment. If she didn't get herself somewhere warm and dry, the next thing that would happen would be hypothermia.

She should have gone straight back to the cottage when she left the house, but she'd thought they might follow her, so she'd decided to go for a quick walk across the fields instead and think things through. Which had sounded fine in theory, but now she was very cold and very wet.

Before she'd fallen in the ditch, she'd thought that maybe she'd head to the village that Dorothy had described and tuck herself away in a cozy café for a few hours while she digested all that had happened. But she couldn't do that now. She was soaked and filthy.

She was going to have to go back to the cottage. But to do that she had to figure out where she was.

Squinting through the steadily falling snow, she could just about make out what looked like a narrow road winding its way through trees at the end of the next field. Presumably that was going in the right direction. If she could cross that field without killing herself, she could walk along the road back to Winterbury.

She trudged across the field, feeling colder by the minute, and followed the snow-covered hedge until she found a gate. Her feet were so cold she could no longer feel her toes, but she managed to clamber over the gate without further mishap. The road was narrow and covered in snow. The absence of car tracks suggested that no one had driven this way for a while.

Did she go left or right? Right, surely.

She started to trudge back along the road and she'd been walking for about five minutes when she heard the sound of a vehicle approaching. She tucked herself in by the hedge and waited for it to pass, but instead it pulled up next to her.

The driver lowered the window. "Are you all right?"

"I'm fine, thanks for asking." She kept her head dipped, because she didn't want whoever it was to see that she'd been crying. She wasn't in the mood to be sociable.

"Are you sure?" His voice was deep. "Because it's snowing, and you're not exactly dressed for the weather. You're soaking wet. Did you fall? Are you lost?"

She heard the concern in his tone and knew she had to reassure him if she wanted him to drive on, which she did. She was not in the mood for company, even concerned company. "I had a slight accident. But I'm fine."

"Where are you heading?"

Oh, go away! She didn't have the energy for this conversation. She turned to look at him, ready to put him firmly in his place, and her gaze locked with his. She felt a jolt of shock. He was younger than she'd expected, just a few years older than her, she guessed, and his eyes were the bluest eyes she'd ever seen. Also the most tired. His jaw was dark with stubble, and he looked as if he'd been up all night.

The stab of attraction was unexpected. She didn't have that kind of reaction to men. No fireworks. No insta-lust. She was far too controlled and careful for that. And her response to him irritated her. Or maybe what irritated her was meeting someone like him at possibly the lowest moment of her life.

She could just imagine how Janie would react if she were here. She'd be flicking her hair, giving him her most dazzling smile and begging him to rescue her. But it was hard to be dazzling when you'd just climbed out of a frozen ditch.

And Imogen was used to rescuing herself. She'd made it her mission in life to be totally independent. She couldn't play the part of the damsel in distress even when she was, quite literally, distressed. She didn't want to lean on those shoulders of his, however broad they were. One of the few advantages of her somewhat barren childhood was that she'd learned to pull herself out of ditches.

And anyway, if his slightly battered, haven't-been-to-bed-all-night look was anything to go by, he was already living his best life.

Her ingrained sense of independence asserted itself and she almost didn't tell him where she was going, but the sensible side of her decided it might be helpful to know that she was at least heading in the right direction. "Holly Cottage. It's—"

"I know Holly Cottage." He frowned. "You're going the wrong way. How did you get here?"

"Across the fields."

"In this weather?"

"I fancied a stroll." It sounded ridiculous even to her. "I like snow. I find it...bracing."

"Bracing?" Disbelief mingled with humor. "Mmm. Why don't you hop in. I can drop you at Holly Cottage."

She saw then that his eyes weren't just tired, they were also kind. Instinctively, she backed away from that kindness. She didn't want kindness. She was holding it together by a thread, and kindness might just snap it.

"No thanks, I'm fine." Now that she'd been given the option, she realized she didn't want to go back to the cottage. There was a strong chance that Dorothy and Sara would be waiting.

Her stomach churned at the thought of it. She couldn't face them. Not yet. Maybe not ever.

Tears clogged her throat and she looked away again. "Thanks for stopping. I appreciate it."

She was about to walk on and hope he took the hint when she heard a whimper from the back of the car and the man turned and stretched out a hand to something in the back seat.

"I know. Life sucks, but you're going to be fine."

She could identify with the first part of that statement. Life did indeed suck.

Wondering who he was talking to, she peered into the car. Underneath a bundle of towels and blanket something moved. "Is that a...*dog*?"

"Somewhere under all that the muck. He's hiding. He knows he's in big trouble. He belongs to Valerie Kelly, a retired pharmacist who lives in the village. Her brother died six months ago and she promised she'd care for Ralph, but she has had health struggles of her own, poor thing, and there is no way she can handle him. He escaped again this morning so she called me, worried he was going to get himself run over. I was driving near to where he was last seen, and there he was, having a party for one in a very muddy ditch." He glanced at the dog, who cowered guiltily under the blanket. "Don't be fooled. He knows no one is going to hurt him. That look he's giving you is pure emotional manipulation."

The dog looked so pathetic she almost smiled. "Do you run a dog rescue or something?"

"It sometimes feels that way, but no, I'm a vet. Mostly farm animals, which is how I knew Jim Kelly. He was a farmer. I looked after his herd of prize cattle. For as long as I can remember Jim had a dog. The moment the dog died he got another one, and each one was called Ralph."

"Why Ralph?"

"I think he just had the one name. Moved it from dog to dog. Anyway, Ralph is now the responsibility of his sister, and she's not coping well. The dog is giving her the runaround. Her arthritis means she can't walk him as much as she should. He needs to be rehomed, but she can't bring herself to do it, because then she'd feel as if she was letting her brother down. But this little incident was the final straw. She's worried the dog will end up dead."

"That's so sad." She turned her attention back to the dog. There was something about him that tugged at her. "What will happen to him?"

"Well, he belongs to me now, which means he will have a life of being dragged around farms at inhuman hours and being fed when I remember to do it."

"You're keeping him?"

"Seems that way. I'm taking him home so we can get properly acquainted and I can figure out what he needs, but transporting him is difficult. He has some behavioral issues, because Valerie just couldn't handle him. I'll deal with those, but that's not going to solve my immediate problem. He keeps trying to climb out of the car. I've been out on calls and wasn't expecting to have a dog in the car so I didn't come prepared."

Out on calls. Was that why he looked so tired?

He was looking at her, contemplating something. "I don't suppose you'd help? I've had to stop four times already. If you could sit in the back with him, that might settle him down.

Once I have him safely at my place, I'll drop you back to Holly Cottage. It's not far."

"I—"

"I can understand you're cautious. You were probably raised not to get into a car with a strange man, but I can call any number of locals to vouch for me if that would help."

Over the years she'd learned to trust her own instincts. Also, she really did have a black belt in jujitsu, and even though she hadn't trained since April, she was still pretty confident that she could do damage if she needed to.

The fact that she was inclined to refuse had more to do with the fact she didn't want company than any wariness of stranger danger, but then the dog poked his head through the blankets and looked at her with soulful eyes. His fur was matted and so caked in mud it was impossible to tell what color he was, let alone what breed.

She felt a pressure in her chest.

He was too much trouble for Valerie. He'd already lost his master, and now he was having to leave his home for a second time. From the look on his face he wasn't too happy about it.

He probably felt lost and lonely.

I don't want to be your mother.

She felt a flash of kinship, and before she could talk herself out of it, she was opening the car door and climbing into the back with the dog. The rejected needed to stick together.

The dog raised his head and gave a thump of his tail, as if agreeing with her thought.

"I hear you've been naughty." She stroked his head, feeling caked mud under her fingers. "You're certainly filthy."

The man turned to look at them both and nodded approval. "He likes you. Good. That will help. If you could just keep your hand on him to reassure him, that would be great. It will take me under ten minutes to get home. I'm Miles, by the way. Miles McEwan."

"Imogen." And then the name suddenly registered. "Miles. You're Dorothy's vet."

He glanced in the mirror. "You know Dorothy?"

How was she supposed to answer that?

She'd thought she knew Dorothy, but apparently she didn't know her that well at all.

Her throat thickened and she stroked the dog's matted head. "Sort of." The dog nudged the palm of her hand, and she felt ridiculously comforted. He couldn't possibly know how upset she was, of course, but it felt as if he knew.

Or maybe he did know and was thinking *you think you've got trouble? Look at me! No one wants me.*

She gave a half smile and felt him lick her palm in solidarity.

Miles shifted his gaze back to the road. "You're staying in Holly Cottage so of course you know Dorothy. She's great, isn't she? One of my favorite people."

Dorothy definitely wasn't Imogen's favorite person right now, but she couldn't resist the opportunity to find out more from someone who knew her well.

"You've known her a long time?"

"Forever. She and my mother were best friends. They were each other's bridesmaids. Also, Dorothy was my primary school-teacher for a while."

"You're kidding." She tried to imagine him as a six-year-old.

"That was a long time ago. Before her husband died. Before she took over the running of the vineyard full-time."

Before her husband died. *Her grandfather.*

Dorothy had mentioned being a widow, but Imogen had never probed for detail. It hadn't seemed appropriate. But now she tried to work out where that information fitted with everything she knew about her mother's family. What was the timing? Had he died after he'd thrown her mother out?

She caught Miles's questioning glance and realized she was expected to respond.

"Our relationship is mostly professional. I work for an events company. Dorothy is a client." Or was. Was a client. There was no way Imogen would be working with her again, but that was far too much detail to share.

He nodded. "You live in London? I suppose someone has to."

"You don't like London?"

"On occasion, but I generally prefer having space and clean air to breathe. Whenever I visit, I'm always glad to get home."

Glancing out of the window at the wintry landscape, it wasn't hard to understand his point of view. They were driving steadily along the narrow road, through an avenue of snowy trees.

If she wasn't so cold and miserable, she'd be admiring it. It looked like a Christmas card, not that she ever sent Christmas cards.

"So Dorothy was your teacher and a family friend, and you look after her animals."

"She didn't always have animals. It started with a donkey. She rescued it and called me to take a look. That was quite a few years ago. I was just starting in the practice. Newly qualified. It was my father's practice."

"He retired?"

"My parents were killed five years ago." His voice roughened. "They were on their way home from an anniversary dinner when their car hit a patch of ice."

He gave no more detail than that, but he didn't need to.

She felt a flash of sympathy and also frustration with how unfair life was. He'd clearly had a wonderful family, and they'd been taken from him. "I'm sorry. That must have been tough."

"At the time it was, yes. But everyone in the village was a great support, Dorothy in particular. Partly because she felt she owed it to my mother, I suppose—they were close friends— and partly because that's just who she is. Dorothy is the kindest person I know. Always there for anyone in trouble, and that includes animals. She takes in anything unwanted."

Unless it was her own daughter, Imogen thought bleakly. Then she wasn't so generous. Did Miles know that part of her history? Presumably not.

"You see a lot of her."

"I check on her animals from time to time. And I drop in for cake when I'm passing. If she offers to cook for you, say yes. She's a brilliant cook. I'd cross the country for her chocolate cake."

Imogen thought about the meal she'd left congealing on the table.

Where was Dorothy now? Probably waiting for her at the cottage.

She'd probably been calling, but Imogen had left her phone in her coat pocket so she had no way of knowing.

"We're here—" Miles took a left turn up a bumpy track and pulled up outside a converted barn.

Imogen stared. "This is yours?"

"It's more impressive from the outside than the inside, so don't get your hopes up." He switched off the engine. "I spend most of my time in muddy fields, and when I'm home I'm sleeping, not mopping the floor. Right. Let's get this chap inside and clean him up. Then we can start teaching him some manners."

She opened her mouth to point out that she wouldn't be teaching him anything, but Miles was already out of the car and opening the car door.

Imogen stepped out. The freezing air penetrated her damp clothing and she shivered, feeling the lack of a coat.

The dog whimpered and gave her a forlorn look.

"Imogen isn't going anywhere," Miles told him, "but I'm going to carry you indoors."

"I'll take him." Imogen didn't want the dog to think she was abandoning him.

Miles frowned. "Are you sure? He's not a small dog. He's fine, really. He's only looking at you as if the world is ending because he wants your sympathy."

"He has my sympathy." Imogen gently scooped him up,

blankets and all, and hoped she wasn't hurting him. She wasn't used to handling an actual dog, and he weighed more than she'd anticipated. The dog lay against her, and she wasn't sure which of them was shivering the most.

"Here—" Miles removed his coat and draped it around her shoulders. She was immediately engulfed in warmth.

"You don't have to—"

"Let's argue about it inside." He closed the car door and walked with her to the barn. "We'll use the side entrance. That way I don't tread mud all over the place."

"This barn is amazing. How did you find it?"

"I bought it from a farmer who owed me a favor." He opened a door that led into a large utility room. "This is where I clean off before I go into the house."

He tugged off his muddy boots and then took the dog from her as she did the same.

The floor underneath her damp socks was blissfully warm. She could see how practical the room would be for a vet. There was a large stainless steel sink, and everywhere she looked there were coats and boots and signs that the occupant lived an active, outdoor life.

He gently lowered Ralph into the sink. "Let's start by washing off that mud so we can check he's all right."

Again he used "we." As if she was part of the dog's future. She wished badly that she was. "You think he might be injured?"

"Hopefully not, but there was some barbed wire close by, so I want to check." He pulled away the muddy towels that were wrapped around the dog. "I couldn't see signs of injury, but it was snowing and we were both in danger of freezing to death so I prioritized getting him back here and calling Valerie to tell her he was safe." There was a shower attachment on the sink, and he turned on the water and tested the temperature. "Let's give him a shower."

Imogen stroked the dog's head to reassure him. "I've never seen so much mud. What breed is he?"

"Golden retriever." He glanced at her. "You look cold. Why don't you go and take a hot shower yourself? You're wet and cold. I can find you something to change into."

Golden retriever. She almost laughed at the irony. But not Midas. Ralph.

"I'll stay with him until we're done here."

"I suppose you're already soaked, so a bit more water isn't going to make much difference. And at least this water is warm." He gave a good-natured grin and rolled up his sleeves, revealing muscled forearms.

She turned her focus back to Ralph and covered the dog's eyes as Miles carefully aimed the jet of water over his head.

They were just arms, for goodness sake. Arms.

Miles soaped the matted fur, loosening caked mud and rinsing and rinsing until finally the water started to flow clear and the dog's coat started to appear.

"That's better." Finally, he turned off the water and ran his hands over the now-clean dog, examining him thoroughly. "He's none the worse for his adventures as far as I can tell." Miles checked the dog's ears and wrapped him in a clean towel.

The dog looked almost as pathetic wet as he'd looked muddy.

Imogen felt a rush of compassion. "Is he going to be all right?"

"He's going to be fine. You might want to stand back in case he shakes and soaks you."

"I don't care." She stroked the dog's head and he rewarded her loyalty by licking her palm.

"Okay, enough. This love affair between the two of you is going to have to wait." Having wrapped the dog in towels, Miles focused his attention on Imogen. "You need to warm up. That door over there leads to a shower. Everything you need is there, including clean towels. Go and stand under the hot water and by the time you're done I'll have found you some dry clothes."

Imogen didn't want to leave the dog, but she was truly freezing and the last thing she wanted was to be ill. She needed all her energy to handle what was coming next in her life.

She gave Ralph a last stroke. "I'll be back in a moment. I'm not going far."

Ralph whined and watched her until she'd disappeared through the door Miles had indicated.

It led to a surprisingly smart shower room, complete with towels warming on a rail.

She stripped off her soaked, muddy clothes and dropped them on the floor. Her skin felt icy to touch and she realized how very cold she was. She stepped under the jet of hot water and closed her eyes, allowing the water to stream over her hair and body. She wondered if Ralph had felt the same way. Did he know Valerie couldn't keep him? Did he miss Jim?

Feeling sad for the dog, she reached for the shampoo, lathered her hair twice and then stayed under the scalding jets of water for several minutes. She wondered if she'd ever feel warm again.

Or maybe the chill came from the inside.

What was she going to do? Was she really going to leave without having another conversation with Dorothy? Was that even an option?

Even as part of her wanted to run as fast as possible in the opposite direction, another part of her had questions. So many questions.

"Imogen?" Miles's voice came from the doorway. "I'll leave some clothes by the door for you."

She turned off the shower.

If he had spare clothes, then he was probably married, or at least had a partner of some sort. And why wouldn't he? He was good-looking and seemed like a decent human. Also he was kind to animals, so it seemed likely some sensible person would have snapped him up long ago.

She stepped out of the shower, wrapped herself in one warm towel and rubbed at her hair with another.

Once she was dry, she reached for the clothes he'd left in a neat pile.

There was a pair of jeans that fitted surprisingly well, and a soft sweater in a shade of pale pink. She found a hairdryer in one of the drawers and finished drying her hair.

She emerged from the bathroom and almost fell over the dog.

"He's been sitting there waiting for you since you closed the door," Miles said, amused. "At some point I need to break the news to him that I'm his new owner and not you."

She crouched down next to the dog, who was now also clean and dry, his fur a soft pale gold. She felt a lump in her throat. Here, right in front of her, was the dog she'd imagined. Only this dog was the real thing.

Right now he felt like the only real thing in her life.

She stroked his head. "Good boy. Aren't you beautiful?" She smiled as he thumped his tail and pressed his nose into her hand. "He looks so much better without all that mud."

"He's a good-looking dog. I'm going to find him something to eat." He glanced at her. "You look better."

"Better?"

"Your lips were turning blue. For a moment there I was as worried about you as I was about the dog. I thought I was going to be dealing with a ripe old case of hypothermia. The clothes fit." He nodded approval. "Good."

"Yes. Thank you. And I do feel better." She also felt self-conscious. He was probably wondering why she'd been stumbling along a snowy lane with no coat. "Do these clothes belong to your wife or something?"

"My sister, Lissa." He piled the towels he'd used for the dog into a large washing machine. "She was doing some work on the place for me and left clothes here. I'm pleased to see them put to good use instead of cluttering up my home. Come through to the kitchen and warm up properly. I need coffee. I'm sure you do too."

She followed him through to the living room and stopped as she saw the large Christmas tree that had pride of place by the window. "Wow. That's—big. You're a Christmas lover, obviously."

"I don't know if I'd describe myself that way. I'm usually working at Christmas." He glanced at the tree. "It's a bit over-the-top, isn't it? I'm willing to bet that you can see it from space when I switch the lights on. You can blame my sister for the decorations. She worries that I spend too much time working, so she arranged for one of her interior design team to come and set up a tree for me. Can you believe that is actually someone's job?"

She stepped closer and took a closer look at the tree with its artistically arranged decorations. She could smell the forest, and for the first time in her life understood how such a thing might lift your spirits. There was something magical about bringing the outdoors indoors. She reached out and touched one of the branches. "What do they do for the other eleven months of the year?"

"They work for my sister, which means they won't even have time to breathe. Ironic, given that she tells me off for working too hard."

She glanced back at him, remembering how tired he'd looked when he'd picked her up. "Do you work too hard?"

"Probably." He shrugged. "But I'm happy. I love my job, except perhaps at three in the morning when I'm out in freezing snow and howling winds with my arm up a cow's backside."

She laughed at the image. Actually laughed, which seemed like something of a miracle, given that only a short time ago she'd been ready to hide in a snowdrift.

"I can see why your sister would be worried." She glanced around her and felt a twinge of envy. "This place is like something out of a magazine."

The living room had a vaulted ceiling and exposed beams.

Like Holly Cottage, there was a wall of Cotswold stone and large windows that overlooked the snow-covered fields. Two comfortable sofas were arranged either side of the fireplace, and in the middle of a large rug (in an impractical shade of cream) there was a coffee table stacked with books.

The place looked tidy, as if the person who lived here spent very little time sitting down.

"Ridiculous, isn't it?" He rolled his eyes as he gestured to the duck-egg blue sofas. "It's all Lissa, obviously. I stupidly gave her free rein with the furnishings. I asked for practical, but as you can see I didn't get what I asked for. She got a little carried away."

"It's gorgeous. Elegant and stylish, but still cozy." And between Holly Cottage and this place, she was starting to rethink her life choices. Maybe it was time to stop saving and finally buy somewhere of her own.

"As I said, Lissa is an interior designer and she decided that as my work life involves me up to my thighs in mud half the time, my home life should be more civilized. I pointed out that my lifestyle isn't compatible with pale blue, and that's when she converted that room we just used into a mudroom/utility room. I'm supposed to scrub off the dirt before I enter my own house. I'd ignore her, obviously, except that I'm convinced she has installed CCTV somewhere, just to check that I'm not ruining her work by living in the place."

Imogen felt Ralph nudge her leg, and she bent to stroke him. "Do you want to leave him in the other room in case he breaks something or jumps on something?"

"Definitely not. A home is to be lived in, and it seems this is his home now. And anyway—" his eyes held a wicked gleam "—if there aren't marks on the duck-egg blue, I won't be able to prove I was right that it was an impractical choice. There's no point in having a sibling if you can't say 'I told you so.' Come through to the kitchen. You need a hot drink and so do I."

She followed him through the beautiful living room and into the kitchen, which did seem more practical with its stone floor and large kitchen island.

"Coffee?" He eyed her. "Or maybe I should make you hot chocolate. It might warm you up."

"Hot chocolate sounds comforting."

He gave her a quick look and she berated herself for her choice of words. Now he was going to ask her why she needed comfort.

But he didn't. Instead, he opened the fridge and pulled out the milk. "Did you eat lunch? Because I'm going to make myself a sandwich so I can easily make you one too."

She relaxed, grateful that he hadn't probed.

"I'm not that hungry, but thanks." She was still too stressed about what had happened earlier to contemplate eating.

"I'll make extra in case you're tempted. Food will warm you up." He frothed some milk and made her a hot chocolate, and then made himself a coffee using a machine that looked as if it could have launched a rocket into space.

He intercepted her glance and smiled. "I don't care what color my sofas are, but I do care about my coffee. So would you if you spent as much time awake at night as I do."

She did spend a fair amount of time awake. Maybe she needed to invest in a coffee machine like his.

She sipped her hot chocolate and instantly felt warmer.

Miles opened the fridge and pulled out random ingredients. "Cheese or ham?"

"I'm not really—"

"Let's go with cheese then." He pulled out a block of cheese and gestured to a cupboard near her. "You'll find some dog food in there. You'd better feed your new friend as you seem to be his favorite."

"I envy you, being able to keep him. I wish he was mine." She slid off the chair and found the food and a bowl.

The dog pressed against her leg, tail wagging in anticipation.

Miles sent her a curious look. "Do you have a dog?" He cut thick chunks of bread from a fresh loaf and added cheese and chutney from a jar with a handwritten label.

"No. I live in London."

"People have dogs in cities."

"Yes, but I work a lot. And unlike you, I can't take the dog along with me. It wouldn't be fair." But she couldn't stop thinking of how it might be to come home to that waggy tail every night. She was starting to understand why her colleagues were obsessed. She watched as the dog devoured the food. "You don't already have a dog?"

"I had a German shepherd for eleven years. Alfie. Brilliant dog. Lost him a year ago. I still miss him." He opened one of the cupboards and pulled out two plates. "I wasn't planning on replacing him, but it seems the universe has different ideas. Although you're the one Ralph is interested in. Time to feed the humans. Here…" He put a sandwich in front of her. "It's not elegant, but the cheese is organic from the farm down the road and the chutney was a gift from Valerie. It's homemade from the apples in her orchard. If you bought that in London, you'd pay a fortune for it."

She really didn't think she could eat, but she didn't want to attract any more attention or questions so she balanced on a stool at the kitchen island and bit into the sandwich, keeping one eye on her new protector. "But you'll keep him?"

"I made a promise to Valerie." He drank his coffee, his gaze fixed on the dog. "He's going to need training. I haven't got time to search the countryside for him every time he decides to go for an adventure. Are we going to stick with the name Ralph?"

She put her sandwich down. He was talking as if she was a longtime friend, and not someone he'd just rescued from the side of the road. "You want to change his name?"

He shrugged. "As I said, Jim only had the one dog name. Maybe this chap would like to have a name that's personal to him. He's had a bit of a sad time, and this is a fresh start. Maybe he'd like a fresh name."

Maybe that was what she should do. Change her name. Start fresh. Get away from her old life.

She brought her attention back to the present. "But does he answer to Ralph?"

"I don't know." He took a bite of his sandwich. "Why don't you find out?"

She slid off the stool. "Come here, Ralph."

The dog shot across to her, tail wagging.

Miles watched while he ate his sandwich. "Now go into the living room and call him Napoleon."

"Napoleon?"

"Just try it."

With a sigh, she walked back to the living room and took a breath. "Come here—Napoleon." She felt like a fool saying it and then moments later started laughing because the dog came shooting toward her, just as he had the first time.

She took him back to the kitchen. "I don't get it. Doesn't he know his name?"

"Possibly, but he's still young, and what he's really responding to is the tone of your voice."

She almost suggested they rename him Midas, but she stopped herself.

Midas was in the past. Midas wasn't real. Her fake dog days were behind her. And if this dog was having a fresh start, so was she. No more pretending. Maybe she wouldn't go as far as changing her name, but from now on she only wanted what was real.

"I like the name Ralph. It suits him. And I don't think he needs a new name just because he's getting a new life." She slid back onto the stool and took another bite of her sandwich. It was delicious, but her stomach felt tight and no matter how gorgeous the dog, or how charming and good-looking his new owner, she was still reeling from the shocking revelation that Dorothy was her grandmother.

That reality hung in her head even while she was talking about other things. Sooner or later she was going to have to stop avoiding the issue and decide what to do.

"Ralph it is," Miles said. "Welcome to your new home, Ralph." He smiled as the dog thumped his tail. "He doesn't seem too unhappy to be here. So now tell me more about yourself. You're spending Christmas at Holly Cottage? It's a great place for that."

"I won't be spending Christmas there." Even as she said it, she felt a stab of regret. "I'm leaving later today."

"Oh, shame. I was thinking maybe you could help me walk Ralph occasionally. When did you arrive?"

He was going to ask for her help with the dog? "Yesterday."

"That's a pretty short stay." His gaze lingered on her face. "I gather you're not impressed with our country ways."

"It's not that." She hesitated. "It's complicated."

"I guessed that when I saw you wandering along a snowy lane with no coat." He glanced at her half-eaten sandwich. "Are you going to finish that?"

"It's delicious, but I'm not really hungry."

"You're upset," he said slowly. "It's none of my business, but if you want to talk about it, I'm a pretty good listener."

She could believe that. She was used to being with people who were usually doing several things at once, including glancing at their phones. Miles had a way of giving you all his attention. It was a little unnerving.

"Let's just say my life is a bit of a mess right now. And that's probably an understatement." There was something about his calm, strong presence and his gentleness with the dog that made her want to blurt it all out. "I found out something today. Something that shocked me."

She was emotionally raw from her earlier encounter and

hadn't yet managed to seal the gaps in her armor. The only thing stopping her from telling him everything was the fact he knew Dorothy. He obviously thought Dorothy was an exceptional person, and she didn't want to be the one to expose Dorothy's secrets.

She'd be gone from here today and she'd never see any of them again.

That thought depressed her more than it should have done. It felt as if she was losing something, which made no sense because all she'd lost today was the last of her naivety.

And a friend. Because she'd considered Dorothy a friend.

She was hit by a wave of exhaustion. She felt tired and despondent, and maybe Ralph sensed it because he stood up and rested his head on her lap.

Miles glanced at him. "He knows you've had a bad day." He paused. "Anything I can help with? I'm a champion problem solver when the problems belong to other people."

That made her smile. "I'm a champion problem solver too. Unfortunately, this isn't really something that can be solved. More something I have to learn to live with."

"Right." He studied her, his expression sharp. "Does Dorothy know you're going? Because if you leave early, she's going to blame herself. She prides herself on making sure her guests have the best time. Is there something wrong with the cottage?"

"It's not the cottage. The cottage is perfect." A little too perfect. It made it all the harder to leave. Despite her initial reservations, her mood had lifted from the moment she'd stepped through the front door. The thought of returning to her place in London wasn't appealing. It was definitely time to rethink her life plan. If this trip had given her nothing else good, she at least had that. She'd realized that it was time to make a move. She'd saved hard, worked multiple jobs when she was studying and she had enough money for a deposit on somewhere half-decent if she was willing to commute. Perhaps she could re-create the "feel" of the cottage in an apartment in London.

Miles finished his sandwich. "Holly Cottage is usually booked up with people wanting to take lifestyle shots for social media. Last year she rented it to an advertising company for a Christmas shoot for a major brand. Whenever I turned the TV on, I saw Holly Cottage. They used it for a movie a few years ago too. Covered the place in fake snow, which irritated the locals."

"I can imagine."

He stood up and put his plate into the dishwasher. "Dorothy is pretty commercial. She's had to be. She has learned how to monetize what she has, but that's so that she can give back. Most of her money is poured into community projects and rescuing the animals."

She realized now how little she knew Dorothy.

"Why does she rescue animals?"

He hesitated. "Trying to compensate for the one she couldn't save?"

"Excuse me?"

"Sorry. I was thinking aloud." He shook his head. "I'm not a psychologist, but I'd say it all goes back to a family tragedy. It's public knowledge, so I'm not betraying a confidence. We're a pretty tight community here. Which can occasionally be irritating, but mostly it's a good thing. Everyone keeps an eye on everyone."

"Family tragedy?" Her heart was thumping hard. "You mean losing her husband?"

"No, although that was a tragedy too of course, and what happened had to have contributed. You don't know about her daughter?"

"You mean Sara? I saw her this morning."

Sara, her aunt. *Her aunt.* That was something she hadn't even started to get her head around. And Ava and Iris were her cousins. Did her mother know about Ava and Iris? Presumably not.

She'd never been given the chance to know them. And neither had Imogen.

She felt a pang. The two little girls were so engaging it would have been nice to have them in her life. She imagined Ava on Christmas morning, her excitement brimming over like lemonade poured too quickly into a glass.

Miles frowned. "I'm not talking about Sara. I meant her other daughter."

Other daughter?

She kept her hands in her lap and tried to keep her expression neutral. "Tell me about her other daughter."

"I don't remember much about her, but my sister was—still is—a close friend of Sara's and I know she hated going round to the house when Tina was there. Tina used to keep alcohol and cigarettes in Sara's bedroom because she knew her mother wouldn't search there. She once stole money from Lissa's coat pocket, but Lissa didn't tiptoe around her in the way Sara did. She took it right back and Tina never bothered her again."

"Tina stole money?"

"Yes. And that wasn't the only thing she stole. She hung around with people who weren't a great influence, I think. She and one of her friends were arrested once. Then at sixteen she got pregnant and after that everything unravelled."

Imogen's mouth felt dry. "That's the tragedy? You're saying that the shame of her getting pregnant killed Dorothy's husband?"

"What? No. Dorothy and Phillip loved that baby and they tried hard to support their daughter too. But Tina didn't want their help. She rejected them. Left home and didn't get in touch for four years."

Imogen felt a flicker of outrage. That wasn't right. Her mother had told her so many times that it was her family who had rejected *her*. They hadn't supported her or given her a chance.

You ruined my life.

"Maybe she knew they didn't want her in their lives." She

tried to keep her voice normal. "Maybe she left because she knew they didn't want the baby."

"No, that wasn't how it was." He looked confused by the suggestion. "And anyway, she didn't take the baby. The baby stayed with them."

Those words hung in the air for a moment and then slowly sank into her head.

"Excuse me?"

"Tina didn't take the baby with her. She walked out on her family and the child too. Just left. Dorothy cared for the baby for four years and not once did Tina get in touch. I've never understood how a mother could just walk away from a baby like that. But that was Tina. She just did what she wanted and didn't care about anyone else. I suppose she knew the baby would be safe with Dorothy."

Imogen's head spun.

Miles was saying her mother had left her with Dorothy?

No. That couldn't be right. She had no idea where he'd got this version of the story, but she *knew* it wasn't right. She hadn't lived with her grandmother, she'd lived with her mother. It had been just her and her mother against the rest of the world. Her mother had told her that so many times.

But she wanted to hear the rest of his version, so she forced herself to keep listening. "And what happened after four years?"

"Tina came back. She just turned up one day, right before Christmas, and said she was taking the baby." He shook his head as if the logic behind the whole incident defeated him.

"Took the baby?" Her lips were so dry she could hardly move them. "What do you mean?"

"She turned up without warning, took the baby and that was that. Poor Dorothy." His voice softened. "I can't even imagine it. She and Phillip loved that baby. So did Sara. They cared for her as if she was their own. And then she was taken away from them. They were heartbroken. Are you going to finish your sandwich?"

She'd forgotten about her sandwich.

What he was telling her couldn't be true. She knew it wasn't true. "Didn't they try and stop her?"

"Yes, but Phillip had a stroke that night. Everyone assumed because of the stress of it. And that part I do remember because my mother took the phone call from Dorothy. She wanted to go with him to the hospital, but she didn't want to leave Sara in the house on her own. Sara was in a bad state. Her dad had just collapsed in front of her, and her sister had taken the child that Sara had been doting on for four years. Dorothy asked my mother to stay with her. My father was out on a call and my sister was on a school trip somewhere, so my mother put me in the car and took me with her to Winterbury. I've never forgotten that night."

She felt lightheaded. "How old were you?"

"Nine? And totally ill-equipped to deal with so much emotional trauma. Sara was distraught. She sat on the sofa sobbing, which is a bit disconcerting when you're a nine-year-old boy. I was relieved my mother was there to handle the brunt of it. Sara just kept saying *she took Immy*. Over and over again. *She took Immy*."

She took Immy.

Imogen's heart was thundering against her ribs. "It's not true. If it had happened that way, she would have told me." But even as she said it part of her was wondering. Remembering all the other untruths her mother had told. But not this, surely? This was huge. No. She couldn't believe it.

But what reason would Miles have to lie? He wasn't repeating something he'd heard; he'd actually been there that night.

"Who would have told you what?" Miles frowned briefly and then stilled. Understanding dawned. "Imogen." He said her name softly. "Immy."

"Yes." She croaked out the word. "I'm the baby. And this is the first time I've heard that story."

16

Dorothy

"Should we call the police?" Dorothy paced across the kitchen and back again. "She's not in the cottage, but her car is still there. Her bag is here. Where could she be?"

"She must have gone for a walk, but I drove around the local roads for a good ten minutes and there was no sign of her." Sara closed the kitchen door. She was looking strained and exhausted.

They'd given the girls lunch and the two of them were now safely curled up in the TV room with Bailey, watching cartoons.

"A walk?" Dorothy couldn't bear to think about it. "But it's freezing out there and she has no coat! And she's been gone for hours. Maybe she has had an accident. She was very upset. What if she slipped and fell?"

"I'll take the car and drive around again. I'll go in a different direction this time. See if I can spot her." Sara grabbed her keys. "I'll call Patrick and ask him to come over and look after the girls."

"I don't want you to drive. One person in trouble is enough. You're upset and there is ice on the roads." Now that she was more in control of her emotions, Dorothy was almost as worried about Sara as she was about Imogen. Sara's coping mechanism had been different to hers. Sara chose not to think about that time, not to talk about it, and now Dorothy's actions had forced her to confront a traumatic part of her life. "I'm so sorry, Sara."

"There's no need to apologize. We just need to deal with it."

Dorothy didn't know how to deal with it. "Should we call the police?"

"No, not yet." Sara put her keys down. "I can't bear the idea that all these years she thought we'd rejected her." Sara's voice broke. "She hates us."

Dorothy was shaken by it too. "No. She is angry with us because of what she thinks we did. But once she knows the truth, that will change."

"Will it? If she has grown up thinking we deserted her and Tina, it won't be easy to persuade her otherwise. And it doesn't seem as if she'd be keen to sit down and have a heart-to-heart over a cup of tea." Sara rummaged in her pocket for a tissue and blew her nose hard. "Sorry. Reliving this whole thing is my nightmare."

"I know, sweetheart. And I feel terrible about it. I should have told Imogen right away who I was, but I was so shocked to see her that first day in that meeting and I missed the moment, and after that I was just enjoying spending time with her. I didn't want to risk it all going wrong."

"I know. I understand." Sara took a deep breath. "I need to keep it together. The girls are already asking difficult questions. What do I tell them?"

"The truth." Dorothy felt bone-tired, but no matter how exhausted she felt, her concern for Imogen was greater. "Let's find Imogen first, and then sort everything else out later. She can't have gone far. What if she was walking along the road and was hit by a car? It's icy out there and the roads haven't been cleared. Call the hospital, Sara. Once you've done that, I'll call the police. I think it's time. Maybe if we do that, she'll turn up. You know what life is like."

This time Sara didn't argue. She reached for her phone, found the number and dialed.

She was on hold, waiting for someone to answer when Dorothy's phone rang.

She snatched it up with a surge of hope, and then sighed as she saw the caller ID. "It's Miles. I don't know why I would have thought it was Imogen given that her phone is here."

"Answer it," Sara said, "if Miles is out on visits you can ask him to keep an eye out for her."

It was a vain hope, but at this stage she was willing to cling to anything no matter how fragile. She answered the call.

"Hello, Miles."

"Dorothy? I have Imogen here."

"Imogen?" Dorothy grabbed the nearest chair and sat down hard. She waved a hand at Sara. "Imogen is with Miles." She turned back to the phone. "Miles? Where are you? How do you have Imogen?"

"It's a long story. We'll tell you when we see you, but I wanted to let you know she's fine. I thought you would be worrying."

He knew her so well.

"Thank you, Miles." She could barely speak for the relief. "Is she all right?"

There was a pause. "Yes."

She wondered about that pause. "Are you at your place? I'll come right now and pick her up."

"No, don't do that. We'll come to Holly Cottage. We'll meet you there in twenty minutes."

Holly Cottage. Why not the house?

Oh, what did it matter? All that mattered was that Imogen

wasn't lying in a ditch or worse. For now, that was enough. The sense of relief was enormous.

"Sara and I will go straight there now. And Miles—" she swallowed "—thank you." She ended the call and looked at Sara. "He's bringing her to Holly Cottage. Let's go." She stood up and looked round the kitchen, flustered. "She didn't eat anything at lunchtime. She must be starving. I'll wrap some of the chicken and take the loaf I baked this morning. There's chocolate cake in the tin. Sara, could you grab that?" She glanced at Sara and saw her typing a message into her phone. "What are you doing?"

"I'm asking Patrick to come straight here and take the girls." Sara pressed Send.

Dorothy felt guilty. "I can do this without you. Patrick is Christmas shopping, and you have to take the girls to their party soon."

"I'm coming with you. There's no avoiding it now. Imogen needs to know the truth, and it might be easier if two of us are telling it. And I need to see her, and talk to her, and tell her—" She gave her mother a helpless look. "I don't want her feeling badly about us. And also, now that we've come this far, I want to find out more about her life. I hope that's not going to be upsetting." She rubbed her fingers over her forehead and gave a wan smile. "Who am I kidding? The whole thing is upsetting." Her phone buzzed and she checked it. "There. Patrick says he'll be here in five minutes. He was already on his way home from the village, so good timing. He can spend an hour with them and then take them on to the party."

"That's kind of him." This time Dorothy didn't argue. She wasn't sure she could do this without Sara. She *needed* Sara. Was that wrong? Sara was a grown woman, but she was still Dorothy's child. Her job was to protect her child, wasn't it? Although she'd failed utterly in that goal with Tina. How did you protect a child who had no wish to be protected? Who seemed to embrace the very things that kept Dorothy awake at night?

She and Sara had been together through all of this, right from the beginning. Sara was the one person who knew all of it. Maybe it wasn't wrong to accept the support she was so freely offering. Maybe this was something they both needed to do.

Sara put her phone down. "How did Imogen come to be with Miles?"

"I don't know. But I'm relieved that she is. She was so very upset when she left here." It broke her heart to think of it. "I was afraid something had happened to her."

"If she's with Miles, she'll be okay. He's good with anything distressed, animal or human. I still remember that night he stayed with me while you went to the hospital." Sara stood up and stuffed a few of her belongings into her bag. "Is she going to talk do you think? Or is she coming back to Holly Cottage to pack up her things and leave?"

Dorothy felt her stomach lurch. That was her biggest fear. That Imogen wouldn't listen, or that she'd listen but not believe them.

"I don't know. But we're going to tell the truth and hope that's enough."

She packed the loaf, the chicken and the cake into a bag, and by the time she'd finished, Patrick had arrived.

He brought with him an air of calm capability, as well as a fair amount of new snow. He tugged off his boots in the doorway.

"Anyone home?"

Both girls heard his voice and emerged from the TV room.

"Daddy! Why are you here?" Ava was delighted to see him, but suspicious. "You said you were doing your Christmas shopping."

"I've finished my shopping and the village is looking so Christmassy with the snow and the decorations I thought I'd take you and Iris there for a treat." Patrick scooped up Ava and held out his hand to Iris. "It's a Daddy and his girls trip. And then I'll take you to your party afterward. Who is excited?"

Iris beamed and slid her hand into his. "I am."

"Me too." Ava put her arms around his neck. "Can we go ice-skating? I want to see if I can twirl on the ice."

"Not today. We'll keep that treat for a different day." Patrick grabbed the girls' coats from Sara and also the bag with their change of clothes.

"Will Imogen be here when we get back?" Ava was clinging like a monkey. "She said she'd make Christmas decorations with me. Where *is* Imogen? She didn't eat her chicken."

"Perhaps we'll see her later." Patrick brushed the question aside with a light touch. "Now let's get going so that we can see those shop windows before everything closes." He shifted his gaze to Sara. "Call if you need me."

She nodded, and Dorothy felt a lump form in her throat as she saw the look they exchanged.

She was pleased that Sara had Patrick. That the two of them had each other.

Patrick had been more of a son to her than Tina had ever been a daughter. It was funny how life turned out. Sometimes it was the people closest to you who disappointed you the most.

Patrick left with the girls, and Sara picked up her coat and then put it down again.

"I'm scared."

"Of Imogen?"

Sara looked at her and her eyes said everything. "Of reliving the past. And that's what we will be doing if we tell Imogen the truth. I don't really want to go there. It took so long to get my life into a good place after Tina left."

"Oh, sweetheart—" Dorothy felt her chest tighten. She didn't want to relive the past either, but it was a little different for her. Unlike Sara, she'd never managed to block it out. She'd carried it with her and learned to live alongside it. She was almost relieved that things were finally in the open. And she was feeling more optimistic than she'd been an hour ago. At least Imogen hadn't left. They were going to have another chance at a proper conversation. "It's going to be fine." She said it with more conviction than she felt. "We don't have to go through every detail. Just give her the chance to ask any questions she wants to ask."

"That's what worries me. I don't want to talk about Tina. I don't want to *think* about Tina. I've worked hard not to give her any space in my life, and I love the life I've built. I won't let thoughts of her spoil it, but seeing Imogen has opened it all up again. I realize that I haven't moved on or forgiven. All I've done is learn to ignore it." Tears spilled over, and Sara pressed her palm to her cheek. "Oh God, I can't believe I'm letting her get to me like this. But you lost so much because of her, and so did I. You lost your husband, and I lost my dad. And Imogen—" Her voice broke. "She didn't care how we felt about Imogen. She didn't even ask what we needed, or what Imogen needed. She dumped her daughter when it suited her, and she took her away when it suited her. Everything was always about her. She was the most selfish person on the planet back then, and there is no reason to believe she has changed. I'm not sure I can sit there with Imogen and say nice things about Tina."

Dorothy crossed the room and hugged her daughter. "You don't have to. We are going to tell the truth. How much of it we tell, we can decide when we talk to her." She stepped back and picked up Sara's coat. "I think this could end up being the best thing that could have happened."

Sara sniffed and took the coat from her. "You don't know that. You're just trying to be an optimist."

"At least everything will be out in the open." No more sleepless nights wondering if she should tell Imogen who she was.

When she should tell Imogen. "Let's go. I don't want them to turn up and find we're not there."

She picked up her coat and the bags, had a quick check of the kitchen and hurried to the car. It seemed ridiculous to drive such a short distance, but she didn't want to waste a moment.

Once inside the cottage, she and Sara unpacked the food in the kitchen and put the kettle on.

Then they lit the log burner in the living room and turned on the fairy lights that snaked along the beams so that the place looked cozy and welcoming.

"I wish we'd bought her a tree, or wrapped a garland around the banister." Dorothy fretted as she looked around. "Something to make the place festive."

"I don't think a fir tree and a few decorations are going to make this any easier," Sara said and then paused as they both heard a car outside. "She's here."

Dorothy felt her heart give a frantic pump. "It's going to be fine." She hurried to the front door and saw Miles pull the car into the space next to Dorothy's.

Imogen's rental car was now covered in a thin layer of snow.

Miles was first out of the car and then Imogen slid out of the passenger seat.

Dorothy couldn't remember ever feeling more nervous.

She noticed that Imogen was dressed differently. She was wearing a pair of jeans and a sweater in a soft shade of pink that brought out the flush in her cheeks and the blue of her eyes. She looked vulnerable and unsure, and Dorothy had to stop herself rushing across and hugging Imogen tightly, as she'd done when she was a young child.

Imogen was clutching a large bag stuffed with what looked like clothes, and in the other she was holding tightly to the lead of a dog. Dorothy took a closer look.

"Is that Ralph? Has something happened to Valerie?"

"Valerie is fine, but Ralph has had an exciting morning."

Miles strode round the car and bent to pat the dog. "He took himself on a solo countryside walkabout and frightened poor Valerie to death. We've agreed that he is going to come and live with me."

"But—" Dorothy struggled to keep up with this new development. "Valerie said she would never let him go. She felt she owed it to Jim." And she'd worried about it because she knew Valerie wasn't coping. "I offered to take Ralph myself, but she wouldn't have it. How did you persuade her to let you take him?"

"I told her I was heartbroken after Alfie, and I needed another dog." He gave Ralph a pat. "She took pity on me."

Dorothy felt a lump in her throat. He'd done that? "But you said you didn't want another dog after Alfie."

"I had a rethink, and now I have Ralph. It pays to be adaptable in life." Miles scratched the dog's head. "You should have seen him when I pulled him out of the ditch. He was a mess. Imogen got soaked trying to bathe him with me, which is why she's now wearing Lissa's clothes."

By focusing on the dog, he'd successfully smoothed over the initial awkwardness, and Dorothy felt a burst of gratitude. He'd made it so much easier for everyone.

"You're very generous. Valerie will be relieved. And Ralph is lucky."

"I'm not sure he agrees." Miles straightened. "Ralph has fallen madly in love with Imogen. I'm a poor second choice." He smiled at Imogen, who returned the smile tentatively.

It was a relief to see that smile. Also a relief that Imogen no longer seemed angry. If anything, she seemed nervous.

They were all nervous.

"Well, thank you for bringing Imogen, Miles."

She assumed he'd leave, and Imogen seemed to make the same assumption because she gave him a strained smile and held out the dog's lead to him.

"Thanks for everything."

But he didn't leave and he didn't take the lead. Instead, he gave her shoulder a quick squeeze and stayed by her side.

"Ralph is not going to want to be parted from Imogen and he has already had a pretty stressful day, so I'll hang around for a bit if that's all right." He glanced at Imogen with a smile. "I'll be right here for a while. Moral support. For Ralph. If that's okay with you."

Moral support. For Ralph.

Dorothy caught Sara's eye.

"I—yes. If you're sure." Imogen looked startled, as if this was the first time anyone had ever been in her corner, and Dorothy felt a lump form in her throat.

She and Sara had been focusing on how they were feeling, but it must be a million times worse for Imogen, who was finding out things for the first time.

How much had she told Miles?

Some of it, surely, or why else would he be insisting on staying?

"Let's go inside. It's cold out here." Dorothy headed back into the cottage, but Imogen didn't follow.

She clung to the dog's lead. "What about Ralph?"

"He can come too! Dogs welcome." Right now she wouldn't have cared if Miles had invited a herd of elephants into her home. She was just relieved Imogen was here and not showing any signs of leaving. "Come into the living room. It's cozy with the fire going."

They all joined her inside and Imogen sat down on the sofa. Miles settled himself next to her, his long legs half filling the room, and Ralph immediately lay across Imogen's feet.

Sara vanished toward the kitchen. "I'll make us some tea."

Dorothy decided that the only way to do this was to dive right in.

"First I need to apologize," she said, "for not telling you

exactly who I was right away. It was a shock seeing you, to be honest, that day last year in the conference room where we had that meeting. I was taken by surprise."

"How did you know me?"

"It was when you smiled. You have the same little dimple in your cheek that Sara has. Your grandfather had it too. It doesn't sound like much, but I knew. I knew right away."

Imogen sat rigid, and Ralph raised his head and looked at her, sensing tension. Then he took a sneaky look at Miles, jumped onto the sofa and sprawled across the two of them, his head on Imogen's lap.

Miles rolled his eyes. "These were clean jeans," he murmured, "but you just make yourself at home."

Imogen rubbed the dog's fur and Ralph thumped his tail and settled in for some serious attention.

Sara returned with a tray loaded with mugs of tea. She put it on the low coffee table that formed the centerpiece of the room.

"I shared some of our history with Imogen." Miles took the mug Sara offered him with a smile of thanks. "I didn't know who she was."

Dorothy was still wondering how the two of them had met, but there would be time to discover more about that later. For now she needed to keep the focus on the things that needed to be said.

"There is a lot to say, so why don't I start at the beginning." It sounded logical, but identifying the beginning wasn't easy. "Tina was my first child. Phillip and I doted on her. Perhaps a little too much—"

Sara sighed. "Mum—"

"I'm sorry. It's impossible not to rake over every minute of the past and try and work out how things went so wrong. You convince yourself that there must have been something you did, or didn't do." She felt Sara's hand pressing her knee, a gentle prompt that she should move on. And she was right. This conversation wasn't about her failings as a parent. "Everything was normal until Sara arrived. From the moment she was born, Tina resented her, and nothing Phillip and I did seemed to change that. Everyone told us that older siblings often resented younger, and it was just a question of time and patience. We did everything we were advised to do. We made sure we gave Tina special time so that she didn't feel pushed aside, we praised her, we encouraged her, we involved her. We thought that maybe we were getting somewhere, but then at five months old Sara contracted meningitis." She rarely thought about it now, but at the time it had consumed them. "She was in hospital for a month and I was by her side almost constantly. I tried to make sure I saw Tina too, but it was hard. We thought we were going to lose Sara. I don't want to linger on that part of the story, except to say that when we returned home, things were worse. Tina wouldn't let me out of her sight, and she hated me spending even a moment of my time with Sara. We spoke to doctors and did everything they suggested, but nothing seemed to help."

"It wasn't your fault," Sara muttered. "How could you possibly think it was your fault? The jealousy was there before I went into hospital. You said so yourself."

"That's true, but afterwards it was worse." She turned her focus back to Imogen, reminding herself to try and stick to facts, not emotions. "We couldn't leave her alone with Sara for a moment. I turned my back to take a phone call on one occasion—it was seconds, that was all—and when I looked back, Tina was holding a cushion over Sara's face." She stopped, conscious that this was Imogen's mother she was talking about. "I'm sorry. This is so difficult. Maybe I should—"

"I want you to carry on." Imogen's voice was barely audible. "Please carry on."

"We hoped that if we kept showing love and consistency, eventually she'd settle down, but she didn't. She broke Sara's toys, she shouted at her—that was the worst part. We never raised our voices, but Tina became verbally aggressive. It started to affect Sara. She was quiet at school, afraid to speak up or draw attention to herself. She hid in her bedroom if Tina was around." Looking back now, she wondered how they'd got through it. It was funny how time had the ability to blunt the razor-sharp edges of pain. "We took Tina to a psychologist. He advised us to set firmer limits and hold her accountable for her behavior, but all that did was make her reject us more. Things got worse when she became a teenager. She stole from us, she lied, she skipped school and spent time with a crowd of kids older than her. Soon she was coming home drunk or high. Frequently, she'd stay out all night and we wouldn't have a clue where she was. She was arrested for shoplifting, even though there was no reason for her to do that. I sometimes thought she chose to do the things she knew would worry us most." She felt Sara's hand on hers, squeezing.

"It's okay, Mum."

"Everyone said it was a teenage phase. That she was testing the limits. But she didn't grow out of it. We considered moving to get her away from the people she hung around with, but in the end we decided that wasn't fair on Sara, or indeed practical. This was our home, and also our business and there was no guarantee that moving would help." She didn't even realize she was crying until she felt Sara push a tissue into her hand. She blew her nose. "Phillip and I blamed ourselves, of course. We assumed there was something we must have done wrong."

Sara inhaled sharply. "Mum—"

"The truth is we think we have a strong influence over who our children become, but perhaps we don't. And that's hard to accept. As a parent you tend to blame yourself for everything." Dorothy took a deep breath. "She got pregnant and that seemed to calm her down. She never told us who the father was, and we didn't push her. We were just so relieved that she was spending more time at home. She took a job in the local shop and worked until she had you. For a few months we were hopeful this was the beginning of a fresh start."

Imogen stirred. "But it wasn't."

"You were a week old when she walked out." It still stunned Dorothy. "She'd met someone, she said. And she was moving to London. She didn't want to have any contact with us." She stared down at her hands. She would rather have not relived this part. "We had a terrible argument. I said things—awful things, I admit it. I lectured her on responsibility. Told her that she had a child now and had to step up. I wish I'd handled it more sensitively. I wish I hadn't said the things I said."

"She still would have left," Sara said quietly, "It would have made no difference. And she said awful things too. Truly awful."

Dorothy glanced at Sara, both of them remembering.

"It was terrible, but we had to keep going because we had you. In the middle of all that stress and anguish, you were the joy. And you were such a sunny baby right from the beginning. We raised you as our own. You adored Sara. We tried to put you in your own room when you turned eighteen months, but you just wanted to sleep in the bed with Sara."

"That's true." Sara gave a hesitant smile. "Wherever I was, there you were."

"You used to wait by the door for Sara to come home from school." Dorothy blinked several times. "Despite everything, it was a happy time. We were all settled. This was our life. And then four years later, a week before Christmas, Tina suddenly appeared with no warning and said she was taking you. She was in a new relationship, she was living in London and had a job. She picked you up, and oh, you were screaming—" Dorothy broke off. She could still hear those screams. Feel the anguish. "Tina was a stranger to you. You didn't know her. You clung to Sara. I remember she was wearing a scarf around her neck and you almost strangled her because you just wouldn't let go.

We tried to talk to Tina, to persuade her to at least stay with us for a while and get to know you, but she said she didn't want us judging her, and telling her where she was going wrong the whole time. I told her we wouldn't judge her, we just wanted to support her, but she wouldn't listen. She had a car waiting outside and she took you. Clothes, toys—she left them all behind."

"She wouldn't even take Bunny," Sara said, and Imogen looked at her, confused.

"Bunny?"

"I gave it to you when you were born. You slept with it every night. You wouldn't let us take it away long enough to wash it. I knew you wouldn't sleep without it so I raced after her car, but she wouldn't stop. I could hear you screaming in the back seat. It took a long time to get that scream out of my head."

"Maybe we would have driven after her." Dorothy kept talking. She knew that if she didn't finish the story now, she never would. "I don't know. But Phillip collapsed about half an hour after she drove off. Massive stroke." She took another breath. "He had blood pressure problems, and the additional stress of losing you proved to be too much. He died after three days in the hospital and our whole world changed."

"I'm sorry." Imogen had tears in her eyes. "I'm so sorry."

Dorothy knew she couldn't crumple. Not now. Not having come this far.

"I'll keep this part short. We contacted social services and a lawyer. We didn't even know where Tina lived. Where she'd taken you. Eventually, we did find her and we sent a message, letting her know that her dad had died. She didn't respond." And that had been the lowest point. She'd wondered then who Tina was, because she felt like a stranger. "She didn't come to the funeral. It was an incredibly tough time. As well as processing the loss of your grandfather, and you, I was trying to keep the company going."

"I honestly don't know how you did it," Sara murmured. "You were incredible."

"You just do," Dorothy said. "You get out of bed every day and do what needs to be done and mostly you don't even know yourself how you're doing it. It was weeks before we were able to focus on Tina properly. Anyway, social services decided you should stay with her. She was your mother and they saw no risk to you. She was in a steady relationship. Getting married." She tried to keep her voice steady. Tried not to let the despair and upset of that time invade her words. "We tried to stay in your life. We visited once and you were so upset and confused. Tina decided she didn't want us visiting at all. She said it unsettled you. That you needed to learn that your home was with her. And it's true that seeing us did unsettle you, but I was never sure if that was more because you picked up Tina's tension."

"You were so little," Sara said softly. "And you looked so confused by everything. It was horrible."

Dorothy reached out and gave Sara's hand a squeeze. "So we stayed away. We stayed away because that was what Tina demanded, but don't think for a moment that it was easy. And I blamed myself. If I hadn't spoken to her the way I did when she walked out that first time, maybe she would have seen us as a support instead of the enemy."

Sara opened her mouth as if she was going to say something, but then shook her head. "Go on."

"I saw a lawyer." Dorothy paused. "Did you know that grandparents have no automatic right to see their grandchildren? There are ways, but I decided that all the conflict wasn't good for you. We agreed to take a step back. Tina promised she'd pass on letters, so I wrote to you every month, and on your fifth birthday Sara and I traveled to see you with presents and a cake, hoping that this might be the start of something more regular. Time had passed, we hoped things would be different, but Tina had taken you out. You weren't there."

"I wrote to you too." Sara glanced at Dorothy, who nodded.

"Tina returned those letters. On your seventh birthday we turned up unannounced, hoping to see you. You were on your way to the park with Tina and a man who presumably was her husband. We tried to talk, but you didn't recognize us and Tina wanted us to leave. She said she wanted a chance to make her own family, without us breathing over her. And that was it."

"We kept writing to you," Sara said. "But we never heard anything back."

"And we assumed that if you wanted to make contact when you were older, then you'd do it. But you never did. And that's fine," Dorothy said quickly. "It was a difficult situation, I can see that. And we lived with it. We tried to accept it, although I thought about you constantly and wondered how you were doing. Sometimes I thought about reaching out again, but the fact that you hadn't reached out to us made me think it wasn't something you wanted. When you walked into the meeting room that day, I couldn't believe it. I knew it was you."

Imogen had been sitting frozen to the spot as she listened, but now she shook her head. "How could I have reached out? I didn't know anything about you. And I didn't see any letters." Her voice sounded strange. "There were no letters. Whenever I asked my mother why we didn't have family, she said you'd rejected her. She said you didn't want us in your life."

The sudden punch of emotion made it hard to breathe.

Even though Imogen had implied as much in the kitchen earlier, it was a struggle not to react. Dorothy reminded herself that this wasn't about her, it was about Imogen. "I sent you money—"

"She must have kept it." Imogen looked embarrassed. "I'm sorry."

Dorothy noticed the lack of surprise in Imogen's voice. She sounded more resigned than shocked. World-weary and older than her years.

"It's not your fault. None of this is your responsibility." Dorothy was quick to reassure her. "And the money didn't matter. What mattered was you. It breaks my heart that you thought we'd abandoned you."

"That was what she told me." Imogen was holding tightly to Ralph. "I thought I didn't have a family."

The words tore at Dorothy. "You do have a family, Imogen. You have a family who loves you very much and would like the chance to get to know you better. But that's up to you, of course." Her throat was so thickened by tears it was hard to speak, but she held the emotion back because she didn't want to make this worse for Imogen. "We can't do anything about the past, but we can do something about the future. You'll have questions, I'm sure. You'll want to think about what I've said. Perhaps you won't believe—"

"I believe you. And I have a million questions, but perhaps for later. Not now." Imogen looked exhausted, and Ralph lifted his head and licked her hand.

"You should have this." Sara reached into her bag and pulled out a slightly battered stuffed bunny. "It's yours."

Dorothy stared at the familiar bunny. "Where did that come from?"

"Home. I asked Patrick to bring it for me when he came to take the girls. I thought it might—I don't know." Sara gave a helpless shrug. "It belongs to Imogen."

Dorothy hid her surprise. She'd had no idea that Sara had kept the bunny. She knew her daughter had worked hard to block out memories of that time, but still she'd kept that bunny safe. *A reminder of Imogen.*

Imogen was staring at the toy on Sara's lap, a strange expression on her face. Then she leaned forward and took the bunny from Sara.

"I remember this," she said finally. "I didn't think I had any memories of the time you've been talking about, but I remember this."

Dorothy felt a surge of hope.

"You loved that bunny," Sara said softly. "I wanted Tina to take him because I knew you'd be upset without it, but she said she'd buy you a new one."

"I don't remember a new one, but I remember this." Imogen gazed at the bunny and then looked at them. "Can I keep this? For now?"

"Keep it forever. It's yours." Sara's voice shook. "It has always been yours. I was just taking care of it."

Imogen wedged the toy between her leg and the sofa. "I don't want Ralph to eat it."

"Neither do I," Miles said dryly, "or I'll be the one removing it from his stomach."

Imogen smiled, as he no doubt intended, but then looked at Dorothy. "Thank you for your honesty. I'm sure that wasn't easy to relive. And I owe you an apology. I was rude earlier. I'm sorry."

"You have nothing to apologize for. You didn't know any of this, and I'm partly to blame for that."

Sara sighed. "Mum—"

"I know." Dorothy lifted a hand to stop her saying what she was about to say. "No blame." Although she didn't believe that of course. Not for a moment. She knew she was always going to blame herself, but she could do it quietly. "The past is what it is. I do hope you'll stay, Imogen. Holly Cottage has always been a very happy place. It has been good to me. I hope it will be good to you, too."

Imogen's hand was gripping Ralph's collar tightly. "You're very kind—"

She was terrified, Dorothy thought. Terrified and overwhelmed.

"I know Ava and Iris would love to spend time with you." Sara sounded tentative. "You are cousins, after all."

"Cousins." Imogen said the word as if it was foreign. "Yes, we are."

Dorothy felt a rush of relief. She'd been afraid that Sara might hold herself back to protect herself, as she'd done so many times before. But she was reaching out, even if her approach was a little cautious and careful. It meant that she was thinking about a future, instead of focusing on the past.

"And you must get to know Patrick," she said, and Sara nodded.

"Yes. We live about five minutes from here."

Dorothy was aware that this must all seem like too much. Imogen had gone from believing she had no family to suddenly discovering she did indeed have family and that they were all keen to meet her and spend time with her.

"If you stay, you'll have complete independence and you can come and go as you please. I don't like to think of you on your own, though. I know all this is a lot to take in. But I'm just up the driveway." She had a sudden inspiration. "And of course you're welcome to have Ralph here whenever you want to. I'm sure Miles would appreciate the help when he's out on calls. Wouldn't you, Miles?"

To give him his due, Miles didn't falter. "It would be a great help, if you're sure it isn't an imposition. Just while I find the rhythm of having a dog back in my life."

Imogen looked at him and then at Dorothy.

"Ralph could stay with me? Here?"

"He seems rather attached to you." Dorothy gave a faint smile, because that had to be the understatement of the century. "He's probably feeling a bit lost with all these changes happening in his life." *Like you*, she thought. "If you want to have him here with you and Miles doesn't mind, I think that would be wonderful."

She understood how comforting a dog could be. How healing all that unconditional love and affection. She respected Sara's wish not to talk about the past, so whenever she felt the need she talked to Bailey.

Imogen wrapped her arms round the dog. "I'd love him to stay here with me occasionally. If you're sure, Miles?"

"You'd be doing me a favor."

Dorothy wanted to hug Miles. "There, that's settled."

Imogen still didn't look convinced. "He's very active. Your beautiful cottage—"

"Has had plenty of canine visitors." Dorothy swiftly waved away that concern. She'd redecorate the entire place if she had to. It was the least of her worries. If Ralph was giving Imogen comfort, then he was welcome as far as she was concerned, even if he shredded the place. "I lived here for a while after Sara left for college. I was rattling around in the house, trying to find my bearings, so I decided I needed a change of scene. I hope you'll be as happy here as I was."

"Well, in that case, thank you." Imogen turned to Miles. "Will it confuse Ralph if he spends some time here with me?"

"I don't think so. It's the people, as much as the place, and he has certainly taken a shine to you. I'll have him when I'm not working and drop him off with you when I need to go out and about. I think it's a great idea." He reached out to rub Ralph's ears, and Dorothy noticed that his fingers brushed against Imogen's.

A thought crept into her head, but she immediately pushed it away. There would be no interfering from her. She was just grateful to Miles for his help and for making what should have been a difficult encounter much easier.

Imogen stroked Ralph. "I don't actually know much about looking after dogs."

"I know a lot," Miles said, "so that will make us a good team. I'll pop back home in a minute and bring you some things. But he likes you, and he feels safe with you, so that's a start."

"He can have Bailey's spare basket." Dorothy stood up. "And we have a few other things up at the house that we can bring down here. You missed lunch, Imogen. There's cold chicken in your fridge, a fresh loaf on the side and chocolate cake in the tin."

She was conscious that Sara probably wanted to join Patrick and the girls in the village for the party, but Sara showed no signs of rushing off.

She was studying the living room of the cottage.

"We need to decorate this place," she said. "Starting with a tree. Do you have a favorite type?"

"A favorite type of Christmas tree?" Imogen looked blank. "Er—no. I've never had a real tree before. It's never really been an important time of year for me. I always find it difficult, although last year I did put a set of lights on my plant. It's fake, so I didn't singe the leaves or anything. And I treated myself to a turkey pizza, although it was a bit gross, to be honest."

A set of lights on my plant.

A turkey pizza.

Dorothy felt a pang. "You don't spend Christmas with your mother?"

"Tina? No. Not since I left home for college. We don't really—" Imogen paused. "Family get-togethers aren't really our thing."

Dorothy thought about the many family occasions when Tina had refused to leave her room and join them.

She tried not to think about how many Christmases Imogen must have spent alone.

"Christmas is very much our thing, so I think it's past time you learned what it means to go completely over-the-top at Christmas." She didn't add that they'd worked very hard to make Christmas their thing after that awful Christmas years ago. "I happen to know a couple of experts in tree hunting.

Sara? Didn't Ava suggest that Imogen should join you tomorrow?"

She wondered if she'd gone too far issuing that invitation, but Sara smiled.

"She did. What do you think, Imogen? Do you fancy joining our crazy, family tree-finding trip? It usually involves Patrick complaining that the tree is too big and then the girls begging him until finally he relents. And we end up with a tree that scrapes the ceiling. But we go to a farm where they grow their own trees, and there's hot chocolate and it's all very festive." Sara paused, suddenly uncertain. "No pressure, obviously. If it all feels like too much and you'd rather have a quiet day, that's fine."

"I'd love to come," Imogen said quickly. "But I wouldn't want to leave Ralph."

"Bring Ralph! The girls would love having him there. And Miles—" Sara turned to him "—if you're free tomorrow, why don't you come too?"

"For once I'm free, and the answer is yes. I can help Imogen transport the tree home. You and Patrick will already have a full car with the girls and trees."

"Come to the house for dinner after, all of you." Dorothy was already planning. She'd make it special. Festive. And later perhaps, when Imogen was a little more used to them, she'd invite her to spend Christmas Day with them. She wanted to make up for all those Christmases Imogen had missed. No more fake plants. No more turkey pizza.

Her spirits lifted.

A few hours ago she never would have predicted this outcome, but now she was feeling ridiculously hopeful. This wasn't about the past, it was about the future.

There was still much to unravel, of course. Still so much to work out and discover. She wasn't going to pretend that any of this was going to be easy. They didn't really know Imogen, and she didn't know them. But the fact that Imogen was staying and planning on joining Sara for a Christmas tree trip, was all good. It gave them a chance. A way forward.

And what better time of year was there to bring a family together than at Christmas?

17

Sara

The snowfall had transformed the village. Snow clung to roofs and dusted the cobbles, softening edges and adding a magical atmosphere that compensated for the cold. The lights strung across the street glowed cheerfully, and shop windows were laden with festive goods designed to entice the casual shopper inside.

Sara pushed open the door of the village hall and kicked the snow off her boots before she walked in.

The hubbub of noise told her that she was probably last to arrive and did nothing for the throb in her head. The day had been utterly draining, but inside she felt calmer than she had in a long time. She'd been worried that seeing Imogen would take them all backward, but that wasn't how it felt. It felt more like taking a step forward.

And she was so ready for that.

"Sara!" One of the doctors who worked in the local practice

spotted her and hurried across. She was wearing a pair of antlers that kept sliding over her eyes. "How are you?"

"I'm well, thanks, Nadia. You?" Sara hugged her and then reached out and straightened her friend's antlers. "You have something growing out of your head. You should probably see a doctor about that."

"Can't get an appointment." Her friend winked at her. "The doctors around here are terrible, haven't you heard?"

"In fact, I hadn't." Their local surgery was fantastic, and Sara knew how lucky they were. "Those antlers suit you."

"They are my protection." Nadia adjusted them. "It's harder for people to corner me and tell me their health problems when I'm looking ridiculous. I keep meaning to tell you how much we loved that mixed crate of wine Patrick sent us in the summer. The red was sublime."

"Anytime you want a top-up just give us a call."

"I will, and—" Nadia broke off as she saw someone over Sara's shoulder. "Oh no, I see someone I need to avoid or I'll be talking about body parts at a children's party. I'll catch you later. Good to see you, Sara. You look gorgeous by the way. Love the coat." She flew off across the room and Sara watched her go with a smile.

This was her life.

Living here, knowing everyone, was so important to her. After the devastating events of her childhood, the community had wrapped itself around her and her mother and provided a warm and comforting layer of protection between her and the world. Sara felt as if she belonged here. This place, and the people, felt like family. She had no secrets from them and their generosity and acceptance at the lowest point in her life had helped heal the scars left by her sister's rejection.

"Hey, Sara." Paul, her friend who owned the bookshop, appeared by her side. "Before that husband of yours notices you're here and monopolizes you, I just wanted to say I tracked down that book."

"Book?" Her mind was still full of Imogen and where this might lead, and it took Sara a moment to work out what he was talking about.

"Volcanoes?"

"Of course! Volcanoes. You found it?"

"And gift-wrapped it. All Shona has to do is write the label, and no doubt she'll do that with her usual artistic flair. Are you and Patrick still on for our post-Christmas gathering?"

They'd managed to find a date that worked for all of them and she was already looking forward to it. "Definitely. My mother is babysitting."

"Good, because you're in charge of drinks." He leaned forward and gave her a quick kiss on the cheek. "Take care of yourself, beautiful. I need to dash. I've left Rick struggling in the store by himself and you know what it's like this close to Christmas. He'll be stressing. Hope the girls enjoy the party." He headed for the door, and Sara finally took a proper look around her.

Someone had taken time to make the place as festive as possible. A huge tree sparkled in one corner, and curtains of tiny stars cascaded over the usually plain walls.

People milled in small groups, parents dropping off children, then pausing to chat and catch up.

Sara spotted Ava and Iris among the crowd and then Patrick, who was talking to Mrs. Parsons, the owner of the local riding stables. She was a brisk, no-nonsense woman, who had taught Sara as a child.

Sara found her as scary now as she had back then. Even though she was now a grown woman with a family of her own, she still called her "Mrs. Parsons."

Patrick excused himself from the conversation and strode across to her.

"Edna says that Iris is a born rider, which is high praise coming from her. She thinks we should consider buying her a pony."

"Edna? Why are you calling her Edna?"

"Because that's her name? And because she told me to call her Edna. I could hardly say 'actually, my wife is terrified of you and I'd rather call you Mrs. Parsons.'"

Sara rolled her eyes. "We are not buying Iris a pony. Thelma will do fine for now."

"Great. You can tell her that." Patrick saw her expression and grinned. "Just kidding. I already told her that."

She batted her eyelashes at him. "You're so big and brave."

"What can I say? Edna and I are besties. She's a great big pussy cat underneath that frightening act she puts on. Also, it helps that I keep her supplied with wine." He drew her to one side, and his tone changed. "I've been worrying about you. How was it?"

Where to begin? "It was…interesting."

"But not awful?" He studied her face, and she felt a rush of love for him.

"Bits of it were awful, but she did listen to us and she's still here, so that's a good outcome." And more than she'd hoped for when Imogen had stormed off at lunchtime. She heard a shriek and saw Ava chasing Iris and their other friends round the room as they waited for the party to start. "How much sugar have they had?"

"Enough to keep them hyperactive until Christmas. Don't judge." He slipped his arm round her, ignoring the fact that they were in public. "That's what happens when you leave me in charge. You're the disciplinarian. I'm the fun parent. I say yes to everything."

It made her smile even though she knew it wasn't true.

"I'm not judging. I'm grateful to you for riding to the rescue. Hi, Ellen—" she greeted a mother from school who was dropping off her daughter. "Everything okay?"

"Great, thanks. Hi, Patrick." Ellen's gaze lingered on Patrick fractionally longer than appropriate and then she drifted away with a smile and a vague invitation that they should have coffee "sometime."

Both of them knew they wouldn't be grabbing a coffee anytime soon. It was small talk. But it didn't bother Sara. She liked living here. Liked knowing that if she walked down the high street, she'd bump into at least six people she knew.

She slipped her arm through Patrick's. "Why does she always look at you as if she wants to sweep you into a dark corner?"

"Because she knows I'm unavailable—" he lowered his head and kissed her briefly "—and therefore I'm a challenge."

Sara had a feeling it was more than that, but she didn't say anything. "Sadly for her I'm not letting you go anytime soon."

"Because I'm all that stands between you and Edna?"

"Of course. Why else?"

"Seems I need to up my game." His tone was light, but he gave her a searching look. "Are you going to give me the details of what happened today?"

"Yes, but not here. Too many listening ears."

He checked his watch. "Their party starts in ten minutes. We have a whole two hours to ourselves. I thought we could go wild and go and have tea and cinnamon cookies at the Bakehouse."

"I like that idea." Even after so many years together, the prospect of spending time with him always lifted her spirits. "And I need to pick up a couple of things for Ava's stocking if we have time. I'll tell the girls we're leaving."

It took another five minutes to extract themselves, and then she and Patrick emerged onto the high street.

The cold air slid across her skin, and Sara shivered and buttoned up her coat. "It's freezing."

"Yes. More snow coming, I think." He took off his scarf and

wrapped it around her neck. "So where did Imogen go when she ran off earlier?"

"I'm not sure, but she somehow ended up with Miles and Ralph."

"Ralph? Who is Ralph?" Patrick frowned. "Oh—you mean Jim's dog?"

"Yes. His sister can't cope anymore, so Miles is taking him. But for some reason Imogen was with Miles too."

They strolled along the high street, dodging families and Christmas shoppers.

"You think he picked her up when she was out walking?"

"I'm assuming so. Although why would Imogen climb into a car with a strange man?" Sara hated the idea of that almost as much as she hated the idea of Imogen wandering on her own, upset.

"If she's been living with Tina, she's probably pretty street-smart."

"Yes. She's tough." Sara thought about the way Imogen had confronted them. "Anyway, I'm glad they bumped into each other, however it happened. And she has bonded with Ralph too, so that's good."

"You don't think she's going to drive back to London?"

"No. We had a long talk. Mum told her everything. She didn't know any of it, Patrick. Tina had told her so many lies." She stopped walking. "She didn't remember me. She didn't remember how much I loved her, or that we were almost insepa-rable for the first four years of her life."

He hugged her tightly. "But she's going to get to know you now." He eased her away from him and cupped her face in his hands. "You're upset, aren't you? Maybe the café isn't such a great idea. Do you want privacy? We can go and sit in the car, or buy a coffee and drink it by the river?"

The river wound its way through the middle of the village and was a favorite place to walk during the summer months.

"I'm not really upset. Just a bit emotional. The café will be fine." She needed the warmth. Needed the familiar buzz of the village. But most of all she needed him. "We'll try and grab a table away from everyone if that's possible."

They were lucky and managed to get the best table in the café, nestled on its own in the curve of the window overlooking the high street. The street outside was dusted in snow, and she was transported back to childhood and all the times she and her mother had come to the same café for a treat. She'd treasured that time together, the moments of calm away from the drama created by her sister.

Sara took off her coat and settled herself in the seat by the window while Patrick went to order.

He returned moments later with two mugs of tea and a thick slice of cake.

He sat opposite her, his wide shoulders effectively blocking her from view.

"Perhaps it's not such a great surprise that Imogen didn't remember you." He put a mug of tea in front of her. "She was only four when Tina took her."

"Yes." Sara curved her hands around the mug. "The funny thing is she remembered Bunny."

Patrick smiled. "I was scared it was going to fall apart when I retrieved it from the back of the drawer. That thing is practically an antique. It was clever of you to think of giving it to her. How is your mother? It must have been a pretty horrible day for her too."

"It was difficult." Sara stared into her mug. "I've always had a bad feeling about her being in touch with Imogen, as you know, but listening to her tell the whole story I realized what an impossible situation it was. When would have been the right time to tell her the truth? Sometimes things just aren't that clear-cut, and this certainly wasn't. But now she knows, and although it has been a horrible, hideous day, I feel relieved and I think Mum does too. No more secrets."

"You look exhausted. You need to eat something." Patrick pushed the cake toward her. "It can't have been easy for Imogen, either, discovering that her mother has been lying for all those years. How did she react? Did she believe you?"

"Yes." Sara took a sip of tea. "I expected her to argue and become defensive, but she didn't. She had an odd look on her face. It was almost as if she wasn't surprised by the fact her mother had lied."

"Maybe she wasn't. Still, she must have been very upset."

"She was very upset earlier, which was why she stormed out. But that was partly shock, of course. She saw photographs of Tina and recognized her. Not the best way to discover the truth. We were lucky she ended up with Miles. And Ralph." She gave a half smile as she thought about it. "You should have seen them. She held on to Ralph the whole time she was listening to the story. Didn't let go of him once. And he seemed completely besotted with her."

Patrick smiled. "Sounds as if Ralph is a bit of a hero."

"Yes. And Miles was brilliant. He asked her if she'd mind taking care of Ralph for a few days while he gets things sorted in the barn. He said he wasn't ready for a new dog."

Patrick lifted an eyebrow. "The guy's a vet. How much more ready can he be?"

"Well, exactly. But he wasn't doing it for himself. He was doing it for Imogen," Sara said softly. "I think he could see how much comfort that dog was giving her."

"Miles is a good guy. Now eat." Patrick picked up the fork and speared some cake. He held it out to her. "You missed lunch."

She leaned forward and ate the cake he offered. "Mmm. That's good." She took the fork from him and ate half the cake, then pushed the plate back toward him. "You have the rest."

"I'd rather you ate it."

"I've had enough. I'm not that hungry."

He watched her for a moment. "You've told me a lot about Imogen. Now tell me about you."

"What about me?"

"How do you feel about the whole thing? I know how much you hate talking about it."

"I do, and that's the funny thing. It was difficult of course, but not as difficult as I thought it would be." She paused. "I've spent so much of my life deliberately not giving it space in my life, running away from it, ignoring it. Then I was finally forced to confront it, and I didn't feel anywhere near as bad as I thought I would. Talking it through with Imogen was almost freeing. As if it was the end of a chapter. Does that make any sense?"

"Yes. And it sounds good."

Sara took a sip of tea. "I love my life. The life we have built together. And it feels as if Imogen might become part of it. A positive part, rather than the part I'm constantly trying not to look at."

"And Tina?"

Sara put her mug down. "I used to feel so bad that I wasn't close to my sister. It felt unnatural somehow. I even blamed myself for some of it. Was I needy? Did I demand too much of my parents' attention? Was it my fault that she was jealous?"

He sighed. "Sara—"

"I know! But even when you know it's not your fault, you can still think it. But today when my mother was telling Imogen all of it, I didn't think any of those things. At some point over the years I've stopped thinking of Tina as my sister. Or maybe I've lost that idealistic belief that sisters should be close. I don't know when that happened. The people I love, the people I'm close to, aren't my sister. And that's okay."

"You may not be close to your sister, but you have friends who are as close as family."

"Yes." She thought about her exchange with Paul earlier and how much she was looking forward to catching up with them all over the holidays. She knew that in a crisis, she could call on any one of them and they'd drop everything and come to her. And she would do the same for them. She'd come a long way. Further than she'd ever acknowledged. "And now I have a niece. And the girls will have a cousin." She watched as he finished off the cake. "Imogen is coming with us tomorrow. Is that okay with you? I probably should have checked before I invited her. It was an impulse."

"It was a good impulse." He grinned. "Providing we're not too much for her. If she's never had experience of family, our Christmas tree trip might be a bit of a shock to the system. We'll have to try and rein Ava in so she doesn't scare Imogen back to London."

"I think Ava may break the ice."

"And there will be actual ice if it doesn't stop snowing." Patrick glanced out of the window. "Can you believe we might have a white Christmas? The kids would love that."

"The kids?" She tilted her head and looked at her husband. "You wouldn't like it at all, of course."

"Me? No. Total pain. I can't stand snowmen and snowballs, sledding and all those other fun—I mean terrible things." He narrowed his eyes and a faint smile played around his mouth. "When did we last have a snowball fight?"

"I'm too old to have a snowball fight." She leaned forward. "I forgot to tell you—Miles and Ralph are also joining us tomorrow."

"Miles? That's interesting. Is there something going on do you think?"

"I don't know. He hasn't been involved with anyone since Zara, and he only just met Imogen. But he seemed almost protective."

"Perhaps he was just being kind."

"Maybe." It had seemed a little more than that to her. "He's never come with us to get a tree before. Lissa always chooses his tree and decorates it. She complains that he doesn't know a fir from a fern."

Patrick laughed. "He's not the only one. Do you think Imogen talked to him? Told him everything?"

"I don't know. I don't know her well enough to guess. Miles is a pretty good listener, so maybe. Although I get the sense Imogen is very independent and used to surviving on her own. Either way, he's coming along tomorrow."

Patrick sat back in his chair. "Whatever else, it promises to be an interesting day. And hopefully it will be a chance to get to know Imogen better."

"I hope so." There had been a time when she'd known everything there was to know about Imogen. She'd been able to interpret every cry and every laugh. But now Imogen was an adult, and Sara hadn't been part of her life for a long time. She'd had experiences Sara knew nothing about. She had hopes and dreams that she'd never shared with Sara.

She would need to get to know her all over again.

18

Imogen

"I don't normally share a bed with someone just a few hours after I met them, but you're just so easy to talk to. I've never met anyone I connected with so quickly. It's as if you know exactly how I'm thinking and feeling. I am so, so glad I met you right in my moment of need." Imogen blew her nose and snuggled under the duvet. She'd lit the fire in the bedroom and it glowed cheerily in the semi darkness. She could have put the light on, but it was easier to talk in the dark.

She hadn't pulled the curtains, and she could see the soft fall of snowflakes drifting white and silver against the midnight blue sky.

"I'm sorry to go on and on about it, but it's been a bit of an upsetting day, that's all. Talking about it helps me process it. Is that okay? The truth is I feel betrayed. How could my mother have lied about her family? I want to believe there has been some horrible mistake, but I know there hasn't been. And I feel so mixed-up about it. Part of me is really angry, because she basically made the decision to deprive us both of family. And part of me is sad because although I've done okay, and actually I'm pretty proud of who I am and what I've achieved, it has been hard—" Her voice cracked and she felt him press closer to her. She appreciated the silent comfort. "There have been times when it has been *really* hard, and knowing now that it didn't have to be that way is really tough to deal with. I could have had Dorothy and Sara in my life the whole time. Family. I almost can't think about that because it's too upsetting. Why did she do it? Don't bother answering that. I don't understand my mother, so I certainly don't expect you to. But it's outrageous, don't you think?"

Also mystifying, because unless there was some side to Dorothy and Sara that she wasn't seeing, they were good people. Why on earth wouldn't her mother want them in her life? It made no sense at all.

They'd seemed so nervous when they were talking to her, and she knew she was partly to blame for that, because she'd yelled at them when she'd seen the photo. The whole thing had been such a shock.

But once she'd calmed down and listened to what they had to say, she'd known instinctively that they were telling the truth. And it wasn't all instinct. Some of it was experience. She knew her mother lied when it suited her. She'd lied to Imogen on plenty of occasions. It just had never occurred to her before that her mother would have lied about *this*.

"Also it doesn't make a lot of sense. In that last horrible meeting, the one that resulted in me almost losing my job, she told me I was the worst thing that had ever happened in her life." Saying the words aloud was actually harder than she would have imagined. "But if that's true, then why wouldn't she have jumped at the chance to leave me with my grandmother? That would have been the perfect solution, wouldn't it?"

She saw nothing but sympathy in his eyes and pulled him closer.

"You're a brilliant listener. Most people judge, or you know they're just going to go and gossip about what you've told them, but you listen and sympathize. You really care, I can tell." She looked at him and met his gaze. "I shouldn't be letting you sleep in my bed, I know that. There are probably going to be consequences, but I don't care. Being with you makes me feel better, and for now that's all that matters. And how can something that feels so right possibly be wrong?"

Her phone rang and she reached for it and checked the number. "It's Miles. I'd better take this. Do not make a sound!"

Ralph thumped his tail on the bed and put his paw on her arm.

"Hi, Miles, are you okay? How is the sick cow?"

"He's going to be fine, but the whole thing took longer than I thought it would." His voice sounded distant and she could tell he was driving. "I assume you've already gone to bed. I hope I didn't wake you."

"No. I was just lying here thinking about today."

"I can imagine. That's why I called, really. Wanted to check you're okay. You had a difficult day."

"I'm fine." She put her hand on Ralph's head.

"You're sure?"

She was touched that he cared. The truth was he was almost as easy to talk to as his dog. "Yes. It's been great having Ralph here. He's a real distraction. Thanks for letting me borrow him."

"You did me a favor. I couldn't take him on my call. I was going to pick him up on my way home, but is it too late?"

She felt something close to panic. No way did she want to lose Ralph. Not tonight. "I've already settled him down for the night, so why don't you just come here tomorrow for our Christmas tree trip and pick him up then. It seems a shame to disturb him."

"Are you sure that's okay?"

"It's fine." It was a relief to know Ralph was staying. "Come early if you like and I'll cook you breakfast."

"Sounds good. And thanks, Imogen."

"You're welcome."

"One thing—whatever you do, don't let him sleep on the bed."

Imogen stroked Ralph, who was very much awake on the bed. "Why would I do a thing like that?"

"I'm sure you wouldn't. I only mentioned it because if he thinks that's okay he will try and sleep in *my* bed, and that's not going to happen. Nothing is guaranteed to stifle your sex life as a dog in the bed."

She laughed, but part of her was curious. "Your girlfriend doesn't like animals?"

"Currently single because, in fact, it turned out that my last girlfriend did *not* particularly like animals. She especially didn't like the fact they had a tendency to get ill in the middle of the night, resulting in my frequent absences. How about you?"

His willingness to share personal information so freely made her feel better about the fact he already knew more about her than anyone else.

"Me?" She pulled Ralph closer. "I like animals."

He laughed. "Sleep well, Imogen. I'll see you in the morning."

"I'm looking forward to it."

And she was. Who would have thought she could actually have smiled after the day she'd had? It was mostly down to Ralph, of course. Nothing to do with Miles, even if he did have kind eyes and a good sense of humor.

Oh, who was she kidding?

Grinning, she put her phone back on charge and picked up the herbal tea she'd made before coming up to bed.

"You're not supposed to sleep in the bed, but surely one night isn't going to hurt. Don't tell him, will you?"

Ralph thumped his tail and snuggled down with his head on his paws.

"I did try and get you to sleep in your basket. But that didn't really work out, did it?"

She'd put his basket under the window in her bedroom so she could see him. He'd sat in it for less than a minute, looking hurt and sorry for himself, before joining her on the bed. He'd tried to do it stealthily, perhaps hoping she wouldn't notice, but stealth and bouncy retrievers didn't really go together, and his efforts had made her smile.

She knew she probably should have sent him back to his basket, but she'd been feeling horrible after the conversation with Dorothy and Sara, and she'd found the warmth of his solid body unbelievably reassuring. No wonder all her colleagues were crazy about their dogs. She'd had no idea a dog could be such a perfect companion.

She took a few photos of him, just so that she had something to remember him by when she was back in London.

She didn't want to think about being back in London. Nor did she want to think about her mother. She was so tired of it all.

She turned her head and looked at the stuffed bunny Sara had given her, now on her nightstand.

As ridiculous as it sounded, that bunny felt like a connection between the past and the present.

Ralph whined, and she shifted her attention from bunny to dog.

"We should get some sleep. Christmas tree hunting tomorrow." And she already felt nervous about it. They might be her family, but she didn't really know these people and they didn't know her. What if they didn't like her? There were no rules that said family members had to like each other, her mother's behavior was evidence of that. "Not sure I'm looking forward to it that much to be honest, but at least you'll be there. And Miles. That should help." She put the tea down and snuggled under the covers.

Ralph had apparently decided he'd done enough listening for one night and was already asleep with no sign of guilt or regret that he was on the bed.

Imogen had no expectations of getting any sleep at all after the activities of the day, but she closed her eyes and next time she opened them it was morning and Ralph was scratching at the door.

Bleary-eyed, Imogen glanced at her phone. "I cannot believe I slept all night!"

Ralph wasn't interested in her sleep patterns. He whined, and she forced herself out of bed and pulled a sweater over the T-shirt she'd worn to bed.

"I'm going to let you out into the garden right now." She grabbed socks and followed him down the stairs into the kitchen.

The floor was warm underfoot and she opened the back door. Snow covered the trees and the garden, glinting like sugar crystals in the weak sunlight.

The cold snaked its way into the cottage, and she wished she'd taken the time to find her jeans or better still, the fleece-lined leggings that she'd packed.

She let Ralph out and pulled on socks and her fur-lined boots. Then she stood in the doorway shivering and watched Ralph investigate his new surroundings, his explorations leaving paw prints in pristine snow. The garden of the cottage was surrounded by a high wall, making it both private and safe, but still she watched Ralph carefully. He was her responsibility, and she didn't want him to come to any harm, although right now she was the one risking frostbite.

"Hurry up, Ralph!" Her teeth were chattering. "Otherwise I'm going to be greeting Miles in my nightwear."

"I have no problem with that, so don't rush on my account." Miles's voice drifted over the garden gate, and Ralph barked with delight and sped across to him.

Imogen was conscious of her bare legs and the fact that her T-shirt stopped at midthigh. The sweater she'd pulled on was almost as long. It certainly wouldn't have been her first choice of outfit for a meeting with Miles.

Why hadn't she heard the car? "You're early."

"We didn't exactly fix a time, so I can't be early." He bent to make a fuss of the dog. "Someone seems to have enjoyed his sleepover. Was he good? Did he behave himself and sleep in his basket?"

"He was perfect." She evaded the question. "We both slept late, which is why there was a bit of a rush to let him out." And she was still surprised by that. She never slept through the night, but last night she had.

"Sleeping late is good. I bet you needed it after yesterday." He straightened and scanned her bare legs. "That is a cute look."

"Ralph was desperate. Obviously, I had planned to get dressed before I saw you."

"Don't rush on my account." He gave her a slow smile and she felt that smile right down to her bones.

"If you make the coffee, I'll go and dress in something warmer."

"Probably a good idea. Christmas tree hunting definitely can't be done with bare legs." He encouraged Ralph into the house. "I'll get breakfast started."

She didn't argue.

Ten minutes later she was showered and dressed in warm clothes. Before joining Miles, she quickly straightened her bed and rumpled the blanket in Ralph's basket to make it look as if he'd slept there just in case anyone checked.

At least dogs didn't drop earrings or other personal items that might give away their presence.

She walked into the kitchen and was greeted by the delicious smells of bacon and fresh coffee. Through the windows she could see snow glistening on the trees.

"I love this room."

"I love it too. Any room that has food in it is always my favorite room." Miles was standing in front of the stove frying bacon. He'd slung his coat over the chair and rolled up the sleeves of his shirt.

As he had his back to her, Imogen allowed herself a moment to study him. She was glad Janie wasn't around. *Smoking hot*, she would have said, and Imogen would have struggled to disagree, but she knew the attraction went much deeper than that. He was strong and capable and, most important of all, kind.

"Can I help?"

"Everything is in hand. I was going to make you a healthy bowl of oats, but then I spotted the bacon Dorothy left in your fridge. You won't have tasted anything like this. Organic, grass-fed—" He forked a few crispy strands onto slices of bread and put the plate in front of her. "Try it. And don't say you're not hungry because Christmas tree hunting is hard work, particularly when it involves Ava. That girl knows what she wants and she is not going to stop until she finds it. This could be the last meal you have for a while. This trip could take until Christmas Eve, so you need fuel."

"She seems like a real character." She sat down and bit into the sandwich. "Oh that's delicious—"

"Isn't it?" He sat down next to her, and Ralph settled himself by Imogen's chair.

There was something strangely intimate about sitting here together sharing breakfast. It should have felt uncomfortable, but oddly enough it didn't.

He picked up his mug and then put it down again. "You're looking at me in a funny way. What's wrong?"

She put her sandwich down. "I'm thinking that I don't do this."

"Eat bacon? I know it's not something one is supposed to do often, but moderation in all things I always say. Particularly when I'm justifying something I want to do."

"Not the bacon. You. This. Breakfast."

"You don't eat breakfast? That's a shocking habit, Imogen." He gave her a reproving look. "It's the most important meal of the day."

She smiled because she knew he was deliberately misunderstanding her.

"I mean having breakfast with a man I met just the day before."

"Yes, well, it was a pretty intense day. And now we share custody of a dog—" he glanced at Ralph "—so that brings us together."

Her heart gave a little skip. "We're going to have him every other night and every other weekend?"

"That is yet to be worked out, but I'm hoping we can keep the lawyers out of it." He took a mouthful of coffee. "How's the bacon sandwich?"

"Incredible. I suppose you make breakfast for women all the time."

"Hardly ever. I don't even make it for myself that often."

"So what did I do to deserve this?"

He put his mug down. "I thought you needed fuel for the trip ahead. Also company, because I didn't want you sitting here all alone eating a lonely bowl of cereal and worrying about whether the day is going to be awkward or not."

And that, of course, was exactly what she would have been doing.

"That's why you arrived early? For moral support?" She

couldn't forget the fact that he'd stayed with her the day before, when there were probably a hundred other things he could have been doing with what seemed to be a rare day off. "You're probably thinking I'm the most high-maintenance woman you've ever met."

"No." He held her gaze. "But you're definitely the bravest person I've ever met."

She swallowed. "Me?"

"Yes. When I stopped my car next to you yesterday you were shocked and upset—presumably because you'd just found out that Dorothy was your grandmother—and the last thing you wanted was company. You didn't want to get in my car, but then you saw Ralph and you climbed in so that you could help."

"That doesn't make me brave. It makes me a sucker for a dog in need."

"Maybe it's both. But when we'd finished sorting out Ralph, you could have gone home, back to London, but you agreed to hear what Dorothy and Sara had to say, and none of that made easy listening. I kept thinking that if that was me, I probably would have walked out because it would have felt like too much, but you sat there and let them say what they needed to say. Not only that, but you accepted what they said as the truth when it would have been easier to deny the whole thing. Not easy to deal with something that difficult."

She thought back to the day before.

There had been a moment, after Miles had told her his version of the story, when she almost had left.

"Leaving would have been the easy decision. No difficult conversations." But she'd known that if she did that, if she walked away and blamed her family for everything that had happened, she'd be denying the truth. She'd be turning herself into a victim like her mother. She'd stay locked in the past, instead of moving forward. It would make her life feel less real, and after embracing fake for so long, she badly needed her life to feel real.

She'd thought about what she'd said to her mother in the hospital that day.

You choose to blame me for everything instead of taking responsibility for your own bad choices.

"I knew that however hard it was, I needed to hear their side of the story. Give them a chance to explain."

He nodded and took another bite of sandwich. "So, as I said, brave."

"Having Ralph there was good." She hesitated. "And having him there meant you stayed too, and that also helped."

"I didn't stay because of Ralph."

She felt her heart thud a little harder. "Miles—"

"And even after that conversation, you could have left. You could have told them that you needed time to digest everything they'd told you, but you didn't. Sara invited you to join them and you could have said no, but you didn't." He finished his coffee. "I'm guessing today is going to be a bit overwhelming for you."

She opened her mouth to issue a denial, but instead found herself telling the truth. "I'm a bit nervous, that's true. Scared." She expected him to be flippant, or make another joke, but his gaze was serious.

"What scares you the most?"

Where to start? "I suppose the fact that they don't know me. What if they don't like me? My mother obviously hurt them a great deal, and I feel responsible."

He frowned. "Imogen—"

"I know that's illogical, but sometimes it's possible to feel things even if you know it's not logical."

"I can tell you without a doubt that however nervous you are, Dorothy and Sara are equally nervous, if not more so."

"More? That's not possible."

"They lost you," he said softly. "They're probably terrified of losing you again."

Was that what they'd thought when she'd walked out the day before? That they'd lost her? "They lost me because of my mother. That's not going to happen again."

"Maybe not in the same way, but see it from their point of view—" He paused. "You're an independent woman with a busy life. Maybe you don't have room in that life for family. Maybe you'll enjoy a few weeks at Holly Cottage, share a few meals with them and then take off back to London and send a Christmas card every year. I know plenty of families who barely see each other from year to year."

She felt something shift inside her. "That's not going to happen. And I've never sent Christmas cards, so I don't suppose I'll start now."

"But they don't know that. It must have been very hard for Dorothy to work with you for so long and not tell you who she was. I'm guessing that was partly because she was afraid it might all blow up and she'd lose you."

She'd been angry that Dorothy hadn't told her the truth right away, but she could see now that it wasn't that simple. "I'm glad in a way that I got to know her a little bit before I found out."

"And now you're going to get to know her properly." He finished his coffee. "All right, let's make a deal. If you want to bail at any point the code word is—" he paused for a moment "—fir tree."

"Code word?"

"Yes. If it's all too much, you say the word and I'll make an excuse and we'll leave."

She was touched. "You'd do that for me?"

"Of course. Just say the word."

She smiled. "Fir tree is two words. Also, I assume we're going to be looking at a lot of fir trees so maybe we should pick something different."

"Good point. I'm willing to admit that code words might not be my strength. You choose."

She probably should have said that there was no need for a code word, but she actually liked the idea of being able to escape if she felt the need. "How about we say we're going to visit Valerie, to put her mind at rest about Ralph?"

"Great idea. An even better idea would be to *actually* visit Valerie. She'd like to meet you, I'm sure. And it will make her feel better to see how happy Ralph is. Right. That's agreed. If you say 'don't we need to visit Valerie?' I'll know I need to do a rapid exit." He paused. "But you're going to be fine, Imogen."

"I hope you're right." She looked at Ralph. "I'm glad he's going to be there."

"Hey, I'll be there too. And I'll be more support than Ralph."

"You think?" She tried to make light of it. "Ralph offers a lot of support. He's very emotionally intuitive."

Miles grinned. "No, that's just him knowing you're the last person who fed him."

Flustered by his smile, she stood up and cleared both plates. "Thanks for breakfast. I suppose we should leave? How long will it take to get there?"

"About half an hour if the roads aren't too bad. It's a pretty place."

"Sounds great." Part of her wished she could just spend the day here, with Miles and Ralph. Maybe go for a walk in the country (dressed appropriately this time, of course, and also with someone who hopefully knew the way), or to explore the village.

He picked up his coat and produced a lead for Ralph. "You'll like it. It's very festive."

Usually, she avoided *festive* because it made her imagine a life she was missing, but today she was actually stepping into that life. How many times had she imagined what it must be like to choose a tree with family? Many times, and today she was going to do it.

"I've never done Christmassy things before. I'm looking forward to it."

She intended to embrace it. Even if it turned out that they just didn't have anything in common, that it was too hard to forge a relationship when so much lay between them, she should make the most of this moment.

She'd always wanted a family and it turned out she'd had one all along, so was she really going to turn down the chance to get to know them just because she was nervous of the outcome?

No, she wasn't.

And in the end it was much easier than she'd predicted, mostly because of Ava.

"The first rule of finding a tree is that it has to be big." Ava held tightly to Imogen's hand and tugged her from tree to tree. She was wearing a pink padded jacket and green boots and her ponytail poked out from under her warm hat. "I like the ones that smell. Do you like the ones that smell?"

"I don't know. I'm relying on you to advise me."

"What's *advise*?"

"It means you tell me what you think I should do."

"Oh." Ava brightened. "I can definitely do that."

"She definitely can," Iris said as she walked past with her hand in Patrick's. "Another word for it would be *bossy*."

"I'm not bossy. Oh, *look*!"

Imogen almost lost her balance as Ava suddenly hauled her toward a tree on their right.

"Ava—" Sara reached out and rescued the scarf that was threatening to abandon contact with Ava's neck "—you can't just drag Imogen everywhere."

"Why not? We're having fun."

"I know you're having fun and that's great," Sara said, "but maybe have fun a little more gently."

Watching Sara interact with her children brought a lump to Imogen's throat. She was so warm, loving and patient. She would never send a child away if she'd had a bad dream.

We tried to put you in your own room when you turned eighteen months, but you just wanted to sleep in the bed with Sara.

What would her life have been like if her mother hadn't taken her away?

She snapped herself out of that thought. What was the point in going there? All they had was now, and hopefully the future. The past was gone, and she wasn't going to let it contaminate the present.

But she wondered, maybe, if Sara's and Dorothy's warmth and strong sense of family had somehow seeped into her, even though she had no memories of it. Were those early days of security and safety part of the reason she had remained so steadfastly loyal to her mother?

The question vanished from her head as her arm was almost pulled from its socket by Ava.

"This one!" Ava didn't like being reined in.

"Ava!" Sara sounded exasperated. "Stop pulling Imogen."

"I wasn't *exactly* pulling her. It's just that I wanted her to walk faster. I like her, Mummy."

"I know you do. We all like her, but we don't want her to fall on her bottom on the ice, otherwise she won't like us! And she won't want to come with us next time." Sara secured the scarf and gave Imogen an apologetic smile. "She is so excited. So is Iris. We all are, to be honest. I hope you're not finding us too overwhelming."

We all like her.

"It's wonderful." She realized that Sara was as nervous as she was, and she was grateful to Ava, who was so open and accepting and blissfully unaware of the potential for awkwardness. Ava's total absence of emotional caution somehow made the whole situation easier. "You do this every year?"

"Yes. It's one of our favorite family traditions. I did it with my parents, and so did Patrick, so I suppose it was a natural thing to repeat it with our own children. It's something we all look forward to."

Bored with listening to adult conversation, Ava skipped ahead to take a look at another tree.

Family tradition.

Imogen wanted to ask if her mother had done it too. If she'd joined in the Christmas tree trip, but she didn't want to risk killing the mood by mentioning her.

"Tina never joined us," Sara said softly. "She hated family trips. She was happier spending time with her friends."

Imogen wondered how she'd known what she was thinking. "That must have been hard on you all."

Sara shrugged, her gaze fixed on Ava. "It's life, isn't it? You make the most of the parts that are right, and do what you can about the parts that aren't so great. I suppose we got used to not having her with us for things like this. We accepted it." She glanced at Imogen. "And that probably made things worse. No one forced her to join us, but by not joining us it just deepened the divisions. Maybe we should have tried harder."

The others had strolled ahead, and Imogen saw Patrick lift Ava onto his shoulders so that she could get a better look at the trees.

Miles was talking to Iris, who was holding tightly to Ralph's lead.

It was a perfect family scene, but not in a million years could she picture her mother here.

"You can't make someone do what they don't want to do."

"No." Sara smiled. "That is very true. I remind myself of that every day when I struggle to get Ava to bed."

"The girls are close."

"Yes. And obviously Patrick and I hope they always will be.

We encourage them to look out for each other and be thoughtful, but the truth is their affection is genuine and natural."

Imogen had always thought it would be nice to have had a sibling, but she found herself wondering how it must feel to have a sibling who wanted nothing to do with you.

Parts of her life hadn't been easy, but that was true of Sara too. And also Dorothy.

"Would you tell me a little about your childhood?" Sara was hesitant. "I've lain awake at nights wondering where you were and if you were okay. Was it bad, Imogen?"

Bad.

How was she supposed to answer that? Her instinct was to lie. To put a gloss on it. She was used to disguising her past. To hiding it. To inventing a life that made her fit in and made others comfortable.

But there was no point in doing that now. This was Sara, and Sara knew Tina. There was no need for fake dogs or fake boyfriends or a fake family. Sara was her real family, and she already knew much of the truth.

"Sometimes it was difficult. Tina didn't want to be a mother, so she wasn't very hands-on or involved—" She was surprised how good it felt not to have to pretend or put on an act. To just tell the truth and be who she was for a change. Acknowledge her life instead of spinning a fictional version.

"I noticed yesterday that you called her Tina. Why?"

"She insisted on it. Firstly, I think it meant she could pretend she wasn't a mother, and secondly because she liked to present herself as a young, single person with no ties."

It was where she'd first learned that it was possible to invent a life. After all, wasn't that what Tina had done?

Sara listened. "What happened to the guy she was with the last time we saw you?"

"Terry." Imogen had good memories of Terry. "He was kind. He used to read to me. But they weren't happy together.

I was too young to understand the detail, but they had a lot of fights and eventually he left." And she hadn't blamed him. She remembered wishing that she could have left too. "They divorced. She didn't have a long relationship after that. Men came and went."

"Did you stay in touch with Terry?"

"He moved abroad. He sent the odd postcard, but that didn't last long. He wasn't really the type to write letters. And I suppose it was awkward. He built a new life, and I wasn't part of that."

"It must have been difficult for you."

"Sometimes." There was plenty she could have told Sara, but how was that going to help? Sara was trying to build a bridge between them, not probing for dark details. Maybe she'd talk about it one day, but this wasn't the time. "It wasn't so bad. It made me self-reliant and that's a good thing." She made a point of always trying to find the positive. Focus on the things she could influence. Not because she was some ridiculously naive optimist, but because it helped. If you turned the spotlight onto the good, if you were lucky the dark stuff faded into the background.

"You've done so well," Sara said. "You should be proud of yourself. Do you have anyone special in your life?"

"No." Imogen stared at the trees, at the snow and the peek of ice blue in the sky. "My fault. I'm not that good at getting close to people." Was she even capable of it? She'd never had a relationship where she was truly herself. She showed people what she wanted them to see, and she was miserly with the information she shared. She'd learned to rely on herself from an early age and she'd spent her life protecting herself, careful not to make herself vulnerable. Was she able to lower her guard sufficiently to get close to someone?

Her gaze slid to Miles, who was listening intently to Ava. She thought about how easily she'd talked to him the day before, and how comfortable she'd felt with him when he'd cooked her breakfast earlier. He already knew more about her than anyone else in her life.

And that made her feel nervous, as if she'd been wearing a costume that had suddenly been stripped away from her.

Sara gave her arm a squeeze and leaned closer so that only Imogen could hear her. "You can trust him."

"Oh!" Was she that transparent? She felt herself blush. "I wasn't— I mean—"

"I know. I'm just saying he's fantastic, in case you were wondering." It was Sara's turn to look uncomfortable. "Sorry. I shouldn't have said anything."

"It's fine." Imogen looked at her. "I'm not used to having conversations like this, that's all."

"Then it's probably good to practice on someone like me, so that when it gets to someone important, you're already an expert."

"You're important."

"But I'm family," Sara said. "You can say anything to me. There is no wrong thing. You don't have to watch your words or protect yourself."

"Family." The word felt unfamiliar on her lips. "I suppose I haven't really got used to the idea yet."

"I know. It feels strange, doesn't it? Being related and yet barely knowing each other. I suppose the answer is just to relax and spend time in each other's company and not overthink it. And Christmas is a great time for that, of course." Sara's voice softened. "But I want you to know that you can talk to me. About anything, at any time. I'm here for you, Imogen. It's important to me that you know that. Even when you're back in London. If you want to talk to someone, just pick up the phone."

No one had ever said anything like that to her before. Never offered that level of support. And she knew Sara was genuine.

She'd seen the way she was with the girls, with Patrick and with Dorothy. Even the fact that she'd come to talk to Imogen, given how badly Tina had upset her, was a measure of how loyal she was.

Tears scalded her eyes. "Thank you."

"I mean it. This must be so difficult for you, and it's important that you can talk to someone you trust, and you can trust me. I wish I'd been there for you through your whole life—your wise old aunt, giving you advice you probably didn't want. Knitting you sweaters that didn't fit." Sara grinned. "Just kidding. I can't knit to save my life so you're safe. No lumpy Santa sweaters from me this Christmas, I promise."

Despite the emotion, Imogen laughed too. She thought about all the difficult times she'd dealt with on her own. *She could have called Sara.* "There were definitely occasions when a wise old aunt would have been helpful."

She thought about the last thing her mother had said to her.

Go and live out your happy family fantasy somewhere else.

If she'd known, she could have done that.

"I feel angry." The words tumbled out, surprising her. "Angry that she lied. And I feel guilty about that."

"I don't think you have any reason to feel guilty. I'm angry too," Sara said. "And I'm sure my mother—your grandmother—feels the same way, although she might not admit it. She is more generous and forgiving than I am, but maybe that's because she is Tina's mother. Maybe it's hard to give up on a child and accept them for who they are. I don't know."

"I don't know either. And I don't understand why she did what she did."

"I'm no psychologist, but I think she always felt inadequate somehow. As if she didn't fit." Sara watched as Miles lifted Ava onto his shoulders. "Will you talk to her about it?"

"I don't know. Our last encounter wasn't great." It was an

understatement, but she didn't intend to share the details of that, particularly not today. "I'll think about it."

Sara slid her arm through Imogen's. "I can't do anything about the past, but I'm here now. Whatever may have gone before, we're family, Imogen, and we're part of your life now. Remember that."

Family. The word made her dizzy.

Her mother considered it a fantasy, and yet standing here with Sara by her side, it felt real for the first time.

"Come on," Ava yelled at them across the frozen landscape, and Sara laughed.

"You may yet live to wish you hadn't rediscovered your family."

"That's not going to happen."

"We'd better focus on the tree or we'll be told off by my exceptionally bossy daughter. We have all the time in the world to catch up. Also Ralph is watching you anxiously. Let's enjoy our day."

Imogen's phone rang at that moment and she pulled it out of her pocket and checked the number.

Tina.

No way. The happiness that had filled her a moment earlier rushed out of her like air from a punctured balloon.

Why was she calling? After everything that had happened the last time they'd met, all those awful things she'd said, why would she want to speak to Imogen?

She stared at the screen and felt Sara's gaze on her.

"Is everything okay?"

"Yes." Imogen rejected the call and put the phone back in her pocket. "It's just work."

"Right." Sara gave her a long look, and Imogen felt a pressure in her chest.

"Actually, it wasn't work. It was Tina. And I have no idea why she is calling. The last time we met she virtually told me she didn't want anything more to do with me, so something must have happened. She probably needs money." The moment she said the words, she felt Sara's shock.

"Oh, Imogen—" Sara stepped a little closer. "Does this happen often? Her calling you for money?"

"It happens. Don't worry, I don't give her money anymore, but I do sometimes pay her rent or pay for repairs." She waited for Sara to tell her what a fool she was, but she didn't.

"She knows just how to manipulate, doesn't she? She behaves badly, but somehow you're the one left feeling awful."

"That's it exactly." And the fact that Sara knew how she felt made it all a little easier. For the first time in her life she felt as if she wasn't alone with it.

"Do you want to talk to her? We can give you privacy." Sara hesitated. "Or I could talk to her for you if you prefer."

Imogen looked at Sara. "You'd do that?"

"If it would help you, yes, although I can't guarantee to be as generous as you are. I might say something rude and regrettable, but that wouldn't be your responsibility."

Despite everything, Imogen smiled because she simply couldn't picture Sara being rude to anyone.

She was about to say as much, but then her phone rang again.

Her gaze met Sara's briefly, and then she turned her attention back to her phone and switched it off.

There were plenty of things she couldn't change and couldn't control, but she could control whether or not she spoke to her mother.

"This is my first family trip to buy a Christmas tree. I'm not going to let her spoil that."

Sara studied her for a moment and then nodded. "Good decision. So let's do it. Let's choose a Christmas tree. I should brief you on the family rules and tradition. You choose a tree that is far too big for the space. Completely impractical. And then you let Patrick point that out."

"And then what?" She pushed back against the dark cloud that had threatened to engulf her. "You back down?"

Sara smiled. "What do you think?"

"I think that against the three of you the man doesn't stand a chance."

"You are so right."

They walked toward Ava, and Imogen reflected on how much easier a problem was to handle when you had someone you could share it with.

At some point she'd have to think about how she was going to deal with her mother, but right now she was surrounded by snow and laughter and Ava's excitement, and she didn't want to waste a moment of this experience thinking about her mother, or the past.

It could all wait.

19

Dorothy

She spent all day preparing, determined that the evening was going to be perfect.

They'd invited her to join them on the Christmas tree trip but she'd declined, partly because she already had three trees for the house and wanted to focus on the evening ahead, but also because she wanted to give Imogen and Sara time together.

She'd thought it would be good for them, and perhaps a little easier and less overwhelming for Imogen than dealing with all of them at once, but then she'd had moments during the day when she'd questioned that decision. Sara hadn't asked for any of this, and it was only because of Dorothy that she'd been forced to confront it all again. How was she handling it?

The trip to choose a Christmas tree was one of Sara's favorite days of the year. What if having Imogen there had spoiled that for her daughter?

She had to stop herself messaging Sara to check everything was all right and reminded herself that Patrick and Miles were both there, and the girls. It was hard for anything to be too awkward or serious when Ava and Iris were involved.

Maybe it would go well, but she was careful to keep her expectations in check. She knew she had a tendency to romanticize family life, even now after everything that had happened. It was one of the reasons she still blamed herself for much of what had happened. A part of her still believed that if she'd done things differently, the outcome might have been different. But would it? Maybe Sara was right. It was fanciful to think she had the ability to control everything that happened. At some point maybe a parent just had to accept that you could raise a child in a certain way, but in the end their choices were their own and you had no control over that.

Instead of blaming yourself, you should try acceptance.

Sara's words had settled in her brain.

She'd spent so much time regretting what she'd said to Tina, the way she'd dealt with it, and blaming herself for all that had happened. And by taking the blame, she'd essentially excused Tina, which she knew Sara found frustrating.

Dorothy stared out of the kitchen window, watching as Benson ventured out of the barn to explore his snow-covered field.

Sara was right. It was Tina who had made the choices. The choice to leave Imogen, the choice to return and take Imogen with her, the choice to exclude her family from her life.

Perhaps acceptance was the right way to go, but how were you supposed to achieve that?

At some point maybe you just had to acknowledge that it was possible to love your child with every fiber of your being, but dislike their behavior and their choices.

Exhausted with worrying about it all, she wrapped up warm and went out to feed a few treats to Benson and the other alpacas. The fields were coated with white, snow crystals gleaming as they caught the sunlight. The beauty of it took her breath away, although it was hard to breathe at all in the bitter cold.

And really she shouldn't be out here talking to Benson when there was so much to be done indoors. She should be focusing on the present, not the past.

Feeling a little better for the fresh air and five minutes with her animals, she returned to the house and busied herself in the kitchen.

An hour later she'd made a rich winter casserole, and delicious smells wafted through the kitchen.

As it was a special dinner, she laid the table in the dining room and took extra care over the presentation. Candles flickered on surfaces and the tree she'd chosen a few days before took pride of place in the curve of the window. She stored the decorations carefully from one year to the next and all of them were precious to her. Everything she hung on the tree came with a memory.

This was where she'd serve Christmas lunch, she decided.

When Phillip had been alive, they'd loved to entertain. Dorothy had brought together people from the village and they'd enjoyed noisy evenings full of laughter and conversation. After he'd died, the idea of doing the same things alone that they'd done together held no appeal for her. She still cooked and enjoyed it, but her gatherings were almost always informal and often impromptu.

But today they had a reason to celebrate.

As a concession to Ava and Iris, they'd eat early. She could hardly believe that Imogen would be joining them at the table.

She'd barely finished her preparations when she heard the sound of car engines, then voices and a shriek of laughter from Ava.

They crowded into the house, bringing cold air, smiles and snowy boots.

And noise. So much noise. It echoed through the house and filled Dorothy's heart.

Sara and Imogen were laughing together, and Dorothy glanced at her daughter with relief but also a touch of curiosity.

Sara had so rigidly protected herself from the past that Dorothy had been worried she would hold herself back with Imogen, but that didn't seem to be the case.

"Well, at least your tree fits in the living room," she was saying to Imogen as they shrugged off coats and piled up scarves and gloves on the side. "The one the girls chose for us is too tall. Even I think that. Patrick is going to have to trim it."

Ralph chose that moment to chase Bailey into the kitchen, and Miles tried to call him back.

"Ralph. Ralph! Sorry, Dorothy," he muttered. "Why did I let myself get talked into this? Imogen? You need to call your dog."

"My dog?" Imogen hung her scarf on top of Sara's and turned to look at him, cheeks glowing. "Since when is he *my* dog?"

"Since you're the only one he will listen to."

Imogen pushed her hair back from her face. "Ralph! Come here."

Ralph rocketed toward her and screeched to a halt at her feet, a dopey look on his face.

"Sit," Imogen said, and Ralph sat, tail wagging.

"You see what I mean?" Miles shook his head in disbelief. "That's it. You're taking him back to London with you."

"Don't tempt me," Imogen said, and Ava looked crestfallen.

"I don't want Imogen to go back to London. I want her to stay here forever and ever and be my friend. Do you have a star for the top of your tree, Imogen?" She twirled on the spot, almost falling over Bailey, who wanted to be part of the fun.

"I don't have a star." Imogen reached out and steadied Ava before she could lose her balance.

"What about the other decorations?"

"I can help with that." Sara produced a box tied with a big red bow and handed it to Imogen. "A little gift."

"For me?" Imogen took it, bemused. "What is it?"

"You have to open it to see! I'll help." Ava reached for the ribbon, but Iris pulled her away.

"Be gentle! You have to let people open their own presents."

"Let's do it together." Imogen crouched down in front of Ava. "You pull the ribbon and I'll take off the paper."

Ava pulled, and the ribbon slithered to the floor, followed by the packaging.

Inside the package was a box of silver decorations. Some were plain and some had a delicate snowflake motif.

"They're gorgeous." Imogen lifted one out of its packaging and looked up at Sara. "You bought these for me?"

"I assumed you didn't have any, and you're going to need them year after year, so—" Sara gave a self-conscious shrug "—this is the beginning of your collection."

Imogen gazed at the box for a moment and then blinked and stood up. "Thank you."

"You're welcome. And you'll find it's an advantage that Miles is tall because he'll be able to reach the top of the tree."

"I'm intrigued to see how much damage Ralph can do," Miles said. "So far it seems he has a loose relationship with 'sit' and 'stay.'"

"Come into the living room and warm up. I thought we'd eat early, but there's time for a drink first. I made a batch of mince pies." Dorothy ushered them all into the living room, and the children headed straight for the tree and the presents underneath.

Ava grabbed one and shook it.

"Stop it." Iris took it from her. "You're going to break it, and it might not even be for you."

"It has my name on it."

An hour passed in excited chaos, and when Dorothy excused herself to make some last-minute preparations in the kitchen, Sara followed.

"What can I do?"

"Mash the potatoes?" Dorothy drained them and put the pan down for Sara to finish them off. She was desperate to know how the day had gone, how Sara had felt about it and whether it had been awkward. But given that they could be disturbed at any moment, she kept her question simple. "How was your day?"

"It was magical. The snow helped, of course. I don't think we've ever had snow before on our Christmas tree day. The forest was pretty. Imogen seemed to enjoy it. She found a great tree. Or rather, Ava found a great tree she insisted Imogen should have." Sara mashed the potatoes, tipped them into a dish and slid them back into the oven to keep warm. Then she looked at her mother. "It was good. Better than I was expecting. Easier. How about you? You've been in the kitchen all day."

"For some of it. And I did some thinking."

"About?"

"Life." Dorothy wiped her hands and turned to look at her daughter. "I've decided you're right. I do take too much responsibility for Tina's choices. And you're also right that I make far too many excuses and allowances for her. I owe you an apology for that."

Sara's expression softened, and she reached out and touched her mother's arm. "You don't owe me anything."

"Yes, I do. The truth is Tina behaved badly and hurt an awful lot of people, including you and Imogen. I should have acknowledged that a long time ago. Accepted it as a fact, instead of always blaming myself." Instead of feeling responsible, she felt sad. Family life might not always be easy, but it offered so much, and Tina had rejected that.

If Sara was surprised, she didn't show it. "What caused this change of heart?"

"I couldn't stop thinking about the fact that she told Imogen such terrible lies. That we didn't want her." It had played on her mind. "She chose to deprive Imogen of wider family." And the only person responsible for that decision was Tina.

"It's a testament to Imogen's maturity that she chose to believe what we told her."

"Yes. She doesn't shy away from the truth, however difficult." Sara hesitated. "I owe you an apology too. I gave you a hard time over Imogen. I was scared that building a relationship with her was the wrong thing to do, but it wasn't. You did the right thing, Mum."

"I'm glad you think so. It could have gone the other way, of course, if Imogen was a different type of person. This could have been much more difficult."

"I suspect she has had rather too much practice at handling the difficult."

"Yes. Do you think Imogen will get in touch with Tina? Challenge her on it?" It was another thing that had been worrying her. That Tina might do something to damage the fragile shoots of this new relationship.

Sara's expression was neutral. "I don't know. But I think just as we have to accept Tina's choices, we have to trust and accept Imogen's. I don't think she has any illusions about what Tina is like."

Something about the way she said it made Dorothy think that she and Imogen had exchanged more than small talk on their trip to the forest.

But that was between them. It was important that Sara and Imogen forged their own relationship, and if that had already started to happen, then she couldn't have been more delighted.

"I'm sure you're right."

"Hopefully, Imogen has the strength to make her own decisions and choices about what is right for her no matter what pressure, if any, Tina puts on her. I think she does."

"Yes." Dorothy lifted the casserole out of the oven. "At least now she knows the truth."

Maybe as a parent you didn't have anywhere near the influence you thought you had. You raised your children the way you believed to be best and taught them right from wrong, but after a certain age their decisions were their own. And sometimes all you could do was accept things the way they were, and not waste time wishing they were different.

Imogen was here now, about to have a meal with the family, because she'd made a choice. Her own choice.

And it sounded as if she had been making all her own choices for a long time.

"How did she get on with Miles?"

Sara raised an eyebrow. "You're not interfering, are you?"

"Definitely not."

"Good. Because as it happens, Ralph is all the matchmaker those two are going to need."

"In that case I shall forgive Ralph for hiding my slippers the moment he came into the house."

And at that moment, Imogen appeared in the doorway, Ava by her side.

"Do you need more helpers?"

Delighted that she wanted to join in, Dorothy took the plates out of the oven where they were warming. "You can tell everyone to wash hands and head to the dining room. We're ready to eat."

"It smells delicious."

Ava reached for Imogen's hand. "Nanna is the best cook."

"I've heard that. I'm looking forward to dinner."

"Christmas is the best," Ava said. "You will be here on Christmas Day, won't you, Imogen?"

There was a slightly awkward pause.

Sara glanced at Imogen and then at Dorothy.

She hadn't planned to issue the invitation quite yet, but maybe it was better this way. Spontaneous.

"If Imogen would join us, then of course we'd all be thrilled."

She held her breath. She wasn't going to pressure her. She wasn't going to coax or cajole. If Imogen felt uncomfortable with the idea, if she didn't want to do this, then Dorothy would need to accept that. Imogen had listened to what they had to say, she'd spent time with Sara and her family and she was here now. No one would blame her if she felt that was enough to begin with. A full-on family Christmas so early in their relationship might be too much to ask of anyone.

She was going to allow Imogen to make whatever decision she felt was right for her.

"I'd love to spend Christmas with you," Imogen said quietly, "if it's not too much trouble."

"It's no trouble at all," Dorothy said. "It would make our Christmas if you were to join us."

"Great! I want to sit next to you." Ava danced off to tell her sister the good news, and Imogen crossed the kitchen to Dorothy.

"Let me take those." She relieved Dorothy of the plates. "And you must let me know what I can do to make Christmas Day easier. I'm no expert in the kitchen and I've never cooked a Christmas lunch before, but I can follow instructions. I want to help."

"In that case, you can persuade my girls to eat brussels sprouts," Sara said cheerfully, "preferably without the commentary on how much they hate them."

Imogen grinned. "I can try."

"You take the plates, Imogen, and I'll bring the casserole." Sara picked up the heavy cast-iron pot. "I'll send Patrick in to help carry the rest."

"I'm here." Patrick appeared, the girls by his side, and soon everyone was helping out, carrying plates and food to the table.

There were plenty of compliments when they saw what Dorothy had done to the room, and Sara gave her a smile.

Dorothy returned the smile, understanding.

Yesterday when Imogen had discovered the truth and walked out so abruptly, neither of them had expected this outcome.

It was more than Dorothy had hoped for. More than Sara had hoped for too.

Imogen, it seemed, was happy to put the past behind her and embrace this new development in her life.

Dorothy settled herself at the table and gave herself permission to stop worrying and simply enjoy this moment with her family.

If Imogen could leave the past behind, then so could she. She could choose to move on and finally forgive herself for whatever part her actions had played in past events. She could accept that the responsibility for everything that had happened was not all hers.

And she could be grateful for what she had right now.

20

Sara

"The girls are finally asleep, and frankly I might be joining them soon. I'm exhausted." Sara flopped down onto the sofa and took the glass of wine Patrick handed her. "Thanks. You're a lifesaver."

In the corner of the room their newly cut Christmas tree sparkled. Even though it had been late when they'd arrived home from Dorothy's, the girls had insisted on decorating it.

"I want to wake up tomorrow and see it all sparkly," Ava had said, and Iris had supported her sister in that wish.

They'd played Christmas music, and Sara had made the girls hot chocolate before finally persuading them to go to bed.

"To another successful Christmas tree trip." She raised her glass to Patrick. "It looks great, doesn't it?" The lights from the tree softened the room and made it seem even cozier than usual. The sharp scent of fir permeated the air and made it feel even more Christmassy. It was like bringing the outdoors indoors.

"It looks big." Patrick sat down next to her and stretched

out his legs. "Why do I always let you three talk me into a tree that's taller than our ceilings?"

"Because you're a pushover?"

"That could be it." He leaned forward and kissed her. "It was a good day, wasn't it?"

"The best."

"You and Imogen had a lot to say to each other."

"Yes." Sara took a sip of wine. "Yes, we did."

"It wasn't awkward? I thought it might be."

"So did I, but it wasn't. She made it easy. She's not afraid to talk about things, the good and the bad. I think it helped that she was so honest. We weren't tiptoeing around the past, pretending it hadn't happened." Imogen didn't hide from things that were difficult in the way she did. It made her want to do better.

"Did she talk about Tina? You usually prefer to avoid the subject."

"Tina called while we were talking, so it was a little hard to ignore her existence."

"She *called*?" Patrick shifted so that he could look at her properly. "You're kidding."

"I'm not kidding. I get the sense she calls Imogen whenever she wants something."

"That sounds like the Tina we once knew. And what did she want? Money?"

She sometimes forgot that he'd been part of it all. That he'd witnessed firsthand the destruction her sister had caused.

"Imogen didn't answer it. She chose not to."

"Surprising," Patrick said, "but good for her."

"Yes. I think she does it often. Chooses the moment to respond so that Tina doesn't have all the control." Sara stared at the tree. "I've been thinking."

"When you use that tone, I start worrying."

Normally, his comment would have made her smile, but

not tonight. "I'm thinking I might offer to go and see Tina with her."

"What?" Just as she'd anticipated, he looked horrified. "She wants to see her?"

"She hasn't said so yet, but think about it, Patrick. Tina lied to her. She doesn't understand why. This has all come as a shock to her. She's going to want to talk it through with her mother at some point. She probably wants to try and understand."

"I get all that, but why do you have to go with her? You've always done everything you can to avoid thinking about Tina. You have more self-discipline than anyone I know. Why would you want to see her?"

"I don't want to see her, but I want to support Imogen. If she wants to talk to Tina, then I'd like to be there—if she wants me."

"But that's between Imogen and Tina, surely."

"Yes. But why should she handle that alone?"

"You're not doing this because you're afraid Tina might lie again?"

"No. I'm doing it because Imogen has no one." Her voice softened. "All these years, she was on her own with it. I don't know the details, but I do know it wasn't easy. Imogen is fiercely independent. I suppose she has had to be because she has never had anyone she could share this with. But now she has."

He looked troubled. "But it's so hard for you—"

"Harder for Imogen. I want her to know she has someone in her corner."

"But I'm sure she knows she has your support."

"I've told her that, obviously, but words don't mean much on their own, do they? Words are easy. I don't want to just tell her I'll be there for her, I want to actually be there for her."

Patrick didn't look reassured. "I understand, but up until a few weeks ago you refused to think about Tina, or talk about her."

"And in the past few days I've been forced to do both." She took another sip of wine and then put her glass down next to his. "I used to think I'd handled the whole Tina situation well by blocking it out. Ignoring that part of my life. Moving on. I was proud of myself—can you believe that? I was frustrated that my mother couldn't do the same."

"You have every reason to feel proud. You moved on from a horrible situation."

"No, I didn't. Not really." She rubbed her hand over the back of her neck. "It was avoidance, Patrick."

"Avoidance is a perfectly legitimate coping mechanism."

"Maybe. But it's a fragile coping mechanism. When it all came out yesterday and I was forced to confront it, I almost had a panic attack. That whole time was so difficult that the idea of reliving it terrified me."

"So feeling that way, why would you want to see Tina?"

"That's just it. I don't feel scared anymore. I keep telling my mother that she should stop blaming herself and just accept what happened, but today in the forest when I was talking to Imogen, I realized that I need to do the same thing. Not avoid it, but accept it. Imogen has lived with this her whole life. She hasn't had the luxury of being able to block it out, or run away from it, and nor has she had the comfort of family support. She did what needed to be done, and she did it alone and with great courage, it seems."

"It sounds as if she has inspired you."

"Maybe she has. I certainly felt humbled. And a bit cowardly, if I'm honest. Talking to her made me think about the person I am, and the role model I want to be to our girls. I want life to be smooth for them, of course, but we both know that's not likely to happen, because life is so rarely smooth. I want to give them the confidence that they can navigate whatever challenges come their way. I don't want them to hide from things, the way I have."

"I think you're being hard on yourself." He reached out and brushed his thumb across her cheek. "You were young, and it was a tough time. Not surprisingly it had a huge impact on you."

"Imogen was young too. But she handled it."

"So are you going to suggest it? Seeing Tina?"

"No, I'm going to take my lead from her. Maybe she'll decide she doesn't want to talk to her mother. But if she does, then I want her to know I'm there to support her. That's what families do, isn't it?"

She was determined to make up for all the years Imogen had been forced to face life on her own.

He let his hand drop. "If you do this, then I'm coming too."

Her insides softened. "I appreciate that, but I don't think that will be necessary."

"Indulge me. If you're going within a kilometer of Tina, I want to be there."

"Why?"

"You need to ask? Because I love you. Didn't you say a moment ago that words don't mean anything without actions? Call this an action."

She leaned forward and kissed him. "I'm a lucky woman."

"You are." His mouth lingered on hers. "Come upstairs and I'll show you how lucky."

It was the perfect end to an almost perfect day.

21

Imogen

"You haven't told me where we're going." Imogen grabbed her thick coat and her hat and gloves. Miles was leaning against the front door, waiting for her.

"I thought you'd be ready. Am I early?"

"No, I'm running behind. I overslept. Again." The sun was shining, but she knew it was bitterly cold outside. "It's becoming a habit."

She'd gone from barely sleeping at all to sleeping deeply. And she'd started to wonder whether Rosalind might have been right. Maybe she had been on the edge of burnout. Over the past few days the knot of tension in her stomach had eased, and that feeling that she was running full speed ahead with nothing in the tank had disappeared. She no longer had thoughts of work racing around her head. She didn't scribble on notepads in the dark or send herself emails at three in the morning. There was no one to manage, no deadlines to meet and no to-do list waiting for her. She switched her phone off in the evening and didn't look at it again until the morning.

And she slept. She didn't know if it was the comfortable bed, or the way the soft down duvet wrapped itself around her, or the lack of city noise, but it felt as if she'd had more sleep over the past few nights than she had over the past year. Even the two missed calls from her mother hadn't been enough to keep her awake.

So far she hadn't responded, and she wasn't sure whether she was going to.

She was upset and confused. Also, angry. She needed time to calm down a little and think carefully about how she wanted to handle it.

With an effort, she pushed that thought out of her mind. She wasn't going to think about it now. She was going to enjoy her day with Miles, and she was not going to allow her mother to spoil that.

After the Christmas tree trip and dinner at Dorothy's, Miles had dropped her back at Holly Cottage. There had been a few breathless moments when she'd wondered whether to invite him in, but then she'd lost her nerve and simply given him a hug and then made a fuss of Ralph to cover her embarrassment.

She'd barely been in bed for five minutes before Miles had called to ask her if she was free on Tuesday because he had a special day planned.

She accepted immediately (of course!) and they'd proceeded to spend the next two hours talking, which made her think she probably should have been brave enough to invite him in.

But now here they were, about to spend the day together. If she'd been Ralph, her tail would have been wagging.

Not sure whether that level of delight might be off-putting, she settled for a smile.

"I'm looking forward to our day, although you still haven't told me what we'll be doing. You've been evasive."

"It's a surprise. You don't like surprises?"

The last surprise she'd had was discovering that Dorothy was her grandmother and Sara her aunt, so she wasn't sure how to answer that.

The past few days had felt like stepping into another life. Miles had worked the day before, so she'd had Ralph with her at the cottage and she'd taken him for a long walk and visited Dorothy at the house. She'd helped her wrap garlands around the staircase, decorate the room the girls would be staying in and ice the Christmas cake. They'd spent the afternoon cooking meals for the freezer so that they didn't have to spend the whole of the holidays in the kitchen.

Imogen had never bothered much with cooking, but with Dorothy by her side she discovered that chopping, frying and producing meals could be surprisingly relaxing. And it also made conversation easy. Imogen had asked her endless questions, keen to discover everything she could about this family she hadn't even known she had. All those years she'd missed. All those birthdays and Christmases and celebrations, as well as the normal ordinary days that came and went without note. She wanted to know what they cared about, what made them laugh, *who they were*. She was trying to cram twenty-eight years of knowledge into a few days so that she could catch up. She'd discovered that Dorothy was a talented pianist, that she was addicted to crossword puzzles and de-stressed from the demands of business by spending time with her animals.

Trying to compensate for the one she couldn't save.

When Miles had first said those words to her she hadn't understood, but she understood now. And the more she got to know Dorothy, the more she knew that her mother's version of events couldn't possibly be right. Her account had been colored by her own insecurities and weakness. Dorothy would never abandon a family member. Or a friend for that matter. Imogen knew that for sure, not just because of what people had said to her, but because of her own observations. Dorothy was a giver. Generous.

And then there was Sara. Sara loved the outdoors, and particularly horses. She'd ridden often as a child, a passion Iris seemed to have inherited. But Sara also loved clothes and flowers and her family. Watching her with the children during the Christmas tree trip, Imogen had wondered how it was possible that Sara and her mother shared the same genetics, because they couldn't have been more different. The more time she spent with them, the more she learned. Like pieces of a jigsaw, she was gradually getting a picture of her family.

But today wasn't about her newfound family, it was about Miles.

"I love surprises, but it's hard to know how to dress when I don't know what we're going to be doing." She grabbed her bag and checked she had her keys and phone. "Where's Ralph?"

"I've dropped him off with Dorothy. My plans for today aren't all dog friendly."

And now she was intrigued. "You won't even give me a tiny clue?"

"Dress warmly," he said. "We'll be out for the whole day, and the evening."

Imogen gave him her hat and gloves to hold while she pulled on her coat. "Just the two of us?"

"Just the two of us."

Her heart thudded a little harder. "So this is like a date?"

"It's not like a date." He smiled. "It *is* a date."

She felt a flicker of something that might have been nerves. "In that case I should probably warn you that I'm not that great at dates."

"I didn't know you could pass or fail dating. You think I'm going to give you a grade?"

"I hope not, because I'd probably average around a D minus.

I'm just warning you so that you can keep your expectations in check."

She tried to zip her coat, but her fingers fumbled and she couldn't get the teeth to bite.

Yes, she was definitely nervous. Could he see that?

Maybe he could, because he tucked the hat and gloves she'd handed him under his arm, gently nudged her hands aside and carefully zipped her coat for her.

"You're talking to the guy who once left a woman in a restaurant to go and deal with a difficult calving, so I don't think you need to feel anxious." His hands lingered on her jacket, and for a wild moment she wondered if he was going to pull her in and kiss her.

And she wanted him to. *She really wanted him to.*

"That sounds like a legitimate reason for date abandonment." Maybe she was misreading the whole thing, which was entirely possible. "Were the cow and calf okay?"

"Yes, thankfully." He let go of her jacket. "But my date was not. She questioned my priorities."

"What were you supposed to do? Ask the cow to hold on for a few hours?"

"Perhaps I should have tried that. I've never found cows to be great listeners, but maybe I just don't have the knack." He retrieved her hat and eased it onto her head. "Would it help if I confessed that this is unusual for me too? I haven't really dated since my last disaster."

"So why are you doing it now?"

He smoothed the stray strands of hair away from her eyes. "I don't know, but I think it's probably a measure of how much I like you."

His words and the light brush of his fingers made her dizzy. "You do?"

If it had been hard to breathe before, it was almost impossible now. She was so *aware* of him. Her skin tingled where he'd touched her, and the air around them was charged with an almost unbearable tension that was wholly unfamiliar.

She was in the process of trying to work out what to do next when he stepped back.

"Yes, I do." He handed her the gloves he'd been holding. "And we should probably get out of here or this date isn't going to happen."

She almost told him that she didn't care what form their date took as long as they were together, but she didn't. He'd clearly given a lot of thought to today. And either he'd feel the same way about her by the end of it, or he wouldn't.

But if he did—

She smiled to herself as she tugged on her winter boots.

There was something deliciously exciting about anticipation.

She locked the cottage and together they headed to his car.

The sky was a perfect blue and the snow sparkled under the winter sun.

Miles headed out of the drive and onto the narrow country road that ran past the Winterbury Estate.

"I'm assuming you haven't done any Christmas shopping yet?"

"You mean shopping for gifts? No. Apart from the usual Secret Santa at work, which is always a painful experience, I've never had anyone to buy presents for. I should probably take a look online for inspiration." She felt a flicker of panic as she realized how close Christmas was and dug in her bag for her phone. "I should have thought of it sooner."

"You didn't know you were going to suddenly acquire a family. And don't worry, I have a plan, so you can put your phone away." Miles drove confidently along the narrow road, occasionally raising his hand to passing motorists.

"Do you know everyone around here?"

"Quite a few people. That's what happens when you've lived in the same village for most of your life."

They drove along small winding roads through countryside, past snowy fields and farms and the occasional church. Trees were frosted with white and stone walls were coated with a layer of snow. It felt a long way from London.

She tried to imagine what it must be like to live here and be part of this community.

"You never moved away?"

"Only to do my vet training. It was an interesting experience, but I missed this place. We're here." They'd reached the edge of a village and he slowed down and swooped into a vacant parking space next to a picturesque pub. The roof was dusted with snow and tiny lights had been strung along the eaves. "This place serves great food, as you will discover later."

The pub looked so inviting, Imogen wasn't sure she wanted to wait until later.

"I don't suppose we could discover it now?"

"You want lunch at ten in the morning?"

"I'm hungry."

He grinned. "The more I know you, the more I like you."

Her heart skipped a beat. She felt the same way about him, but she was too unsure of her own emotions to say so. This all felt so different. Her life was too busy to ever meet anyone organically, and for the last few years she'd used dating apps and become more and more disillusioned. It felt as impersonal as applying for a job. In the end she'd decided to give herself a break from the stress of it.

"Does your plan for the day include grabbing a coffee somewhere? I'm no good without coffee in the morning. Sorry. I should have set an alarm so that I woke up earlier. Then I could have consumed my coffee before you arrived."

"Don't panic. Coffee is definitely the first thing on the agenda. How do you feel about chocolate cake for breakfast?"

She blinked. "It's a new one on me, so maybe I can tell you after I've eaten it?"

"Sounds good. Wrap up. It's cold out there." He opened the door and a blast of frigid air blew through the car.

"You're not kidding." Imogen pulled on her hat and zipped up her coat. "Chocolate cake is sounding better all the time."

They walked out of the car park and onto the cobbled street that ran the length of the village. A stream meandered next to the road, the surface partly frozen.

The village had a nostalgic appeal, as if it was from a different time.

"I can't believe there are ducks." Imogen paused to watch them. "Aren't they cold?"

"Ducks are hardy. They're generally fine in cold weather, although you need to watch their feet."

"Have you ever had a duck as a patient?"

"Most of the animals I deal with are a little bigger than that." He reached out and took her hand and she glanced at him.

"You're afraid I might slip?"

"No. I just like holding your hand." He tugged her closer to let someone pass. "Unless you have something against holding hands in public?"

"No—" she cleared her throat "—I don't."

He was so easy with it all. So comfortable, whereas she overthought every word and gesture. But maybe this wasn't as new to him as it was to her. She'd been alone for so long she'd forgotten how it felt to hold someone's hand.

It felt good.

"Miles!" A woman in her forties crossed the road to greet him. She sent Imogen a curious look. "How are you doing?"

"I'm great thanks, Pippa." He held Imogen's hand firmly, showing no signs of releasing it. "How's Ted?"

"Better, thanks. Recovering. The doctor has him on a strict diet and he's moaning about it, so that's fun, particularly as we're in the gorging season. Melissa tells me she's travelling this Christmas?"

"Yes. She was here last month and hopes to make it for New Year's Eve. This is Imogen, by the way. Imogen—Pippa."

Imogen gave a polite smile and they exchanged a few words before Pippa reached out and touched Miles on the arm.

"Are you working over Christmas? Because you're welcome to join us for lunch."

"That's kind, Pippa, but I've already accepted an invitation to Dorothy's."

Pippa smiled. "Then I know you'll be well-fed. Good. If I don't see you before, I hope you have a great Christmas."

She leaned in to give him a spontaneous hug and then turned and hurried in the opposite direction.

Imogen watched her go. "She was giving me funny looks."

"It wasn't personal. She was just interested because we were together and I was holding your hand. She had a million questions that she will now no doubt fire at my sister, who won't know the answers. I await the phone call." He seemed to find it amusing rather than irritating, and she felt a pang of envy that he had such a close family relationship.

Her mother had never shown the slightest interest in her love life. She'd never shown the slightest interest in anything Imogen did.

Imogen had been on her own.

But not anymore.

"Did you get on well with your sister when you were growing up? She wasn't jealous of you?"

"No. If anything, she mothered me. I suppose she still does in a way. And yes, we got on fine, although better now that we're older. We didn't share many interests when we were growing up, apart from a love of food. We used to fight over the last slice of my mother's chocolate cake."

His mother's chocolate cake. Chocolate cake came with happy memories.

She smiled. "Who won?"

"My mother always insisted on cutting it in half. She was a born diplomat."

"Your appetite seems to be something of a local legend. Do you always have multiple invitations to Christmas lunch?"

"Always. I've perfected a certain helpless look when people talk about Christmas, and it works a treat. I haven't had to cook for myself on Christmas Day for at least five years. In my defence I invariably cover Christmas, and I often get called out, so I wouldn't risk roasting my own turkey. If I can grab a few roast potatoes at someone else's table, that works for me."

"Why do you cover Christmas?"

"Because my colleagues all have families. It's important that they're at home for Christmas."

"That's thoughtful."

"They cover for me when necessary." He pulled her closer. "I negotiated for them to cover today for me."

"What reason did you give?"

"I told them the truth. That I had a hot date with a hot girl." He smiled at her. "Although you look pretty cold right now, so we should probably get ourselves to that coffee shop before you freeze."

They carried on walking, and everywhere she looked she saw charm and character. Rows of cottages, their stone walls gleaming pale gold in the winter sunlight. Creeper wound itself around doors and windows and snow dusted the sloping roofs.

"This whole place looks like a movie set. It's so Christmassy."

"That's why I brought you here." His hand tightened on hers. "You said you'd never done anything Christmassy before, so that's what we're doing today. We're spending the whole day doing Christmassy things."

"I thought you didn't usually make much of a fuss about Christmas?"

He smiled. "This will be a first for both of us. Also it's a cunning way of getting you to help me choose my Christmas gifts. Left to my own devices I'd buy everyone a woolly hat. Do you need a woolly hat by any chance?"

"Is it possible to have too many?"

"Not in my opinion and I'm glad you agree. But before we go shopping, we need sustenance. This place has a Christmas market and a coffee shop that sells the best cakes anywhere. Except, maybe, Dorothy's kitchen." He pushed open the door of a pretty café and she stepped inside.

Immediately, she was engulfed by warmth, delicious smells and the soothing sound of a coffee machine in action.

"What can I get you?" Miles unzipped his coat and gestured to the counter. "Choose something."

"I'm not sure about chocolate cake." She scanned the display. "Almond croissant please. And a cappuccino. I'll pay."

"No, today is on me. Call it a thank-you for helping me out with Ralph. You can treat me to a day out in London some-time. Go and grab that table by the window. It has a great view of the street."

Imogen sat down at the vacant table. It was nestled in the curve of the window, and she gazed out over the snowy street, feeling as if she was starring in a Dickens novel.

You can treat me to a day out in London sometime.

The knowledge that he was already hoping they'd see each other again gave her a dizzying buzz.

"Why are you smiling?" Miles unloaded the food and cof-fee from a tray and sat down next to her.

"Because I'm enjoying myself."

"That's a relief."

"The last woman you dated—" she kept her voice casual "—was it serious?"

"No. Definitely casual." He ate a mouthful of chocolate cake. "She didn't like my lifestyle. The last serious relationship I had was three years ago. She also didn't like my lifestyle. Nor did she like living in the countryside. How about you?"

She took a sip of coffee, wondering how honest to be. "My dating history is pretty sparse and unimpressive."

"Tell me about your last boyfriend."

She put her cup down. "That would be Jack." She felt color heat her cheeks and he raised an eyebrow.

"And Jack was—don't tell me—a successful banker with an income the same size as his ego?"

"Not exactly." She hesitated. "Jack was fictitious."

There was silence as he digested that. "Fictitious? You mean he doesn't exist?"

"That's right. I made him up. I got tired of using dating apps, but it was occasionally convenient to have a boyfriend, so I invented a guy called Jack."

But it was time to let him go. Jack, Midas—she was clearing the fake out of her life.

"Why was it convenient to have a boyfriend?"

She stared out of the window for a moment, wondering why she was telling him this. "I wanted to fit in. I invented a life I thought would make me seem like everyone else."

"Why would you want to be like everyone else?"

"Because growing up I always felt different. Other people seemed to have homes, and even though plenty of them had separated parents, their parents still seemed to be interested in them. I didn't want to stand out, so I used to make things up. It wasn't just a boyfriend." And soon she was telling him all of it. How she'd tried to blend in when she was at school and then college, how she'd learned to present herself in a certain way in order not to draw attention. She told him about her first day at RPQ when everyone had personal items on their desk. "They all talked so openly about family and friends. What was I supposed to say? That my mother insists I call her by her first name because she dislikes any suggestion that we're related? It was too personal. And I suppose deep down I was afraid that if they knew me they'd judge me. If your own mother isn't in-terested in you, why would anyone else be?"

"I think that says more about your mother than you."

"Maybe. But if they thought that, then they would have been sympathetic, and I didn't want that either. I didn't want peo-ple feeling sorry for me. I just wanted to fit in and do my job."

He nodded slowly. "So you invented a family and a dog to avoid the questions and make it easier. Did the dog have a name?"

"Midas. He was an accident, really. I mentioned him in passing one day because everyone had pets, and I thought that would be a simple way of bonding. I didn't think for one mo-ment anyone would expect to meet him. It escalated, and it wasn't easy to extract myself. The email about 'Bring your dog to work day' was a low point."

"Bring your dog to work day?" He smiled and she frowned at him, affronted.

"Are you laughing at me?"

"No. I'm wondering if any of your colleagues understand just how much havoc a group of dogs can create. I'm also try-ing to picture your face when they told you they'd sent out 'missing dog' notices."

She groaned at the memory. "The gods of lying certainly weren't smiling down on me, particularly when the actual owner of the dog called the number. Next time I won't use a photo from the internet." But she was smiling too because he was right—looking back on it, it was funny. And it felt good to finally be honest with someone. To share it. Good, and also unnerving. She'd never been her true self with anyone before. She poked at the foam in her coffee, wondering what he really thought of her. "So now I've told you all of it, you can leave if you like. No hard feelings."

His smile faded. "Leave? Why would I leave?"

"Because I just told you all about myself." She put the spoon down. "You must think I'm batshit crazy."

"For wanting to fit in? No, of course not. That's a pretty human need. We're herd animals. And as for not wanting to talk about your mother—" he shrugged "—why would you? Plenty of people have things in their lives they prefer not to share, Imogen." He was so relaxed about it, so unfazed by her honest confession, that she started to relax.

"But making up a dog—"

"Sounds like a creative solution to me. And it's not as if 'Bring your dog to work days' are common. How were you supposed to anticipate that? What kind of dog was he?"

She broke off the corner of her croissant and ate it. "He was a golden retriever, just like Ralph."

"Of course. Midas." He nodded. "I should have guessed."

"The weird thing is I made him up because I wanted to seem like a dog person like my colleagues, and it turns out I am a dog person. I didn't even know I loved dogs until I met Ralph. I didn't have a pet growing up, and I only invented Midas because everyone at work is obsessed with their pets." She sighed and sat back in her chair. "And I still have to confess to them that it was all lies. I'm not looking forward to that part."

"They don't know Midas was fictitious?"

"No. I was sent on extended leave before I could tell them the truth. That joy awaits me in January, along with a load of other unpleasant things."

Like dealing with her mother.

She felt a cloud descend as she thought of returning to her life in London. She couldn't bear the thought of leaving Holly Cottage, but that was only hers for Christmas, of course.

The Christmas cottage. Just for the holidays.

In the new year Dorothy would be making it available as a rental property again.

Miles reached across and took her hand. "You don't have

to tell them if you don't want to. There's no rule that says you have to reveal all the details of your life."

"I know, but I'm learning that if you never let anyone see the real you, then no one knows the real you." She paused. "I suppose I was afraid they wouldn't like me."

"I know the real you, and I like you." His tone was rough. "I like you a lot."

How was it that she could be so confident in some areas of her life, and so unsure in others?

Like now.

She felt herself blush. "I like you a lot too."

"Good." His hand tightened on hers. "And now let's think about Christmas, because that's what today is all about. If you could have any gift for Christmas, what would it be?"

She didn't have to think about it. "Having a real family Christmas is probably the best gift. Dorothy has hung a stocking for me on the fireplace. Can you believe that? Actually, it was Ava who insisted on it. And tomorrow is Iris's school play—we're taking Benson along. I'm in charge of making sure he behaves himself, although I don't know how I'm supposed to do that because he has a mind of his own."

"If I were you, I'd take an expert with you. Just to be safe."

She looked at him. "You'd come?"

"If I'm invited."

"You're definitely invited." She paused, remembering all the times she'd performed with no one in the audience rooting for her. "Iris would love it. And so would I."

"Then I'll be there. And returning to the subject of Christmas, apart from being with family, what would be your dream gift?"

A dog.

But not any dog. Ralph.

She didn't say it aloud. What was the point? Ralph was

Miles's dog, not hers. And anyway, she couldn't have a pet with her current lifestyle.

"I don't know. What's top of your list? Have you written to Santa?"

"I bought myself a weatherproof jacket that is going to keep me warm when I'm out in the fields at two in the morning in January."

"That doesn't sound particularly exciting."

"It is if you're the one getting frostbite." He pushed his chocolate cake toward her. "Try a mouthful. I insist."

She did as he instructed and closed her eyes as she savored it. "Okay, I admit it—that's good. Too good. So what's next on our agenda?"

"We are going to do all our Christmas shopping at the Christmas market. Then we're having lunch."

"And after that?"

"We're going ice-skating."

She put the fork down. "Seriously? I had no idea you could skate."

"I can't. I've never done it before, but Lissa assures me we will have fun."

"You discussed our day out with your sister?"

He finished his coffee. "I wanted some tips on what would make a perfect Christmas date, so I consulted an expert. My sister is obsessed with Christmas. She visits at least two Christmas markets in Europe every winter and starts decorating in November. She says it brightens the winter months. I wanted you to have a good time."

He'd wanted her to have a good time, so he'd asked his sister's advice.

"For the record, I am having a good time, so her advice was good." Her gaze met his across the table and she felt something shift between them. "I don't suppose your sister gave you a list of gift ideas? I need to buy presents for Ava and Iris, also Sara, and I've never bought anything for children before."

"I didn't ask for that level of detail, but if we get stuck we can always call her. Are you ready?"

They left the warmth of the café and ventured out into the street.

They passed a gift shop and an independent bookstore and then turned a corner and found that the street had been transformed into a bustling Christmas market. There were wooden stalls offering handmade crafts, jewelry and ceramics, as well as specialty food and drink.

"It's pretty. I hadn't realised there would be food."

"Lissa tells me that this is the best Christmas market around here because they bring together local producers, and the quality is exceptional. This is why I couldn't risk bringing Ralph," Miles said. "He can't resist a good artisan sausage, and I didn't want to risk the possible humiliation of dealing with a rampaging dog in a Christmas market. I have to carry on living in this place."

"Poor Ralph. I'll buy him a treat to make up for it."

"You've been treating him by letting him sleep on your bed."

She wondered whether to deny it, but a glance at his face told her there was no point. "How did you guess?"

"Because he tries to do the same when he is staying with me. The difference is that I don't let him."

"What can I say? I like having him there." She refused to apologize for it. "Ralph is pretty much the perfect companion."

"Are you setting me a challenge?"

"No. So far you're doing pretty well too. Can I ask you something?"

"Anything."

"Was it true what Dorothy said about you not wanting another dog after Alfie?"

"Yes. That's how I felt. Alfie was one in a million." He

picked up a hand-thrown pot from the stall next to them, checked the price and then put it back again. "I couldn't bear the thought of replacing him. I wasn't emotionally ready to move on. But then I saw Valerie struggling with Ralph, and I decided it was time."

She felt a twinge of envy that he and Ralph would be living together. Sharing their lives.

"Ralph is lucky. I hope you're buying him something special for Christmas."

"That depends."

"On?"

"Whether he'd look good in a woolly hat."

Imogen laughed and strolled along the street searching for gift inspiration from the many stalls.

She chose a pair of earrings for Sara, and on impulse bought the same for Janie and Anya. They'd been good friends to her. Whether they'd still be good friends after she'd confessed the truth about herself remained to be seen, but she wasn't going to think about that now.

At the next stall she chose a beautiful notebook for Rosalind by way of a thank-you. If it hadn't been for Rosalind, she wouldn't be here. She wouldn't have met Miles. Dorothy wouldn't have lent her the cottage, and maybe she wouldn't have known Dorothy was her grandmother, although that would no doubt have come out eventually.

And maybe, if Rosalind hadn't insisted she take a long break, she would have burned out. She saw now that she couldn't have carried on working at the pace she'd been working, not just because it was unsustainable from an energy point of view, but also because it made her life so narrow.

She paid for the notebook, and Miles took the bag from her and slid it into one of the other bags he was carrying.

"Who is this for?"

"My boss."

"You like her?"

"Yes, she's brilliant. Inspirational, but also insightful. When she told me I had to take a month off, I was devastated. I had no idea what I was going to do without work to fill my days, particularly over Christmas."

He looked at the number of parcels she'd amassed in a short time. "You seem to be doing fine with that."

"Yes. And I'm sleeping well, which is a miracle. It took me a while to switch off, but now I have, I can't imagine switching it back on again. It has made me realize that I need to do more. Get a better balance in my life. All I thought about was work. I'd send emails in the middle of the night."

"Why? That fictitious boyfriend of yours should have made you leave your laptop at the bedroom door."

She laughed. "He was useless. It's over."

"The breakup was bad?"

"Terrible. He won't speak to me."

"I feel for the guy. So why was your workload so heavy you had to answer emails in the middle of the night?"

"That was my own fault for never saying no to anyone. I took on more and more. I was always the first in the door and the last home. I told myself it was ambition and that's partly true, but it was also fear." She could admit that to herself now. "The drive to succeed came from a place of insecurity."

"It sounds as if you're good at your job, so why would you feel insecure?"

"I think it's hardwired into me. It was tough when growing up. Money was tight. Tina sometimes had work, and sometimes she didn't."

He winced. "Hearing you call her Tina feels so wrong."

Almost everything about her relationship with her mother had felt wrong.

"She insisted on Tina. We moved frequently when I was a child, usually because she couldn't afford the rent. We never had anywhere that was ours. Nowhere that felt like home. I badly wanted something different. I'd visit friends and see their homes, and I wanted that. Nothing big or elaborate, just a place that was mine. At college, lots of the students had help from their parents, but I never had that. I had three jobs, which is why I got used to working in the middle of the night, I suppose. I've always known I have to be financially independent, and that's been a driver for me." She paused by a stall selling soft toys.

"Does Dorothy know how hard it has been for you?"

"I'm sure she has guessed some of it. I've given her a few details, but not all of them." She picked up an alpaca. "This is very soft and cuddly. Do you think Ava would like this?"

"No idea. Probably. So you're protecting Dorothy?"

"Partly. I know she feels guilty and I don't want her to feel worse than she already does. But also I prefer to look forward. I thought I had no family and it turns out I do have family, and a loving family at that. I don't want to focus on the time I didn't have it. I want to enjoy the fact that now I do have it. Does that make sense?"

"It does. And in the spirit of looking forward, are you going to change things when you get back to London? Are you going to carry on working for Rosalind or will you look for something else?"

Something else. The thought hadn't occurred to her.

"I love my job. I'm good at my job. I just need to learn to do it differently. To switch off. Maybe delegate more." She thought about Anya and Janie, and how hard she found it to release control over work. "I need to give it some thought. But not now."

She didn't want to think about going back, not with the lights from the Christmas market sparkling around her and Miles looking at her as if she was the only person there.

She wanted to freeze the moment and make it last forever.

She bought the stuffed alpaca for Ava, and on impulse bought the same for Iris.

"I need to find a gift for Patrick. Any ideas?" She glanced around, lacking in inspiration. "I had no idea Christmas shopping was so mentally exhausting. This will be my first Christmas with them. I want to get them something really special."

"I think having you there will make it really special. I'm pretty sure gifts won't matter."

"They matter to me. I want to get it right."

"If I can't buy someone a woolly hat, I buy them food. That way they can either eat it, or give it to someone else to eat. How about chocolates? Iris loves chocolate. I'm sure she'll be more than happy to help him. Wait a minute—I'll message Lissa and see if she has any ideas. She's known Patrick forever." He pulled his phone out and sent a message to his sister, and they strolled past a few more stalls as she looked for something special.

The problem was that she didn't know them that well yet.

She was pondering a pair of cashmere gloves for Dorothy when Lissa replied.

Miles scanned the message. "She says to go to the bookshop and ask Paul and Rick. Patrick loves books, that's true. It's a good idea. I should have thought of it, and the fact that I didn't is just one of the many reasons I won't be applying to be Santa anytime soon. We'll head to the bookshop when we've finished with the market."

"Paul and Rick? You really do know everyone."

"Lissa has a really tight group of friends from childhood and they're good at staying in touch. Patrick and Sara you know, obviously. Then there's Paul and Rick, and also Shona. She's a florist. Lives in Cheltenham and spends her life doing posh weddings. We had a drunken kiss on my eighteenth birthday, but don't ever tell my sister that."

His frankness made her smile and she thought how nice it

was that they were all knitted together, their lives intertwined and overlapping, their history shared and stored.

She bought the cashmere gloves, and at the next stall she chose some art materials for Ava and Iris.

She added a box of Belgian truffles as a thank-you to Dorothy for inviting her for Christmas and bought large chocolate Santas for the children.

"Does Sara mind them having chocolate?"

"At Christmas, anything goes. Given that you've never really done any Christmas shopping before, you seem to be mastering the art pretty quickly." Miles grabbed her purchases before she could drop them. "We're going to need to offload some of these at the car soon."

"What about you? Aren't you going to do any shopping? Are you buying something for Lissa, or is she getting a hat too?"

"Cheese."

"Excuse me?"

"My sister loves cheese, particularly French cheese. That's what I buy her."

The Christmas market turned out to be a memorable and magical experience. She sampled fudge and chocolate and carried on buying gifts until Miles called a halt to it on the grounds that they couldn't carry any more.

They headed to the bookstore, where Paul and Rick sold her a book they assured her Patrick would love, and then they headed to the pub, an old fourteenth-century coaching inn complete with beamed ceilings, stone floors and a roaring log fire.

The place was crowded, but the owner managed to find Miles a prime table near the fire, muttering something about him never buying a drink for himself again after what he'd done for the Hendersons' prize cattle the previous summer.

She was fast discovering that he was something of a hero in his local community.

"We should have asked to have those presents gift wrapped." He settled next to her and stretched out his legs. "It would have saved you a job."

"I didn't want them gift wrapped. I'm going to wrap them myself when we get home. It's all part of the Christmas experience. You don't wrap your own?"

"If you'd ever seen my wrapping, you wouldn't be asking that question."

She hung her coat on the back of the chair. "I've been watching videos on how to wrap a present perfectly."

"You don't think you're taking this a little too seriously?"

"No. It's my first proper family Christmas. I want it to be just like the movies." She laughed and then felt her phone buzz. She took it out of her pocket and the joy from the day faded.

Miles watched her. "Your mother?"

"Yes. She's called a couple of times, but I haven't answered her calls or called her back. Last time I saw her she told me to get out of her life, so that's what I'm doing. Except it's not that easy." She rejected the call and put her phone back in her bag. "Part of me wants to speak to her and get some answers."

Over the past week she'd told him all of it, revealing far more than she had to Dorothy and Sara. It was easier, somehow, to talk to someone who wasn't directly emotionally involved. Or maybe it was just that Miles was easy to talk to.

"Would answers help?" He spoke quietly and she looked at him for a moment, wondering how he always knew the right question to ask.

"Probably not. No. Whatever she says, nothing is going to change the past."

"Maybe it's not answers you want. Maybe it's an apology."

She took a sip of her drink and thought about it. "Yes. But I know I wouldn't get one. I feel so angry with her." She blurted the words out and felt his hand cover hers.

"That's understandable."

"Not only because of the things she said last time I saw her, but because she made a choice for me that she never should have made. And maybe that was acceptable when I was a baby, although I don't understand that part at all because if she hated being a mother so much, if I was really the worst thing that had ever happened to her as she told me that night, then why didn't she just leave me with Dorothy and Sara? That makes no sense. But the part that makes me really angry is that she lied about them for my whole life. She spent years stoking my resentment toward them, telling me they'd abandoned her. She didn't want them in her life and she made that decision for both of us, and that's what I'm finding hard to deal with. Even that last time I saw her, she didn't tell me the truth."

He kept his hand on hers. "It sounds as if she's the master of emotional manipulation. I can't imagine how upsetting that episode in the hospital must have been."

Imogen thought back to the hurt she'd felt that night. She'd felt totally alone. She could have lost her job. "It was bad. But it's funny how life works out, isn't it? I kept beating myself up for going to the hospital that night, but if I hadn't gone, then I wouldn't have messed up my job, and if I hadn't messed up my job, Rosalind wouldn't have insisted I take a month off. If I hadn't had a month off, I wouldn't be here now. I never would have met my real family. Isn't that ironic?"

He stroked her hand with his thumb. "You don't think Dorothy would have said something eventually?"

"Maybe. I suppose so." She frowned. "When I asked her, she just said that she didn't have a plan. She was taking it day by day."

"It can't have been an easy thing to raise with you."

"No. I can see that now."

He let go of her hand and reached for his drink. "If Tina isn't calling you to apologize or wish you a happy Christmas, why is she calling?"

"She probably wants money. That's the only reason she calls. Anyway, enough of that. We're having a perfect Christmassy day, and my mother isn't going to be part of that." She was determined that she was not going to let her mother spoil the day. She couldn't control what her mother did, but she could control how she responded to it.

They ate lunch and it was several hours before they could drag themselves away from the warmth of the pub.

She slid her arm through his. "What's next?"

"Ice-skating." They headed to the small ice rink that had been set up on the edge of the village and watched for a few minutes while children circumnavigated the rink held by wobbly parents.

Imogen winced as a woman in a blue hat lost her balance and crashed down hard on her bottom. "Ouch."

"Mmm. Lissa thought this would be romantic," Miles said. "I'm not sure why. We could both end up in hospital. She probably thought it would give us an excuse to hold hands, but as we've been doing that for most of the day, I'm not sure we need to go to those extremes. Unless you're desperate to show off your ice dance skills, we could move on to our next Christmassy activity."

"I don't have any ice dance skills, so moving on sounds good."

They headed back to the car and he drove away from the village and deep into the countryside.

It was dark by the time he turned into the entrance of a stately home.

"Won't it be closed?"

"Inside, yes, but we're not doing a tour of the interior. They have a festive light trail. I believe officially they call it an enchanted trail, so if you don't feel enchanted I'll demand a refund. A client of mine mentioned it to me. I thought that if you wanted to feel Christmassy, this is probably the place."

She was touched by how much thought he'd put into their day, and from the moment she stepped out of the car, she knew this had been a good choice.

He took her hand and they walked past the stands selling hot chocolate and toasted marshmallows and followed a lantern trail through the gardens. They wandered through tunnels of fairy lights and past a lake illuminated by lasers of different colors.

She'd spent most of her life trying to ignore Christmas. Her focus had been on making it through to the other side and normality, but here, surrounded by lights and trees, excited children and an almost otherworldly atmosphere, she could finally understand why people might love this time of year.

She loved it.

"It's beautiful." She tilted her head back, admiring the twinkling snowflakes and stars above her head. "I am definitely enchanted. No refund necessary."

"Having real snow on the ground doesn't hurt."

"That's true."

The shimmering light bathed the snow in iridescent colors, adding a magical quality to the landscape.

They followed the snowy trail into the woodland, where trees were lit with different colors.

Laughter drifted toward them, but for now they were alone, cocooned by snowy branches and soft, intimate lighting, and when he lowered his head to kiss her she lifted herself onto her toes to meet him halfway.

His mouth settled on hers, his lips cold, but his kiss warm and unhurried. Pleasure raked through her, the sensation so intense and unexpected that she would have lost her balance had he not been holding her. She wrapped her arms around his neck and moved closer. She had no thoughts of pulling away. Why would she? Kissing him felt so blissfully right that for a moment she wondered if the forest might indeed be enchanted.

The slow seduction of his mouth felt like so much more than a kiss. A delicious, erotic prelude to something more. A promise.

Sounds of approaching children interrupted them, and he lifted his head reluctantly, but kept his arms tightly around her, holding her close until the children had passed and they once more had the forest to themselves.

She leaned against his chest, waiting for her heart rate to steady.

Kissing him had made her feel as if she'd discovered something about herself, as if this moment was something more than just a romantic interlude under the stars.

He cupped her face in his hands and kissed her again.

"If you've had enough of Christmas, I could take you home?" He murmured the words against her mouth. "And maybe you could invite me in?"

Something in his eyes and his tone made her catch her breath.

In a way, she'd already invited him in. She'd shared things with him she'd never shared with anyone else. Opened herself up and let him see who she really was.

There was nothing fake between them. No lies. Nothing that wasn't honest and true.

And now she was here in this magical winter wonderland, hovering on the edge of something that felt more real than anything she'd ever encountered before.

She didn't hesitate.

"Let's go."

22

Dorothy

"I have news!" Sara burst into the kitchen and dumped two bulging shopping bags on the kitchen table. She stripped off her coat and threw it over the nearest chair. "You will *never* guess what."

"What? You've spent all your savings in the farm shop and now you need a loan?" Dorothy put down the tray of freshly baked mince pies she'd pulled out of the oven and grabbed the bags from the table before the contents could spill across her kitchen floor. "Why are you shopping there? Everything costs a fortune. Why the sudden extravagance?"

"It's our treat. If we're spending Christmas with you, then we need to contribute. Between Patrick and the girls, we eat a lot. And Imogen will be here too, and maybe Miles. It's just a few bits and pieces—Lissa's favorite artisan crackers that go so well with cheese, some of those olives you love, those cute marzipan animals that Iris adores—anyway, forget about that. I have something much more exciting to talk about."

"Ah yes, you said you had news that I'm never going to guess?" Dorothy transferred the mince pies to a cooling rack.

"I just spoke to Lissa, who had a call from Pippa last night." Sara pulled off her wool hat and pushed her hair out of her eyes. "Guess who she saw holding hands in the Christmas market yesterday?"

Dorothy tried not to smile. "You don't really want me to waste time guessing, do you? And I'm sure I don't know why we need bother with a local newspaper given the extraordinary powers of observation displayed by the locals."

Sara was vibrating with excitement. "Pippa bumped into Miles and Imogen. And they were holding hands."

"I thought we agreed we weren't going to interfere?"

"I'm not interfering, exactly, just showing an intense interest."

Dorothy dusted the mince pies with icing sugar. "It is lethal underfoot at the moment, so that was probably a good decision from a health and safety point of view. Does anything in those bags need to go in the fridge, Sara?"

"Health and safety? They weren't holding hands because it was icy, Mum. They were laughing and talking and generally having fun. Those mince pies smell delicious. Are they for eating?"

"Later. I've made them for Imogen. She told me they're her favorite." And right now she would have baked anything from a six-tier cake to a soufflé (and she hated making soufflé) if Imogen expressed a preference. She wanted to spoil her. To make up for all the years she hadn't been able to do that. "It's good to know they were having fun. If you're going to spend the whole day with someone it's best to enjoy it."

"How did you know they were spending the whole day together?" Sara's eyes narrowed. "Lissa only told me about it this morning."

"This sounds more like interference than interest, Sara."

"Fine. I'm interfering, although to be honest they seem to be doing fine without any help from us. Tell me how you know!"

"Miles told me he'd planned a day of Christmassy things for Imogen. They were going to the Christmas market, walk in the country, lunch in the pub and then I think they were doing the light trail. I thought it was a lovely idea. Very romantic. And perfect for Imogen. It will be good for her to get into the spirit of Christmas for once. All that talk of pizzas made me shudder." Leaving the mince pies to cool, she started to unload Sara's bags. "I get the sense she hasn't had anywhere near enough fun in her life. She's been so focused on making sure she can earn money and be independent."

Not that Imogen had said much, but she'd said enough for Dorothy to work out that it hadn't been easy for her. And she felt both guilty and frustrated about that.

"Wait—Miles told you?" Sara stared at her. "When?"

"He dropped in for a quick coffee very early yesterday morning. We had a little chat, but that's not unusual."

"And you didn't tell me?"

"I didn't see you yesterday. And anyway, I always treat my conversations with Miles as confidential. I'm his mother figure. I like to think I'm filling in for poor Sheila—" Dorothy felt the usual pang of loss as she thought of her friend "—and anyway I didn't want to draw attention to it and possibly make them both feel awkward."

"From what Pippa said, they are way past feeling awkward. I was really hoping they'd spent the night together, but his car wasn't there this morning when I took the kids to school. Gutting. And Imogen was definitely in because I saw a light on, so she didn't stay over at his." Sara paused for breath. "Mum?"

Ralph chose that moment to charge into the room, carrying one of Dorothy's slippers, and Sara looked from the dog to her mother.

"Ralph is here? Why is Ralph here?"

"I looked after him yesterday while they went on their date. Miles didn't want to leave him alone for that long, which given the chaos this dog can cause was probably a wise decision." She bent to make a fuss of him. "But you were a good boy, weren't you? Yes, you were, although I'm going to need that slipper back now, thank you."

Ralph dropped it at her feet, tail wagging.

Sara was frowning. "But why did he stay overnight? Why didn't Miles just pick him up when he dropped Imogen home?"

"I expect he was late and didn't want to disturb me. And that was fine with me. Ralph is a sweetheart, although for some reason he wanted to sleep on the bed with me, which is a little strange because I'm sure Valerie never let him into her bedroom." Dorothy rubbed the top of his head. "I don't know where he would have picked up that habit."

"Do you think Miles stayed the night and hid the car?"

"Goodness, why would he hide his car?" Dorothy straightened. "They're both consenting adults. If they chose to spend the night together, then that's their choice. I've invited Valerie to join us for Christmas lunch. I didn't like the idea of her being on her own, and she is very easy company. She always tells great stories from her pharmacy days about people's 'drug habits' as she calls them. I hope that's okay with you and Patrick. Ellen is going to pick her up on her way over.

"At this rate the entire village is going to be spending Christmas here, but that's fine by me. And as for Miles and Imogen— I'm not judging. Just hopeful, that's all." Sara sneaked a mince pie from the rack. "I love Miles like a brother. Can I help it if I want him to be happy? Although Imogen lives in London, and Miles isn't moving from here, so how would it work in the long-term?"

"I don't know, and I don't need to know because it's not my business. And it's not your business either."

Sara took a bite of the mince pie and closed her eyes. "This is delicious. And London isn't a million miles away."

"Sara!"

"What? Sorry. I was thinking aloud, that's all."

"Well, maybe think quietly." Dorothy gave her a look. "In my experience it doesn't pay to matchmake or interfere in any way. When Imogen arrives, you're to behave normally. You're not to interrogate her."

"I'll try not to." But Sara was smiling. "Lissa would be thrilled if something happened between them. She has been so worried about him ever since Zara left. He's barely dated."

"He's been careful, that's true. But I don't blame him for that. And as I said, it's not our business. Now stop talking about it because I don't want Imogen to arrive and find us gossiping. Have you finished your Christmas shopping?"

"All done. How about you?"

"I just have Imogen left to buy for. I've bought fun things for her stocking—Iris and I chose a few things together, but I want to give her something special. Can you think of anything she'd like?"

Sara was still smiling. "Er—a certain super-hot animal doctor, maybe?"

"Sara!"

"Okay, sorry. No meddling." Sara sat back and thought. "Clothes? No. She lives in London so she'll have plenty of clothes. And she always looks stylish, even when she's dressed for arctic weather. A necklace? Something special?"

"I hadn't thought of that. Maybe." Dorothy pondered. "This is her first Christmas with us, and it's a fresh start. A beginning, if you like. I want to give her something meaningful. Something that makes her feel like part of the family."

"I think just being here with us will make her feel like part of the family," Sara said, "but I'll keep thinking."

The dogs suddenly shot out of the room barking, and Dorothy watched them go.

"Someone at the door. Imogen, no doubt. No more talking about Miles. And do not give her the third degree on her love life."

"My lips are sealed."

Imogen walked into the room moments later, an adoring Ralph at her heels.

"Thank you so much for keeping him, Dorothy." She hugged Dorothy tightly, and Dorothy felt a lump build in her throat. All the love she'd been holding back threatened to spill out.

"You're so welcome. Anytime."

Imogen made a fuss of Ralph. "Was he good?"

"Good as gold." Dorothy eyed Ralph, and Imogen glanced at her with a smile.

"Was he a handful?"

"Well, he did keep wanting to share the bed with me, but once we established that it wasn't going to happen, he slept down here with Bailey and all was well."

Imogen turned pink. "That's my fault. I may have spoiled him a little when he was staying with me."

"And this is why we don't have a dog," Sara said. "Having two children climbing into bed with me is more than enough. Did you have a fun day yesterday, Imogen?"

"It was brilliant. I bought a gift for Ralph. And one for Bailey too. No favoritism." Imogen put her hand in her pocket and presented each dog with a new chew toy shaped like a bone. "The Christmas market was so festive, and the light trail was magical. I'm still thinking about it."

"You were lucky with the weather," Sara said. "It was a clear night. It must have been romantic."

Dorothy sighed. "Sara—"

"It was romantic." Imogen leaned against the countertop, a dreamy look in her eyes. "I had the perfect day. Normally

I avoid everything to do with Christmas, but yesterday I embraced everything and I had the best time. Miles is so great."

"He is," Sara said. "He really is."

Imogen watched as Ralph played with the bone. "Did you know he asked his sister for ideas for the best Christmassy date ever?"

"Well, actually I—" Sara caught her mother's eye. "No. Didn't know that. Tell us all about it."

Dorothy reached for a cake tin. "Imogen might prefer to keep it to herself."

"No, I wouldn't. It was so amazing I want to talk about it." She gave them an apologetic look. "Sorry. I've never felt like this before. You're probably bored. You don't want to hear it."

"Trust me, we want to hear it. The more detail, the better," Sara said, and pulled out the chair next to her. "Sit down, Imogen. Eat a mince pie. They're delicious. Mum will make us both coffee while you tell us everything. Where is Miles, by the way?"

"He's working today and he was called at six." Imogen sat down next to Sara. "He did tell me which farm, but I've forgotten the name."

"At six?" Understanding spread across Sara's face, along with a smile. "He left the cottage at six? That explains it."

"Explains what?"

Sara caught her mother's eye. "Why you're—er—looking a little tired. How maddening for you not being able to have a lie-in and a slow start to the day."

"I don't mind. That's his job, isn't it?"

"True."

"I like the fact that he cares about his work so much. I'm the same."

"He's a good person. Also smoking hot—"

Dorothy gave a start. "Sara!"

Sara grinned at Imogen. "We'll have that conversation when your grandmother isn't in the room."

"I'm not a prude," Dorothy said, "just more respectful of people's privacy than you are."

"I'm respectful of people's privacy normally," Sara protested, "but Imogen is family so that gives me probing rights."

Dorothy was about to contradict her when she saw the glow on Imogen's face.

She'd been racking her brains for something special she could buy to make Imogen feel part of their family unit, and Sara had managed it with a few intrusive words and one emphatic statement.

Imogen is family.

Dorothy cleared her throat. "Just remember, Imogen," she said briskly, "that being family gives you the right to tell your well-meaning but interfering aunt to keep her questions and observations to herself."

Imogen stole another mince pie. "It's good to have someone to talk to about it."

"It's a shame Miles was working today," Sara said. "But I suppose at least one of you had a lie-in."

"Not really. I got up at six and made him coffee and a bacon sandwich. It's cold out there and you know how hungry he gets." Imogen finished the mince pie. "These are the best, Dorothy. I'd happily eat nothing else for the rest of my life. Do you know how to make boeuf bourguignon? And if so, will you teach me?"

"Yes. But why do you need to make it?"

Imogen blushed. "Because yesterday when we were talking about our favorite foods, Miles mentioned that he loves it. I'm cooking him dinner tomorrow and I thought I'd surprise him. And I hope you don't mind, but I invited him to the play tonight and he said yes. He said he'd help with Benson."

Dorothy stared at her. "Miles is coming to the school play? Are you sure?"

Sara was laughing. "Oh, Imogen, Imogen—"

"What? Should I not have invited him?"

"I invite him every year," Dorothy said, "particularly if they want to borrow animals. He always refuses."

"In the past he has found himself either dodging amorous mothers or questions about pets," Sara said dryly. "He probably thinks that if he's with you, he has protection."

"I do have a black belt in jujitsu." Imogen flexed her biceps. "Not that I think he'll need my protection. He has muscles of his own."

Sara rested her chin on her palm. "Tell us more, Imogen."

"Ignore her," Dorothy advised. "Now back to that casserole. It's all in the quality of the meat and wine. We could go to the farm shop together to buy all the ingredients, and then we could make it in your kitchen at Holly Cottage."

"Are you sure you have time?"

"Absolutely. We'll make extra for the freezer." Dorothy walked to the kitchen shelves, selected a book and opened it to the right page. "This is the recipe I use, although I adapt it slightly. You'll see my notes in the margin. You'll need to make a shopping list."

Imogen studied the recipe and started making notes in her phone. "I want it to be special."

"I'll get Patrick to choose you a good wine," Sara said. "How about candles? Do you have candles?"

"There are candles in the cottage."

Imogen looked doubtful. "Do you think candles will be too much? I don't want to scare him."

"He's not the sort of guy who scares easily. Unless you expect him to attend the school play unaccompanied. Also—" Sara leaned forward "—candlelight is very forgiving. If the food isn't perfect, he won't be able to see."

Dorothy gave her a look. "The food will be perfect. Do you want us to keep Ralph here?"

"No, but thank you." Imogen bent to stroke him. "We love having him around."

"Well, I'm sure Ralph would happily devour a boeuf bourguignon, so make sure you don't leave him alone in the kitchen." Dorothy grabbed a sheet of paper and a pen and started scribbling a shopping list for their trip. "The meat benefits from marinating overnight so we should probably shop this afternoon if we have time. Do you have plans?"

"Just wrapping the Christmas gifts I bought yesterday and getting ready for the play." Imogen paused. "And I need to go and buy a stamp."

"A stamp? For a card? I can give you one of those." Sara opened her purse and found a stamp. "I thought you didn't send cards."

"I never have before. This is a first." Imogen hesitated. "I had another call from Tina."

Sara's smile faded. "Oh."

"I ignored it. I was on my dream date."

"Good for you."

Sara scooted her chair closer to Imogen's and put her hand on her arm. "Did she leave a message?"

"Just that I should call her," Imogen said. "Which means she must want something."

Ralph dropped his bone on the floor and crossed the room to her.

"Are you going to call her?"

"I almost did this morning. Partly because that's what I always do—it's hardwired into me—and partly because I'm upset and I want answers. She made the decision to cut you out of her life, and she made that decision for all of us. She didn't give me a choice and she didn't give you a choice." Imogen stroked Ralph's head. "I considered going back to London for the day and hammering on her door so that I could get those answers face-to-face."

"If you want to go and talk to her in person, then I'll come with you," Sara said immediately, and Imogen gave a wavering smile.

"Thank you. You have no idea how much it means to know that you'd do that. But you don't need to, because I'm not going."

Dorothy felt a huge wave of relief. She'd been so afraid that Tina might somehow manage to disrupt the new tender shoots of their relationship.

"You're not?"

"No. I talked it through with Miles, and I realized that getting answers won't make any difference to how I feel. There is nothing she can say that will change anything, so in a way her reasons don't matter, do they? It's done. It happened. It's in the past. Even if she were to say she was sorry and that she regretted it, it wouldn't change where we are now. And I'd rather focus on where we are now."

"So are you going to return her call?"

"No. I've written her a Christmas card. My first ever card." Imogen gave a half smile. "And in the card I told her that I'd met you, and that moving forward you're going to be part of my life. A big part. And if she would also like to be part of my life and have a proper relationship, then she can get in touch. But if it is to stand a chance of working she needs to stop blaming me, and also you, for the choices she made, and start taking responsibility. Obviously I'd love an apology, but unless Santa can work miracles, I don't suppose that will be coming my way anytime soon."

Dorothy felt a rush of respect and something close to awe. "You're really quite incredible." Her voice broke a little and Imogen pulled a face.

"I'm really not," she said. "I should have said it years ago, but I couldn't bear the idea of cutting ties with the person I believed to be my only family, even if she was only interested in me for what I could provide. I wish I'd done things differently, but I'm not going to beat myself up about that. I did what felt right at the time, and that's all you can do."

I did what felt right at the time.

Dorothy felt a lump gather in her throat. That was true of her, too. She'd done what felt right at the time. And she'd beaten herself up about it ever since.

No more. She'd always believed in second chances. Maybe it was time to give herself a second chance.

She was going to follow Imogen's example and leave the past where it belonged, in the past.

She was going to forgive herself for any mistakes she may have made. She was going to acknowledge that Tina's choices were her own.

And instead of regretting all those years she hadn't had Imogen in her life, she was going to be grateful for the years they had ahead.

And suddenly she knew. She knew exactly what she was going to give Imogen for Christmas.

23

Imogen

Imogen loaded her gifts carefully into the back of the car. She'd spent hours wrapping them, folding perfect creases in festive paper and tying elaborate bows with shimmering ribbon, and she wasn't going to risk ruining all her hard work now. It felt a little ridiculous to be driving the short distance to Dorothy's, but there was no other way of transporting the presents. And also herself. She'd treated herself to a new dress at one of the boutiques in the village, and it wasn't exactly designed for a snowy trek up to the house.

She'd assumed she'd be going with Miles, but after spending a romantic Christmas Eve together, sipping champagne and talking about everything under the sun as they always seemed to do when they were together, he'd vanished before it was light.

She'd been half-asleep when he left, had dimly heard him wish her a Merry Christmas, but when she'd woken enough for a conversation, he was gone and so was Ralph.

He'd left a note on the kitchen table saying he had things to do, and he'd meet her at Dorothy's.

And she was already looking forward to seeing him again, even though it had only been a few hours. They'd spent every available moment together since their Christmassy date, and she'd never been happier.

She loaded the last of the parcels, locked the cottage and drove carefully up the snow-covered drive to the house.

Dorothy had told her that she was welcome to stay at the house for Christmas Eve, but given that Ava and Iris were also in residence, Imogen and Miles had decided it would be more appropriate for them to stay at the cottage. Also, she was conscious that she and Miles didn't have that much longer together, living like this, and she wanted to make the most of it.

"Imogen!" Ava was in the doorway, waving madly. She was wearing a red dress with green tights, her cheeks were flushed with excitement and she already had traces of chocolate around her mouth. "I'll help you with your presents."

"Don't let her help," Iris advised, appearing next to her. "She either drops them or opens them."

"I do not."

"We'll all help Imogen." Sara stepped past the girls and together they unloaded the car and transferred everything into the house. "Where's Miles?"

"Being mysterious. He muttered something about an animal."

"He did warn us he might get called out," Sara said, and Ava's eyes were round.

"Maybe it's one of Santa's reindeer that's sick. They must be very tired because going round the whole world is a very long way."

"That could be it." Sara closed the front door and they deposited all Imogen's gifts under the tree.

Imogen took off her coat and Ava gasped.

"You sparkle! Look, Mummy."

"I can see." Sara stood back and admired Imogen. "That is a stunning dress."

"You look like the star on the Christmas tree. All silvery." Ava touched Imogen's dress reverentially. "Can I have one the same?"

"A fashionista at six." Patrick gave Imogen a quick kiss on the cheek by way of welcome. "Pity me. Or at least, pity our bank balance."

"I'm not sure the dress comes in your size," Imogen told Ava, "but we can take a look later."

She'd been nervous that she'd overdone it, but Sara had also made an extra effort and was wearing an elegant dress of midnight blue velvet, with her hair swept into a casual updo. Her nod to Christmas was the pair of silver robin earrings that dangled from her ears, catching the light each time she moved.

Ava lifted her arms up to Imogen and she scooped her up and felt the child's arms lock around her neck.

"So did Santa come?" She felt a rush of affection for the little girl. "Was your stocking full?"

"Yes! I had lots of things. I'll show you. And chocolate. I've already eaten it."

"I can see that."

"Can we open your presents now?" Ava wriggled out of Imogen's arms, shot over to the Christmas tree and began shaking and squashing the parcels Imogen had brought.

Imogen could feel her excitement, but she could also feel everyone else's excitement.

There was a level of energy in the room that wasn't usually present.

"How about you open one now," she suggested, "and the rest later?"

"Yes!" Ava read the labels carefully and handed one to her sister. "This is for Iris."

Iris blushed and smiled at Imogen. "Thank you." She sat down next to Imogen and carefully untied the ribbon.

Ava, meanwhile, ripped the paper from her gift in her haste to get to whatever was inside. "It's an alpaca!" She held it aloft. "I love it. I want to show Benson." She was on her feet and halfway across the living room when Sara stopped her.

"What do you say to Imogen?"

"Thank you." Ava shot back across the room and gave Imogen a chocolatey kiss. "I'm going to call it Benson."

"Nanna is just bringing a snack," Sara said, "so maybe show Benson later."

Dorothy came into the room carrying a tray of coffee and homemade cinnamon biscuits. "I thought you'd need to keep your strength up with all these parcels to unwrap." She saw Imogen and smiled. "You're here!"

"Just arrived. Merry Christmas." It felt strange saying those words, because normally she didn't have anyone to say them to.

"Merry Christmas." Dorothy put the tray down and gave Imogen a big hug. "This is going to be the best Christmas ever, as Ava would say."

"It already is. Nanna, look!" Ava waved her alpaca and Dorothy dutifully admired it, while handing around coffee to the adults.

They'd opened half the presents and almost devoured the cinnamon cookies by the time Miles appeared in the doorway.

Imogen felt her heart miss a beat.

Seeing him made her so *happy*.

Was this love? It couldn't be, could it? Not after such a short time. But it was something, she knew that. Something important. Something exciting and good.

His gaze held hers for a few intimate seconds before he turned his attention to Ava, who was tugging at his arm.

"Come in, Miles." Dorothy gestured to a gap on the sofa.

"Ellen and Valerie are coming for twelve, so we'll open our gifts now, but I just need ten minutes in the kitchen before we start."

Imogen was about to ask Miles where Ralph was, but he'd struck up a conversation with Patrick about a book they'd both read, so she followed Dorothy into the kitchen along with Sara.

"What can I do to help?"

"Nothing at all," Dorothy said. "You're a guest. Sara? Could you peel some more potatoes and parsnips please? I'm nervous that I didn't do enough. Miles and Patrick eat so much and I don't want anyone to go hungry."

"There is absolutely zero chance of that. And Imogen is not a guest, she's family." Sara handed Imogen a potato peeler. "You do the potatoes, and I'll do the parsnips."

Imogen laughed. Who would have thought that being handed a potato peeler would have given her such a high? "Whatever you say, Aunt Sara."

Sara winced. "You make me feel old. Also, on second thought, maybe you shouldn't be peeling potatoes in that silver dress."

"It's fine."

"It's more than fine. Did you see the expression on Miles's face when he saw that dress?" Sara winked at Imogen. "He definitely wanted to unwrap you."

He'd unwrapped her many times over the past week, but she didn't tell them that.

She was discovering that there were some things that you didn't share, even with family.

They worked side by side in the kitchen until Dorothy was satisfied that lunch could look after itself for a while and then they returned to the living room, where Ava's excitement levels were almost off the scale.

"Everything is under control in the kitchen," Dorothy said, "so let's take a few moments together before our guests arrive. I think it's time for Imogen to open some of her gifts."

"Ava and I will get them for you, Imogen." Flushed and excited, Iris scrambled under the tree with her sister, checking labels and emerging with boxes of different shapes and sizes.

Imogen watched, feeling self-conscious.

A stocking with her name embroidered on it was placed on her lap, lumpy and stiff with gifts.

She squeezed it in awe. "This is—" she swallowed "—my first stocking."

"What?" Ava was astounded. "Why? Didn't Santa know where you lived? Did you not write to him?"

"I never wrote to him."

"Never? From now on we'll write together." Ava launched herself onto the sofa next to Imogen. "Shall I help you open them?"

It was only a few weeks before that she'd been dreading another lonely Christmas, and now here she was, surrounded by family and presents and more warmth than she'd felt in a long time.

"I'd love some help."

"I'll help too." Iris sat down on the other side of her.

"You're taking too long!" Ava thrust a gift at Imogen and she laughed and unwrapped it, and then another and another, until she was feeling completely overwhelmed by their generosity.

And then they opened their presents from her, and she felt a glow of happiness at their excited response. She was grateful to Miles for their Christmas shopping trip, and not only because it was one of the happiest days she could remember.

She hadn't had a response from her mother to the Christmas card she'd sent, but it didn't matter. Maybe she'd be in touch, and maybe she wouldn't. But Imogen knew that with the support of Dorothy, Sara and also Miles, she'd handle whatever happened.

"By the way, this came for you yesterday, by special delivery." Sara handed her a big box. "The postmark is London."

London?

Mystified, Imogen opened the box and found a card from Rosalind, Anya, Janie, Sophie and the rest of the team.

Happy Christmas Imogen. We miss you! Can't wait to have you back—we're sick of doing all your work ☺

Imogen swallowed.

We miss you.

She felt a lump in her throat. When she'd sent the Christmas card to her mother, she'd sent another to her colleagues, and she'd included a letter that told them everything. It had felt easier to do it in a letter, somehow. To write it down. She'd been dreading their response, but now they'd sent her this.

"They've sent you a present." Ava dug her hand into the box and pulled out a soft toy. "It's a dog. I love it, although not as much as the alpaca you got me! It looks a bit like Ralph."

"It's not for you." Iris pried it from her sister's grasp and handed it to Imogen.

The stuffed dog did indeed look like Ralph, but round its neck was a tag that read Midas.

She smiled and suddenly felt that everything might, after all, be okay.

They'd accepted what she'd told them. They'd accepted *her*.

She glanced at Miles, who was the only person who knew the whole truth about her complicated life with her colleagues.

He smiled back. "That's the best kind of dog to have at work. Also the vet bills will be low."

"Now it's my turn." Dorothy held a small, prettily wrapped parcel in her hands. "I spent a lot of time thinking about what I could give you, Imogen. I wanted it to be special, to mark our first Christmas together. Something that you would always remember."

Imogen was touched. "I'm always going to remember today." How could she not? "I don't need a gift for that."

"Well, I hope you're going to like this." Dorothy gave her the gift and Imogen unwrapped it carefully, wondering what it could be.

She opened the box and inside she found a key. She lifted it out, mystified. "A key?"

"It's the key to Holly Cottage." Dorothy's voice was husky. "It's yours, sweetheart. I want you to have it. I know you live in London, and your life is in London, but I thought maybe that if you had somewhere that was yours here, you might come for weekends occasionally and visit us. Maybe you could work the occasional day from home if Rosalind would allow it. Or better still, come and work for us. We could use someone with your skills."

Imogen was silent. She couldn't speak.

"There's no pressure," Sara said quickly. "We know you're really busy and once you get back to work you'll be snowed under again and you probably won't even have time to think about us. But there are probably times when you feel like getting out of London, so hopefully this will allow you to do that. And just to be clear—you don't have to join the family business, just because you're family."

Join the family business.

"I don't know what to say." Her eyes filled, but she blinked back the tears because today was supposed to be happy and she didn't want to confuse her little cousins. And she *was* happy, of course. Incredibly happy. "It's such a generous gift."

And the gift was so much more than bricks and mortar, and she had a feeling Dorothy knew that.

Her grandmother wasn't just giving her a cottage, she was giving her security.

For the first time in her life, she had a safety net.

For the first time in her life, she wasn't alone.

"I'm going to stay here as often as I can." Imogen felt the weight of the key in her hand. "I've already decided to change things when I go back."

She'd given it a lot of thought and she'd emailed Rosalind a few days before and been surprised when Rosalind had immediately called her. She was conscious that Rosalind would already have seen the letter she'd written, so there were no more secrets.

They'd had a frank conversation during which Imogen had admitted that Rosalind had been right—she had been near burnout. She knew she had to find a way of working that still allowed her to perform at her best, without veering into the unhealthy. She also wanted to find a way to spend more time with Miles. Rosalind had proposed a compromise. Imogen could work from home whenever it fitted with her schedule (it helped that they had a couple of clients based in the Cotswolds) and would try and delegate more, so that she didn't have to be present at every event. Rosalind hadn't mentioned the card Imogen had sent, or the embarrassing saga of Midas. Imogen had been feeling mortified, but now she had this funny and thoughtful gift from her colleagues and she felt so much better.

She'd go back in January and it would be a fresh start. A new way of working.

It was enough for now, and maybe, at some point in the future, she would consider taking a job with the family business.

She looked at Dorothy. "You're not going to believe this, but I was going to ask you if I could book Holly Cottage for a few weeks next year."

"This way you won't have to book anything, and I'd much rather it was a home for you than a rental."

A home.

She imagined herself drinking her morning coffee outside in the spring, with daffodils and tulips all around her and lambs in the fields beyond. She imagined taking summer walks across the fields to the village. Spending time in the bookshop, meeting Miles for lunch in the pub.

And when she needed to work, she could do it at the desk in the spare room, overlooking the glorious countryside and maybe take Ralph for a walk on her lunch break if Miles would let her.

"I don't know what to say." Overwhelmed, she stood up and hugged Dorothy. "Thank you. This means the world. I'll be coming here so often you'll probably live to regret your generosity."

"Never." Dorothy hugged Imogen tightly and then let her go and cleared her throat. "Now then, if that's all the present opening finished, we should do some last-minute lunch prep and perhaps Iris and Ava could check the table."

"One minute—" Miles interrupted her. "The present opening isn't quite finished. I have something for Imogen."

She'd expected a woolly hat, so she was surprised when he left the room. She heard the sound of the front door opening, the slam of a car door and then a familiar bark.

Ralph came thundering into the room and skidded to a halt in front of Imogen, an adoring expression on his face.

Ava frowned. "Why does Ralph have a big red ribbon around his neck?"

"Because I'd be accused of animal cruelty if I tried to wrap him in paper." Miles dropped to a crouch beside the dog and looked at Imogen. "I know you can't take him back to London, but I also know how much you love him. And he loves you right back."

The way Miles was looking at her made her wonder for a moment if he was talking about more than the dog. But she wasn't going to pursue that thought, not with her entire family watching in fascination. She could see Sara grinning and exchanging "I told you so" looks with Patrick and even Dorothy was observing them curiously.

Ralph was wagging his tail and he put his paw on her leg.

"Watch her silver dress!" Sara was horrified, but Imogen didn't care about the dress.

"I do love him." But what exactly was he suggesting?

"So here's what I thought—" Miles took her hand. "We have joint custody. He lives with me during the week, and when you're back here, either staying with me or in Holly Cottage, as that seems to be your new home, he's yours. Ours."

Ours.

She and Miles. Together.

She had no idea how they were going to make it work, but she knew that they would. They'd find a way. And although she knew it was far too early to be thinking long-term, eventually maybe they'd be living under one roof.

"That sounds perfect."

"Good." His gaze held hers. "There's just one rule."

"There is?"

"Yes. You promise not to let him sleep on the bed."

She was so happy she couldn't resist teasing him. "Even when he looks at me with sad eyes?"

"Especially then. It's important that he knows who is boss."

"Ralph is the boss." Imogen hugged Ralph, and Miles grinned and dropped a small parcel into her lap.

"And because it might take a while to figure out the logistics, I bought you this."

"It doesn't feel like a woolly hat." She opened it and saw a framed photo of her and Ralph taken in the snow a few days before. She was laughing up at the camera, her arms around the dog and her smile was so huge she barely recognized herself.

"It's for your desk," he said softly. "Because everyone should have a picture of their dog on their desk."

She felt so much emotion she almost couldn't speak. "I'm just disappointed it isn't a woolly hat," she said finally, and everyone laughed.

"Right, enough of this family togetherness. We really should get ready," Sara said. "Mum has invited half the village for lunch. But first let's have a family toast."

Patrick came into the room with brimming glasses on a tray, and they all took one.

Sara raised her glass. "To Imogen. And family." She smiled at her girls and at Patrick. "Merry Christmas."

Imogen raised her glass too, mostly because Ralph's wagging tail was in danger of knocking it out of her hand.

"Merry Christmas."

She was starting to understand why this time of year was special to so many people.

Here, among her family, she felt cocooned by love and happiness. Getting to know them had been like putting together pieces of a jigsaw and building up a picture, but now she realized that she was a piece of that same jigsaw. The missing piece.

And she fitted perfectly.

* * * * *

Acknowledgments

It takes a team to put a book into the hands of readers and I'm fortunate enough to work with excellent publishing teams. My continued thanks to the brilliant Margaret Marbury, Susan Swinwood and the rest of the team at Canary Street Press for working so hard to put my books into the hands of readers. Lisa Milton, Manpreet Grewal, and the whole team at HQ Stories have championed my work from the start and it's thanks to their hard work, creativity and enthusiasm that more and more readers are discovering my books. Hitting that coveted number one slot on the *Sunday Times* bestseller list with *The Christmas Book Club* was a career high for me, and I have them to thank for it. Also working with them is FUN, which is always a bonus!

My talented editor, Flo Nicoll, continues to cast her particular brand of magic over every book I write. I've worked with Flo for so long she feels more like family than a colleague, and

I'm convinced we have the perfect editor/author partnership. All authors should be so lucky.

My agent, Susan Ginsburg, is simply the best. I value her wise advice (and her sense of humour!) more than I can say. I'm grateful to her, Catherine Bradshaw and the whole team at Writers House for their tireless advocacy and support.

I have the best family anyone could wish for, not least because they always produce food and chocolate when I'm nearing a deadline.

My biggest thanks go to my readers who continue to buy my books, send kind messages, post beautiful photos and generally encourage me. I hope this book is a welcome addition to the collection.

Love
Sarah

Turn the page for a sneak peek of
USA TODAY *bestselling author Sarah Morgan's next novel,
coming this spring from Canary Street Press!*

1

Milly

Why had she said yes?

Milly sat in her car outside the railway station, although it seemed generous to call it that given that it was in the middle of nowhere and consisted of nothing more than a single platform and a shelter. There was no ticket office. No buzz of waiting people. Just one train an hour.

It was the last place on earth you'd expect to encounter a movie star, which was presumably why Nicole had chosen it.

Milly understood the need for discretion and privacy, but still, this felt like overkill.

There was one other car parked farther down the narrow country road, but other than that, there were no signs of life and she sat in the darkness, trying not to be spooked as she waited for that one train, the last train of the day. She'd opened the car windows, but even at this late hour it was stifling. It had been the hottest June on record and there was no sign of the weather breaking. Back in March when it had rained every day, Milly had dreamed of sunshine, but the sunshine had brought with it a smothering heat that made her dream of rain.

She'd already sweat off the makeup she'd carefully applied before leaving, but she didn't bother renewing it, because what was the point? It was dark and there was no one to see her anyway. It didn't matter how she looked. But when you were meeting someone who many considered to be one of the most beautiful women in the world, it was hard to resist the urge to make an effort.

Not that anyone noticed her when Nicole was around. They never had.

She sighed and checked the time.

Maybe Nicole had changed her mind. *Please let her have changed her mind.*

She'd heard nothing since that single phone call the night before. Was she wasting her time sitting here? She thought about her child, safely asleep in her grandmother's house. Milly hated asking her mother for help and this time she hadn't even been able to explain why she needed last-minute babysitting because Nicole had sworn her to secrecy.

She felt guilty because her mother had assumed Milly was finally going on a date and hadn't been able to hide her delight. "Good," she'd said. "It's been eighteen months since Richard walked out and the divorce has been final for six months. I'm pleased you've finally moved on."

Moved on?

Milly hadn't moved on. If she'd admitted that the *last* thing she wanted was another romantic entanglement when she was still tied up in knots about the last one, she would have caused her mother even more worry and she didn't want to do that. She kept those thoughts to herself, but the effort required to pretend she was coping well was exhausting.

All she really wanted now was to be the best mother possible to Zoe, but she was pretty sure she was failing at that too.

She'd read so many books and articles on how to make divorce easier on kids, the advice swirled around in her head. She was trying hard to put everything into practice. She'd been careful not to say a bad word about Richard in front of Zoe (although she used plenty of bad words when she was alone in the shower), and she tried to keep everything around them as normal as possible. She forced herself to get up in the morning, and smile and pretend to be fine when she really wasn't fine at all and would gladly have spent the whole day in bed.

Between lying to her mother, putting on a brave face for her child and forcing herself to be polite to Richard even when he was being frustratingly unreasonable and unapologetically selfish, she'd forgotten what it felt like to actually express her true feelings.

There had been a time when the prospect of Nicole coming to stay would have lifted her mood because if there was one person in the world she could be honest with, it was Nicole. But not anymore.

What was she doing here when the last thing she needed was more emotional stress? She didn't know if she was a fool, or if this was the very definition of friendship—showing up no matter what.

Promises made when you were fifteen didn't seem to make as much sense when you were thirty-five. They certainly hadn't meant anything to Nicole.

She reached for her phone and sent a message.

Are you on the train?

A flash of headlights caught her attention and she froze in her seat as another car approached. It drove past without stopping and she let out the breath she hadn't realized she'd been holding. She wasn't built for subterfuge.

When Nicole had called her asking for help, she should have said no.

She was particularly frustrated with herself because she'd recently done an online course on assertiveness, thanks to a twenty-minute wait at the hairdresser, where she'd foolishly fallen into the trap of doing one of those magazine questionnaires.

If you answer yes to more than three questions, you may have a problem with being assertive.

Milly had answered yes to all ten questions and had decided right then and there that she needed to do something about it. Her tendency to say yes was the reason she felt pressured all the time. It was the reason she lay awake at night, stressed and hyperventilating with her to-do list racing around her brain. It was the reason she never felt able to call out Richard's unreasonable behavior (he'd already humiliated and divorced her, so really what more could he do?). She didn't know if the way he behaved was a hallmark of ex-husbands generally, but she knew she wasn't handling it well. It had to stop. She had to change.

She was too busy to take a class in person, largely because of her inability to say no, so she'd enrolled in an online course and for two weeks had spent an hour every evening practicing ways to be more assertive. She'd learned about boundaries, about the importance of standing up for her rights and respecting other people's, she'd filled out worksheets where she'd practiced ways of saying no. Assertive, but not aggressive. Use the *I* word, not *you. When you do (fill in particular behavioral aberration here)… I feel (describe, without swearing, how it makes you feel)…*

She'd passed with flying colors and thought that maybe this would be a new beginning. And then her phone had rung.

The caller display had said Sister.

Milly had stared at it for so long it had stopped ringing. But it had immediately started again and this time she'd answered it, even though part of her didn't want to.

It wasn't her sister, of course. She didn't have a sister, but when Nicole's career had taken off, she'd insisted that Milly store her number under a different name. It had felt exciting at the time. Clandestine. It had made her feel special, because all of a sudden everyone wanted a piece of Nicole and Milly had her number in her phone.

They'd been in their early twenties, but even at that tender age their lives couldn't have been more different. Milly was married to Richard and had just discovered she was pregnant. She spent her days helping her mother run the family business, a small but exclusive resort of lakeside cabins nestled close to the water in the beautiful Lake District.

Nicole, on the other hand, had dropped out of college to pursue acting seriously and by the age of twenty-one had achieved global fame after starring in a movie about a teenager who traveled back in time to save the planet from destruction. It had broken all box office records. Milly had seen the film and agreed with the critics that Nicole had been captivating in the role but that wasn't the point where she'd recognized just how talented her friend was. That moment had come a few months later, when Nicole had all but floated onto the stage to accept the most coveted best-actress award wearing a custom-made gown that somehow managed to make her look both innocent and alluring. Her speech had been heartfelt and moving and many of the people in the audience had cried.

Milly had cried too, and that was when she'd realized that her friend wasn't just going to be big—she was going to be huge. Because the speech was all lies, and Milly knew it was lies. She was, quite possibly, one of only two people who knew it was lies, the other being Nicole's mother, who was unlikely to be watching.

But still, Nicole had made her believe every word and still she'd cried.

Nicole had called her afterward. "Did you hear my speech?"

"Yes, I heard your speech."

"You know the truth. People would pay you to tell my story."

Milly had rolled her eyes. "Don't be ridiculous."

"You have no idea how far people will go to get information on me and tear me down."

"You're sounding paranoid."

But Nicole had said the same thing a few days later when Milly had met her in her suite in a London hotel where she was staying for a premiere of her latest movie.

She'd been escorted to the room by unsmiling security guards with earpieces and overdeveloped muscles, and she'd sat stiffly on one of the white sofas in the ridiculously opulent suite, feeling out of place and desperate to find common ground with her old friend.

She remembered ten-year-old Nicole saying *one day I'm going to be famous*, and here she was—famous.

And fame had changed everything.

"Seriously, Milly, you can't have my name in your phone anymore. Someone might see it. We need to agree on a different name." Nicole had been wired, nervous, talking too quickly, sipping a glass of wine even though it was three in the afternoon. Her hair fell in dark silky waves down her back and those famous eyes, *eyes that made you lose your powers of speech*, as one smitten critic had put it, were huge in her pale face. In real life she seemed thinner than ever, and Milly, almost eight months pregnant by then, had felt like a baby elephant next to her.

She'd shifted slightly, trying to get more comfortable, which was almost impossible with a baby stuck under your ribs. "Who is going to see it? And what are they going to do? Mug me and steal my phone? I live by a lake in the middle of nowhere, Nic. I'm surrounded by trees and mountains. When I open my windows, I hear nothing." That wasn't quite true. She frequently slept with the windows open and she lay in the darkness and listened to the plaintive call of the birds on the lake and the occasional hoot of an owl, thinking how much she liked her quiet, predictable life. Unlike Nicole, she'd never had a desire to be famous, and nothing about her friend's life had given her reason to revise her opinion. "My home isn't exactly paparazzi central."

Nicole had looked at her with a mix of envy and pity, as if she was wondering how anyone as unworldly as Milly made it through the day.

"Indulge me." She'd put down her wineglass and taken the phone from her friend. Her slim fingers had flown over the keys. "There. Fixed."

Milly had stared at it. "Sister?"

"Why not? It's what we are. It's the way I feel about you. The way I'll always feel about you." Nicole had hugged her then and Milly had hugged her back and for that brief moment their old connection had flickered to life. This was the Nicole she'd grown up with, not the new glamorous Nicole who couldn't walk down a street without being recognized. Still, she hadn't been able to shake the uneasy feeling that their relationship was about to change in a big way and it made her sad because nothing was more important to her than their friendship.

"You're going to forget about me."

"Don't be ridiculous." Nicole had said exactly what Milly had hoped she'd say. "You're my best friend. You'll always be my best friend, and when we're both old, you're going to come and spend winters with me in California and we'll sit on the deck and watch the sunsets and talk about that time I drank half a bottle of vodka and dyed your hair purple. You were so mad at me you threw my favorite bag in the lake."

Milly knew those weren't the moments she'd remember when she looked back on their friendship. She'd be thinking of all the times Nicole had walked into a room first because Milly had been too shy to enter on her own. She'd remember the patience Nicole had shown when teaching Milly how to project confidence even when she was quaking inside. She'd think about the nights Nicole had stayed over at her place after Milly's dad had walked out. The hours they'd lain awake talking about the future and what they both wanted.

And despite Milly's fears, their friendship had endured. There were frequent phone calls and messages where Nicole would send photos of herself being transformed by hair and makeup into an assassin, an FBI agent, an art thief, a superhero.

Milly had sent back photos of Zoe. Zoe at six months. Zoe taking her first steps. Zoe's first day at school. She'd sent photos of the four new luxury cabins they'd built by the lake and then felt embarrassed because Nicole owned properties around the world and Milly's cabins, modest by comparison, were probably of little interest to her.

But despite their very different lives, they'd been in regular contact until eighteen months ago when Nicole had suddenly ghosted her.

Thinking about that brought her back to the present.

Milly checked the time again. The place felt so dead it was hard to believe a train was due to arrive any minute. But even if it did, there was no guarantee that her friend would be on it. Maybe Nicole was going to ghost her again. Maybe she wasn't going to show up and Milly would drive back home alone, feeling more of a fool than she already did.

And if Nicole did happen to arrive, what was Milly going to say?

Why have you ignored me for the past eighteen months?

Where were you when I needed you?

It had happened right after Milly, Richard and Zoe had visited her in LA. Milly assumed there was a connection and had spent hours going over the holiday in her mind, but couldn't identify a reason. Initially, she hadn't worried because she knew how busy Nicole was, but a few weeks later when Milly had left a message telling her that Richard was having an affair and divorcing her and there was *still* no response, she'd started to worry. More than worry. Her friend's silence had hurt. It had been a bitter blow, coming so soon after Richard's betrayal.

The one person she'd always thought she could depend on, her safety net in life, had let her down.

Milly still couldn't believe Nicole had ignored something so life shattering. When had they ever not supported each other?

Nicole's silence hurt more than it should have because not only had she been dumped by her husband, but it seemed she'd been dumped by her best friend too.

There was no more pretending that Nicole would be there for her in a crisis. No more pretending that the word *sister* in her phone was anything more than a way of disguising Nicole's identity.

Even now, so many months later, that reality hurt.

"Maybe it's me." She spoke aloud, as she sometimes did when she was alone in the car. It was the one time she felt able to speak her mind. "Maybe I'm just the kind of person people leave."

First her father, then Richard and then Nicole.

She'd assumed that was the end of it, and then the night before, Nicole had finally called.

The call should have woken Milly up, but Milly had been lying awake, stewing about Richard, having conversations in her head that she knew she'd never have in real life despite the assertiveness course because she was determined to keep things civil for her daughter.

She'd answered partly because it was Nicole, and Milly had never not answered a call from Nicole, but also because a small hurt part of her hoped that maybe Nicole was finally getting in touch to apologize.

But there had been no apology, just a plea.

I need your help.

Nothing for eighteen months, not a squeak, and now she was expecting Milly to help.

During the conversation, admittedly short, not once had she asked how Milly was doing. She hadn't mentioned Richard's affair, or the divorce, or acknowledged how hard it must be for Milly to be going through exactly what her mother had gone through.

I wouldn't ask if it wasn't important. Please, Milly. I'm desperate.

Desperate? What did desperate look like when your life was pretty much perfect? Just how desperate could you be when you were rich, beautiful and the toast of the moviegoing public?

Nicole didn't know the meaning of the word, but Milly did, although she worked hard not to show it. She was determined not to put that extra pressure on Zoe.

She was just about holding it together, which was another reason she should have said no to Nicole. She should have put into practice everything she'd learned from her assertiveness course. She should have said, *No, sorry, I'm struggling enough with my own life right now, as you'd know if you read your emails*, or better still (as she'd been taught that it wasn't necessary to give lengthy explanations), *Sorry, I can't help.*

But she hadn't said any of those things. She'd said yes.

Yes, she'd pick her up. Yes, she'd drive at night to lessen the chances of being seen. Yes, Nicole could stay with Milly. Yes, she'd find a way to hide her.

Which was why she was now, against her better judgment, sitting in the middle of nowhere, waiting for a train that was late and a friend she wasn't sure she wanted to see.

The assertiveness course clearly hadn't worked. If she was more assertive, she'd demand a refund.

A sound cut through her thoughts and she realized the train was approaching. Finally.

She felt a slight stirring of dread. The fabric of their friendship had been stretched by their diverging paths and was now torn in places and barely holding together. It would have been disingenuous to pretend their relationship hadn't changed.

Usually the only emotion she felt before seeing Nicole was excitement, but tonight her stomach churned with an uncomfortable mix of hurt and resentment.

Where had Nicole been when Milly had needed her?

She was upset and a little bit angry, but most of all disappointed that their friendship had fallen short of what she'd believed it to be.

The train slowed down and stopped and Milly peered into the dimly lit station, but there were only two people visible. One was a man in his fifties who immediately strode toward the parked car that Milly had noticed earlier, and the other was a woman of significantly advanced years wearing a coat that had seen better days and a hat that concealed most of her white hair. She was stooping badly, so bent over she was struggling to walk even with the help of her stick.

There was no sign of Nicole, which was confusing because it had been Nicole who had insisted Milly be poised for a quick getaway.

A quick getaway. Was that even possible in a small family hatchback? Milly hadn't been in the mood for drama. *We're not in a movie now, Nicole.*

And Nicole's response to her. *You have no idea what my life is like.*

Milly couldn't argue with that.

She had no idea what it was like to be one of the most in demand actresses of her generation, commanding millions for each movie. And as if acting talent and looks (voted most beautiful woman two years running) weren't enough, Nicole's last blockbuster had required her to sing, and she'd stunned the world with her voice.

Milly sighed.

The last thing you should do when your life was a total mess was to spend time with someone whose life was perfect.

She glanced at the train again. Still no Nicole, and no sign of anyone else leaving the train. Maybe she was hiding in a dark corner, waiting for these other people to leave before emerging. Or maybe she'd changed her mind.

The old woman teetered slightly, almost losing her balance, and Milly shot out of the car, concern for the woman's safety overriding her promise to keep a low profile.

"Can I help you?" She put a hand on the woman's arm. "It's very late. Is someone meeting you?"

The woman lifted her head and looked directly at Milly and Milly stared into those unmistakable eyes and thought, *I really am a fool.*

"You have to be kidding me. N—"

"Shh. Not until we're in the car."

Milly would have been impressed if she hadn't been so frustrated. Part of that frustration was directed at herself for being so easily duped. "We're in the middle of nowhere and there is no one around."

"They're always around." Nicole slid her arm into Milly's and adopted her stoop again. "Help me into the car."

"Help you?"

How long was this charade supposed to continue?

But she wanted to get out of here as much as Nicole, so she dutifully put her arm around her friend and felt a flicker of shock as she registered how thin she was.

She guided her to the passenger side of the car, hoping no one was watching because she was pretty confident her acting abilities would fool no one.

Nicole handed her the stick and Milly tucked it into the back of the car.

She took another quick glance around the station. "There is no one here." She slid into the driver's seat and closed the door. "You're going to bake inside that coat. Why the heavy disguise? Have you robbed a bank in real life or something? If I'm harboring a criminal, I'd like to know."

Nicole's eyes were closed. "Can we talk about it later? I'm really not—" her voice shook a little "—I'm not feeling too good. And I'm freezing. I need the coat."

Freezing?

Milly had been feeling hurt and angry. There were things she'd planned to say, but there was something about seeing Nicole looking so fragile that sucked all the heat out of her emotions. But then she remembered her assertiveness course.

Her feelings mattered too. This wasn't only about Nicole.

"There is no one around, Nicole. This place is empty. We are the last people here. And before I drive anywhere, I want to know what this is all about. Why the sudden phone call and why the urgency?"

"You seriously don't know?"

"If I knew, I wouldn't be asking."

"Oh, Milly." Nicole gave a choked laugh and opened her eyes. "You haven't changed one bit and I'm so happy about that."

"What's that supposed to mean?" Since Richard had walked out, taking most of her confidence with him, she felt as if every part of her had changed. She could barely remember the person she used to be, but Nicole didn't know that because she hadn't asked.

She felt a pang of loss as she remembered how it used to be. There was a barrier that had never been there before.

Nicole turned her head to look at her. "When we were young you always refused to read scandalous stories about celebrities. You thought it was distasteful that someone was making a career out of exploiting someone else's misfortune and you didn't want to be part of it. You were always kind, even to people you didn't know."

Was that why she'd ended up where she was, with everyone taking advantage of her?

"These days it's less about my principles and more about the fact I don't have a moment in the day to draw breath, let alone read gossip. I have a life, Nicole!" A life she was holding together by her fingernails. And suddenly the heat flared to life again. Maybe Nicole was hurting, but she was hurting too. "I don't have time to read much at all. I wish I did, but between raising my child alone and worrying what all this is doing to her, dealing with my ex-husband, running a business at a time when everyone is watching what they're spending and wondering if I'm going to be alone for the rest of my life, there's not a lot of spare time left for lounging around reading about people whose lives quite frankly seem pretty good from where I'm standing." She stopped, breathless and mortified. Why had she said all that? She'd blurted out far more than she'd intended to. She'd told herself that she was going to be reserved and polite and give nothing of herself. She was going to show Nicole that this friendship didn't matter to her any more than it did to Nicole. That she'd moved on just as Nicole had.

But she hadn't, had she? She'd had Nicole in her car for all of two minutes and already she'd been more honest with her than with anyone else in her life.

Some things didn't change.

She sat there, miserably embarrassed, and then Nicole reached out and touched her arm.

"I've missed you."

Milly felt something soften inside her, but she forced herself to ignore it. "Sure. You missed me so much you didn't get in touch for eighteen months."

She was so surprised to hear those words coming out of her mouth that she almost turned around to check there was no one else in the car.

Maybe the assertiveness course hadn't been such a waste of money after all.

Nicole removed her hand from Milly's arm. "Don't be angry. I know there are things we need to talk about, but the whole world is angry with me right now. I couldn't stand it if you were too."

"Why would 'the whole world' be angry with you?"

"Perhaps *angry* is the wrong word. I should have said the whole world hates me." Nicole's voice shook a little. "I am currently the most hated woman on the planet."

Milly felt suddenly exhausted. "Please, for once, can we leave the drama at the door?"

"For you it's drama, but for me it's my life."

Milly clamped her jaws shut to stop herself from saying something she might regret. "Nicole—"

"I want you to know that what they're saying isn't true. Well, some of it is—but not the way they've told it. It's all twisted." Her voice was barely a whisper. "I'm not sure which is worse— having people make up lies about you, or knowing that people believe those lies without question."

Milly was starting to wish she'd taken the time to do an internet search. She'd been up since dawn and hadn't stopped all day. Her body was tired, her brain was tired and she didn't have the energy for this. "What lies? What do people believe?"

There was a pause. "According to the press, I've broken up the happiest marriage in Hollywood. I'm a home-wrecker. The Other Woman."

Milly went cold. She thought of Richard. *There's someone else...* "You—what?"

"Go to any news site and you can read all about it. Two truths and a lie. Or is it two lies and a truth? I can't remember. And it doesn't really matter because no one is interested in the truth anyway. The people who write all that stuff about me just want clicks, and the people who read it want proof that my amazing-looking life isn't so amazing. Celebrity downfall is a great cure for envy, didn't you know? *Yes, she's rich, but is she really happy?* Well, no, she isn't." Nicole slurred her words slightly and Milly felt a growing wave of nausea.

I'm a home-wrecker.

Why did it have to be that? Nicole had a colorful dating history, with a reputation for falling for her costars, but to the best of Milly's knowledge, she'd never been involved with anyone who was married. For Milly the topic was something of a trigger given recent circumstances, but she knew plenty of people wouldn't have shared her disapproval.

And this wasn't about her.

"You are overthinking this, Nicole. Most people are too busy handling their own problems and making it through each day to worry about what is happening to you."

"That's where you're wrong. When people have problems, they look around them for someone who has it worse so that they feel better about their own lives. They think 'well, at least I'm not her.' My problems are a source of entertainment. Remember when we used to play three wishes?"

And just like that she was right back in her childhood, curled up on her bed, watching Nicole paint her nails.

If you could have three wishes, what would you wish for?

Milly frowned. "We haven't played that game for at least two decades."

"If I had one wish it would be to put the clock back and start again." Nicole's gaze was fixed on Milly's face. "How about you?"

One wish.

"I don't know. I don't waste time wishing for things anymore."

"Why not?" Nicole spoke softly. "Wishing tells you what you really want."

"Or else it just shows you what you don't have, and dwelling on that isn't helpful." Milly fastened her seat belt and started the engine. "We need to go. I have to be up at five tomorrow. My life doesn't go on hold just because you're here. How long are you planning to stay?"

"I don't know." Nicole's voice shook. "Maybe forever."

That was a joke, surely? Milly glanced quickly at her friend, but Nicole's eyes were closed again and there was no hint of a smile on her face.

Forever.

Milly tightened her grip on the wheel. If she had to wish for one thing right now it would be patience.

Don't miss Sarah Morgan's new book, available soon!